THE HELL BENDERS

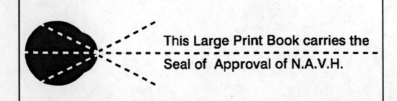

This Large Print Book carries the
Seal of Approval of N.A.V.H.

THE HELL BENDERS

KEN HODGSON

WHEELER PUBLISHING
A part of Gale, Cengage Learning

GALE
CENGAGE Learning·

Farmington Hills, Mich • San Francisco • New York • Waterville, Maine
Meriden, Conn • Mason, Ohio • Chicago

GALE
CENGAGE Learning·

Copyright © 1999 by Ken Hodgson.
Wheeler Publishing, a part of Gale, Cengage Learning.

LIBRARY OF CONGRESS CATALOGING-IN-PUBLICATION DATA

Hodgson, Ken.
   The hell benders / by Ken Hodgson. — Large print edition.
     pages ; cm. — (Wheeler Publishing large print western)
     ISBN-13: 978-1-4104-6650-1 (softcover)
     ISBN-10: 1-4104-6650-7 (softcover)
     1. Bender family—Fiction. 2. Murder—Kansas—Parsons—Fiction. 3.
Frontier and pioneer life—Kansas—Parsons—Fiction. 4. Parsons
(Kan.)—Fiction. 5. Large type books. I. Title.
   PS3558.O34346H45 2014
   813'.54—dc23   2013051119

Published in 2014 by arrangement with Ken Hodgson

ACKNOWLEDGMENTS

I would like to give heartfelt thanks to my editor, Karen V. Haas for making it happen. To Felton Cochran, Scott Claremont, and my wife, Rita, kudos for looking over my shoulder and not letting me mess up too badly. Then I need to thank the friendly people of Labette County, Kansas, for their many kindnesses during my research of this book.

Last, but not least, The San Angelo, Texas, Writers' Club for their unwavering support. See guys, it really can come true.

■ ■ ■ ■

PART 1
THE INN ON
THE PRAIRIE

■ ■ ■ ■

'Will you walk into my parlor?' said a spider
  to a fly;
' 'Tis the prettiest little parlor that ever you
  did spy.'

Mary Howitt
The Spider and the Fly

The heart is deceitful above all things,
And desperately wicked: who can know it?

Jeremiah 17:9

PROLOGUE

Royce heard the wagon coming long before he saw it. A heavy blanket of fog hung oppressively in the chill, April morning air along the Verdigris River in Southeast Kansas.

From long habit, he checked his Colt. Satisfied that it was loaded, he snapped the loading gate closed, making sure the single, unloaded chamber was under the firing pin.

He slipped the gun under his belt. His battered revolver fit much looser than it had three years earlier. He was a lot harder and leaner now than when he had first traveled this same route on his way to the Colorado gold camp of Central City.

Royce Dickinson had nearly starved or frozen to death on several occasions that first winter in those unfamiliar, rugged mountains. Gold nuggets were supposed to be lying around just waiting to be picked up.

He and thousands of greenhorns like him had learned the hard way that a lot of plain, hard work was necessary to glean a single ounce of gold from those cold, clear waters.

With more determination than most, Royce had stayed on. He finally partnered up with Chalmer Utley, a Georgian who had mined some gold in his native state. Using Chalmer's knowledge of mining and what little money he had left, they had managed to win two thousand dollars' worth of gold each over two long summers of shoveling tons of gravel through a sluice box.

Six worn leather bags that contained his future were carefully stashed in his saddlebags. He didn't expect any trouble this far east, along the Osage Mission Trail, but people being what they were he was taking no chances.

When the wagon finally creaked into view from a heavy patch of fog, it looked as if it were coming out of a cloud. Royce scrutinized the occupants with a practiced eye, and relaxed. It was just a family moving to somewhere new; not an uncommon encounter.

Their old wagon was a sight. The two front wheels had obviously been salvaged from another, smaller conveyance, and they were set in a foot closer together than the rear. This made a distinctive double track in the dusty Kansas prairie.

The driver was a huge man wearing faded overalls. Gray, streaked, black hair spilled out from under his battered hat. The younger man alongside him was a smaller copy of the older one except that he didn't seem to be able to keep his mouth closed, and a stream of brown tobacco juice ran down his chin.

The large, older woman in the rear seat reminded him of a turkey buzzard the way she was dressed, all in black with a red scarf wrapped around her neck. Royce ignored the way she stared at him, cold-eyed, from underneath her black sunbonnet. His attention was focused on the lithe young girl by her side.

Even the gray felt coat she wore couldn't cover the promise of her body. Her bright, auburn hair and smiling, red lips caused his mind to go back to Virginia Mowbray, the fianceé he had left waiting for him in Arkansas.

Royce took little note of the obviously pregnant, doe-eyed, Jersey milk cow that was tied behind the decrepit wagon. It just added to the picture of a harmless farm family, moving on.

The younger man hopped down from the

wagon, smiling, an open hand thrust out from under his long, black coat.

"John. John Bender," the man said pleasantly.

"Royce Dickinson," he answered, shaking the proffered hand.

"Do you happen to know where the road turns off to Parsons?" the young man asked, causing a fresh stream of tobacco juice to run out the corner of his mouth.

"If I remember right, about four miles north. It'll be the first trail you come to heading east."

"You ain't from these parts?"

"No, sir. I was through here a few years ago on my way to Colorado. Now I'm heading back home to Arkansas."

"A fellow traveler," the young girl said pleasantly.

"My sister Kate," the young man said, then added, "and my father, William, and my ma, Almira."

"Glad to meet you," Royce said, beaming.

Royce's attention was focused on Kate. It had been a long time, too long, since he had seen such a lovely girl. There had been places along his route home, like Dodge City, where he had been sorely tempted to stop and sample the favors of a young lady. However, those places were notorious for robbery. He wanted most of all to keep his hard-won gold until he could reach Arkansas, and his fianceé. Then he could buy a good farm and make a life for them. But this girl's smile was so full of promise —

"I've got some coffee on the fire, if you'd like a cup?" Royce offered, looking at Kate Bender.

"Right neighborly of you," John answered. "You on your way back from the goldfields?"

"Yeah, been there three years," Royce answered absently, still staring at Kate.

A couple of cranes were standing on a sandbar a few hundred feet upriver from where Royce was standing. Kate batted her wide, green eyes and pointed at them.

"Look at those beautiful birds. Royce, what *are* they?"

When Royce turned to look at the focus of Kate's attention, John reached with his right hand under his long coat with a practiced fluid motion and extracted a mushroom-headed claw hammer. He drew back, using a full swing, and struck Royce hard in the back of his head. The sweeping blow took away part of his brains, causing a spray of circular rings to appear in the still waters of the Verdigris River.

Royce Dickinson fell heavily on the muddy bank and lay unmoving, his head facedown in the water. John Bender calmly placed the hammer in his belt and brought out a Bowie knife. Without hesitation, he cut the dead man's throat from ear to ear.

John watched the murky river water start to turn crimson for a moment. Then he turned to the older woman, still holding the bloodstained knife in his hand, and said, "It's done, Ma."

"Well, get to looking. Try the saddlebags first."

After he washed the blood from his knife he returned it to its hidden sheath, then ambled over to where Royce's saddlebags were lying alongside the saddle the dead man had used for a pillow last night. He took a tin cup and, using his coat to keep from burning himself, he picked up the blackened coffeepot from the coals of the campfire, filled the cup with steaming, hot coffee, and set it on a log to cool.

"Get to it, son," William Bender said with a note of irritation in his voice.

John shot a sharp glance at his father, then masked it with a smile. It wasn't a good idea to rile the old man. It took him a moment to undo the brass clasp on the saddlebags. Then he threw back the leather flap and reached inside. A genuine smile crossed his face when he felt the heavy gold bags inside.

He gathered up all six of the pouches. Carrying them in the crook of his arm, he brought them to the wagon and handed them one by one to his mother.

"The Lord always provides," the woman said without emotion as she felt the heft of the bags.

"Amen," William mumbled.

"How much did we get, Mama?" Kate asked cheerfully.

"Maybe two thousand dollars. We'll have to get it weighed."

"Why, that's enough to pay for us going back into business, without going into our savings," Kate squealed.

"Yeah, like your Ma says, the Lord always provides," William Bender said. Then he directed a frown at John, who had gone back to see if the cup of coffee had cooled down any. Finding it still too hot to drink, he blew on it, sending off clouds of steam.

"Son, set that coffee down and see what he's got on him," he said impatiently.

Obediently, John set the cup back on the log and rolled Royce's body over. He glanced momentarily at the open, sightless, eyes that were staring blankly upward, then went about his search.

Aside from the worn Colt pistol, Royce Dickinson's pockets yielded only two dollars in coin and a pocketknife with one broken blade.

John started to stick the money in his pocket. Then, remembering the whipping he had received the last time he had done such a thing, he thought better of it and handed the coins and gun over to his mother. She promptly placed the Colt under her seat in the wagon.

"Choctaw Charlie'll buy that saddle. Toss it on, then get the horse," his Pa told him.

Kate looked over at the roan that was tied to an oak tree by the river with greedy eyes, then asked, "Ma, can I keep it? I'm going to need a horse, you know."

The answering slap to her face left a red handprint on Kate's cheek and tears in her eyes.

"Don't you ever learn *anything,* you stupid girl?" Ma said in her low, gravelly voice. "Remember what happened in Missouri? A little thing like someone recalling seeing a horse could hang us all." Then, with a syrupy voice, she purred to a teary-eyed Kate, "We'll buy you a horse with the money the Choctaw'll pay us for this one."

"Yeah, Ma. You're right, as always," Kate answered with tears still in her eyes from the stinging blow.

John had made room, among their cluttered belongings in the back of the wagon, for Royce's saddle and camp gear. He tied the roan to a lead rope alongside the pregnant milk cow. Then, picking up the tin cup of coffee from the log, he smiled when he found it was finally cool enough to drink. Taking a sip, he slowly climbed on the wagon alongside his pa, being careful not to spill his coffee.

When the wagon started up, a squeak from an ungreased wheel caused the cranes to take flight.

William watched the birds flapping their way upriver and into a fog bank.

"Choctaw Charlie told me once that the Indians believe a crane takes your soul to the next world when you die," William stated.

"Heathens have strange ideas," Ma replied over the creaking of the wagon and continued, "We live by the Good Book, not some savage's beliefs, and the Lord always provides."

Ma Bender glared intently at John for a moment, then reached in her pocket and took out a white handkerchief and handed it to him. "John," she said heavily, "you've got some blood from that man on your cheek. Wipe it off. Cleanliness is like Godliness, you know."

Kate, looking complacently over her shoulder, watched the open-eyed corpse of Royce Dickinson fade away as the wagon passed into a white cloud on its way north.

ONE

"Chatterhorn, over at the bank, said you had some land out on the trail for sale," the burly William Bender said.

Neely Wells looked up from the ledger book he had spread out on the wooden counter of his general store. This was one of his least-liked jobs, adding up what were jokingly called profits, and bills he likely would never collect. In a dry-land farm town like Parsons, Kansas, in the hard frontier year of 1872, you did what you could to make a dollar, or a nickel.

Neely, at thirty-one years of age, owned a general store on the dirt main street of town. He subsisted by selling whatever the settlers needed, from seeds to cast-iron cookstoves — nearly all of it on credit. In a good year, when it rained, he received enough to make a living. Most years, however, had been shaping up like this one. The wind had been blowing hard, and only an occasional shower sprinkled them with light rain; a tease, like the promise of a harlot.

The two husky men standing in front of him took him aback. They were striking in appearance. The larger and older of the pair stood at the counter. A smaller man, hands in his pockets, was at the front of the store browsing through a glass case, looking at carpenter tools.

"Yeah, I do have some land on the trail I'd like to sell, a full quarter section," Neely said to the unsmiling, black-haired man.

"My son John, here, and my wife and daughter would like to see it. We'll pay cash if the price is right."

"For cash, nearly anything in these parts is reasonable," Neely said lightly, hoping to break the old man's scowl. It didn't work. "I can't make it until tomorrow morning. If you'd like to meet me there say around ten? It's nine miles west of here. Just the other side of some hills."

"The banker told us where it's at. We'll be there."

"My name's Neely, Neely Wells."

"Bender's our name. I'm William. My son and Ma and Kate'll see you there in the mornin'."

The older man turned to leave. The younger man was holding a blacksmith hammer in his hands, looking at it as a father looks at a newborn baby. "Pa, we could use this for our blacksmithin'," he said.

"How much?" the old man asked out the side of his mouth.

"Just four bits."

William Bender reached into his overalls, extracted a silver liberty half-dollar, and tossed it to Neely, who caught it in midair.

"Thanks. See you in the morning."

Well, at least one of them can smile without his face cracking, Neely thought as he watched the strange pair leave his store. Young John was grinning from ear to ear, staring at his new hammer.

Neely closed his ledger book when they left. He'd lost interest in book work. The hope of selling that remote piece of land and paying off some long past due bills took his attention.

Robert and Mary Albertson had tried to make a go of it homesteading out there. A hot, dry summer killed their crops. An overheated cookstove caused their cabin to burn to the ground, taking the life of their year-old baby, and destroyed all their possessions. The combination of the two tragedies was more than they could overcome. The grief-stricken pair had dropped by his store last fall on their way back to Iowa and deeded their homestead to him for the bill they had run up.

Neely had grudgingly accepted it. He had real doubts that he could sell the land for the three-hundred-dollar tab he had on his books. But it was that or nothing, most likely.

When he had ridden out to examine the place he'd found nothing to salvage. Even the cookstove that had caused the tragedy had been loaded up and hauled off. Only ashes and a dry, half-completed attempt to dig a well remained.

Neely had a strange uneasiness about these Bender folks. He thought briefly he might have seen a picture of the old man on a Wanted poster.

Last fall the citizens of Labette County had elected him sheriff. It really wasn't much of a race — he was the only candidate. No one wanted a thankless job that paid only twenty-five dollars a month. But to Neely that was enough to live on, and mostly his duties consisted of arresting drunks or simmering down some trailhand who had too much tarantula juice under his belt.

Lute Thompson, the town undertaker, had rented a small building from him out back

24

of his store. Lute was a good hand — when he was sober, which wasn't too often. After a death in town it was a sure bet that Lute would be drunk for a week — usually after the funeral, when he got paid for the wooden coffin he had made and for digging the hole.

When Neely needed a deputy he gave Lute a dollar a day for his services, providing no one had turned up their heels, of course. When he wasn't on the whiskey Lute was dependable and fearless. A slender, mild-talking, whiskerless man who was always impeccably dressed, he had gained a local reputation by disarming a cowboy who was shooting up The Rose Saloon and nearly beating him to death with his own pistol. No one, it seemed, wanted to find out if he could do it again.

Neely walked over to his varnished oak rolltop desk, opened the right-hand drawer, and extracted the pile of Wanted posters it contained. After thumbing through them, he was relieved. Nothing in there contained a description of the Benders. It would be bad business to have to arrest someone who wanted to buy property from him. He tossed the papers back in his drawer and went to wait on a pimply-faced kid who was greedily eyeing the penny candy.

Later that day, before the bank closed, Neely walked the half block down the plank boardwalk of the street to see old man Chatterhorn. The bony, hawk-nosed, silver-haired banker looked at him with a wide smile. Then he asked casually about the Bender family. "It'll be nice to have some citizens with some money to spend, won't it, Neely?" he said, then added cheerfully, "I cashed in nearly two thousand in gold dust for them. The youngun' had been out west mining and found his fortune."

"They're a lookin' at the old Albertson place, the one I got when they burned out last fall."

"Well, sell it to them. They've got the money on deposit right here."

"You know, that young John doesn't look like a goldminer. I'm really not too sure he's not a few logs shy of a full cord of wood."

"Don't let that sheriff job go to your head and cause you to start distrusting people with cash. Those Bender folks may be a little odd, but you haven't seen their daughter Kate. She'll change your whole attitude. Come to think of it, it's probably time you thought about a wife."

On his way back to his general store Neely reflected on what Ben Chatterhorn had said. Perhaps he *was* becoming too suspicious, and just on looks, to boot. And this Kate, well it would be a welcome change in the line of settler's daughters if she was a looker. Those wooden coffins that Lute hammered out of rough-cut lumber were built better than most of the local girls he knew.

Neely was in a downright good mood by now. He opened the door to his store, smiling inwardly. Tomorrow would be a very interesting day.

Day broke clear and blue, not a sign of a rain cloud on the horizon. No one had died overnight, and Lute was downright depressed by the fact. It had been nearly a month now since anyone had cashed in their chips. He was more than ready for a celebration. It was of little consolation to him when Neely offered to pay him a half dollar to watch the store while he was gone. Since he had a good supply of coffins of all sizes made and lined up on both sides of his shop, like whiskey bottles in a saloon, he readily agreed. Perhaps he could hear some good gossip or hopefully, find out someone was bad sick.

■ ■ ■ ■

Neely reined his horse to a stop and pulled his old pocket watch out when he came within sight of the low hills that bordered the old Albertson homestead to the north. His mother's picture looked back from the opened case top. He found himself hoping that this Kate would look like her; dark hair and a haunting beauty. He had only been twelve when she died of the flu, but Neely remembered her well — her sweetness and laughter, and the light manner she used to cope with him when he disobeyed.

He snapped the case closed and placed the watch back in its pocket of his jacket, alongside the sheriff's star he had pinned on for some reason. It was not his custom to wear it. Everyone around there knew he was the law.

Neely frowned at the thought that he was early. It wasn't good business to show up ahead of time. They might take that as being desperate to sell, which he certainly was. He stopped for a while to let his horse graze on some grass that seemed to be greening more than the rest. *It'll be bad if we don't get some rain,* he thought. *One more dry year will break a lot of homesteaders, and most of them owe me money.*

After a while Neely grew tired of listening to the meadowlarks twittering, and he spurred his horse away from its small patch of food and headed to the north of the hills.

He couldn't suppress a grin when he saw that old wagon the Benders had come out in. The way the two front wheels set in gave it a comical appearance.

Then he saw Kate Bender. Old man Chatterhorn might have snow on his roof, but he knew a good-looking girl when he saw one. As Neely came closer he ignored the old woman sitting in the back of the wagon, her face hidden under a black sunbonnet, and focused on Kate.

Kate Bender was chasing an early spring butterfly across the prairie. The insect seemed to be traveling in circles, Kate skipping happily in pursuit. Neely Wells was having a *very* hard time keeping his mind on the business at hand. Then Kate stopped for a moment and undid the top two buttons of her tight-fitting, print dress, smiling invitingly at him. That was almost more than Neely could take.

With a pained, pinched look on his face he turned away from the frolicking Kate, dismounted his horse, and walked over to the stern-countenanced John and William

Bender. *The way those two look could sober up the town drunk,* Neely thought to himself. Then a memory came from the depth of his consciousness.

Years earlier, after his mother's death, he had accompanied his father to Kansas City to buy some livestock. A traveling circus was in town, and he had talked his father into taking him to see it after much urging.

Nothing had frightened and fascinated him more than a pair of gorillas that were on display behind what looked to him like woefully frail iron bars. The gorillas had simply sat together taking turns picking through each other's fur. He had expected them to let out a snarl at any moment, crash through the cage, and rip him and everyone else to pieces.

Even though those gorillas hadn't actually done anything, he had been unable to get them out of his mind. They dripped with power and cruelty. All they needed to kill was the opportunity. Certainly no conscience would be around to bother them later.

Looking at the two Bender men, Neely felt some of that same, unreasoning fear trickle its way down his back. *Perhaps it is just the way they look,* he told himself, *the coal black, unkempt, long hair, heavy, black eyebrows — like large, fuzzy caterpillars.* This and their wide muscular shoulders and powerful bodies, along with an unusually stoic quietness was what brought back those memories of the gorillas. All they needed to do to complete the picture was to start picking each other over for cooties. But now there were no steel bars between him and the beasts.

"One hundred and sixty acres?" William asked, shaking Neely from his reverie.

"Yeah. We're in the Southeast quarter now. The property goes about a third of a mile north and takes in part of Spill Out Creek, so you have a good supply of stock water," Neely replied. He was glad to be able to get back to his business of selling land and push his unreasonable fears to a more comfortable place in the back of his mind.

"And the main road, the Osage Mission Trail, cuts across this quarter?"

"Yes, it does. We're on it now, and the corner of this land is about six hundred feet over there," Neely answered, pointing to a wooden post sticking up from the grassy plain in the distance.

"What about neighbors?" John asked.

"Brock O'Malley and his family are the closest. Just about a mile east over that low

31

ridge. They have a full section, and grow some of the best wheat you ever saw."

William surveyed the steep spray of tree-studded hills that bordered the south of Neely's land. A thin smile crossed his lips as he said, "Well, we won't have any close company in that direction."

"You planning on just farmin'?" Neely asked, friendly like. The sharp way William's eyebrows shot up told him that these people weren't the type to be questioned. There was nothing new about that. A lot of people settling in the Osage Country of Labette County wanted to leave their pasts behind them, whether their pictures were on Wanted posters or not.

William Bender's looks softened into a narrow smile, and he said, "No, not really. Ma and me, well, we plan on running us a boarding house and restaurant, kind of a nice little way station where a man can stop and get a good meal and a cold drink, then bunk up in a nice feather bed if he's so of mind.

"Of course, we'll run some stock. John and me will do some blacksmithing. And Ma kind of fancies an apple orchard. She likes to plant things." William Bender stuck his fingers in the straps of his overalls and slowly surveyed the property. Then, with his usual unsmiling countenance, he turned to Neely. "Chatterhorn said you'd be askin' six hundred dollars. I'll go five, cash, right now."

It took all the reserve Neely could muster to keep from smiling. Then he remembered the note he had with Ben at the bank. Old Chatterhorn could squeeze a penny until the Indian sang soprano. He was just making sure he got paid.

"Reckon I could take that," he replied flatly, then added, "Welcome to the county."

When Neely reached inside his jacket to get the sales agreement that he had brought with him in hopeful expectation, the flap came open just enough to expose his sheriff's star. William Bender's eyes fixed on it a moment. Then he asked, with the thinnest of smiles crossing his face, "You the law around here?"

"Yeah. The only law this side of Independence. Not a lot to do along those lines. This is a peaceful community."

"Glad to hear it. Ma and me can't abide violence. Nice to have some law around."

Neely felt a lot better about these people. Their appearance had dredged up old memories, that was all. And he *had* sold the Albertson's place. And there was Kate.

He handed the paperwork to William, who

33

looked it over uncomprehendingly.

"Just sign here, and this afternoon or tomorrow when you get back to town we can go the bank and have the papers notarized. Then you can pay me and get your deed."

"Got something to write with?" Bender asked.

Neely pulled out a pencil from his shirt pocket and extended it to him. "You sign right here," Neely said in a helpful tone, pointing out a blank line on the paperwork.

William Bender took the pencil full in his hand, scribbled a large X in the indicated space with a flourish, then handed the papers and pencil back to Neeley.

This was really no surprise to him. A lot of people in this part of the country couldn't read or write. Their mark was legal in any court.

"Let me say good-bye to your wife and daughter. Then we can get on with the day," Neely said. Both William and John accompanied him to the wagon. Ma Bender looked him over from under the black bonnet with cold, deep-set eyes.

"We got the place for five hundred, Ma," John told her.

"Should've been for less, but we need to get to buildin'," Ma grumbled.

Neely was glad to see Kate walking up to him, holding the colorful orange and black butterfly in her hands. His gaze fixed on her open dress top. Then he quickly shifted his looks to her face. His cheeks felt red with embarrassment. Close up, this girl was simply beautiful. He felt that if he opened his pocket watch the picture inside it would pale next to Kate Bender.

"It's going to be awful lonely living way out here, Mister Wells," she said, batting her eyes.

"You'll have to come into town once in a while. I'll be glad to show you around," Neely said, feeling downright awkward.

"Mister Wells here is also our local law," William interjected.

Kate's smile fled from her face for the barest instant and then returned, followed by a pretty pout on her red lips, and she said, "I'd like that, Mister Wells. I'm *sure* we'll get to be good friends."

Neely made his good-byes, climbed on his horse, and — with a final tip of his hat at Kate — rode off across the grassland toward town.

Ma was looking at Kate as Neely rode off, becoming just a dot on the grassland. Kate was smiling vacantly, holding the butterfly's wings in one hand. With the other, she was

slowly pulling off its legs.
One at a time.

Two

Lute was not in a good mood when Neely arrived back at his store. It seemed everyone in town was in disgustingly good health. Even the Harper boy, who most people thought had appendicitis, was now all right. It turned out he had gotten into the fruit cellar and eaten a whole jar of canned green apples.

The only highlight was when Goosey Hooper came in to buy a nickel plug of chewing tobacco. He had mentioned that word was the new faro dealer at The Rose Saloon was cheating. Maybe someone would shoot him tonight. One could never give up hope.

When Neely added up the sales Lute had made, he joined him in his doldrums. Six dollars was the day's take, and five of those were added to the already padded tabs. He carefully entered the new debts into his cloth-covered ledger book, being very glad that the Benders had bought the Albertson's homestead.

"Heard that new girl is a real good looker," Lute said to get Neely's mind off his credit sales.

"That she is. Prettiest thing in these parts."

"You ought to go after her, then. A man's got to dip his wick once in a while."

Neely ignored Lute's comment and made a sincere effort to look busy at his ledger. Lute, he knew all too well, wouldn't pass up anything female as long as she still had a pulse. When he had gotten some "count-ing" money from his job as undertaker, he was off on a drunk. If he just had a small amount of money in his pocket, like the fifty cents he was waiting to be paid now, he would be off to see Slanty Annie.

Annie had a room upstairs in The Rose Saloon. She was a hard-faced blonde who catered to anyone who had some money to spend. She wasn't the only whore in town. Lute said she just seemed to enjoy her work more than most. For some reason, Annie had taken a liking to him, too.

Slanty Annie had received her nickname due to the fact that a disgruntled customer had pushed her down a flight of stairs a few years back, breaking her leg. When it healed, it turned out to be a couple of inches shorter than the other, giving her a decided list to one side.

Neely went to his cash register, keyed it, opened the drawer, took out a couple of quarters, and tossed them out on the counter for Lute.

With a satisfied smile, Lute scooped up the coins and stuck them in his pocket. "Thanks, ol' buddy. Think about what I said," he added, as he was on his way out.

Neely watched as Lute turned to go up the street in the direction of The Rose Saloon. Then he went about his business, dusting off shelves of canned goods.

Less than a hour had passed when Neely heard the sounds of hammering out back of his store. Lute was back making another coffin, whistling while he worked.

Then, through his single front window, he saw the Bender men pull their strange looking wagon to a stop. He took off his apron and hung it on a nail behind the counter by his cash register.

He turned over the OPEN sign in the window to read CLOSED on his way out, locked the door, and accompanied the stoic men to the bank. He was genuinely sad that Kate hadn't come in with them.

"Womenfolk stay at the place?" he asked.

"Yeah. They wanted to stake out where we'll put the business," William answered.

John had a large chaw of tobacco in his mouth, and the front of his overalls showed where it had overflowed on occasion, giving credence to Neely's theory about him not being all too bright.

Ben Chatterhorn welcomed them like long-lost relations, fawning over old man Bender, catering to his every whim. Neely was thankful when it was over. He transferred the five hundred dollars into his account, knowing that Ben would come by later today and ask for most of it on his note.

William Bender also took out another five hundred in cash. This amount brought tears to Ben's eyes.

Once they got back to the store the Benders spent over three hundred of it for building supplies, paying him cash for a wagonload of plank lumber, nails, and shingles. Lute had come around to see what was going on and he wound up helping load a cookstove on the wagon. He was still whistling. Neely felt like joining him once the Benders had left, driving off in that strange-looking and overloaded old wagon of theirs.

"Sure don't say much, do they," Lute said.

"Nope, but they didn't ask for credit."

"They buildin' a house?"

"Said they're putting in a business — a way station out on the Osage Mission Trail."

"If they put out a good meal and don't water the whiskey, they'll do all right. Especially if that Kate's there. A good looker will draw like bees to a flower."

"Yeah, I reckon."

"If you don't chase after her, you'll be awaitin' in a long line, Neely."

"I'll ride out in a few days and see how they're doin'."

"Just don't take too much time. There's those who won't," Lute said as he left to go back to finish his optimistic coffin building.

Neely envied Lute his view of life. In the story of the ant and the grasshopper, Lute sure wouldn't have been that ant, but he seemed happy, taking what he could when he could. He was a good ten years older than Neely. Word was that he had been married and had some family "back East." He never spoke of them, and Neely never asked. He considered Lute a friend, and if friends wanted him to know something, they told him. He didn't ask.

Lute made his home in the single-room frame building he rented from Neely. Come bedtime, he would lay a couple of coffins out side by side and pitch his bedroll on them. He cooked his meals on the black, potbellied stove that stood in the middle of the shack.

A lean-to had been built on one side of the building to house a customer, when Lute had one. On occasion, one of them was a little ripe, and ice wasn't always available, at least not enough of it to keep the smell down. Sometimes it took several days before relatives could travel the distance for the funeral.

Lute had built the lean-to on what was generally considered the downwind side, but in Kansas one could never be sure of which way that would be from one day to the next. Last summer, during a heat wave, he had gotten a cowboy who had been bucked off his horse and broken his neck. He had lain two days in the beating hot sun before was found.

From even as far away as The Rose Saloon, Lute had gotten complaints about his "customer." As a last resort, he had purchased a sack of quick lime. This solved the problem, and it was cheaper and lasted longer than ice. The side effect of this was that some people had started calling him "Limey Lute," a nickname he hated. The drover that he had beaten half to death with his own pistol had called him that. No one called him "Limey" anymore.

When William and John Bender got back to their new land purchase, the women had already staked out a building site. It was laid out by four wooden sticks driven into the ground, and a clothesline was strung around the tops of the posts, making a rectangle in the grassland.

The area staked out was directly over the half-dug well the Albertsons had started. It was a hand-dug hole about five feet around and nearly twelve feet deep. White sandstone rocks from the nearby hills had been laboriously broken into slabs and used to line the sides of the well.

William smiled when he saw where the stakes were placed. The area was about a hundred yards south of the main road; just right for a little privacy when it was needed. The well would certainly be usable for their business. If they'd had something like that in Missouri, they might not have had to leave so suddenly.

William pulled the wagon alongside the stakes. He and John climbed down. Before they went to unhitch the horses and hobble them so they could graze, John took a plug of Kentucky tobacco from the front pocket of his overalls and cut a fresh chew, using

43

the Bowie knife he kept in a sheath sewn inside his pants.

"Cut me off a piece," Pa said.

John extended the plug to him and whacked off a generous portion, which Pa tucked into the side of his whiskerless mouth.

Many men wore beards, but William had insisted that he and his son stay clean-shaven. "You can grow a beard and your own Ma won't recognize you," he had counseled. "It just takes a couple of weeks. That could come in real handy."

While John busied himself with the team Pa walked over to where Ma and Kate were standing by the old well. Kate was simply beaming, and even Almira had a rare smile on her face. He spit a load of tobacco juice in the direction of a horned toad, and missed. Turning to Ma he said, "We'll be in business in two or three days. This is a good place, Ma. We'll do right well here."

"Don't I always say the Lord will provide?" Ma said, looking at the well.

A dust cloud coming down the main road took their attention. A buckboard drawn by a single horse pulled up alongside them. The lone driver looked down with a friendly expression and said cheerfully, "I'm Brock O'Malley, your neighbor. Good to have

44

someone out this way. My wife, Nell, will be glad to have womenfolk to visit with. My boy, Seth, and I'll be over here at first light and help you put up your house. He's only fourteen, but strong as a mule."

"Why, that's right neighborly of you, friend," Pa answered. Then he caught O'Malley looking hard at the stakes surrounding the old well. Not waiting for the unasked question, Pa said, "It's gonna be a fruit cellar for Ma. Make a good cyclone hideout, too. We're planning on diggin' a new well out back, where we can water the orchard."

William could see that his answer had settled any questions about them building over the well. He really hadn't expected any company this soon.

"Orchard?" Brock asked, surprised.

"Apples. We hope to start plantin' pretty soon."

"Well, that *will* be a treat. Most people just run some stock or raise wheat."

"The Lord gives us all different tasks," Ma said.

"You churchgoin' folk?" Brock questioned.

"Yes, sir," Pa answered proudly. "We plan on being right regular after we get things organized."

"That'll make Nell real happy — to have someone to go to church with."

"We'll look forward to it, neighbor."

"Well, I'll be getting home. You folks are probably tuckered out. See you in the morning."

"Thank you again," William said as the wagon started, kicking up a dust cloud on its way out.

"People are really anxious to help us get back in business," Kate said after the wagon had left.

"Yeah, ain't it nice?" Pa answered, smiling.

True to his word, Brock showed up with Seth at the Bender's camp while the sun was still red in the East Kansas sky.

Ma and Kate had a blackened enamel coffeepot on the fire and bacon sizzling in the iron skillet. The O'Malleys gratefully accepted the coffee, but refused the offer of breakfast, saying they had eaten a couple of hours ago, before milking the cows and coming to help them.

Seth, even though he was but fourteen, couldn't seem to get his eyes off Kate as she pranced around serving up bacon and eggs and keeping everyone's tin cups of black coffee full.

Brock made a mental note that it was time

to have that little talk with his son about the birds and bees. After raising the boy on a farm, he'd figured it'd be a brief talk, but seeing the way he was staring after Kate he decided he wouldn't be able to put it off much longer.

After the Bender clan had been fed Ma started cleaning up the dishes and Kate went to milk their Jersey cow, which had begun bawling, complaining about being left unattended.

By dinnertime, the building had been framed. Two rectangular windows and a lone door faced to the north, toward the main road. One solitary window to the left rear of the house and another door in the back opened to what Ma had taken to calling her "orchard," though only stunted grass was struggling to grow there now.

Ma and Kate had made a surprisingly good dinner — roast beef sandwiches with homemade bread that had come from a box in back of their sorry looking wagon. Brock kept up a lively conversation with his new neighbors. They were somewhat quiet, but he scarcely noticed he was the one doing most of the talking. It was just so nice to have someone new to talk to. He'd been married to Nell for fifteen years. There wasn't much to say after that much time that hadn't already been said.

They had started framing the single peaked roof. Seth was clinging to a joist, nailing the crossbeams fast, when Kate came walking through. Heat had begun to build in the cloudless day, and she had undone the top buttons of her blouse, showing more cleavage than the young man had ever dreamed of.

He swung hard at the nail while looking at Kate's bosom, smashing his thumb into the rough lumber. Seth yelled and jumped down, blood spurting from his damaged appendage. Kate made over him like a hurt puppy. Purring in his ear, she smeared his thumb with axle grease and wrapped it with a piece of cloth torn from an old pair of what he knew only as "unmentionables."

Young John Bender took Seth's place, nailing rafters. Seth got little sympathy from any of the men, who knew full well why he had hit his thumb. The boy didn't mind at all. Every time he handed up a new piece of lumber, he could see his bandage and remember where the cloth for it had come from.

Reluctantly, Seth climbed on the buckboard in late afternoon to sit alongside his dad for the drive back to what he felt was a perfectly boring farm.

When Kate mentioned that she would stop by their place when the family went into town tomorrow to see how he was doing, Seth felt better. The throbbing in his thumb didn't return until they pulled into their barn.

The Bender clan lined up, facing the skeleton of their new home and business.

"We'll go into Parsons tomorrow," Pa said, "and we'll get the rest of the lumber, windows, doors, and roofing material. Ma, you make up a list of what you need to run the kitchen. Better get a good supply of whiskey. I think we'll have need for it."

During the day probably twenty travelers had come down the main road. Most of them slowed long enough to look wonderingly at the building that was sprouting from the grassy plain. All they needed were some finishing touches, and a sign.

"It'll be *so* nice to be doing business again," Kate said.

"Won't it, though?" Pa answered.

Another day broke clear and blue. The Benders paid it no mind. Rain wasn't necessary for their success. After the Jersey was milked, John caught the hobbled horses and

49

hitched them to their decrepit wagon.

Seth ran to meet them when their creaking conveyance pulled into the O'Malley farm. He still had the same bandage on his thumb. Last night his mother had grown tired of trying to talk him into a new dressing. At her husband's urging, she had just let the matter drop.

Kate brightened the boy's day when she pecked a small kiss on his cheek before climbing back on the wagon. Not only would his bandage remain the same, but he promised himself never to wash his face again.

Neely was glad to see the Bender's wagon pull to a stop in front of his store, doubly so when he saw the beautiful Kate was sitting on the plank rear seat alongside her taciturn mother.

Lute was in the store with him, sipping on a cup of coffee from the large, enamel pot that was always kept hot, no matter what the weather was. He had decided to quit building coffins until there was a reduction in his inventory. The one he'd made yesterday took up so much room in his little shack that he was unable to stretch out properly when he made his bed last night. His neck was still stiff from his cramped sleeping position.

His taut neck was instantly forgotten when he saw the young girl come into the store. Neely made his introductions, then busied himself filling the Benders extensive order. The old wagon was again overloaded with supplies. This time, in addition to building materials, several cases of foodstuffs, and a couple of cases of good whiskey were added to the sale.

Kate and Ma were waited on by Lute, who obviously was having a difficult time restraining himself. The beautiful Bender girl was no Slanty Annie. Occasional scowls from Almira, however, were sufficient to keep his mind on the business at hand.

The women had bought glassware, bedding, and enough pots and pans for a decent restaurant. Kate had also purchased candles and a goodly supply of sugar, salt, pepper, and various pie spices.

Their total expenditures were over three hundred dollars. William Bender took the short walk to Chatterhorn's Kansas State Bank, returned, and paid the smiling Neely Wells cash for their purchases.

Old Ben will be in a bad mood for a week, Neely thought as William counted out the pile of cash that went promptly into his cash register.

The Bender men were securing their load with ropes, crisscrossing them over the numerous crates. When Ma had taken up her usual perch on the back seat, scowling straight ahead, Kate bounced back into the store and approached Neely, a pouty smile on her face. "Mister Wells?" she asked, batting her eyes.

"Yes, Ma'am?"

"Ma was wondering if you could order in some apple trees for her? About two dozen — half Golden Delicious and the other half Jonathans."

"Why of course, but it might take a week or so."

"That'll be fine. Please do it."

"Consider them ordered."

"And Mister Wells —."

"Neely, please. Everyone calls me that, especially my friends."

"It's Neely, then. I'm *sure* we're going to be good friends."

Neely felt his cheeks flush; never before had such a lovely girl talked to him so.

"We'll have things pretty well ready to go by Friday. That's only three days from now. Would you do us the honor of coming out for supper? I'd surely love that."

Neely swallowed hard. He knew his face must be the color of a beet. "I wouldn't miss it for the world. Thank you and your folks for asking."

He only started breathing again when Kate strolled out the door. Lute's gaze followed her all the way to her seat on the wagon alongside her mother, his sore neck forgotten.

"That Kate's sure a piece of work," Lute said as the wagon pulled out and headed down the dusty, dirt street. Then he added, "She sure didn't get her looks from her Ma, that's for certain. I've planted people who had bigger smiles on their face than she can muster."

"I guess that's just the way they are. I've noticed that the old man seems to have an accent. German, I think. Maybe it's just that they're from Europe or somewhere."

"Wherever they're from, that old woman was beaten by an ugly stick, for sure."

"You know Lute, come to think of it, they never *did* say where they're from."

"Well, I guess it's none of our business. They sure pay their own way."

"That's for sure, and a nice change from most of the newcomers. The older ones, too, come to think of it."

Lute was getting uncomfortable with the direction the conversation was taking. Last month's rent on his shack was unpaid. To get his friend's mind off money matters he said, "You know, those Bender men are sure rough looking. Strong as an ox, too, especially that John. He loaded that cookstove mostly by himself yesterday. I really wonder if he's playing the game with a full deck of cards, the way he drools tobacco juice all over."

"They claim to be some kind of blacksmiths. Guess you don't need a lot of brain power for that job."

"They don't look like they'd have any problem pounding metal, for sure."

"I reckon they wouldn't, at that," Neely answered absently. He was thinking back on the gorillas.

In the heat of a Friday afternoon, the Benders lined up in front of their newly built home and business. Young John had hung a sign he'd made on the clapboard siding of the building, above the door. The sign was a large one, painted on a single piece of pine wood. John had whitewashed the raw board several times to give it a good base for the red letters he had carefully painted on it. John was inordinately proud of the fact that he made it to the third grade before he had been thrown out for fighting.

The lettered sign read GROCRY, then

below, in smaller letters, Meals and Drinks.

John was admiring the sign with a rare smile on his face. This caused a fresh issue of tobacco juice to add itself to the collection already in evidence on the front of his overalls.

"I don't think you spelled grocery right," Kate mentioned.

The thin smile fled John's face and he stared at the sign, a quizzing look on his face as if he were studying the situation but really didn't understand the question.

"Never mind," Ma said. "The drinks and meals are what we want, anyway."

"Come inside, Ma — it's hot out here," William said.

Kate followed her folks into the building, leaving John standing in the sun squinting at his sign with one lowered eyebrow, as if he had never seen it before.

Just inside the door, on the left, a long table had been built coming out of the wall. Wooden benches lined both sides. Three people could sit on each side in comfort. A white oilcloth covered the rude, wooden tabletop, and two candles were set in glass pie dishes in the center.

Behind the back bench, separating their living area from the front of the building, a wagon canvas had been stretched tight from floor to roof, the entire distance of the table bench.

On the right side of the door, a long narrow, rough plank made a countertop of sorts. Numerous shelves running along the wall behind the plank were filled with various canned foods and assorted dry goods. A glass jar on the end of the counter, next to the wall, was filled with penny candy for any children who might drop by.

Another piece of canvas wagon covering was stretched from ceiling to floor behind the store area. A walkway between the end of the plank and the canvas gave access to the shelves.

A loose flap of canvas, which could be dropped to cover the entranceway to their living area, was tied open with a piece of rope. At the far end of the building, directly in line with the open canvas, was the cookstove they had purchased from Neely.

Alongside the stove, a small table had been built for preparing meals. Two rude wood shelves above it contained flour, sugar, salt, coffee, and other cooking supplies. Another shelf below the table held various skillets, pots, and pans. To the right of the table was the back door, which opened out to the "orchard," and a hole that had been dug for an outhouse to fit over.

To the left of the stove, a closet had been built of clapboard. Another piece of canvas hung loosely over an opening, making a "door" of sorts. Twin bunk beds stood alongside each wall of the living quarters. Each had a wooden crate nailed by its bottom to the wall, providing storage shelves for personal belongings.

The two women had the bottom bunks. The men had taken the two top ones. With all the various items contained in the crates, such as tobacco for the men and perfumes for Kate, each one also held a single item in common — a black, gold-lettered, King James version of the Bible — in prominence, for anyone to see who looked into the kitchen area to check on how the meals were coming along.

"Now for the best part," William said as he pulled the front bench back from the table and scooted a hand-braided rug from underneath.

A leather strap was protruding from a semicircular cut in the wood floor, just under the bench that was backed up to the wagon canvas.

William got down on his hands and knees. Stooping under the table, which was built too low for a man of his stature, he grabbed up the strap and raised the door on its hinges. A half circle of darkness looked back at them. The door in the floor was built over Albertson's old, unfinished well.

A large timber ran under the floor, in the center part of the table. The door to the old well was hinged to it. On the bottom of the timber, a block and tackle had also been fixed to it with a strap of metal, the ropes running through the pulleys dropping off into darkness. A wooden ladder made of two-by-fours could be seen leaning up against the top, resting on a slab of white sandstone.

Kate walked up close and looked down into the darkness with a satisfied smile.

Almira stood her ground in the front of the room, but her lessened scowl showed she approved of the apparatus.

William lowered the door back into position, rolled the rug back, smoothed it out, and set the bench back where it had been. He stood and stretched his back to get the kinks out. Old man Bender checked out his handiwork, then looked at his wife and daughter. They were obviously impressed. Not a sign of the trapdoor was to be seen.

"We could have used that in Missouri," Kate said simply.

Almira Bender crossed the distance between her and Kate with amazing speed for a woman of her bulk, surprising even Kate, who had grown used to her mother's outbursts.

Ma grabbed a fold of flesh on the bottom of Kate's upper arm with her thumb and forefinger and twisted it viciously. A bruise there wouldn't show. She was always careful to never make a mark on Kate where it showed for any length of time. *You can't do business with damaged merchandise.*

Kate let out a cry of pain, but made no effort to move or get away from her mother. It was never a good idea to upset her more.

"You are never to say the word *Missouri* again."

"Yes, Mama," Kate sobbed. Almira still had a twist of her arm skin, her fingers like lobster pincers.

Almira then took her fingers away, and what passed for a smile crossed her face.

"Darlin', it's for your own good. Like it says in the Good Book — 'Spare the rod and spoil the child.' We'll *all* hang if they find us. You're far too pretty for a rope, girl."

"Yes, Mama."

"From now on if anybody asks, we're from Michigan," Almira said, directing her look at William, who had watched the incident without emotion. He'd seen a lot worse from his wife.

"You're right, Ma, it's Michigan," he said. "We've never even been to Missouri."

"You make sure that halfwit son of yours knows that."

"Yes, Ma'am," William answered obediently.

Ma Bender redirected her gaze at Kate, who was rubbing her arm, keeping some distance now from her mother.

"Girl, I want you to keep that tinhorn sheriff happy, no matter what you have to do. We're good, churchgoin' people, the last ones he'll ever suspect. Make sure of it."

"Yes, Mama," Kate answered.

"And that boy, he's been over here too much. Do something about it."

"Whatever you say."

Seth O'Malley had walked over from his farm the last two days. Kate had rebandaged his thumb, using regular cloth and tape bought from Neely's store, much to the young boy's chagrin. He had been as helpful as he could with his wounded hand. Yesterday, he and John had dug the hole for the outhouse. They had just sent him home, saying they had company coming.

"We could use his help to dig the well, Ma," William said.

"OK. *Then* he goes. We can't have outsiders about," Ma replied.

"John and I'll see to him, Ma."

"We'll run the place just like we did before," Ma continued. "Nothing will happen until I say so. We don't want people dropping out of sight as soon as we open. Patience is a virtue. Kate dear, help me fix a good supper for your sheriff fellow."

Kate obediently went to the cookstove and started stoking the fire. William went back outside into the hot, clear blue heat of the Kansas afternoon with a lightness to his step. It felt good to be ready for business again.

John was still standing in front of the house, staring blankly at his sign, drooling tobacco juice on his bib overalls.

THREE

Neely's spirits were high. There was money in the cash register, and thanks to the Benders he had paid off the $250.00 note he had at Chatterhorn's Bank. The old crook had been charging him four percent interest.

He allowed himself the luxury of a barber shop trim and shave. His muttonchop sideburns were now severely reduced in size, and his brown moustache was waxed and turned up at the ends.

A long nine cigar was protruding from one side of his mouth, and two more were stuck in the front pocket of a boiled shirt with a starched collar he had borrowed from Lute. Both men were about the same size, but this was the first time he'd had occasion to beg the loan of some of his friend's "dandy" clothes.

He stood in front of the seldom used mirror on an oak dresser in his bedroom. Neely had the entire upstairs of his two-story, false-fronted store for his living quarters. Only the rear room was ever used. A double-size, rumpled bed along one wall, the dresser he was standing in front of, and a wardrobe made of maple that had come with the building when he bought it all completed what he felt were adequate furnishings.

Three other rooms stood vacant, like unfulfilled promises. The front room was a large one, with two windows overlooking the main street. Neely seldom went there. It was what he called a woman's room. Frilly lace curtains tied back at the sides framed the windows. Colorful, blue, Victorian-style wallpaper covered the walls. The other two rooms were small children's bedrooms.

Bill and Marie Nolon, the folks he'd bought the business from two years earlier, had had three kids, a girl and two boys. They'd needed all the rooms, and then some. Neely, being a lifelong bachelor, was satisfied with the single, sparsely furnished back room. When he had money he took most of his meals at The Grand Hotel. If times were tough he cooked on the black, potbellied stove in the back of the store, contenting himself with a can of beans or, on occasion, making a large pot of stew that would last him for days.

Kate Bender had him giving some thought to those unused rooms. He could, in his mind's eye, see Kate accompanying him up the walkway built alongside the south side of his wood frame store. The stairs began on the main street and ran up at an angle to a single door that opened to his bedroom.

His eye caught sight of his silver sheriff's star lying starkly on the dresser, taking him back to the business at hand. He was getting way ahead of himself. He hardly knew this girl. He took the badge in his hand, looked hard at it, then placed it in the upper right-hand drawer. Tonight was not a time for business. He closed the dresser drawer with a slam, checked himself over one more time, lit a match, fired up his cigar, and headed down the stairs for the livery stable, where he kept his horse.

Goosey Hooper jumped with his usual start when Neely walked into the livery stable. That was how he'd gotten the name Goosey. He was a tall, unusually thin man who could hide behind a telegraph pole. Nervous disposition, he leaped as if he'd been goosed when surprised, no matter how slightly.

"I'm going to need my horse," Neely said.

"Oh, sure thing," Goosey said, calming down. Noticing Neely's fancy clothes, he couldn't keep from asking, "You got a date for a change?"

"Just going out to those new folks' place for supper."

"You mean the Benders? I hear that girl of theirs — Kate, isn't it? — is a real cutie. Maybe that explains the boiled shirt and shave."

"Just being neighborly."

"Yeah, *sure* you are," Goosey said sarcastically as he grabbed up Neely's saddle and headed off to the rear of the livery, where the horses were stabled.

Neely's bay had its head in the feed trough when they arrived at the stall. From the way the monthly oat bill from Goosey had been increasing, he doubted that nag ever looked at anything except that wooden hollow.

Goosey tossed the saddle on, cinched it tight, and turned to Neely with a serious look on his face. "Had a man stop by this afternoon to feed his horse and rest a spell. He come through Oswego, and the place was hoppin'. A homestead east of town was burned out, the settlers killed."

"What? That's the first I've heard of it." Neely was shocked.

"They think it was Choctaw Charlie and his gang."

"Choctaw Charlie? Why he's that half-breed killer from down in the Indian territory of Oklahoma."

"That he is," Goosey answered somberly. "Also, they say he's got a couple of bad ones ridin' with him."

"Reckon he wouldn't be in the company of any *good* ones. How do they know it's him?"

"The man was shot full of holes, and his throat cut. They had two little ones, a couple of girls, maybe two and four years old. They didn't bother to waste a bullet on them, just sliced their throats."

"Jesus," Neely said through pinched lips, the color gone from his face. "What of the woman?"

"She's missing. They must have taken her with them."

"That sounds like what I've heard of Choctaw Charlie, but he's never struck in Kansas before."

"Well, seems he's here now," Goosey replied.

Neely tied his horse to the hitching rail in front of his closed store. He climbed the wooden stairs back to his room, the spring gone from his step. He went to his dresser, not looking in the mirror. The silver star he took from the drawer seemed a lot heavier and more conspicuous now as he pinned it on the left front pocket of Lute's shirt.

Neely took out his pistol belt from the lower drawer and strapped it on. The gun in the oiled, leather holster was a .36 Colt Navy revolver. A peaceable man at heart, he had never taken to packing a gun — he had mostly been a shopkeeper — but he'd been around enough to know that sometimes there was no other answer.

Neely went out back to Lute's shack and found his friend napping in his usual bed on a pair of coffins. He woke Lute and filled him in on what Goosey had said. The undertaker was fully awake and wide-eyed before Neely finished his tale. "Check with Peeples at the telegraph office," he said. "Maybe there'll be something on the wire about it. Oswego is not in our jurisdiction, but they'll probably let us know, killings like this."

"Sure, Neely. You headed out to the Benders?"

"Yeah. They'll need to know to be on their guard with that bunch around."

Then Lute asked, "Do they have a gun?"

"Never seen one. I'll take one out with me."

"Good idea. I'd hate to think of what that bunch would do with Kate."

Neely went back to his store, unlocked the door, and walked behind the counter to where he kept the guns lined up along the wall. He picked out a double-barreled ten-gauge shotgun with scrollwork on the hammers. All someone had to do was cock the hammers back, point it in the general direction, and pull the triggers. With a load of double-O buckshot, it would tear a man in two without a lot of aiming. Handy for a woman.

Neely took a full box of shells from the shelf by the guns, tucking it under his arm. He leaned the shotgun by the open door of his shop, placed the box of shotgun shells in his saddlebag, returned, and locked the store.

Carrying the shotgun across his saddle, a somber Neely Wells rode down the dusty street of Parsons, heading to what he had planned on being a good night to get better acquainted with a beautiful girl.

Dry, white clouds that promised little rain blotted out a lowering sun when Neely rode his bay up to the new hitching rail in front of the Bender Inn. The ride out had been uneventful, but Neely found himself checking out every draw and tree he rode by. He had also taken the precaution of loading the ten-gauge before he left town.

He dismounted, carrying the shotgun in the crook of his arm, and tied the reins to the wood rail with a half hitch. Then he spit out the cold nubbin of his long nine cigar and ground it into the dry earth with the heel of his boot.

Neely looked at the sign that had been placed over the door and grinned when he saw the word GROCRY. *That looks like John's handiwork,* he thought.

He took the stiff, brown felt bowler hat that Lute had assured him was the style these days from his head. Carrying it in one hand and the loaded shotgun in the other, he headed for the door. It opened before he got there.

Kate Bender stepped out, her long auburn hair cascading over her shoulders and down her back. It glowed with a glint of copper in the subdued sunlight. Rouged cheeks and red lipstick set off her pouty lips. A blue skirt — the shortest skirt Neely had ever seen on a woman — nearly showed off her knees. Kate had on a tight-fitting blouse with a frilly chemisette accenting her cleavage. He swallowed hard. Neely had never in his life seen a more beautiful girl.

Kate stepped back, staring wide-eyed at the star-wearing man packing a pistol and carrying a shotgun.

"There's been some trouble down Oswego way," Neely said.

William Bender pushed his way in front of Kate, who was still fixed on Neely's guns. "What kind of trouble?" he growled.

"Some settlers were burned out and killed, the woman kidnapped. I brought you folks a shotgun to protect yourselves with."

Both William and Kate relaxed.

"Neighborly of you to think of us, Neely. Ma and me can't abide with violence. The gun's a good idea, though, if there's criminals about."

"These are the worst — Choctaw Charlie and the pair that rides with him."

Kate's eyes opened wider for a brief second at the name.

"Well, come in, friend," William said. "Supper's about ready. I'll pay you for the shotgun next time we're in town. We could use one for shooting ducks and rabbits, anyway. I doubt that half-breed'll bother us."

Neely quickened, he'd never said Choctaw Charlie was a half-breed. "You heard of him?"

"We've heard talk of him when we come through the territories. He's a bad one, for sure."

"There's got to be a worse word than *bad* to describe Choctaw Charlie," Neely said as he stepped into the house, closing the door behind him.

Fried chicken cooked in a deep cast-iron skillet, mashed potatoes and gravy, hot biscuits, and green apple pie began to take the edge off Neely's nerves. Kate did the rest.

After supper she sat beside him at the table, their heads resting against the wagon canvas, sipping on steaming cups of black coffee.

The rest of the family had retired to the back of the house and living quarters, leaving the pair alone.

Kate was more charming than Neely believed a girl could be. She laughed at his wit, always smiling and happy. When Neely left later that night to make the lonely ride back to Parsons, he felt he was falling in love. Choctaw Charlie was probably in another county by now. All was right with the world.

In the darkness, Neely wouldn't have been able to make out the forms mounted on four horses, blending in with the trees on the skyline of the low hills behind The Bender Inn. Even if he had looked.

■ ■ ■ ■

The door of the Bender's house was flung open without anyone knocking. Choctaw Charlie walked in nonchalantly, sat himself at the front table, brushed his stringy, long black hair from his face, and looked at William Bender with cold eyes.

"Thought you might be around tonight," William said as he came in from the back room, holding his coffee cup listlessly.

"Why, I've got something for that sweet, young daughter of yours," the half-breed sneered.

"And just what might that be, Charlie?" Kate said as she came through the canvas-framed doorway, after her dad.

"Whatever you want, my dear," he replied in the most perfect English. "First, I'd like to give my wife a little money to buy a horse."

Kate looked at Charlie with a well-practiced smile. *Let him think what he wants. A man can be led by his pecker, like a pet dog on a leash,* she thought.

Choctaw Charlie stared back at her with unemotional gray eyes. He fished in his vest pocket for a moment, came out with a handful of gold coins, counted out fifty dollars' worth, and returned the rest to his black waistcoat.

Kate didn't particularly like Charlie, but she knew neither she nor her folks would be here without him.

When things blew up in Missouri they had barely made it to the Indian territory before the pursuing posse. After a chance meeting, Charlie had agreed to hide them out for the thousand dollars they were carrying on their person, never suspecting there was over forty thousand more hidden in a false floor of their decrepit-looking wagon.

Choctaw Charlie had looked hungrily at Kate and demanded one more condition; he wanted the sweet one any time he asked. Ma had readily agreed for Kate. That was nothing new. Since she turned fifteen, Kate had given men what they wanted most — any time her Ma or Pa told her to. Charlie liked his sex rough, but Kate had never complained. He never bruised her as much as her mother did, anyway.

Choctaw Charlie was not much older than Kate, maybe twenty-five. He wasn't certain on that point, himself. Bora Charlie Devin, he was the product of a riverboat gambler and a Choctaw squaw. His whiskerless face and Roman nose betrayed his Indian ancestry.

His mother died when he was around eight. His dad told him she died of appendicitis. When he got older, he came to the opinion his old man had poisoned her. It was bad for business, having an Indian squaw on a riverboat.

His father had taught him all the tricks of the rougher trades — running whores, dealing cards from the bottom of the deck, quietly getting rid of someone when they complained of being cheated or simply got in the way.

Then, when he was fifteen, a would-be gambler complained about his pa's card cheating. The man was a little faster with a gun than his dad and shot him in the chest with a derringer he had concealed in his coatsleeve.

An orphan half-breed wasn't welcome on the river, he knew. After breaking into the cabin of the man who had killed his father, he cut the would-be gambler's throat. Taking everything of value he could carry, he'd jumped the boat at the next port, stolen a horse, and ridden back to the Indian Territory.

Charlie Devin, half-white and knowing only deceit and trickery, was not any more welcome among the Choctaws than the riverboat people. He followed the only star he knew. Travelers began disappearing, only to turn up robbed, with their throats cut.

After nine years of marauding, he had gained fame of a sort in the northeastern hill country of Indian Territory. Various toughs had joined with him from time to time. Most had been killed off by lawmen, either shot or hung. Two or three, he wasn't sure, had their throats cut by Charlie himself. He'd thought they were holding out on him.

Only two of the worst — or the best, from Charlie's viewpoint — remained. At least they had the good sense to throw all the robbery proceeds into the kitty. They also did what they were told without question, and with zeal for the job at hand.

Greasy Haynes sat quietly, mounted on his horse in front of The Bender Inn, holding the reins of the woman's mount. Greasy had no choice but to be silent. Years ago, the Cherokee had cut out his tongue, at the same time they removed his testicles. The young Indian maiden had been bathing in a small stream when he made the encounter. Greasy was certain she was asking for what followed. The girl's three brothers didn't see things his way. They tracked him down, surprising him one night. They mutilated him and left him for dead, his testicles stuffed in his bloody mouth.

After Greasy nursed himself back to health, he had returned the favor, only he hunted down the girl. It was *her* fault. All he could do by then was cut her with his knife, but he found that was even better than sex. He found he loved it. Cutting women.

Greasy ran his hands over his red hair, slicking it back. That's how he got his name. He carried a jar of bear grease with him at all times, constantly working it into his hair.

Vance Tobe, a wisp of a man, stood alongside his horse, holding a Sharps rifle in the crook of his bony arm. He ignored both Greasy and the woman. Vance was keeping watch with the eyes of an owl. He could see at night as well as a cat, and was always on his guard.

Vance had ridden for a while with Jesse James over in Missouri. He liked killing too much for the James brothers, and they had invited him to leave, or else. Now he rode for a gang that had no such qualms.

Kate took Charlie's money in her hand, bent over the table and kissed him. "Thanks," she purred, dropping the gold coins in her skirt pocket.

"That man who just left — who was he?"

Charlie asked, flashing his eyes at William.

"The local law," the old man replied. "A real hick. Kate and us have got him horn-swaggled. He even brought out a shotgun to protect us from *you.*"

Charlie laughed. When he laughed, it sounded like a shallow, sick cough. "Just so long as he don't touch my wife. If he does, I'll have to introduce him to Greasy."

Kate put her best "trust me" smile on. Looking at Charlie, she said, "I'm just going to keep his mind off sheriffin'. You know it won't be more than that."

"I'm counting on it. When you going to have some goods?"

"Keep an eye on the rear window, the one facing the hills. Two candles there will mean for you to come," Kate said.

"We'll keep an eye out. Well, we're heading off. Greasy might be getting impatient," Charlie said as he got up from the bench.

When he opened the door to leave, Kate saw the woman on the horse in front of Greasy Haynes. Her arms were tied behind her back. She was staring vacantly ahead with dead eyes. In the moonlight Kate could see that one side of her face was swollen.

The screams that came from the low hills of Southeast Kansas later that night might have been taken for a mountain lion's. Or a coyote's. They sounded like nothing human.

FOUR

Neely was awakened by a pounding on his door. He had been dreaming of Kate Bender, and was not happy to be jerked away from his sleep. He pulled on his work pants, threw on a shirt, and opened the door.

Lute was outside, a serious look on his face.

"What is it, Lute?"

"Out back."

"You got a customer?" Neely asked.

"Yeah, but you've got to see him."

"OK. Just let me get my boots on."

Lute stood impatiently outside the open door while Neely finished dressing. As they started down the plank walkway, Lute said, "They found him yesterday on the banks of the Verdigris River."

"Who is he?" Neely asked as they rounded the bottom of the stairs to head in the direction of Lute's undertaking parlor.

"Don't know. And it won't be easy to find out."

Neely saw two men standing somberly by an old mule-drawn freight wagon. A canvas was draped over something in the bed.

The older of the two stepped forward. "You the law?" he asked.

Neely looked down at his shirt. There was no badge. The sheriff's star was still pinned to the pocket of Lute's boiled shirt, the one he had worn last night. "That I am. My badge is upstairs. I was sleepin'."

When Neely checked the position of the sun, he realized it was probably around eight. He had overslept.

"We've been travelin' since first light," the freighter said with a hint of sarcasm in his voice. "I'm Fred Cane, and this is my son, Jason. We found him when we were lookin' to make camp last night. We loaded him up and headed on over. Then it got dark and we went ahead and spent the night. *He* weren't in no hurry, that's for sure," he said, motioning with his head toward the canvas.

Neely remembered seeing the pair and the old freight wagon before. It had been through town several times.

"You run this route regular?" he asked.

"When there's freight, we do. Go all the way to Joplin when we have a call to do so.

We're out of Coffeyville. That's where we call home. Never found nothin' like this before, God knows."

Lute reached over the low sideboard of the wagon and took hold of the canvas. The younger man looked away.

When Lute pulled the covering back, Neely felt a rising nausea building from somewhere low in his gut.

"Buzzards. They always go for the eyes first," Lute remarked.

Neely choked down the feeling rising in his belly and asked, "Anything on him?"

"No, he's been picked over by more'n vultures with feathers."

"Robbery?"

"Most likely. His throat's been cut, and the back of his head ain't there anymore," Lute replied.

Choctaw Charlie! The name burned in Neely's mind. "I'll wire the sheriffs around about. Maybe they'll know who he is. Lute, how long you reckon he's been dead?"

"Hard to say. It's been hot. I'd guess a week, more or less."

"Well, let's get him into a coffin," Neely said.

After they had rolled the dead man into the wooden box and the freighter and his pasty-faced son had left, Neely followed

Lute, who was packing a half-full sack of quicklime under his arm, into the lean-to.

"You thinkin' what I'm thinkin'?" he asked Lute.

"Yeah. Choctaw Charlie's come to Labette County."

Joe Peeples had a telegram from the sheriff in Oswego waiting for Neely when he walked into his small cubbyhole of an office, tucked snugly in a side room off the lobby of the hotel.

It told him little that he didn't already know, except that now he had names to go with the bodies of the homesteaders. Jake Whorton was the father. Tina and Amy had been the names of his daughters. His wife Lisa was yet to be found. He felt even worse now. Having their names made it more real, somehow.

Neely wrote out a short message about what he knew of the remains of the dead man the freighters had found. He directed Peeples to send a copy to the sheriffs in Oswego, Coffeyville, and Independence. Maybe someone would be missing, and they would at least be able to put a name on the dead man's headboard. Neely signed a voucher directing the charges to be sent to the county. Then he left the hotel and walked to the bank.

Ben Chatterhorn had already heard about the Oswego incident. He seemed genuinely shaken by the murdered man found by the river. This was in Labette County. Aside from owning the bank, he was also the mayor of Parsons, and county trustee of Labette County.

"You don't know who he was?" Ben questioned.

"If he don't have anyone lookin' for him, we'll never know."

"That bad?" Ben asked, wide-eyed.

"He's at Lute's if you want to see for yourself."

Ben recoiled and said, "No, that's all right. What are you going to do about it?"

"I've sent telegrams to the law in the area. Not much else I *can* do."

"This is bad for business, Neely, and you *are* the sheriff."

"Yeah," Neely growled. "I *am* the sheriff." *And twenty-five dollars a month ain't near enough,* he thought as he turned and left the bank.

Neely was sitting at his desk puffing on a fresh cigar when Lute sauntered in. He spun the swivel chair around and was genuinely glad to see his friend. It seemed to him that nearly everyone in town had been in his store this morning. They had wanted to know about the killings, and what Neely was planning to do to protect them. No one had bought much except some ammunition. On credit, of course.

"You know, I was in Kansas City once a few years ago," Lute said in his usual jaunty voice. "The trash dump had caught fire, close by the hotel. A bird landed on a tree branch just outside my window. When the smell hit him, it killed him dead. Fell off that limb like a stone. You know, that garbage fire stench was a piker compared to the cigar you're puffin' on."

The smile that crossed Neely's face felt good to him — like an old friend returning. "Long nines, nine inches long and nine for a nickel. Best deal in the store," he quipped.

"Only if you're trying to get rid of mosquitoes, or paying customers."

"Been too dry for skeeters, and cash customers are even more scarce."

"Let me take you to dinner at the hotel," Lute said. Then he added, "And I'll pay you back for it right soon."

Neely ground out the fire from the end of his cigar in an ashtray, got up from his desk, went to his OPEN sign and flipped it over to CLOSED. He looked at Lute, the smile remaining, and said, "Can't pass up a deal like that. Let's go."

The spring was back in Neely's step as they walked the short distance to the hotel.

Luckily, the rest of the week was quiet. The telegrams Neely received in answer to his query about the dead man said nothing. Other lawmen were waiting to see if anyone turned up missing — just as he was doing.

Chatterhorn called an emergency meeting of the county trustees the same night he was told of the man the freighters had brought in. They had appropriated some funds to pay for the telegrams Neely was sending out.

Then, at Ben's urging, they added fifteen dollars to pay Lute Thompson to bury the man.

The wind had been blowing in the direction of the bank and Lute hadn't been very generous in his application of quicklime. Chatterhorn thought it would be better for business if Lute got on with his work.

To Neely's surprise, Lute dropped by and paid him last month's rent. He nearly bit the end off a fresh cigar when Lute also paid him back for that dinner at the hotel.

To add to Neely's astonishment, Lute didn't get drunk this time. But he *had* been seen going into The Rose Saloon a lot. And

85

he was also whistling most of the time.

Slanty Annie was getting Lute's drinking money, a quarter a throw, or maybe it was fifty cents. Neely wasn't sure on the money point. He'd have to ask someone when the time was right. Annie had a lot of customers in Parsons. Slanty Annie's customers were, for the most part, also patrons of Neely's general store. It wouldn't be prudent to ask which establishment gave them the biggest screwing, however. They might tell Neely the truth.

John Bender and Seth were working hard on digging the well out back of the inn. They were urged on by Ma and Kate, who were getting tired of hauling water from Spill Out Creek. It was nearly a half mile trip. Then the women had to boil it just to make sure it was drinkable.

Seth's smashed thumb was recovering, but he still insisted on Kate putting a fresh bandage on it every day.

The boy was there every morning, right after he had done his chores. The O'Malleys had six cows that needed milking, and a garden to be weeded and hoed. They also had half a hundred squawking chickens to be fed, and the boy had to try to figure out where they were laying their eggs and gather them up. Seth found he could get up at the crack of dawn and have his work done by eight. Then he was off for the rest of the day to help the new neighbors out, and see Kate. Even when he watched her from a distance, on the few occasions when she came outside to do some task or another, he could feel his heart skip a beat.

Dinner break was the boy's favorite time. It wasn't because of the downright good food Kate and her ma cooked up. It was the fact that he got to sit at the table alongside Kate. When it was time to go back to well digging, the lovestruck boy was reeling from the smell of her heady perfume.

A wooden windlass with a crank at each end had been built over the hole, which was now over fifteen feet deep. The first eight feet of their diggings had been shored up by peeled logs they had cut from trees growing near the creek. John Bender had scraped the bark from the poles so they wouldn't rot out. Rough cut two-by-fours were scabbed in the corners to hold the logs tight against the sides.

Below the first eight feet they had dug into a flaky, gray shale that held its shape once they had picked through it, requiring no support.

John and Seth had a system worked out.

John stood at the windlass while Seth picked the shale loose and loaded it into a wooden bucket. Then John cranked up the bucket and, using one hand, carried the loaded tub over to one side and dumped it. The last few buckets of clay were muddy. The well wouldn't need to be much deeper.

While the pair were digging the well, William had been building a corral and a shed of sorts, a short distance away. Once the shed and well were completed, they could bring up their horses and milk cow from Spill Out Creek, where they were now kept, either tied or hobbled.

On occasion a wagon or lone traveler stopped at the inn. When Seth climbed the rickety ladder to the surface for a drink of water or to take a brief rest, he looked at them with a jaundiced eye. These strangers' comings and goings caused a great consternation in the boy. Someone else was getting Kate's attention.

Soon the well would be done, and Seth consoled himself with the fact that then he could help out around the inn, and be closer to Kate.

Brock O'Malley broke his son's heart and shattered his world that night when he told the boy that tomorrow would be his last day helping the Benders out. Their wheat was making a valiant effort to grow in spite of the drought, and it needed attention. Also, the two of them were to ride down to Cherryvale and drive back some cattle to fatten and sell. His efforts were needed on their farm for the rest of the summer.

Seth O'Malley picked listlessly at his supper that night, his appetite gone. It just wasn't fair that he would have to abandon seeing his beautiful Kate. But his dad's word was law, and there was always fall, after the wheat harvest.

When the sun had finally set in a clear sky, John Bender took up a long, wooden pole that he had fashioned at Ma's urging. A small rope had been nailed to one end and looped around to come through a staple nailed to the opposite side of the six-foot long pole. It made a usable snare.

Taking an empty potato sack with him, he started out for the low, sandstone hills to the south. In the cooling of the day, it didn't take him long to find the subject of his quest.

A diamondback rattler hissed its warning at John and coiled itself up tightly under a sheltering shelf of sandstone. Carefully, he extended the pole and dropped the rope loop over the snake's head. Quickly, he pulled the other end of the rope, pulling the snake's head tight against the pole.

Once the rattler had been secured in the gunnysack, he scanned the ledge for another. A buzzing by his feet caused him to jump back with a start. He had been standing only a couple of feet from an unseen diamondback while he concentrated on catching the first one.

Regaining his composure, he swallowed hard. Somewhat more shakily than before, he dropped the snare over that snake's head and added it to the contents of the bag.

Taking care to hold the bag away from his body, he carried the sack and its deadly contents to the mouth of the well they had been digging.

He pulled up the ladder and laid the neck of the sack at the edge of the hole. Then he untied the rope that held it closed. Being careful to grab the bag by the corners so he wouldn't get bitten, he pulled the sack upward, dropping the hissing snakes into the dark depths of the well.

Taking the now empty sack and snare pole with him, John Bender went in the back door of their house. It was supper time. When he told his Ma what he had done, he might even get an extra slice of pie. She would be proud of him.

Morning broke gray and cloudy. Black thunderheads were building in the east, and the smell of rain was in the air.

Seth O'Malley paid little attention to the weather as he walked the mile to The Bender Inn with feet that felt made of lead.

Over coffee, before they began work on the well, Seth blurted out the sad news that he would be unable to continue helping them. The boy never noticed that he was the only one upset by that fact. Ma Bender glared at the young man with her usual scowl and said, "There's been rattlers around here, boy. Take care around the well."

John's eyes opened wide, but he said nothing. Ma always knew best.

Seth dropped the ladder into the darkness of the well. Halfway down, he waited until his eyes adjusted to the dark, something he had never done before. A movement at the bottom in the mud caught his attention. Then he yelled up to John that there were snakes in the well.

John already had his snare pole. The shaken boy never noticed that fact. The rattlers were caught and brought to the surface, where their heads were promptly chopped off.

Ma Bender came out. She mumbled something about Seth being lucky, then picked up a headless, writhing snake and peeled its skin away in one swift motion, as if taking off a sock. When she had skinned the other, Ma said on her way back to the house, carrying the still wiggling snakes, "Waste not, want not. This'll make a good supper." Seth was glad she hadn't said dinner. He'd had all the snake he wanted for one day.

By midmorning, thunder began rumbling across the plains, and the sky was growing increasingly black. William came out to the well, called Seth up, and told him to head home. The boy went into the house and said his good-byes to Kate and Ma, then headed home in a fast lope, trying to beat the rain.

"There goes one lucky boy," Kate said after Seth had left.

"Why did you do it, Ma?" John growled. He was upset by the turn of events.

"We don't want any attention. It would have looked like an accident, but people would've thought on it. Better this way. We got what we want, to be left alone."

"Tomorrow's Sunday, Ma. We goin' to church?" William questioned.

"It's the Sabbath, ain't it? All godfearing people go to church. Of course we are."

Heavy rain started coming down in sheets, keeping the Benders inside for the rest of the day. John and his dad contented themselves with cleaning and oiling the six rifles, three shotguns — including the one Neely had brought them — and four pistols that were kept out of sight in the clapboard closet. Kate busied herself starching shirt collars and ironing clothes for the next day.

Ma Bender spent an extraordinary amount of time fussing over a large, cast-iron stewpot. Rattlesnake stew took a *lot* of fixing.

FIVE

Yesterday's rainstorm had delivered just slightly on its promise; only spots along the Osage Mission Trail were muddy enough to show twin ruts in the road when the Bender's strange wagon crossed them.

Reverend Pike Rogers met his flock on the steps of his one-room church. It sat at the north side of town, just off Main Street, surrounded by a clump of spreading cottonwood trees.

When the preacher came to town four years ago, he'd held his first services in The Rose Saloon. Shannon Bell owned the place then, before he was shot by a drover who objected to the five aces he was holding. He'd grudgingly gone along with Pike until he started adding up his Sunday's take. It was down considerably.

Knowing it would be bad for business to give the boot to a man of the cloth, Shannon called in some markers. The lot where the church now sat was donated by Bell himself. He had won it in a crooked hand of poker, anyway, so felt no real sense of loss when he dropped the deed in the collection plate.

A couple of Bell's hired toughs had made sure the word got out — give until it hurt, or else. When Shannon Bell told *his* flock to do something, they did it. His particular brand of punishment was a lot swifter and more predictable than anything the reverend had to offer.

Saloon girls found money hidden in their well-used mattresses. From them to the town drunks, who found they could do without a few drinks, money poured into the stunned preacher's hands. Over a thousand dollars. By the next Sabbath, Pike Rogers had a building for his congregation. Bell went back to fleecing customers on Sundays, immensely happy with himself.

Eppie Rogers, the reverend's wife, stood by his side. Shaped like a turnip, she had flaming red hair and a perpetually contagious smile. Eppie had faithfully produced a son each year since their arrival in Parsons. From her spreading girth and rosy cheeks, it was obvious that this year's offspring was on its way.

Matthew, Mark, Luke, and John were the

names given their sons, in the order that they were born. It was a matter of conversation around Parsons as to whether the new arrival would be called Acts or the Rogers would go straight to James. No one seemed to give any thought to the possibility of girls' names. It was a foregone conclusion that it would be another boy. Anyway, the reverend would have to cross that bridge when he came to it.

Neely had brought up the subject of the preacher naming his kids after books of the Bible to Lute. The undertaker was stretched out, lying on his bedroll over a pair of coffins, reading a dime novel, a cup of black coffee by his hand.

Lute, who never darkened the doorway of the church, cocked one eyebrow higher than the other. With a deadpan expression he said, "The man's goal in life is to screw his way through the New Testament. I admire a man who has a plan all laid out."

Sometimes Neely wondered about his friend's sense of humor, but not this morning. Leaving Lute to pore over his book, he headed on to church and Kate.

The reverend and his wife were welcoming the Bender clan when he got there. When she saw Neely, Kate let out a squeal of delight and ran to him, taking his hand.

The rosy cheeks of the preacher's wife paled beside Neely's flush. Never before had a girl been so forward with him, and in front of half the town, to boot.

Kate insisted that Neely sit by her. During the hymn singing he just mouthed the words, knowing full well his efforts at being a vocalist sounded like a coyote caught in a trap. On the other hand, Kate had the most beautiful voice he had ever heard. Clear and grand, her singing caught the attention of and brought smiles to the entire congregation, especially Pike Rogers, who thought he would finally be able to put together a choir.

Only after the reverend had started preaching in his usual droning monotone did Neely find himself composed enough to look at Kate and the rest of the Benders out of the corner of his eye. Each member of the family carried a black, gold-embossed Bible.

Dressed in a snow-white, neck-high, and ankle-length dress, the girl by his side looked like an angel. Ma Bender still wore a black dress, causing Neely to wonder if she owned any other colors. Dressed in clean overalls and each wearing the same stoic expression as Almira, William and John filled out the oak pew. Obviously giving up chewing tobacco in church, the younger Bender had his mouth half-open, and no brown juice leaked from the corner of his lips.

After the long sermon dragged to a close and a smiling Kate had accepted the reverend's offer to sing in the choir, Neely asked the whole Bender family to join him for dinner at the hotel.

"We've got to get back to the place," William said. Then he added, "I reckon Kate might like to go with you, though."

Neely couldn't believe his good fortune.

"I'd love that. Then, maybe later, we could go to the livery and you could help me pick out a good horse and saddle," Kate purred.

"Sure thing," Neely said, trying hard to keep his smile from showing. "Then I'll give Kate an escort back later today."

"Appreciate that. Can't be too careful, that's for sure," William said.

Neely didn't watch the Benders as they climbed aboard their decrepit wagon for the trip back to the inn. He didn't notice much of anything; Kate was holding his hand again as they strolled slowly to the hotel.

If someone had asked him what he had for dinner, Neely couldn't have answered them. He was floating in an unfamiliar, wonderful haze. By the time they walked into the livery stable it was midday, and shaping up to be a hot May afternoon. Goosey was napping, leaning back on some feed sacks. When Neely placed his hand on his shoulder to wake him up, Goosey put on a bigger show than usual, becoming completely airborne.

After Goosey calmed down enough to do business, Kate finally settled on a lively dun gelding. From the depths of a little used storeroom, the livery man came up with an English sidesaddle. Kate paid a smiling Goosey Hooper with gold coins.

Once Neely's horse was saddled, he realized with a sinking heart that it was finally time to head out to the Benders. After a stop at his store, where Neely went inside briefly to pick up his gun and holster, they rode off together under a blue, cloudless sky.

Time passed all too fast, it seemed to Neely. The ride from Parsons to The Bender Inn had never been shorter. An unfamiliar horse was tied to the hitching rail when they rode up, giving Neely a feeling of consternation. Once they went inside, though, he relaxed. A man, dressed far too well to be a cowboy or farmer was sitting at the table, leaning loosely against the canvas wall. A half-empty whiskey bottle in front of him showed he'd been there for a while.

The man bolted upright, and his eyes fixed on Kate. He straightened his bow tie, and blurted, "Have a drink, friends, I'm buying."

Neely noticed a slur in the stranger's voice. He was well on his way to getting drunk. "And who might you be?" Neely asked.

"Cal — Calvin Olson. Cattle buyer. I'm on my way to Independence."

"You take care, Mister Olson. There's been trouble about."

Cal opened his vest and patted a small revolver tucked into a leather holster. "I can take care of myself. You some kind of law-man?"

"I'm the county sheriff. Choctaw Charlie's been in the area."

"You worry too much, lawman," Cal slurred, keeping his eyes focused on Kate. "Seems any time some little thing goes wrong Choctaw Charlie gets the blame. Why he's been known to hit in three states all in the same day."

Neely realized this man wasn't given to accepting good advice. Kate accompanied Neely outside, closing the door behind her. He had started to say something when Kate wrapped her arms around the thoroughly surprised man and kissed him full on the lips.

"I had a wonderful time, Neely," she said as she untwined her arms. "Maybe we can do it again next week? Right now, Ma's got need of me."

"Yeah, until next week," Neely heard himself say. He was mistaken about the distance from the inn to Parsons. The ride back was the longest of his life.

Calvin Olson's hungry eyes followed Kate as she walked by him. She dropped the canvas doorway closed on her way through to the living area. Her mother was busily kneading bread, preparing to place it in metal loaf pans to allow the yeast to work. The men were not to be seen.

Kate stripped off the white dress, replacing it with her usual lowcut blouse and short, tight skirt. Almira looked at her approvingly. "Ma, I'll go out and see if our customer needs anything."

Her mother, with a thin dry smile, said, "You do that."

Kate liked whiskey. It was only at these times that she could imbibe. Her mother wouldn't allow it normally, saying that the drinking of spirits went against the teachings of the Good Book.

After a few more drinks, Cal Olson was all over the lovely Kate, his hands finding their way inside her blouse, massaging her firm breasts. Kate just giggled happily, making no effort to stop him.

When the whiskey was exhausted Kate straightened up, carrying herself away from Calvin's hands, and pointed to the empty bottle. "Lover," she cooed, "I think we need another bottle."

He couldn't believe his good fortune, finding a lovely, willing girl in such an out-of-the-way place. "Whatever you want, my sweet, you've got," Cal slurred, reaching into his obviously fat wallet and bringing out a ten-dollar bill.

Kate swung herself around on the bench, looking into the back area. "Ma, we need some more whiskey. Have John bring in a bottle of the *good* stuff."

"Only the best for my lady friend," Cal added.

Almira Bender gave Kate a knowing look, then went out the back door.

In a short while, John stood in the doorway holding an opened bottle in his huge hands. Cal Olson, seeing the rough-looking man for the first time, scooted away from Kate, wide-eyed. John simply placed the bottle on the table with his open-mouthed smile, turned, and left.

When the sound of the back door slamming reverberated through the inn was followed by silence, Kate drew Cal closer to her. She filled their glasses. The cattle buyer noticed the whiskey was of the best quality, genuine Kentucky bourbon, his favorite.

Now that they were alone Calvin Olson decided to take full advantage of the situation, only Kate beat him to it. Her soft hands began slowly working their way up his leg, stopping at his growing hardness. When she began unbuttoning his pants, Cal drew back with a lusty sigh, pushing his head back into the tightly stretched wagon canvas behind him.

John Bender, standing silently behind the covering, drew back the heavy blacksmith hammer they had bought at Neely's store. Centering in on the round protuberance in front of him, he swung hard at the canvas, shattering Calvin Olson's skull and driving him to the floor. He lay there, shivering like a clubbed fish.

Kate jumped from the bench to meet John and her Ma on their way in. William Bender came in the back door that he had slammed shut from the outside only moments ago.

"We did it, Mama," Kate said in a happy voice.

"Pull the rug back and open the door, John," Ma commanded.

The younger Bender did as he was told. Once the trapdoor over the well had been raised, he extracted his hidden Bowie knife. Pulling the cattle buyer by his hair until his head was over the opening, he cut the man's throat from one ear to the other, taking care that all the blood ran into the hole.

Quickly, John grabbed the man's shirt collar and gave a pull. The body of Calvin Olson fell to the bottom of the dark, dry well with a sickening thud.

A minute later the door had been closed and the rug replaced. John was leading the cattle buyer's horse off to the not-too-distant hills. Ma and Kate were busy fixing supper. William Bender was out back cutting firewood for the cookstove. All was quiet and in order at The Bender Inn, should someone else happen to stop by.

Late that night, using the block and tackle, the body of the cattle buyer was hoisted to the surface. Kate went straight for the wallet she had seen earlier. When the money had been counted she fumed, "Only five hundred dollars."

"It's a start, daughter," William said.

"He seemed like such a big shot. I thought there would be a couple of thousand, at least," Kate moaned.

"We make do with what the Lord sends us," Ma intoned.

"You're right as always, Mama," Kate agreed.

Grabbing up the swinging body, old man Bender unhooked the rope from the block and tackle that had been tied under the dead man's arms. He dragged him onto the wooden floor and tossed the rope back into the hole to await the next "customer." Pa and John rifled through the man's pockets, finding little of value except the small revolver and holster. "You take the legs, son," he said.

Obediently John took up his burden and helped his Pa carry the overweight cattle buyer to Ma's "orchard."

A small circular hole three feet across and five feet deep had been dug earlier by William and John while Kate had been busily entertaining the drunken man.

After Cal Olson had been forced into the hole and placed in a sitting position, his legs tight against his chest, the two men filled the hole with dirt and tamped it firm with their boots.

"Let's go have us a drink of good whiskey, son," Pa said.

"I'd like that," John answered, happy to take advantage of one of his Ma's rare good moods.

The two Bender men leaned their shovels against the bare clapboard siding of their inn, then went inside to join the women. William was mildly surprised to see even his usually teetotaler and taciturn wife sipping on a glass of bourbon and happily chatting with Kate about the day's affairs.

It *had* been a good day, the old man reflected. At last they were back in business. He felt proud of himself as he went to join his family in celebration. Times were tough. A steady income was hard to come by.

SIX

It was the same nightmare again. Kate Bender bolted upright, instantly awake, sweating profusely, and stifling a scream.

A few moments of breathing deeply. Better. She tried to push the memory back into her subconscious without success. What she kept dreaming of *did* happen. The events coming back to her at night, like an echo that kept growing louder.

It was stone dark inside their little house on the Kansas plain. John and William were in a snoring contest. The bunk bed above her literally vibrated with her brother's snoring. Sometimes he drew in a large amount of air and didn't breathe for the longest time, as if he were dead, only to sputter back to life louder than ever.

Someday, brother, you won't wake up, Kate thought as she rolled herself from under a light blanket to sit on the side of her bed. She was wearing a thin chemise that clung to her like a second skin.

It was still warm. The bulky, flannel nightgown that Kate pulled from its nail hanger in the darkness wasn't for comfort. If John happened to wake up and see her skimpily dressed . . . God knows he had tried enough times before.

Mama said it was just the way men were. The devil himself was a man. Once, back in Missouri, she had shown Kate a picture in a large, ornate Bible. There was a color picture of Lucifer himself, unmistakably a man with cloven hooves for feet.

"Never let a man have what he wants most until you get everything you can from him first." Those words were her Mama's, and Kate heard them often.

But her *brother*. If he ever did do it to her, she'd kill him that very night. It would be a simple matter to cut his throat while he was sound asleep, snoring.

It wasn't fair, anyway, that he was alive and her child, her beautiful baby boy, wasn't.

She slipped on a pair of leather moccasins. They were made of the softest leather. Charlie had given them to her one night in the Indian Territory. They were well worn. She hadn't asked where he had gotten them. It didn't matter. They fit well, and were comfortable.

Moving silently through the dark house, Kate headed for the back door. She would sleep no more that night. She never did after one of her nightmares. The bottle of bourbon was sitting on the cook table by the stove. A ray of moonlight shooting through the single window showed it to be nearly empty.

Picking up the bottle, Kate tucked it into her nightgown and quietly went out, shutting the door carefully behind her. The mound of fresh-turned earth in her Mama's "orchard" shone brightly, sparkling in the pale, yellow light like the whiskey bottle she now held in her hand.

A pile of thin logs that were destined to be a corral lay heaped on the dying grass. Kate sat on them and took a long drink of the bourbon. A strange warmth began from somewhere inside and spread pleasantly. The only times she ever felt this pleasure was on the rare occasions she had whiskey. Maybe business would be good and Mama would allow her to have some more often.

Thousands of stars winked down at her from a coal-black sky. Another drink, and the warmth increased. The bottle was nearly dry. One last sip, and the now empty bottle was tossed aside.

Kate Bender lay back on the logs, clasped her hands together behind her head, stared at the stars, and remembered.

The dream was always the same. A washtub setting on two wooden sawhorses. Mama holding her child close, so he wouldn't kick.

His head in the tub of water. . . .

Kate had given birth twice. The first time, she was only fifteen. Mama had made her do it several times with Alvin Tate, a farmer who had some adjoining land the family wanted to buy. He was old and smelly, reminding her of a billy goat. The man grunted like an animal and stank of stale whiskey. Mama was right. It never took a man long. If you got what you wanted, it was worth it.

When Kate got pregnant, Mama and Pa told old man Tate the baby was his, and he had to marry her or do right by the family for this inconvenience. The farmer was wealthy by the standards of a Missouri river town. He was also married, with six kids of his own. Eighty acres of land was a fair price to pay for Kate's dishonor and the Bender's silence.

The baby was stillborn, her sad-faced Mama told her. Only lately had she begun to wonder. No matter, though. They had the land for their inn.

At first, Mama and Pa had contented themselves with simply watering whiskey or cheating at cards. Then, when she was eighteen, John had killed a customer. It was an accident, really. The man was livid, threatening — angry over her Pa's ham-handed attempt to cheat at poker.

Her brother had glided up behind the yelling man as silently as a cat. Grabbing his head with his hands, John spun it around heavily. There was a dull popping sound, like when someone bites down on a piece of gristle. The traveler was dead. They found nearly ten thousand dollars in his pockets — a fortune. And it was all so easy.

Getting behind someone so John could break his neck was a problem. Then Mama came up with a canvas cloth behind a bench at a table. It was so simple, really. Eventually a customer would lean back against it. Even a small claw hammer swung by Kate from the other side was sufficient to cave in the head of an unsuspecting traveler.

On occasion, the visitor needed some help to put his head back against the curtain. Kate's soft hands applied to the right place, accompanied by lots of whiskey, did the job. Fondling a man down *there* always worked.

Then Sam Klonquist, a blue-eyed, blonde-haired Swede, started spending time at the inn. He focused his attentions on Kate like a dog in heat. A muscular young dock worker, he lived with his family in nearby Cape Girardeau.

Mama and Pa had a rule — never get rid of anyone who had family about or lived in the area. A lone traveler, disappearing on a long trip while carrying a sum of money, was not too uncommon. Also, no one knew just where such men had disappeared. It was a big country. When someone local turned up missing, however. . . .

After losing three prosperous appearing customers, her Mama had given her a handmade quilt with embroidered red roses on it. The next time Sam was hanging around in the way and a customer was at hand, Kate was to take him and the quilt to the woods in back of their inn.

After several visits to the woods with the lovestruck young Swede, Kate found herself pregnant once again. When Sam found out, he packed up and skedaddled down the Mississippi as soon as he could rustle up a job on a barge. Mama was always right. Once a man gets what he wants —

The bouncing baby boy she gave birth to was her delight. He had his father's blue eyes. Kate would sing him to sleep at nights with her melodious voice.

All went well for nearly two more years. The cache of gold and currency kept hidden in a tin lard can underneath the floor of their house grew to over forty-two thousand dollars. A fortune.

At night, after the inn had closed, the family sat around the table, planning. Kate played with her baby and John sat wide-eyed as Mama drew a picture in their heads. A dream that had crystallized over the years led them on like a siren's song.

Once they had fifty thousand dollars they would move to San Francisco, no longer poor innkeepers. They would buy a sprawling, brick home on a hill. A coachman would take Kate riding in the cool evening air, a rich beau by her side. There were lots of wealthy young men there. Kate was beautiful. Wealth could be obtained by marriage as well as other means.

Mama and Pa would entertain royalty in their mansion, throwing lawn parties where only the most elite were invited. The opportunities were boundless. Kate could see a fire building in her mother's coal-black eyes as she described their future life. It was as if she could actually see the house on the hill, hear the music of the piano. . . .

What John dreamed of was a mystery to

Kate. Probably whiskey and a girl to stick his prick into. That was all any man wanted.

It mattered little what her brother was dreaming of. He would never make it to San Francisco. If Kate didn't cut his throat for him trying to poke her, Mama would see to him.

John was not perfect, like Kate was. He was slow of wit, damaged. Only his great strength, which was needed now, kept him useful. In San Francisco, he would be a problem. Mama didn't like problems.

Kate's younger sister, Rachel, had been a lot like John. A half-wit. Dull. She had also been unattractive to men, fat and slovenly. After Rachel developed breasts, she had grown quarrelsome with Mama, refusing to do what a perfect child must do: *Honor thy father and thy mother.* Those words were from the Good Book. Rachel refused to obey God's teachings.

Mama had cooked up a special apple pie for Rachel, her favorite dessert. She ate it greedily, and died that night screaming with pain.

Her worried Pa had fetched a doctor, who was clearly drunk. The sawbones mumbled something about a burst appendix. There was nothing he could do. Kate knew better. Her Pa never suspected a thing. Pa never questioned Mama; she was always right. He was also maybe a little afraid of her.

If only John had heeded the word of God, she would still have her beautiful son. Mama quoted often from the Good Book: "Be willing and obedient and ye shall eat the good of the land."

On a hot Missouri morning, Mama had instructed John to take a man's horse into the woods and hide it. The man, himself, presented no problem; none of them had. The Mississippi River backed up from its course to the ocean, forming a swamp along the back of their eighty acres. A body weighted down and thrown into those murky waters was never to be seen again, crawdads, snapping turtles, and catfish being what they are. Horses were too valuable to waste in this manner. They could be sold to persons not inclined to ask too many questions.

John hadn't done what Mama said. He wasn't obedient like the Good Book instructed. He tarried too long, playing with a king snake he had caught. A lone rider saw the still-saddled horse and recognized it as belonging to his friend, a traveling companion he was to meet several miles down the road.

Pa tried to convince the stranger that his

friend was out back, in the outhouse, and to come in and have a cup of coffee. The man stayed on his horse, asking endless questions, his anger rising, yelling. Mama came to the door carrying a shotgun and fired at the horseman. Pa was planning on shooting quail later in the day, and had taken out the buckshot and replaced it with birdshot. Mama didn't know this, and the man, while wounded, was able to ride off.

There was no way to keep him from reaching Cape Girardeau and the law. All they could do was run. Stashing their hard-won money in a false floor of their wagon, they had been able to take only a few clothes and personal items.

Mama said they had to travel hard and fast. There was no way they could escape while caring for a baby. The washtub had been set out on two sawhorses and filled with water. It was laundry day. Mama liked her tubs set up high. It hurt her back to bend over, especially when her rheumatism was acting up. Taking her little David from her, Mama did what she had to do. Kate felt like crying, but caught herself. Perfect girls never cry. She just watched silently.

It was John's fault, not Mama's. If he hadn't been lazy and playing with a snake, she would still have her precious, perfect, child. Mama just did what she had to do. *Honor thy father and thy mother.*

That was when the dreams began. They came less often now, but they still came. *It's all John's fault,* Kate thought. *He'll have to pay.*

Kate sat up on the log pile. She recovered the empty whiskey bottle. Holding it tightly against her breast, as she had done with David, she began rocking and singing. Kate was still singing sweet lullabies to that empty bottle when a red glow in the east signaled that it was a new day.

SEVEN

On a sultry Thursday afternoon, just before closing time, the bounty hunter came into Neely's store. He was a short, stocky man with a bushy, black beard, and armed to the teeth.

Twin revolvers hung low on his hips, the ends of the holsters tied to his legs with leather strings, gunfighter style. He wore a cartridge belt draped over his shoulder with the familiarity of a banker wearing a tie. A heavy appearing Winchester rifle was cradled easily in his left arm. "You the sheriff?" the man asked flatly. His cold eyes betrayed no emotion.

"Yes, I'm the sheriff. Name's Neely Wells," he answered, offering his hand.

"Wade. Wade Cowell, from Arkansas."

It was like shaking hands with an iceberg. "What can I do for you, Mister Cowell?"

"I'm after Choctaw Charlie and his gang. They're here in this area. I've followed those

118

sons o' bitches all the way from the territories. Wasn't much of a tracking job, just look for new dug graves."

"Are you a deputy?" Neely questioned.

"There's two thousand dollars reward money for the half-breed, dead or alive. Five hundred each for his sidekicks. I expect to collect the whole three grand. After seeing what those three have done, I'd nearly kill them for free."

A bounty hunter. Neely had heard of people like him, men who hunted other men for money. This was the first one he had ever met. It gave Neely a start when he realized this man would kill without emotion as long as there was profit in it. "Two are all that ride with him?" Neely questioned. This was more than the Wanted fliers told him.

"That's what's left. I shot Ralph Berry last month. He only paid two hundred. The worst are still with him."

"Who are they?"

"Aside from Choctaw Charlie himself, there's Vance Tobe and a real mean one called Greasy Haynes. No one knows his first name. They call him 'Greasy' because of the way he keeps his hair slicked back with bear grease. He's the worst of the lot, likes to cut women up real slow like. If they're in no hurry, he'll take days."

Kate. Her name hit Neely like a fist to his gut.

"Vance Tobe is the most dangerous," the bounty hunter continued, "a little weasel of a man, probably weighs no more than a hundred and thirty pounds drippin' wet. He carries a .50 caliber Sharps rifle, and knows how to use it. That rifle will blow a man out of the saddle from a quarter mile away, long before you see him. Must kick the hell out of him, though, such a little man with a big gun."

"What can I do for you?" Neely asked, with the growing hope that this cold man might take care of his problem.

"There was a body found on the Verdigris River. Could you show me where it was?" the bounty hunter asked as he took a map from inside his vest and unfolded it on the oak countertop.

Neely pointed to where the freighters had found the murdered man. In his mind, he drew a line from Oswego to where his finger rested. The Bender Inn was nearly in the center, just to the north. "They must be long gone by now. Nothing has happened for days," Neely said hopefully.

"I doubt it. Once they move in they seem to stay for a spell."

"Well, I hope you get them."

"For three thousand dollars, I'll bring in the devil himself," Wade Cowell said as he refolded the map, stuck it back in his vest, and started from the store.

"Mister Cowell," Neely shouted after him, "do you know who he was — the man by the river?"

"Haven't a clue," the bounty hunter said over his shoulder without turning around.

As Neely watched the armed man leave his store to walk down the dirt street, he found himself hoping more and more that the cold-eyed man was up to the job.

It was too bad the bounty hunter hadn't known the name of the man killed in his county. The wooden grave marker simply said Murdered 1872 on it, lettered in somber black paint by Lute. Everyone, it seemed, who came into his store asked if there was anything new. He still had nothing to tell them.

Neely shook Choctaw Charlie from his mind and went about the business of preparing to close his store, thinking of Kate Bender. Her steamy kiss burned in his mind like a brand.

He had been running his store by rote all week, looking forward to Sunday when he could see her again. He met every freight wagon that came to town, hoping the apple trees had arrived. That would give him a perfect opportunity to go to the Bender's without seeming too forward.

It had been years, since he was just a kid, that Neely had done any sparking. Making a living had grown to be the most important thing in his life. The yearning he felt toward Kate made him feel like a kid again.

He was also wondering if she liked lace curtains.

Lute Thompson ambled into the general store, bringing Neely out of his daydreams. He noticed the time. It was an hour past closing, and the OPEN sign was still out.

"Open a little late, aren't we?" Lute said on his way to the stove. He picked up the blackened coffeepot using a well-stained pot holder and poured a cup. He sipped at it lightly and grimaced, "I think we ought to save this batch, Neely. It'd make, real good coffin varnish."

Then Neely told him about the bounty hunter. Lute's smile faded and was replaced with a distant, faraway look. "They're just a little notch above those they're hunting," Lute finally said.

"He was a cold one, armed to the teeth. Acted like a real tough customer. I just wonder if he's as tough as he thinks he is."

"No one ever is," Lute replied, through clenched teeth.

"Still, if the bounty hunter is right and Choctaw Charlie and his gang are close by, I hope he gets them, Lute. When I pinned on a badge, I didn't plan on runnin' down a gang of killers."

Lute set his coffee cup down, leaned back on the store counter, and looked Neely Wells over as if he had never seen him before.

Neely was wearing a well-stained, white storekeeper's apron, and he had a feather duster in his hand that he'd been using to dust off canned goods. A merchant, not a sheriff, was what Lute saw. "Where's your gun?" Lute asked.

"I keep it in my desk."

"Fetch it, and a box of cartridges. We're going out back and get you some practice. I've just got a feelin' you're goin' to need it. Bounty hunter or not. And you might give some thought to keepin' that pistol of yours a little more handy. If that bounty hunter had been Choctaw Charlie lookin' to get rid of a small-town sheriff, just how much trouble would he have had?"

A suddenly somber Neely stashed the feather duster in its place under the counter, doffed his apron, and grabbed up a box of

Colt .36 caliber cartridges.

After the powder smoke drifted away on a warm evening breeze, all six of the empty whiskey bottles Lute had sat on a log remained unscathed. From a distance of fifty feet, he had missed six shots out of six with his old revolver.

Lute rolled his eyes, forcing a pencil-thin smile, then put his hand on Neely's shoulder. "Thought you might need a little practice with that thing," he said, "I never had any idea you would need a whole education. The side of a barn wouldn't have been in a lot of danger."

"I guess I *am* out of practice," Neely replied sheepishly.

"When you pin on a badge, handlin' a gun is something you'd better learn to do. People are law-abidin' for the most part. On occasion, however, you can run across one that's just plain bad. *They* know how to use a gun. And don't hesitate a second doin' it, either. Neely, I don't want you for a customer. The next guy to own your place might raise my rent. Load up again."

When the box of cartridges was empty, the whiskey bottles were shattered. Lute had showed Neely how to cock the revolver with his thumb as he drew it. Taught him how to take a deep breath, then let it out to steady his aim. Told him to grease his holster well, so the gun would slide out easily.

During the walk back to town to have supper together at The Grand Hotel, Neely wondered deeply where Lute Thompson, an undertaker, had learned so much about gunfighting.

Beneath a sheltering ledge of sandstone in a hidden box canyon, Charlie Devin and Vance Tobe sat by a flickering campfire. Greasy Haynes was a few feet back from them, leaning against a large rock, sharpening one of his knives on a whetstone with slow, practiced strokes. He couldn't add anything to the conversation, anyway, so he kept to himself.

Their hideout was a perfect one. Situated in the low hills south of the Bender's, it was guarded by a narrow entrance and lined by craggy, steep walls. Like the many rattlesnakes of the area, it was impossible to see until it was too late.

A few small trees had been cut and set across the entrance to the box canyon, making a serviceable corral. Of the five horses that grazed peacefully behind the makeshift gate, one had once belonged to a farmer in Oswego, last ridden by his late wife, another by a deceased cattle buyer who had no further use for it. These horses were the cause of a growing argument between Charlie and Vance.

Vance wanted to take the two horses to Fort Scott, sell them, do some whoring, rob a bank, and return. Charlie was in no hurry to leave.

"You've got that Kate to take to the woods when you want, Charlie," Vance said with rising anger in his voice. "When you went down to get that horse, I saw the quilt she had with her and what you two done."

"And just *how* did you manage that?" Charlie hissed.

Vance Tobe motioned toward his saddlebags, "I've picked me up a telescope. I'm gonna try to fix it to my Sharps."

"Fetch it. I'd like to see this."

Vance hesitated a moment, studying Charlie's expression. As always, it was flat, cold, unreadable. He decided that now wasn't the time to confront him. It was better to wait until he had Charlie's back in his rifle sights from a hundred yards away. Then he would kill him.

Vance plucked the telescope from his saddlebag and tossed it to Charlie with a sneer, saying nothing.

"Well, well, Vance, my friend," Charlie said

in his practiced, syrupy sweet voice. Sliding the leather-covered telescope out to its full-length, he looked at Vance, smiling. "This *is* a nice one, Vance old friend," Charlie purred. "I'll bet you could drill a man from nearly a mile away with this fixed to your rifle."

Without warning, Charlie Devin swung the telescope around, striking Vance in the side of his face, cutting a bloody gash in his cheek. Vance Tobe had his hand on his gun when Charlie pushed a cocked derringer into his neck. "Don't do it, *friend.* Just remember who's running this outfit, and the next time you spy on me, keep in mind I'll kill you for it," Charlie said in his cold, measured voice.

Taking care to move slowly, Vance pulled a dirty handkerchief from his pocket, and held it to his cut cheek, and said, "Sure boss. I guess I was wrong."

Watching the argument, Greasy Haynes never missed a stroke on the whetstone with his knife sharpening. He had hoped Vance Tobe would kill Charlie. Then he could go straight to The Bender Inn. That Kate would be fun. She was tough. She might even last for days. He was still upset over the farmer's wife — the one that they had brought from Oswego. Once Charlie and

Vance were done with her, he'd started his cutting. It wasn't fair what that bitch did. He hadn't even worked on her an hour. He was removing her left nipple when instead of drawing back like she was supposed to, she jumped up into the knife, thrusting it deep in her chest, killing herself instantly. He had learned something. When he got his next one, he would tie her so that couldn't happen again.

"Now that we all are in agreement," Charlie said, "here's what we're going to do. We're staying right here for a while. Those Benders are doing more than robbing, and I think they've got money hid away. The longer we wait, the more they'll have. After a time, we'll hit the bank at Parsons. That won't be any trouble. Kate says the sheriff there is a storekeeper. Once we kill him and maybe a few others, the place will be in turmoil for a spell — then we'll ride out here and pay a social call on the Benders. I've got a feeling Greasy can convince them to contribute generously to our travel fund. We'll even bring Kate along with us. Then you and Greasy can have her. It'll help pass the time. It's a long ride to Fort Scott."

Vance Tobe nodded in approval, still holding the handkerchief to his cheek. With his other hand, he slowly picked up the telescope and studied it. At least it didn't appear to be damaged. He slid it closed and placed it back in his saddlebag. All the while, in his mind's eye, he could see Choctaw Charlie's back lined up in his rifle sights. It *was* a long ride to Fort Scott.

Greasy Haynes was sharpening another knife. A grin on his face showed off yellow, crooked teeth in the flickering firelight. He was thinking of cutting on Kate Bender.

EIGHT

Wade Cowell woke at first light. He was camped on the bank of Spill Out Creek. The drought had reduced its flow to a mere trickle. The weather was warm and he had slept on a single blanket, using his saddle for a pillow. He was also angry with himself.

He had been in too big of a hurry yesterday. He should have bought some supplies from that storekeeper sheriff in Parsons. There was nothing for breakfast but some beef jerky and a scant handful of coffee.

Last night he'd a water-fried steak, his lard gone. Wade hated a steak fried in water. They were dry, tough, and tasteless. He had been on the trail too long. All he had thought of these past months was Choctaw Charlie and his gang. He needed a bath, shave, a good home-cooked meal, and some rest.

Wade had been among the first to visit the Whorton place in Oswego. He was close on the trail of those outlaws, arriving there only a few hours after Charlie's gang had fired the buildings. The two little girls' bodies hadn't even been covered by a blanket. He couldn't get the thought of those two beautiful innocent children from his mind. He wasn't just doing it for money, now. Choctaw Charlie *needed* killing. The fact that he would be two thousand dollars richer when that happened only made it better.

He thought briefly about gathering up some wood, building a fire, and boiling a watery pot of coffee, then decided against it. He didn't have enough coffee to boil up a decent pot the way he liked it, strong. Also, the whole prairie was a tinderbox. It obviously hadn't rained for some time. The grass was either dead or dying. He would wait until he got to Cherryvale. There he could treat himself to a good breakfast at a restaurant and stock up on supplies.

The bounty hunter found his hobbled horse a couple of hundred yards down the creek, grazing on a rare patch of green grass. A small spring was what kept it from dying. Choctaw Charlie's bunch would have to be camped near water. When he got to Cherryvale, he would ask around; find out where the smaller creeks or springs were located.

It would be in a little-known and less traveled area where the outlaws could be found. And it would also be near water, that much was certain.

The moon was filling out, up to its third quarter. There was plenty of light to scout by at night. This was when he would check out the waterholes.

Wade Cowell had made his living as a bounty hunter since the end of the Civil War. His job with the Confederate Army during the war was tracking down deserters, bringing them back to be shot or hung. After the war ended, it was a simple matter to keep doing what he did best — what he was trained to do.

Early on, he learned to have no emotion, no feelings toward his prey. What they had done was no concern of his. He was just doing a job, helping out the law and getting paid for it.

He had seen lots of people killed, some brutally. But never little girls, not like those in Oswego. There was no way he would bring any of this gang back to face trial.

After he saddled his horse and stowed his bedroll and camp gear, Wade rode back to the Osage Mission Trail heading to Cherryvale. He felt comfortable with the wide open grasslands he was passing through. No chance of an ambush here. He avoided the tree-covered hills like those he saw in the distance during the daytime.

Every animal has a lair, a home. Any good hunter knows this. When animals or people are home, they relax their vigilance. All Wade Cowell had to do was locate their hideout from a nice safe distance, then wait until they left. When they came back later, he would be hiding, waiting. That little weasel, Vance Tobe, was the most dangerous. He would kill him first. Then Choctaw Charlie. Greasy Haynes was somewhat of a mystery to him. He might be faster on the draw than Charlie, but he doubted it. Greasy was a large man, fat. They were generally slower. No matter. He would get all three so quick they wouldn't have a chance, just like he always did.

Less than a mile after leaving his campsite, the bounty hunter saw a frame house coming into view on his left. From long habit, he scanned for horses, any sign of an ambush. This was the main trail. If Choctaw Charlie's gang were about, they might be watching it.

All seemed in order. A very pregnant Jersey milk cow and a dun horse were in the corral. Smoke drifted lazily from the chimney of the house.

When he got closer, relaxing some but still cautious, he saw a sign above the door — "GROCRY, Meals and drinks." Now he wouldn't have to ride to Cherryvale for breakfast.

Wade Cowell dismounted and hitched his horse to the railing in front of the inn. Once again, he scanned the area. Nothing. From long habit he took his Winchester rifle from its scabbard, cradled it in his arm, then went in to get some coffee and a hot meal.

Kate Bender was alone when the bounty hunter came in. His startled, wide-eyed expression when he saw her was obvious. It was nothing new to her. She was used to it. Men always looked at her like that, hungrily.

"What's a pretty thing like you doing out here by yourself?" Wade asked.

"My family — Ma, Pa and brother John — took the wagon and went to Parsons for supplies."

"It's not a real good idea for you to be alone. Choctaw Charlie's in the area."

Kate's eyes widened slightly. Then she said, "You look like you're a man prepared for anything. I'm sure you can protect me until they get back. Sit down and I'll get you some coffee."

Wade leaned his rifle against the end of

the table and slid onto the bench in front of the canvas. Most folks sat on that bench because it had a backrest. The bench on the opposite side was just a plain wooden plank.

Kate smiled sweetly at the man with her pouty, bee-stung lips as she brought him his cup of coffee. Wade sipped it cautiously — just the way he liked it, strong and black. "You folks been out here long?" he inquired.

"No, not at all. We've only been open a short time."

"There's some bad people around," the bounty hunter said as his brown eyes scanned the inn, "and I don't see a gun. You really should have a shotgun, just in case."

"Ma don't abide with violence. She don't like guns. We're church-going people, Mister —"

"Excuse me, Ma'am. My name is Wade Cowell, from Arkansas."

"Kate Bender," she replied, batting her eyelashes.

"If it wouldn't be a lot of trouble, Miss Bender, could you fry me up some bacon and eggs? I'm powerful hungry."

"Why, of course. I'll get right on it," Kate said as she glided from the room.

Over the rattling of pots and pans from the kitchen, Kate asked, "How do you know this Choctaw Charlie is about?"

"I've tracked him and his gang this far. They're in this area, for sure." Wade started to tell the young lady about what he saw in Oswego, but decided against it. This girl was young and sweet. She didn't need to hear about things like what went on at that farmhouse.

"Are you the law?" Kate asked.

"Not really. I just bring them in."

"And you're after this Choctaw fellow?"

"I'll be here until I get him. Then you'll be a lot safer, believe me."

"You're such a good man. Would you stay with me until my folks get back, in case that horrible Indian comes around?"

"Miss, as long as the coffee holds out I'll be glad to stick around," Wade said.

Kate came through the doorway carrying the metal coffeepot, its handle carefully cradled in a pot holder. She refilled the bounty hunter's cup with a smile and said, "I surely appreciate you being here, Wade. Your breakfast will be out in a minute."

When Kate went back into the kitchen, Wade blew on his coffee to cool it a bit, took a drink, set the cup on the table, and relaxed. It was nice to have a table to eat at for a change, and a beautiful girl to cook a meal for him. He stretched his arms, then

136

leaned back against the canvas with a sigh.

From the other side, Kate quickly switched the coffeepot in her hands. Using her right hand, she slipped a hammer from under her pillow. It wasn't a large, heavy one like Pa or her brother liked to use. Hers was small, light, daintily pointed. A lady's hammer.

Kate Bender struck the bounty hunter's head through the canvas as hard as she could. It sounded as if someone had dropped a sack of flour to the floor. Then silence.

She set the coffeepot down and went through the doorway to inspect her handiwork. The man was in a heap under the table, not moving.

Kate had difficulty dragging him off the trapdoor. He was not a large man, but solid and heavy. Also, he was still breathing, his breaths hitting in heavy, unbroken surges like waves on the ocean.

With added desperation, Kate grabbed one of his boots and pulled as hard as she could. The prostrate man slid a foot. Then with another tug, another foot.

Finally she could grab the leather strap under the rug and throw open the door to the old well.

Wade Cowell's head rolled to hang limply

into the darkness. Kate noticed he was blowing bloody bubbles from his nose when he gasped for breath.

Calmly, with a look of determination, Kate Bender retrieved her hammer. Kneeling by the bounty hunter, Kate laid a half-dozen heavy blows to the back of his head until she was certain he would never bother Choctaw Charlie, or anyone else, for that matter.

It wasn't too difficult for the diminutive Kate to roll the body to where it fell into the hole with a thud. She quickly tidied up — the rifle to the closet, blood washed from her hammer, dishes picked up; just like Mama wanted done.

Kate went outside, untied the bounty hunter's horse, and led it into the small barn her Pa and brother had just completed. Then she closed the door to keep any prying eyes from spying it.

On her way back in Kate saw a wrinkle in the rug over the trapdoor. She got down on her knees and carefully smoothed it out. A vigilant look around showed no trace of the bounty hunter. It was as if he had dropped off the face of the earth. The trap was now reset.

Kate dished up the bacon and eggs she had cooked. Taking them to the table, she

138

sat down to enjoy a late breakfast, proud of what she had done.

Maybe the next time Charlie took her to the trees he would be gentle with her. Her Mama would be proud of her, anyway.

That was for sure.

NINE

The Reverend Pike Rogers was simply beaming. His choir was wonderful. Kate Bender's beautiful voice was what he had been hoping for. Eppie's piano playing needed some practice, he realized, or possibly the piano itself was in bad need of tuning. This was the first time he'd noticed it. But then Kate hadn't been singing before, either.

After the choir finished and returned to their seats for the preaching, it was Neely's turn to feel satisfied. Kate slid her soft hand into his when she sat down beside him.

The preacher's sermon was even longer and more boring than usual. Pike Rogers spoke in a droning monotone that caused more than one parishioner to begin snoring. A quick jab to the ribs shook them awake with a snort. Pa Bender and John both received pokes from Almira to keep them from sleep. Neely could understand;

his eyes felt heavy, too. Only Kate's presence kept him awake.

When the collection plate was passed, Neely noticed that Ma Bender dropped in a twenty-dollar gold piece. That was more than the church received in a normal month. It felt nice to have some folks in town who would help out. The inn must be doing well for them. Several people had mentioned to Neely how good their food was. Also, that Almira Bender made the best apple pies in the county.

This hardworking family had also bought a lot of supplies from Neely's general store, paying cash money. Last week, William even paid him for the ten-gauge shotgun and shells he had left with them. He felt foolish when he thought back on his earlier suspicions about the Benders, and just from the way they looked, at that. As the preacher was fond of saying, "You can't judge a book by its cover."

Neely's heart sank to the pit of his stomach when Kate sorrowfully told him she couldn't stay for dinner. She explained there was work to be done at their inn. He consoled himself with the fact that the apple tree seedlings would most likely be in shortly. Then he could see the beautiful Kate again. It was nice she was such a hard worker to boot. That was a good trait in a lady, or a wife.

With a slight peck to Neely's cheek, Kate climbed in that strange-looking wagon of theirs, taking a seat alongside her mother. She was smiling over her shoulder at him as the Bender family faded down Parsons's main street, making a pair of twin tracks in the dirt.

"We're going to do some more target shooting this afternoon," Lute Thompson told Neely over dinner at the hotel.

Neely flicked a crumb of chocolate cake from his handlebar moustache, cocking an eye at Lute. "You've gotten me to wear a gun. Now you're going to cause me to go broke buyin' shells. Those things cost money."

"Not as much as I'd charge to plant you!"

"Oh, Lute," Neely pleaded, "there's nothing going to happen here. That Wade fellow — the bounty hunter — will most likely get Choctaw Charlie and his gang. That's his profession."

"When he rides into town with 'em draped over their horses and wants you to fetch his reward money, you can count on that. Right now, I'm a lookin' at the only law in these parts, and he couldn't hit a bull in the ass

142

with a two-by-four."

Neely shoveled the last of the cake into his mouth with his fork, depositing a fresh set of crumbs on his moustache, and said, "But it's been so quiet. Nothing's happened lately."

"Always that way before a storm," Lute replied.

"Let's go by the store and get the shells," Neely said with resignation.

Neely's shooting *was* improving. Lute carefully and patiently worked on one thing at a time. "Trigger pull is important. Squeeze it nice and easy. A jerk will throw your aim off. Point your finger at a whiskey bottle." Neely did as he was told. "Now imagine your pistol is your finger. What you have to practice is aimin' your gun like you point your finger. Then squeeze the trigger easy like. If someone is shootin' at you, most of the time they're scared, worked up. They'll likely not take the time to aim proper. The first man to put a bullet where it counts walks away," Lute told him.

Neely made a few slow draws with his Colt, just to get limbered up. Six empty whiskey bottles were setting on a log, swinging in a sea of broken glass. He took a deep breath, blew it out and drew, cocking the hammer with his thumb as the gun cleared leather.

Doing as Lute had said, he pointed the pistol at a whiskey bottle just as he would point his index finger. Then a swift smooth squeeze on the trigger, and the bottle exploded into a thousand fragments. Neely smiled broadly.

Five more times and the rest of the bottles joined the mass of broken glass around the log.

"Not bad," Lute said flatly, destroying Neely's smile. "Now all you've got to do is get a mite faster. If those other five whiskey bottles had been a shootin' back at you, we could rent you out for a screen door."

Lute was gathering up some more whiskey bottles to put on the log. Neely was reloading his Colt, wondering if he would ever get good enough to gain a word of praise for his shooting ability, when a boy's grating voice cracked behind them. "Mister Thompson, Annie from over at The Rose says she needs you to come right away."

Lute wheeled around, dropping the bottles to the ground as he did so. "What is it, son?" Lute said sharply.

Neely knew Albin Marsh well. He was the son of Jake Marsh, the town barber. Albin was a skinny, pimple-faced boy, maybe thirteen-years-old. He made extra money running errands for whores. Most of the girls never went out in "polite society." When they needed something bought or an errand run, they usually hired local boys, like him, for the task, paying them more than they could earn in a week doing other chores.

Albin's face was pinched, ashen. "I ain't certain, but I think it's powerful bad."

Neely dropped his Colt back into its oiled holster and took off after Lute and the boy, running.

The back stairs that led to the second-story of The Rose Saloon, where the girls plied their trade, were taken two steps at a time. A teary-eyed Annie met them in the hallway, standing outside an open door. Lute's face showed relief when he saw her. "It's Letta," Annie sobbed, tears streaming down her painted cheeks. "I think she's dead."

Lute pushed his way past her and went into the room, followed by Neely. When they got to the bed, Doc Clemmons was pulling a sheet over the head of a pretty, slender brunette who couldn't have been much over twenty years old.

"Laudanum," the doctor said simply. He never was a man for a lot of words.

When the men saw an empty, overturned, glass-stoppered bottle lying on the night-stand by the bed, they understood. Laudanum, a derivative of opium, was widely used by girls of the line. In small quantities, it was used to treat everything from nervousness to stomachaches. In larger quantities, it was a simple, painless way to commit suicide. They went quietly and peacefully to sleep and stayed that way. Not an uncommon occurrence among ladies of the night.

"She's yours now, Lute," the doctor said. "There was enough laudanum in that bottle to do in five men."

Roland Langtry, the present owner of The Rose, pushed his way past them to look at the form under the sheet. With a scowl on his face Roland growled, "Well, get her out of here. This is bad for business."

Lute shot him a glance that could have killed an oak tree, causing him to step back, wide-eyed. "Well, what I mean is I'm real sorry about this," Roland sputtered.

"*Sure* you are," Lute mumbled.

"I'll pay for the funeral, and all. Here, make sure she gets a proper send-off," Roland Langtry said, quickly reaching into his pocket and tossing three ten-dollar gold pieces on the bed beside the body.

Lute's icy stare followed Roland as he turned and left the room. When Annie hobbled into the room, his expression changed to one of grief.

Lute put his arm around her softly and said gently, "I know she was your friend. I'm mighty sorry for her."

Annie sobbed, trying hard to keep from breaking down, "Letta was planning on leaving and getting married. Her man was from Fort Scott. All he needed was some money to buy a home for her. She gave him her life savings, then he just took off. It was more than she could take."

"Neely, could you get someone from downstairs to help take Letta to my place?" Lute asked somberly.

"Of course, Lute."

"I'll be stayin' with Annie the rest of the day, once you get Letta taken care of. I expect you to get back to what we were doin'," Lute said.

Hank Johnson, one of the locals who seemed to call The Rose home, helped Neely carry the slight, sheet-wrapped burden down the back stairs. Once Letta was carefully placed in one of Lute's coffins, Neely tossed Hank a quarter and watched as the frail man left to spend it as fast as he could. He closed the door quietly, firmly, on his way out.

As he walked back to the outskirts of town and the shooting log, the Colt felt heavy on his hip. He also knew now that Slanty Annie meant more to Lute Thompson than what a quarter or fifty cents could buy.

Later that night, when darkness was just beginning to envelop the town, Neely Wells watched from his upstairs window as Lute came home for the night. He had a bottle of whiskey with him, carried listlessly in one hand as he opened the door to his undertaking parlor and went in.

Neely turned from the window and sat down at his newly acquired and already cluttered kitchen table with a tired sigh. There was a cup of coffee in front of him. He took a sip. It was cold.

He lit the glass kerosene lamp setting in the middle of the wooden table. Yellow flickering light chased shadows from the room. Earlier this week he had borrowed one of those dime novels Lute was so fond of reading. Extracting it from a pile of papers stacked precariously on the edge of the table, he studied the orange jacketed book.

It was *Dodge City Dan, the Fastest Gun in the West,* by Edward C. Fish. This caused him to wonder if this was where his friend got his knowledge of gunfighting. *My God, I hope not,* he thought. *People who write these things wouldn't know a Colt from a cow chip.*

No matter. He was getting better. Lute was right; being handy with a gun was a good idea, him being sheriff and all.

Neely slid the lantern closer, opened the novel, and began to read. By the time he got to the second page his mind was wandering.

Letta had been her name. No one had called her by her last name. Probably the one she went by was not her real one, anyway. Most girls who drifted into the oldest profession took an assumed name to save their families embarrassment. They had mothers, fathers, kinfolk, somewhere. Neely wondered hard on what name Lute would put on that pitiful brunette's headboard.

He closed the book, placed it back on the table, blew out the light, and went to bed early.

It had been a long day.

TEN

Storms danced around the town of Parsons most of the night. Lightning lit the sky and thunder rattled windows. It was an empty threat. When the light of day came the clouds were gone, and the grassy plains remained powder dry.

Just before the rain clouds decided to head for Missouri, a loud clap of thunder from the departing storm woke Neely Wells from a night of fitful sleep. . . .

He had been dreaming — one of those really weird dreams, where none of it makes sense once a person is awake. All he could remember was dreaming of those whiskey bottles Lute had placed on a log for target practice. Only there had been small, evil, grinning faces where the bottles necked down, and they each had two little guns in tiny holsters, one on each side.

He tried to draw fast, but that Colt of his came out of its holster with the speed of an hour hand on a clock. He tried to draw faster, but the harder he tried the slower it moved, the heavier his gun got. Like lead.

The bottles began to laugh, a mocking, malevolent laugh. Little arms appeared from their sides. Those tiny pistols flew up to aim at him, and began firing.

Just a bad dream, Neely said to himself as he rolled over to sit on the side of his bed. He reached over to the nightstand, picked a long nine cigar from the opened drawer, bit the end off it, and fumbled around in the dark trying to find a match. Finally he gripped one, feeling which end the sulphur tip was on, and struck it against the side of the wooden matchbox, bathing the room in yellow light.

He lit his cigar and a kerosene lamp with the same match. Neely took a deep puff from his long nine. Running his fingers through his hair, he shook the last remnants of that strange dream from his head and decided to get dressed no matter what time it was.

When he came down the stairs to go into his store to make a pot of coffee, Neely noticed a light in the window of Lute's undertaking parlor. That was nothing new. When Lute got on a drunk, he often passed out and left a lamp burning.

When the coffee had boiled, a red glow in the east signaled a new and clear day was coming. The ticking wall clock on the store wall showed it to be just after five A.M. It felt a lot earlier than that to Neely.

Using two pot holders, Neely plucked the still boiling metal coffeepot from the stove. Grabbing a couple of cups on his way out the door, he headed for Lute's.

To Neely's complete surprise, the undertaker was propped up on a coffin, wearing long johns, reading a book. A glance at the table showed the whiskey bottle he'd seen Lute carrying last night to be full, unopened.

Lute didn't take his eyes from his book as he said, "Nice of you to bring the pot over so early. Did you think I might be in need?"

Neely didn't know what to say. He filled the two cups, sat the pot on the table, and mumbled, "I saw you come in with a bottle last night. With what happened yesterday, and all —."

"That's my case bottle," Lute said, placing a bookmark and closing his novel. "It's there in case I need it." Getting up from his coffin bed, he walked over and sat down at the table, pulling a steaming cup toward him. Neely slid out the only other chair out from under the table and joined Lute.

The undertaker's eyes were dark, sunken. He looked tired and in need of a shave. Neely felt he must look the same.

"How's — Annie holdin' up?" Neely asked, barely skirting the word "Slanty."

"Fair-to-middlin', I reckon, considerin' they were good friends and all."

"Where is she?" Neely asked, his eyes searching.

"In the lean-to. We're goin' to have a funeral this afternoon. Ole Pike will say a few words. Most of the girls will be there. I'll try to give her a good send-off." Lute looked Neely in the eye and added, "I couldn't do that if I was drinkin'."

"I didn't think the reverend would be too inclined to want to be there. You know — her profession and all."

Lute took a long drink of coffee and said, "I wasn't really plannin' on offering him a whole lot of choice along that line. He can either do his preachin' or I'll shoot him."

Neely was never too sure when Lute was teasing. He hadn't seen a gun around his place. However, he felt certain the Reverend Pike Rogers would preach at the funeral this afternoon. Lute Thompson had that way about him. When he told someone to do something, for some reason they did it. The last one to challenge that assumption had been the drunken drover at The Rose Saloon. After three weeks, when he was well enough to leave town, the hardest thing he could eat was watery oatmeal. "I reckon I can close the store and come to give my respects," Neely said.

"That'd be right nice of you. Letta Palmer was her true name. I'll put that on her board. She had some family in Illinois. Annie said she would write and tell them Letta died of pneumonia, and also say she was working as a seamstress at the time."

When the coffeepot had been drained, the sun was shining bright in a clear, blue sky. Neely went back to his store and flipped the sign in the front window to read OPEN.

Lute went to the livery stable to make arrangements for Goosey to hitch up his funeral hearse. Lute didn't own a horse. When he had need of one to pull the black carriage, he rented one from Goosey.

The undertaker kept Lute's hearse in a stall at the livery stable, out of the weather. He had completely rebuilt it last fall, after an accident. A green broke horse that wasn't used to pulling a wagon, coupled with the fact that Lute was drunk at the time, had caused the disaster.

The jughead horse had spooked for some

reason or the other and run away, overturning the hearse in front of Ben Chatterhorn's bank. The coffin was thrown out, and it splintered apart and tossed old Ollie Moore onto the boardwalk and rolled him halfway into the doorway of the bank. He came to rest at the feet of Mrs. Cousins, who happened to be leaving the bank at the time. She fainted dead away, landing on top of Ollie's body. At first, it was thought Lute was bad hurt or dead. He lay unmoving alongside his overturned hearse while the panic-driven horse headed out of town, dragging its traces.

Lute wasn't hurt at all, as it turned out, just drunk. He was snoring fitfully, and in no condition to continue with the proceedings. Some not-too-sober patrons from The Rose Saloon and The Kansas Schooner came out to see what the ruckus was about. The funeral was in the late afternoon so most of them had been there for some time. After little discussion, they decided to carry on with the funeral.

Seeing two bodies that looked to be in need of burying, a pair of coffins was brought up from the undertaker's parlor. When the lid was nailed over Mrs. Cousins she woke up, let out a scream that would have done justice to a panther, and scared the hell out of the whole bunch of do-gooders.

There was a hurried meeting among the now sober group as to Lute Thompson's business practices. Some thought a hanging would be more appropriate than a funeral. When Ollie Moore's family came on the scene and told the mob only one was meant to be buried, everyone calmed down except Mrs. Cousins. Some claimed she hasn't been right in the head ever since. Others who knew her said she had been that way before.

Ollie Moore received a decent burial, and Lute's hearse was uprighted by a dozen or so men. Ollie's splintered coffin, along with Mrs. Cousins's little used one, was tossed in the back. Lute was left lying alongside the boardwalk, snoring loudly. It took until the next day for Goosey Hooper to finally recover his spooked horse, on the outskirts of Cherryvale.

Lute was devastated when he sobered up and inspected his damaged hearse. He had it freighted all the way to Kansas City for refurbishing. After a month it came back to Parsons a splendid coach. It was a matter of curiosity around town where the undertaker had come up with the money to pay for all the work done on his hearse. They couldn't remember *that* many people having died.

The new carriage was an ornate work of art, glossy jet black with gold scrollwork. Large, elliptical, leaded glass windows on both sides gave mourners a splendid view of the deceased's coffin. Black-and-white-trimmed ostrich feathers set around the roof completed the decor. A gold script sign on both sides proclaimed, Lute Thompson Undertaker.

At that time the mortician decided that it would be prudent to postpone consuming any whiskey until after the services for his customers were complete. He couldn't afford to rebuild any more hearses.

It was midday, and not a cloud was to be seen in the sea blue Kansas sky when an overloaded freight wagon groaned to a halt in front of Neely Wells's General Store.

Fred Case slowly climbed down to meet Neely when he came out to see what the freighter had brought him. Once on the boardwalk, Fred placed both hands on his hips, arched his back, and said, "I'm getting too old for this shit."

Neely paid him no mind. He was looking at the twenty-four seedling apple trees lined up in a row inside the loaded wagon, burlap sacks wrapped around their roots. "Let's unload them and set 'em alongside the store under the stairs, out of the sun," Neely said.

Seeing he wasn't going to get any sympathy for his aching back, the freighter turned with a sigh and walked to the seedlings. After unloading a few, he asked Neely, "Did you ever find out who that man was — the one the boy and I found on the river?"

"No, not a clue yet. I've got my doubts as to whether we ever will."

"Shame. It upset the hell out of my wife. She won't let Jason come with me nowadays. He was a big help. Anyone else turn up dead?"

Neely thought briefly about Letta Palmer, then answered, "Not murdered, anyway. There's a bounty hunter from Arkansas here after Choctaw Charlie and his gang. I don't reckon we'll have any more problems."

"Sure hope not. Be a lot easier on the ole back if I could get my boy to help out again."

Once the apple trees were carefully set under cover, Fred Case slowly crawled up to his seat on the freighter and drove off down the dusty street.

Neely went back into his store with a satisfied look on his face. At last he had a good reason to go see the Benders, especially Kate.

Letta Palmer's funeral was held at two o'clock. It was a graveside service. In Lute's mind, it was a foregone conclusion that the preacher would have gone for being shot rather than submit to a church funeral. Soiled doves were mostly ignored by the townspeople. Lute understood it would be better to keep it that way. A nice simple service held in the cemetery by an open grave was acceptable to most everyone.

A five-dollar gold coin proved an adequate alternative to getting shot for the Reverend Pike Rogers to deliver a tear-provoking eulogy.

Standing in front of the oval, leaded glass window of Lute's black funeral hearse, Pike preached with more feeling in his voice than usual. Neely, who was watching the proceedings from some distance, wondered if Lute *had* threatened to shoot the preacher. He'd never heard the reverend speak in anything other than a monotone drone before.

Slanty Annie Mitchell stood by Lute, holding tight to his arm, sobbing quietly. A half dozen girls from The Rose were there. Surprisingly, so were Roland Langtry and a couple dozen regulars from The Rose Saloon. He had told them they could have free drinks if they attended, which had effectively cleaned out the bar.

After the preacher said everything good about Letta Palmer he could think of for five dollars, the funeral was over. Annie gave Lute a kiss and left with the other girls to go back to work.

Roland nearly got trampled by the mob's rush back to the saloon, leaving only Neely, Lute, and Pike Rogers to let the coffin down into the open grave. Once Letta was laid to rest the preacher made a hurried retreat, confirming Lute's suspicions that a shovel handle wouldn't fit his hands.

Once the last shovelful of earth had been tamped in place and the headboard set, Neely backed off and looked at the marker. It read simply, Letta Palmer 1851–1872. Looking at Lute, Neely said, "She sure was young and pretty. It's a damn shame she had to wind up like this."

"Life's a fatal disease. She just got tired sooner than most," Lute replied on his way to place the shovel in his hearse. Then he turned, looked at the grave for a long, somber moment, and said, "But you're right. It is a damn shame."

Neely rode alongside Lute in the hearse for the short drive back to town. Neither of the men spoke until the coach pulled to a halt at the undertaker's parlor. "Lute, old friend," Neely said, "I've got some apple tree seedlings that need to go out to the Benders. Since you've got the hearse hitched up and all, do you think I could use it to deliver them?"

"I don't see why not. Shucks, I'll even ride along with you. The change of scenery will do me good." Neely's jaw fell open. The dumbstruck look on his face wasn't lost on Lute, who thought the situation over for a moment and said, "On second thought, I might ought to drop by and see how Annie's doing. You go ahead by yourself."

Lute helped Neely load the seedlings into his coach and tie them down with ropes so they wouldn't roll around.

As a happy Neely Wells flicked the reins to leave for the Benders', he heard Lute calling from behind, "Careful with that hearse, now. You hit a hard dog turd just right and it'll turn over on you."

ELEVEN

John Bender was behind the inn cutting firewood when he saw the black funeral hearse approaching. He leaned his axe against a wooden sawhorse, took a fresh bite from a twist of black chewing tobacco, and walked around to meet Neely as he pulled the coach to a stop.

Ignoring Neely, John walked up to the hearse and pressed his face against one of the oval windows to get a look inside. When he pulled away, twin streaks of brown juice were trickling down the glass. "You got a dead person in there?" John asked flatly.

"No, I just borrowed the hearse to bring your apple trees out," Neely said, climbing down from the coach.

A look of disappointment crossed John's face as he thrust his hands in his pockets, backed off a few feet, and stared at the hearse with a blank, open-mouthed expression.

The front door of the inn flew open, and Kate came running to meet Neely, followed by William. She wrapped her arms around him, gave him a quick peck on the cheek, then stepped back to stand alongside her stoic father.

"I brought out your apple trees," Neely said quickly to stave off any more questions about the hearse.

"Why, that's right kind of you. Ma's been hoping they'd come in," William said.

"It's about time, for sure," Almira Bender shouted from the doorway of the inn. "Well, get them unloaded. It's got to be hot as blazes in that thing. Put them out back."

When Ma Bender turned in the doorway to go back inside, Neely noticed she was as big one way as the other. *That old woman is built just like a pickle barrel,* he thought. Also, she was still wearing the same black dress, causing him to wonder anew if that was the only color she ever wore. Well, it matched her disposition, anyway, he decided. At least Kate didn't seem to have inherited any of her tendencies.

"Well, son, don't just stand there with your mouth open," William said to John. "Let's get to work like your Ma wants."

Neely walked around and opened the rear door of the hearse, untied the ropes, and started handing out trees. He grabbed one up himself and followed the Benders to the back of their inn. Noticing a pair of freshly turned patches of earth in the distance, he made the comment, "I see you're getting ready to start planting them."

William cocked his head in the direction of the spaded ground and said, "Ma has a tendency to rush things. She's in a hurry to get her orchard started. You know women."

Neely Wells *didn't* know women, but he was fast forming some opinions. Ma Bender gave him a cold chill when he thought of her. Kate, on the other hand, was like a dream come true; sweet, luscious, and desirable.

The trees were carefully laid out in the shade of the small barn. The doe-eyed, Jersey milk cow stuck her head over the corral railing to watch the proceedings. Neely thought the Jersey looked different, somehow. A closer examination showed a wobbly legged calf standing in her shadow, nursing on a teat. "I see you've got a new addition to the Bender clan," Neely said, looking at Kate.

"Sure played hob with the milk supply," William growled.

"I miss my milk," John said simply.

Neely rolled his eyes toward Kate. She

smiled broadly at him and said happily, "He was born last night. Come and look at him."

Neely walked over to the corral, bent over the railing, and watched the little bull calf happily sucking away. When Kate came alongside him, she put her arm around his waist, her head alongside his. He could smell her heady perfume, feel her soft, auburn hair touch his cheek. He felt a growing desire to reach over, grab her up gently, and kiss her.

"Ain't he cute?" John Bender said, showing off a set of yellow teeth and jerking Neely back to reality. "I just can't wait until he's big so's we can kill him," John continued, an empty-headed grin on his face. "Then we can have steaks — and milk again."

Kate quickly moved her hand from Neely's waist to take his hand and usher him into the inn, leaving John staring open-mouthed at the nursing calf and William drawing water from the well to soak the tree roots.

Ma Bender, who was busily banging pots around the kitchen, ignored them as they went to sit at the front table. Neely slid into his usual spot, just behind the other side of the curtain. A dark, coffee-like stain on the white wagon canvas caught his eye and Kate noticed, causing an even larger pout to come to her lips. "That John, he can't even serve a cup of coffee without making a mess. You'll have to overlook him, Neely. He's not real smart, but he's a big help to Ma and he's as gentle as a lamb," Kate said in a low voice.

Neely had already figured out the fact that John Bender wasn't much smarter than a box full of rocks. It was the "gentle" part he wasn't too sure about. Never mind about him. Kate was by his side. He leaned back into the canvas, taking care to avoid the stained area. Summoning up all of his courage, he took Kate's hand and looked hard into her green eyes. He had started to speak when Almira came through the doorway and slammed a large piece of apple pie and a steaming cup of black coffee on the table in front of him. "That's for bringing out my apple trees," Ma Bender said with her usual growl. She quickly spun around to go back into the kitchen, then added, "Kate, come in here and help me. Let that man have his pie."

Neely sighed as his beautiful Kate left to do her mother's bidding. The raves Neely had heard about Ma Bender's pies were true. This apple pie *was* the best he had ever eaten. Almira Bender might have the disposition of a rattlesnake with boils, but she sure could cook. Neely Wells was certain that Kate could do just as well as the old woman, only she would be a real pleasure to be around.

When Kate came out to fill his coffee cup, she gave him a passionate smile and, in the wink of an eye, turned and glided back into the kitchen.

Neely finished the last of his pie. He leaned back against the wagon canvas, listening to the busy sounds of the women hard at work in the kitchen. Slowly he spun the half-empty coffee cup on the table, trying to figure out how to get Kate by herself for a little while.

The front door flew open and four burly, rough-looking, bearded men filed in. Through the open door Neely could see a lumber wagon loaded with saw logs, bound for the mill in Coffeyville, he guessed. With a start, he realized he had been so preoccupied with Kate that he hadn't even heard the wagon stop.

Neely slugged down the last of his coffee and slid from the table to make room for the timber cutters. One of the men made a comment about the hearse outside as they sat down. Neely started to answer him when Kate strolled in. The funeral coach was immediately forgotten, and hungry smiles crossed the men's faces. They ordered whiskey and supper without taking their eyes off Kate for even a second.

When she left, some of the men made comments about Kate's good looks, causing Neely to feel a growing sense of anger. He started to tell them to watch their manners. Then he felt Kate's soft hand in his. She led him through the door and closed it behind them. "It's all right, Neely," Kate said, batting her eyes. "I can cope with those men. They're just a little rough, is all."

"I just don't like them talking like that."

"Not everyone is as nice as you are. You're special." Neely swallowed hard and looked at her, speechless. "Well, I've got to get back to work, Neely. Ma needs me. I'll see you Sunday in church."

"Yeah — Sunday," Neely sputtered.

Kate gave him one of her steamy, full kisses, spun around, and went back into the inn. It took Neely a few moments to compose himself before walking to Lute's hearse and climbing up into the driver's seat. In Almira's orchard, he could see John and William hard at work. Already they had two of the small saplings planted where earlier he had seen the spaded areas.

Neely flicked the reins and drove the coach over to where the Bender men were digging. "I forgot to tell you," Neely said from his seat on the coach, directing his gaze at William, "the nursery sent word along that those trees need to be fertilized."

"Thanks, we'll see to it," William said without looking away from the hole he was digging.

On the long drive back to Parsons, Neely thought hard about Kate Bender. Lutc Thompson's words echoed in his head: *If you don't chase after her, you'll be waiting in a long line.*

It was definitely time to find out if she liked lace curtains, he decided, especially if he were ever going to make Kate his wife. There was simply no way he could put off asking the question much longer.

Choctaw Charlie clicked the leather-covered telescope another notch to keep the black hearse in focus as he watched it depart the inn, leaving a cloud of white dust in its wake.

He took the glass from his eye, folded it closed, and handed it over to Vance Tobe, who was sitting alongside him under the cover of a scrub oak tree. "That sure is a nice telescope, Vance. I appreciate you letting me use it," Choctaw Charlie said in his measured, calm voice.

Vance carefully replaced the telescope in its case. He rubbed the small, healing scar under his eye for a moment, remembering how he had gotten it, then said, "That hick sheriff sure has a hankerin' for your woman. Comin' all the way out here in a hearse, of all things."

"I don't think it's going to be a lasting relationship," Charlie answered coldly.

"Nice of your lady to get rid of the bounty hunter for us. That bastard was one determined son of a bitch. And she did it all by herself, to boot."

"Kate's a real tough one to figure out. I thought Ma Bender was the one to watch out for. Now I ain't certain."

Vance spat a wad of tobacco juice at the ground, hitting his boot instead, and said, "That old woman could scare piss out of a grizzly bear."

"I think you boys have been patient long enough," Choctaw Charlie said to Vance. He nodded his head at Greasy Haynes, who was squatting Indian style a few feet from them, and added, "We'll hit the bank at Parsons tomorrow around noon. After we get the money, we'll shoot off our guns a few times to draw the sheriff out. He'll come right down the street to see what the ruckus is about. Vance, you kill him with that Sharps of yours."

"It'll be my pleasure," Vance Tobe said through a thin grin.

"Then we'll ride back out here. The town will be in an uproar. It'll take a day or two for them to get themselves organized, with the sheriff killed and all."

Greasy Haynes looked up, interested now, running his thumb slowly along the back of a Bowie knife with a foot-long blade.

"We'll go straight to the Bender's from the bank?" Vance questioned.

"Yeah. Those people probably have got more money hidden away than we'll get from the bank. All we have to do is convince them to give it to us."

"We kill the men when we get there?"

"That's the first thing we do — shoot them before they suspect a thing. Then Greasy can start working on the old woman. It won't take him long. He can be *real* convincing. Once we get their money, we'll round up all the horses to sell and head for Fort Scott."

"What about Kate?"

"She'll be invited along. You and Greasy can enjoy her company." Choctaw Charlie thought for a moment, then said to Greasy Haynes, "Out of respect for what she did to the bounty hunter I don't want you cutting

171

on her more than a week, now — you hear?"
Then he broke into that sickly, coughing
laugh of his.

Greasy Haynes looked past him. He was
staring at the distant Bender Inn, still lovingly stroking his Bowie knife.

TWELVE

"I'm sure glad you didn't turn that hearse of mine over yesterday. The darn thing costs a small fortune to fix back up," Lute said to Neely, over a pot of black coffee.

This had become a morning ritual with them. Neely would build a fire in his stove at first light. Once the blackened, porcelain-covered coffeepot had boiled long enough to reduce the contents to the consistency of light syrup, Neely would grab it, using two pot holders, and head for Lute's undertaking parlor.

If the conversation was to be one that required some thinking on, the coffeepot was set in the center of the table, the two men sitting on opposite sides facing each other. Should the topic not be one of any consequence, such as politics or religion, the coffeepot was set on a coffin. Lute and Neely would sit side by side on the floor, leaning up against a row of more coffins.

This morning, Neely set the pot on the table. Lute grabbed his cup from a shelf, held it up over his head, and looked inside.

"If anything's livin' in that cup, this coffee will kill it for sure," Neely said, as he sat down.

"Reckon I won't bother checking yours out, then. Any scorpions, spiders, or dead flies will just add flavoring to that weak stuff you boil up every mornin'," Lute said, setting a cup on the table. He didn't bother to look inside it, either. Before Neely could check it out, Lute had the pot in his hand, filling the cup.

When nothing unrecognizable floated to the surface after a long minute, Neely blew on his coffee to cool it and took a sip. Lute just sat quietly across from him, looking as if he weren't awake. His two-day stubble of gray beard made him seem older, and tired. "Women trouble, that's the only thing it could be. Well, you've come to the right place for advice," Lute finally said happily, breaking the silence. "Why, I've known women all my life. Even my mother was a woman."

Neely took another sip of coffee, this time with a grin on his face, and said, "It's nice to have a fountain of wisdom to consult when I've a need to."

"Yeah, I reckon you're one lucky cuss to have a man of my knowledge around."

"It's Kate Bender. I think I want to marry her."

"You sure you're not just in heat? There's a mighty big difference between dippin' your wick and livin' with them for the rest of your life," Lute said.

"You don't find a girl like her every day, Lute. She's pretty and as sweet as they come."

"I'd advise a little caution. I'll bet you don't know her as well as you think you do."

"I really think I'd better ask her soon. You're the one who told me not to waste any time."

"Hell's fire! I was talkin' about jumpin' her bones, not marryin' her."

Neely took a long nine cigar from his shirt pocket and offered it to Lute. It surprised him when his friend took the cigar, bit the end off, and started fishing around on a shelf, looking for a match. Neely plucked another from his pocket, along with a sulphur match. After both cigars began to fill the undertaker's parlor with acrid smoke Lute said, "You won't be able to do this when you get married. A woman hates cigar smoke worse than a lazy husband."

"She knows I smoke."

175

"The only plan a woman has from the time she's a baby is to wait until the time a man puts a ring on her finger. Then she spends the rest of her life tryin' to change him around from the way he was."

"I've never known a harder worker. Why, she's always busy doin' somethin' for her Ma."

"That's another thing. You ever notice how a daughter will grow to look like her mother? I'd think some on that, if I were you."

Neely felt a chill at the idea that a beautiful girl like Kate could ever become as mean and ugly as Almira, but Lute *did* have a point. Ma Bender had to have been young once.

Lute refilled their cups, leaned back in his chair, and said seriously, "Neely, if you're dead set on that girl, I'll give you some advice. Take a little more time. It's a big decision."

"I reckon a few weeks just to get to know her and her family a little better *would* be a good idea."

"There you go," Lute said, grinning as he reached into his pocket, pulled out a couple of quarters, and tossed them on the table.

"What are those for?" Neely asked, surprised.

"There's a new girl at The Rose. Her name's Sadie. You really should go see her and find out if that'll cure your problem."

"I often wondered what it cost. Now I know it's fifty cents."

"No it ain't. It's a quarter. I just figured it might take more than once to see if that's your problem."

Neely smiled broadly, causing his handlebar moustache to wiggle like a bug crawling on his lip. He drank the last of the coffee, took another puff on his black cigar, blew a smoke ring, and said, "Thanks, Lute, for the talk. I'd better get over to the store. I'll think on what you said."

"You do that," Lute said as Neely picked up the now cool and nearly empty coffeepot from the table and headed for the door. He started to say something about the two quarters left lying starkly on the wood table, but decided against it. When a man is in love, no other woman will do. Lute Thompson knew that all too well. So he said nothing as Neely left the undertaking parlor to begin his day's work.

It was just before noon and the sun was riding high in a cloudless, blue sky when Joe Peeples came into the general store, carrying a small, white piece of paper. He went straight to the stove, filled a cup with coffee, and said to Neely, "If we don't get some rain soon, this whole town will dry up and blow away."

Along with everyone that owes me money, Neely thought, but he simply said, "Yeah, it's been another dry one for sure."

Joe never was given to a lot of social life, generally being content to stay in his windowless cubbyhole of a telegraph office. The only time he was known to leave it during the day was when he had a message to deliver. "You have a telegram from the sheriff in Fort Scott," Joe said matter-of-factly, handing the paper to Neely. "It's an inquiry about a man that's come up missing. His name is Royce Dickinson. Seems he sent a letter to Independence saying he was coming through Parsons on his way back to Arkansas. He never got there. They sent along his description."

Neely read the telegram, shook his head, and went to get Lute. The undertaker was busily constructing another coffin. He had rough-cut boards setting across a pair of sawhorses in front of his parlor, cutting them to length. This was a good excuse for him to get out of the sun for a while, so he followed Neely back into the store.

Lute carefully studied the message, expres-

178

sionless.

"Do you think it might be him — the man found on the river?" Neely asked.

"Hard to say," Lute replied. "There wasn't a lot left to identify. But the build and height are about the same. It's a shame there was nothing left on him. They even took his boots, you know."

Neely started to say something when a volley of gunfire erupted down the street. Joe ran to the door, opened it just enough to stick his head out, then turned ashen-faced to Lute and Neely, and said, "My God, I think they're robbing the bank!"

Neely grabbed his Colt from its holster and started for the door. Lute put a firm hand on his shoulder and said, "Not that way. If you head down the street they'll kill you dead, and I'll charge double to plant you for being so dumb. This way."

Neely numbly followed Lute out the side door and to his parlor. "Wait here — I mean it," Lute said fiercely, going inside.

After a moment, Lute came out. Two large revolvers hung low on his hips, brass cartridges glinting in the bright sunlight from the brown leather belt.

Neely was taken aback. He had never even seen a gun at Lute's before. When he looked at his friend's face, he saw that the friendly

179

brown eyes had been reduced to mere slits. "We're going to circle around and come out on the side of them," Lute said, leading the way down the alley.

A woman screamed, and another round of gunfire split the air as the duo made their way past the rear of the bank. There was a space between the barber shop building and the bank. Lute drew both of his revolvers, saying, "Stay close behind me, along the wall. Keep in the shadows."

Neely drew his gun and flattened himself out with his back to the wall as Lute had and began edging to the street. When Lute came to the end of the building, he carefully looked around.

There were three mounted men almost in front of him. All were armed, and two of them had their guns drawn. One man, a small, skinny fellow, had a rifle pointed down the street in the direction of Neely's General Store. Obviously, they weren't expecting anyone to come from their flank.

Another horseman, nattily dressed, was alongside the little man, firing his pistol in the air. Even from his hiding place in the shadows, Lute Thompson could see the man smiling. He also knew he was looking at Choctaw Charlie.

Behind the two mounted men was another. A huge giant with red, shiny hair. There was a double-barrelled shotgun cradled in his arms.

A shaken Neely started to ask Lute what was going on, when Lute sprang from the shadows like a cat pouncing on a mouse. He aimed both of his revolvers at the little man with the big rifle and fired. A red spray erupted from the man's neck, knocking him from the saddle. When the bullets struck him, the man pulled the trigger on his rifle from shock, firing it. The kick of the rifle drove the stock of the gun into his horse, causing it to wheel and bump Choctaw Charlie's mount.

While Choctaw was trying to get his horse under control, Lute's pistols spat fire once more. This time, the giant with red, greasy hair twisted in his saddle, dropping the double-barreled shotgun to the ground as he did so.

Neely came up behind Lute, his Colt drawn. He looked at two riderless horses for a brief second, desperately trying to understand what had happened. Then Lute pushed him to one side and fired a shot that hit Choctaw Charlie's horse just behind its ear. At that moment, he saw a hand grasping the saddle horn, and another holding a pistol, snaking under the horse's neck.

When Lute's bullet hit the horse it reared up, causing the nearly hidden pistol to fire. Neely heard breaking glass, and a cry of pain from the bank building behind him. Then the horse fell over, landing on its rider, causing another yell of pain to rip the air.

Lute then trained his pistols in the direction of the big, fiery-haired man, only to find he had spun his horse around and was riding out of town as fast as he could, with Neely firing wildly at him.

"Neely!" Lute yelled sharply. "Quit wastin' ammo and get over here."

Neely, still shaking badly, looked at his smoking gun, trying to comprehend what was happening. Lute's yell brought him back to the present, the fog lifting from his mind, the reality of the scene in front of him horrifying. Somewhat wobbly, but at least aware of what was happening, Neely finally collected himself and joined Lute.

Carefully, Lute walked around to where he could see under the fallen horse, keeping both of his pistols pointed ahead.

Choctaw Charlie was crumpled under the horse and saddle, his face a mask of pain and rage. The pistol he had carried now lay in the dirt several feet away from his reach.

When Choctaw Charlie tried twisting

around to face Lute, Neely, who was close behind, could see that Charlie's leg was caught under the dead horse.

"You old son of a bitch," Charlie screamed at Lute, "you've broken my leg!"

"I'll do a lot more than bust your damn leg if you don't get rid of it," Lute said fiercely, pointing a gun at Choctaw Charlie's face.

Neely couldn't understand why Lute was getting ready to kill an unarmed man. Then Choctaw Charlie said, "All right, damn you, anyway," and a derringer hidden in the palm of his hand was tossed over to join his other pistol in the dirt. Neely swallowed hard. He'd never seen the gun until now.

Lute took a look over at the little man lying alongside the boardwalk. A spreading pool of thick, dark red blood told him he had nothing more to worry about from him. "Neely, keep your gun on our friend here," Lute said calmly, nodding his head at Choctaw Charlie, "and do us all a favor and shoot him if he does anythin' more than blink."

Neely pointed his cocked pistol at Choctaw Charlie's snarling face. Lute flipped both of his revolvers back in their holsters with an easy motion. A crowd was gathering. "Who else got shot?" Lute shouted the question in the direction of the bank.

183

"It's Ben Chatterhorn," an excited voice from inside squawked. "You better get Doc. I think he's bad hurt."

Lute started to tell someone to go fetch the doctor when he saw the fat man waddling down the boardwalk toward him, carrying a black leather case. Doc Clemmons stopped and looked at the man lying in the street for a moment. "That one's mine, you old sawbones," Lute said. "Someone said Chatterhorn's been shot. You might have better luck peddlin' your services in the bank."

Doc Clemmons looked hard at Lute, started to say something, then apparently thought better of it and went into the bank.

Turning to the building crowd, Lute said, "Well, don't just stand there a jawin', let's get a dead horse off that half-breed."

It took six men to raise the horse enough to drag a screaming and cursing Charlie Devin from under it. Neely could see the leg that the horse had fallen on was cocked at a crazy angle. It was broken, for sure.

"Keep your gun on him," Lute barked at Neely, who had put his pistol back in its holster. He did what he was told, as Lute bent over Choctaw. During a thorough search Lute had taken another derringer from one of his boots and two large knives from hidden sheaths. "That was a good Indian trick you tried to pull," Lute said to Choctaw Charlie in a matter-of-fact voice, "hangin' on to one side of your horse and usin' it as a shield while shootin' from under its neck."

"You weren't supposed to shoot my horse, you old son of a bitch. No one ever shoots a horse!"

"Reckon I didn't know that. An' I ain't old. Tie him up good and proper, then get him to the jail," Lute said to no one in particular.

A suddenly brave crowd realized they were looking at a defeated, captured Choctaw Charlie. All of them had heard stories of this outlaw's vile deeds. Now he lay helpless in front of them, with a broken leg. And it all had happened so fast. Two men came up with coils of rope. The crowd then bundled him up, like a cocoon. As they carried Choctaw Charlie down the street like a sack of potatoes to Parsons's one-cell jail, Neely placed his gun back in its holster and walked over to stand beside Lute. He and Lute listened to Charlie Devin's fading screams for a doctor and threats of what he had in store for everyone in town.

Neely looked at Lute. The same friendly eyes that he had grown to know greeted him. "Neely, for Christ's sake stop shaking. It's all over now. I know you were scared. So was I. It was your first time, and still you did all right. You did try to plug that red-headed bastard when he skedaddled out of town, didn't you? Hell, you might even have winged him." Lute chuckled and added, "By accident, of course. Now, let's go see how bad old Chatterhorn got hit."

Neely nodded weakly, and they went into the bank. A crowd had gathered around a man on the floor. Doc Clemmons had his case of instruments open and was busily working over the prostrate figure.

Goosey Hooper was there, dancing on the outside of the crowd. The wide-eyed livery-man came up to Lute and Neely and said excitedly, "He got shot through the cheeks."

Lute grimaced and asked the doctor loudly — he still couldn't see the victim for the crowd — "Did his face and teeth get busted up bad?"

Doc Clemmons whiney voice answered, "Wasn't those cheeks. He'll be OK. He'll just have to eat standing up for a while, is all." That was a long speech for the doctor, but one to cause more than Lute and Neely to choke down a laugh.

"Goosey, come outside with us," Lute said. Obediently, the livery stable owner followed them out to the boardwalk. "Take the dead man's horse over to your place," Lute said simply.

After Goosey led the terror-stricken animal away, Lute went to the dead man, who was still lying facedown in the dirt, and turned him over. His throat was shot half away. Surprised, unblinking eyes stared into the stark Kansas sun.

"That has to be Vance Tobe. The bounty hunter described him to me," Neely said.

"The bounty hunter sure didn't get to them in time, now did he? Maybe Choctaw Charlie knows what happened to him," Lute said.

"Yeah, if he'll talk."

Lute said nothing. He left the body of Vance Tobe and went to where the shotgun the giant, red-haired man had carried was lying in the dirt. Lute picked it up and, looking the gun over, said loudly, "Damn it!"

"What is it?" Neely asked.

"I must be out of practice. Look here, the shotgun caught one of my bullets," Lute answered, pointing to a black hole in the shattered wood stock.

"But you fired twice."

"I think it'll take more than one bullet to bring that big son of a bitch down."

"That was a guy they call Greasy Haynes,

according to what the bounty hunter told me," Neely said, then added, "He mentioned that Greasy likes to cut on women."

"We ought to get a posse together and go after him. With a bullet in his gut he'll travel slow. But us havin' Choctaw Charlie himself in jail, I think we'd better stay here in case some more of his gang try to break him out."

"The bounty hunter said those two *was* his gang, but you're right, we'd better stay here just in case."

Lute looked at Neely with a serious expression on his face. He handed him the shotgun, then picked up Vance Tobe's rifle, shook the dirt off it, blew dirt from the hammer, opened the action, and took out a large brass shell. "Fifty caliber Sharps," Lute said. "It would blow a hole in a man big enough for a bird to fly through. If you had come out the front door this would have had your name on it." Lute slipped the cartridge in Neely's shirt pocket, smiled, and said, "You might want to keep this." He looked at the milling crowd of people and yelled, "Will a couple of you carry that body over to my place?"

Immediately, several men picked up the remains of Vance Tobe and headed down the street to Lute Thompson's undertaking parlor with their bloody burden. Neely noticed the respect in their faces when they looked at Lute. He felt the same way. Here was a man they all knew as an undertaker and occasional drunk, who had single-handedly stopped a bank robbery. He had killed one outlaw, and shot and wounded another. Choctaw Charlie, one of the most feared killers in the territory, was now in the town jail with a broken leg, all because of Lute's shooting.

Lute had done what he did in the blink of an eye, and now was perfectly calm about it. "My God, Lute," Neely said suddenly. "Do you know what you've done?"

"Yeah, all too well. For sixteen years I wore a badge like yours. Only mine said, Texas Ranger on it."

THIRTEEN

Choctaw Charlie was lodged securely in Parsons's lone jail cell. The prison itself, which sat on a knoll in back of the hotel, was a one-room building constructed of white sandstone slabs set in mortar. One very small, iron-barred window was set in the rear. A heavy, steel front door with narrow slots cut horizontally into it was the other source of light, and the only access to the cell.

Neely had used the single pair of shackles in town to fasten Charlie's left hand to an iron ring which had been anchored to a large stone by the bed for that purpose. A shotgun-carrying guard stood nervously outside.

Doc Clemmons had come by to see about setting Choctaw's broken leg. The furious outlaw lashed out with his good one, kicking the doctor in the groin. If Choctaw Charlie's broken limb was ever going to be set now, it would be by someone other than the town doctor.

Lute Thompson had gotten Vance Tobe well-dusted with quicklime, nailed into a coffin, and set into the lean-to when Neely came to see him.

"Come on up to the store, Lute. I made a fresh pot. Also, it's too hot out here."

"Reckon it is a mite warm out," Lute said, following Neely into his shop.

Neely sat in the swivel chair in front of his rolltop desk. Lute plopped into an oak chair alongside the desk with a sigh, looked at Neely, and said, "I'm gettin' too old for this shit."

Before Neely could answer, the front door of his general store swung open and a half dozen townswomen entered, led by a very pregnant Eppie Rogers.

Lute rolled his eyes, and a look of dread covered his face like a mask.

"Mister Thompson," Eppie said in a syrupy sweet voice, "on behalf of the women of this town I would like to thank you for what you did and invite you to come to our church Sunday."

"Lady," Lute replied in a cold, calculated voice, "a few hours ago I shot a man's throat out, gut shot another, killed a horse, and smashed a man's leg. In a day or two, I'll help your sheriff hang a man by his neck until the life's out of him. If that's what it takes to get invited to your church socials, I'll pass."

Eppie Rogers's mouth flew open, fury in her eyes, and she shouted, "Well, I never!"

Lute made an obvious look at her girth, smiled, and said, "I don't believe *that* statement would hold up in court."

After the shocked bevy left the store, Lute turned to a speechless Neely and said flatly, "Killin' is bad business, old friend. That's one reason I left the Rangers. After a while you don't feel anymore. It's like part of you died. The part that feels."

"I'd have been the one nailed in that coffin, if it wasn't for you."

"I did what had to be done. When you come up against a bunch like Choctaw Charlie's, you can't hesitate — that's what they depend on. Most people are slow to take a life. They think on it for a second too long. You have to be *like* them, or maybe even a little meaner, to beat them. That's the part I hate."

Silence pervaded the room for a long while. Then to change the subject, Neely said, "I've sent out telegrams to the other towns warning about Greasy Haynes and telling them we have Choctaw Charlie in jail."

"Are they goin' to send a judge out for a trial?" Lute questioned.

"The governor wired a message that the circuit judge was busy for weeks. Under the circumstances, he was giving that power to our township trustee."

Lute laughed. "Why, that's old Chatterhorn. I don't see how he could be too awful impartial, after getting shot in the ass and all."

"He'll have to conduct his affairs standin' up, for sure," Neely chuckled. Then he looked at Lute seriously and said, "They're going to hang him, you know."

"There ain't no doubt about it. No one probably knows that better than Choctaw Charlie himself."

"I've never hung anyone before. The whole town's going to expect me to do it."

"It comes with that star on your shirt. If I was you, I'd pick out a good tall tree not far from the jail and start someone buildin' a scaffold under it."

Neely began to say something when Joe Peeples came into the store, walking over to Neely and Lute in his usual, stiff business-like manner. "Ben Chatterhorn's home restin'. The bullet just creased him a little. He'll be fine. He told me to tell you that he'll hold court in the lobby of the hotel at ten o'clock tomorrow morning. After Choctaw Charlie gets his fair trial, you can plan on hangin' him at three in the afternoon," Joe said.

"I can't have a proper scaffold built by then," Neely replied.

"Ben said to just put him on a horse and hang him from the nearest tree. Doc said he would be glad to spur the horse off."

Neely sighed. "Tell Chatterhorn we'll take care of it."

After a period of small talk to ease the strain of the day, Neely asked Lute, "Do you think you could come with me in the morning, say around seven or so? I'd like to take Choctaw Charlie some coffee and breakfast and see if we can get him to maybe tell us who that man was, the one they killed on the river. There's no reason for him not to tell us now. Maybe he's that Royce fellow. Then we can put a name on his grave and wire his folks what happened to him."

"Sure, I'll come with you, but I wouldn't expect much out of Choctaw Charlie. Any conscience he ever had is long dead," Lute answered, getting up to leave.

"By the way, Lute, there's a twenty-five-hundred-dollar reward for the two men you got. I've put in to the governor's office for it. You should have your money in a few days."

"Yeah, thanks, Neely," Lute said flatly over his shoulder as he left the store. Neely watched as Lute turned in the doorway and walked off in the direction of The Rose Saloon.

It was a time of celebration in the town of Parsons that night. The Rose Saloon and The Kansas Schooner were packed. Glasses were clinked together and toasts made to Lute Thompson, the brave Texas Ranger who had captured the famous outlaw.

From Annie Mitchell's upstairs room, Lute listened to the sound of the honky-tonk piano rattling the night air. In the soft, yellow light of a flickering kerosene lamp, Annie's blond hair turned to gold. When she was with Lute her face softened, and a sparkle returned to her blue eyes.

They lay together in silence on top of Annie's well-worn double bed. Lute was wearing his long underwear. He didn't like being naked in front of a woman. During his sixteen years of being married to Margaret he had never gotten used to it — being naked. Somehow, it made him feel embarrassed.

Annie, on the other hand, was wearing what she came into this world with. Lute admired the way it never seemed to bother her, bouncing around the room without any clothes on. He could never remember seeing Margaret that way. Always, she had insisted on the room being dark and the covers pulled over them when they made love. Once it was over, she would wrap up in a shapeless, flannel nightgown.

That was a lifetime ago. Lute was a raw recruit in the Texas Rangers, full of spit and vinegar. Margaret Williams was the daughter of the owner of the town newspaper in Fort Worth. After a brief courtship they had run away to Dallas and gotten married. Margaret's father was livid, but there was nothing he could do about the situation. Married was married. Also, there was the distinct possibility that Margaret was already pregnant. So Lane Williams grudgingly accepted the young Texas Ranger as his son-in-law.

The first few years they spent together were good ones. Margaret had given birth to three children; two boys who were mischievous and full of life, and a beautiful girl with brown hair and green eyes, like her mother.

Lute was gone from home a lot. It was part of the job of being a Texas Ranger. It seemed the longer they were married, the more Lute was away. Margaret resented that fact, and it became a sore that waxed larger throughout the years.

Their arguments grew louder. Lute's answer was to volunteer for assignments that took him into the field for months at a time.

After a long, hard six months of pursuing Mexican cattle rustlers along the Rio Grande near the border town of Del Rio, he had come home to an empty house. His father-in-law refused to tell him where they had gone. However, Lane *was* quick to tell him that the divorce papers were proper and filed.

Lute took a leave of absence from the Rangers. Using detective techniques learned from years of being a lawman, he quickly traced his family to Kansas City.

His first impulse was to storm in and take his wife and children back to Texas by whatever force was necessary. After some thought, however, he took a room near where they lived and watched from the shadows. Margaret was married to a doctor. His children ran to the doctor and hugged him when he came home at night from the hospital.

And he did come home — every night. It was a life Margaret craved, and one he simply couldn't supply. After a week of moping Lute saddled up and rode aimlessly until coming to the small town of Parsons, Kansas.

When he arrived, the town's only undertaker had just stepped on a rattlesnake. He helped bury the man, then decided that he would keep doing it, burying people. The job fit his mood at the time.

That was nearly three years ago. Now, as he lay there in Slanty Annie's bed, stroking her blond hair, he felt for the first time in years that he was back in the Texas Rangers.

Neely Wells was his friend. Lute realized that the storekeeper knew nothing of what it took to be a sheriff. He stayed sober now just for that reason — to keep Neely from getting himself killed.

Perhaps in a day or two he could crawl back into a whiskey bottle. That Greasy Haynes was shot was a certainty. One bullet from his .44 was deflected when it struck the shotgun, the other had hit the outlaw low on his right side, not necessarily a fatal wound.

Greasy Haynes might just den up in the

woods like a hurt animal and quietly die of infection, but Lute doubted that. His experiences had taught him that a man like Greasy could soak up a lot of lead. On second thought, he would stay sober a while longer.

Lute rolled over and kissed Annie. She giggled like a schoolgirl, and had started to unbutton his long handles when the sound of a shotgun blast thundered over the sound of the piano.

"Hellfire and tarnation!" Lute exclaimed, rolling off the bed and fishing hurriedly for his pants. The music went silent, and another explosion echoed through the night air. Forgetting his pants he pulled his boots on, strapped his revolvers around his long handles, and plunged from the room to head down the back stairs. He knew the instant he heard the gunfire where the problem was: the jail.

When he got to the lone cell in back of the hotel, a crowd was already gathering. After a quick look around, Lute holstered his guns. Neely was standing in front of the jail near the door. He looked pale and sick. "What the hell happened?" Lute questioned.

"Roland Langtry. We found him like that," Neely answered, quickly motioning with his eyes to the bloodied saloon owner lying on the ground alongside his shotgun. Doc Clemmons was bent over him, working on his head. "He was guarding Choctaw Charlie while I got some rest," Neely added through pinched lips.

Roland moaned loudly and tried to sit up. The doctor pushed him back down, telling him to take it easy.

Lute pushed his way close to Roland, looked him over and declared, "He ain't shot." Then he asked, "Who the hell got blasted by the shotgun? Did they get Choctaw Charlie out of jail?"

"It wasn't a jailbreak, Lute. Charlie — what's left of him — is smeared all over the cell," Neely said grimly.

"The hell you say," Lute replied, walking over and peering through a slot in the metal door. Even by the sparse moonlight, he could see that shotgun blasts had torn the chained outlaw nearly in two. "Now why would anyone kill a man we were gonna hang tomorrow?" Lute asked, puzzled.

"Maybe family of someone he's killed. My God, Lute, I just don't know," Neely replied.

"You old pillpusher, back off," Roland said, sitting up. A red splotch showed through the white bandage Doc Clemmons had wrapped around his head.

"Who hit you?" Neely asked, taking the words out of Lute's mouth.

"I — I was just sittin' in a chair leaning against the jail, when all of a sudden I see somethin' out of the corner of my eye."

"Well, who the hell was it? Tell us," Lute demanded.

"I never saw who it was. It happened so fast."

"What *did* you see, Roland?" Neely asked.

"A hammer, a small one. That was all, just a hammer."

"Well, son of a bitch," Lute said.

Kate Bender's shoulder was sore and hurting. That ten-gauge shotgun Neely Wells had brought them kicked like a Missouri mule. When she dressed this morning, she was careful to button her blouse all the way to the top to keep the spreading, purple bruise concealed.

With a stiff arm, Kate helped her Ma cook breakfast. This morning they were fixing a large one; eggs, side meat, and cornbread cracklins fried in hog fat. It was a celebration of sorts.

They weren't certain Choctaw Charlie would have talked any about them, but it was a chance they felt they couldn't afford

201

to take. He knew the Benders were from Missouri. Very discreetly, they had checked out Wanted posters, finding they were not on any of them. Perhaps none of the bodies were ever discovered. That would be a stroke of luck. Wounding that man with a shotgun wasn't anything to get the law too fired up about, just a local matter.

Choctaw Charlie *was* a possible problem, however. Almira Bender didn't like problems. Brock and Seth O'Malley had come by their inn late yesterday afternoon on their way back from Parsons. They had been in town for supplies when the shooting started. In an excited voice, the pair told of the bank robbery and how Lute Thompson, the undertaker, had killed Vance Tobe and captured Choctaw Charlie by shooting his horse. Greasy Haynes had gotten away, but he was believed to be badly hurt, a bullet in his gut.

Taking care not to arouse their suspicions, Kate and Almira asked where Choctaw was being held and what was being done to keep that dreaded outlaw from escaping.

After the O'Malleys had left the Benders called a family meeting. This was always done in a crisis, if there was time.

It was decided that the risk of Choctaw Charlie talking was too great a chance to take. He wasn't one given to any type of loyalty, that was for sure. His ability to buy horses and merchandise left behind by their "customers" was a benefit to them, but there were others who would do the same. Also, Choctaw was a possible danger — Ma Bender was certain he planned to kill them eventually. It would be better to extend that favor to him first.

Kate happily volunteered for the task of removing Choctaw Charlie from the face of the earth. He had not thanked her for killing the bounty hunter, and when he took her to the woods after she told him, he was rougher on her than usual. Her nipples were still sore and bruised from his teeth. He always made her scream. It was something he had to do. Choctaw Charlie was never able to get hard unless she was screaming.

John saddled her horse for her. Tucking the small, shoemaker's hammer into the leather belt around her narrow waist and carrying the shotgun across her saddle, Kate Bender had ridden alone by the pale moonlight into Parsons. The single guard had been half asleep. She was fairly certain he never saw her. It was possible that the man had lived. There wasn't time for more blows from her hammer; her mission had been to kill Charlie Devin.

He had smiled when he saw her. He thought Kate was there to get him out of jail.

When he saw the shotgun stuck through the cell door, it was Choctaw Charlie's turn to scream.

Greasy Haynes was holed up in a crevice of rock near the town of Cherryvale, his pain-glazed, dark eyes constantly scanning for danger.

The bullet had gone completely through his right side. Where the slug had come out, above his hipbone, was the worst. The hole felt as big as a silver dollar. He had mixed tobacco juice with mud and packed both holes with it. The bleeding had stopped, but not the pain.

That bitch, he thought, *that damn Kate Bender. It was her fault. She caused Choctaw Charlie to do what he did. We should have hit The Bender Inn instead of the bank. We would have, too, if she hadn't corrupted him. Women do that to men, ruin them. I know what to do to women to pay them back. Always, it's the fault of a woman when things go wrong.*

Greasy bent over to take his Bowie knife out of its sheath to fondle it. When he did so, a sharp pain and a feeling of wetness came to his lower back. He spat several mouthfuls of tobacco juice into a handful of dirt. Working it into a paste, he pushed it into his wound again. The poultice stopped the bleeding.

The pain was worse now. No matter. He had the knife in his hands. Taking the blade in one hand and a sharpening stone in the other, he began to hone the already keen edge with long, loving strokes.

He would heal. He always did. Greasy Haynes had been through worse than this. Much worse. It would take time; he would be strong. Then, when he was healed, he could use his wonderful, razor-sharp knife again. Only now there would be no one to tell him what to do, or when to do it.

Patience is a virtue. Greasy Haynes remembered the wizened silver-haired preacher saying that from years ago. His father always made sure he went to church every Sunday. The old parson was right. He needed patience. Someday he would show Kate Bender what real pain was all about.

FOURTEEN

"Too bad we couldn't have had a proper hangin' for Choctaw Charlie. It would have been a real fanny bumper, for sure. I reckon half the people in the county would have turned out," Lute said in a disappointed voice to Neely, over their morning coffee.

"Why somebody killed him while he was already locked up is a mystery to me," Neely replied.

"Could be that they was afraid of something he might say. I don't think it was Greasy Haynes. He's shot a little too bad to be galavantin' around the country. Why he would have killed him anyway is a mystery. I just don't know."

"Sure made a mess out of my jail," Neely said. "I've got Maude Saunders scrubbin' away on it. That white sandstone will never come clean."

"All that blood will give any future guests somethin' to think on, for sure. Talking about messes, I could save a coffin and use a gunnysack to lay what's left of Choctaw Charlie away in. The shotgun must have been at least a ten-gauge. Two blasts of double-O buckshot from six feet away does a hell of a job, for sure."

"You know, Lute, I think Roland Langtry is one lucky son of a gun. Whoever it was tried to kill him, too — being hit on the head with a hammer, of all things."

"Nope, you can't hurt a bartender by poundin' them on the head. If their skulls weren't as hard as a cast-iron cookstove, they wouldn't be in that business in the first place."

Neely couldn't help but smile. He always admired the way Lute Thompson could find humor in nearly everything. Somehow, he wasn't really surprised to learn Lute had been a Texas Ranger. The way he carried himself with confidence when he was sober spoke volumes. The fact that he drank himself into a stupor on occasion expressed a deep-seated, unmentioned pain. Neely wondered a lot about what past hurts his friend must have suffered, but would certainly never ask. Lute would talk about it when he was ready. He also knew that Lute had stayed sober only because he was afraid something would happen to him.

Lute had been right. If not for his friend having been there and taking charge as he did, Neely knew full well there would be only one person buried today — him. He owed Lute his life. If it took the rest of the time he had left on this earth, he would repay him, somehow.

Things would settle down now, return to normal. By this afternoon the two outlaws would be under six feet of dirt, laid to rest in unmarked graves. His problems solved, he could then go back to the business of courting Kate Bender. Surely, no one would make any attempts at serious lawbreaking around Parsons in the future, not after what happened to the last ones who tried.

Greasy Haynes was either dead or heading for a safer climate. There was no way he would ever bother anyone around here again.

"I've been a thinkin' on that telegram you got, the one about that Royce fellow," Lute said, shaking Neely from his reverie. "We were a tad interrupted when we last talked on it. I'm of the opinion that the man we've got buried *is* Royce Dickinson, but there's no way we could ever identify him. If we tell them we've planted him and he turns up somewhere else, like in jail, that'd be embarrassin' as hell. I'd just send a note that we have an unidentifiable body that was his size and found with nothing in the way of personal items on him. Let them draw their own conclusions."

"You should have been a politician. That's a good way to handle it."

"Ain't no cause to go a callin' me names, Neely. The only difference between a politician and an outlaw is that a politician does his stealin' all legal like."

"I see your point." Neely chuckled. "Well, I guess you've got a couple of holes to dig, and I've got a store to open."

"Yup, I guess we'd better get to it," Lute replied, draining the last swallow of coffee from his cup.

When Neely left the undertaker's parlor he noticed a bank of black storm clouds building in the west. It certainly looked as if it might rain; that would be good news. He needed all the cheering up he could get.

At noontime Neely Wells walked to the front window of his store and flipped the OPEN sign over to CLOSED. When he reached the creaking boardwalk, he turned and locked the door with a skeleton key. As he strode off to The Grand Hotel, he noticed the cloudbank was still in the same place it had been this morning. It was as if God had painted it on the sky and then gotten distracted for some reason and forgot what he was doing. At least some folks west of town were getting a good rain.

When he went into Joe Peeples's telegraph office, the little man spun quickly around in his oak swivel chair, his eyes fixed on Neely's holstered Colt. He bolted back with a jump that would have done Goosey Hooper proud, nearly overturning his chair. Then he saw the badge, and finally Neely's smiling face, and relaxed. "You've been takin' the same nerve tonic Goosey sips on, I see," Neely said jokingly.

Joe, breathing hard and looking embarrassed, spurted out, "My God, I just saw the gun and thought we were being robbed like old Ben Chatterhorn was. Those outlaws had taken over five thousand dollars when your friend shot them."

"Well, Chatterhorn has his money back all safe and sound. How's his butt, anyway?" Neely asked, still smiling.

"He's walking mighty stiff these days. He's at the bank, if you want to see him. I've got to warn you, he's in a really bad mood. He wanted in the worst way to see Choctaw Charlie hung. Whoever killed that outlaw in the jail cell also kept Ben from getting paid as judge for the trial."

"I reckon losin' a few dollars would bother him more than gettin' his ass shot."

It was the telegraph operator's turn to smile when he answered, "That man does love his money. So does Roland Langtry. He was real upset there wasn't a hangin'. That would have brought him in a pile. I expect a lot of folks are disappointed. It could have been a real festive occasion."

"How's Roland doin', anyway?"

"He's had worse headaches from drinkin' that rotgut whiskey he peddles."

"I suspect that's the truth. You know, whoever it was who hit him could have caved his skull in."

"If it had been anyone besides Roland, the blow would have killed them, for sure. I always thought he was one hardheaded scalawag. Now we have proof I was right."

"Any telegrams for me?" Neely asked.

"Oh yeah. You're a right popular man these days," Joe answered, reaching into a pigeonhole of his rolltop desk, extracting a handful of white papers, and handing them to Neely.

Three of the messages were from other sheriffs, congratulating him on getting rid of Choctaw Charlie and asking for a further description of Greasy Haynes.

One telegram was a surprise. It was from

Fort Scott, inquiring about Calvin Olson, a cattle buyer who had gone to Independence on business. He had vanished on the way, never making it to his destination.

Neely remembered the fat man with that name sitting in The Bender Inn getting drunk. He had been surly when he told him about Choctaw Charlie being in the area. Most likely, there would be another body found somewhere between the Bender's and Independence. At least this would be the last. *Calvin Olson should have listened to me. If he had, be might still be alive,* Neely thought.

The final telegram was from the governor's office in Topeka, authorizing him to pay reward money to one Lute Thompson in the amount of five hundred dollars for killing Vance Tobe and two thousand dollars for the capture of Charlie Devin, also known as Choctaw Charlie. He was instructed to make out a voucher, attach the telegram to it, and take it to the bank for payment.

"That one ought to make Lute mighty happy," Joe said as Neely folded the messages into his shirt pocket.

"I reckon it should. He deserves it."

"That's for sure. Who would have thought about him being a Texas Ranger? I expect he'll go on a hell of a toot now, and try to wear out Slanty Annie."

"No way of tellin' about Lute. He's got his own manner of doin' things."

"Ain't that a fact?" Joe said to Neely as the sheriff turned to leave.

After a dinner of pinto beans and cornbread in the hotel dining room, Neely stopped by his store long enough to fill out a voucher form. He took it and the telegram to the bank, presenting them to a stiff-moving, unsmiling Ben Chatterhorn. "Tell Lute he'll have to come by and sign for his money. Then he'll get paid," the banker said through tight lips.

"He's out buryin' those outlaws now. I'll give him the message when he gets done."

"I hope he plants them deep. It'll be a shorter distance for the devil to get them," Ben Chatterhorn said harshly.

"Those two won't cause any more trouble, thanks to Lute." On his way out of the bank, for some reason Neely couldn't control, he said over his shoulder, "You'll have to admit, Choctaw Charlie had a way of keeping you on your toes when he was around."

What Ben Chatterhorn said was mostly unintelligible, but Neely Wells walked down the street with an ear to ear grin. Lute

213

would have been proud of him.

It had rained all morning at The Bender Inn. A nice, slow ground soaker, the type of rain that puts a farmer's spirits high. The Benders, however, were not farmers. The Osage Mission Road that ran in front of their business was becoming a muddy quagmire. This was not good for attracting customers.

The daily stagecoach from Independence to Parsons had passed, leaving deep ruts in the road. That had been the only traffic of the day, so far. Kate was lying in her bed reading the Bible, thankful to be able to rest her sore shoulder. William was lackadaisically sharpening tools and knives. Inactivity never bothered him much. He could sit for hours lost in thought, chewing on a plug of black tobacco, doing nothing.

John Bender was sitting on the side of his bed, strumming on a six-string guitar. He was surprisingly good. Like tobacco chewing or hammer swinging, it was something he had a natural talent for. "Old Folks at Home" was his chosen melody of the day. Over and over, he played the same tune until Kate, or someone, asked for another selection. John knew most of the popular songs. Once he heard a tune he instantly memorized it and could replay it at will. But until someone asked for another song, he played the same ones repeatedly, like a stuck player piano.

Kate occasionally sang along with John's guitar playing, her melodious voice ringing loudly in the little house. Singing was not to be counted among John Bender's talents. Pa said his singing sounded as if someone were trying to skin a live cat.

Almira Bender, always busy, was sprinting around the little house doing first one thing, then another. She had several loaves of bread sitting on the warming oven of the stove, waiting for the yeast to work.

A large, cast-iron pot of beef stew was slowly simmering. On occasion, Ma stirred it while adding more ingredients, such as tomatoes or carrots. Two of her famous apple pies were in the oven, baking. Two more were made up and ready to bake when the first two were done and there was room in the stove for them.

William Bender looked up from his knife sharpening and said to Almira, "We're better off without him. I have a feeling that Choctaw Charlie wasn't one to hold with his word."

"The Good Book says, 'If your right hand offends thee, it's better it be cut off.' Katie

215

was a good daughter, following the teachings we live by," Ma Bender replied, stirring the stew.

"Amen," William said.

Kate folded her leather-covered Bible closed, placed it in the crate by her bed, turned, and sat up. "Mama," she asked sweetly, "I'm awful sore from that shotgun and where Choctaw Charlie was mean to me. Could I please stay home from church tomorrow and rest up a little more?"

"Idle hands are the devil's playground, child," Almira answered sternly. "You'll come along with us, and I expect you to keep that sheriff good and happy, no matter what you have to do."

"Yes, Mama," Kate replied, "but I'm all bruised. I can't let him see me without my clothes on until I'm healed up."

"You're right, child. That might get him to thinking. We can't have that. You'll come to church and I want you to be nice to him, but that's all you have to do for now."

"Thank you, Mama," Kate replied meekly.

Ma Bender was beginning to set the table for their dinner when, she saw a solitary horseman through the rain-streaked window, tying up to their hitch rail. "We might have us a customer," Almira said solemnly.

The lone traveler came inside, took off his

rain slicker and hat, and hung them from nails driven in a plank by the door. When he turned to look at the Benders, they were all smiles; even Ma had managed the semblance of one. This man was a total stranger.

Kate came stiffly to the front and offered the man a seat at the table — the canvas side where he could have a nice backrest.

As most men did, he gaped open-mouthed and wide-eyed when he encountered the beautiful Kate Bender. Quickly composing himself, the slightly embarrassed young man took the proffered seat.

He couldn't believe his good fortune when the pretty girl sat across the table from him. She sipped on a cup of coffee while batting her emerald green eyes invitingly, making small talk, asking questions.

Quince Stallings was the name he gave Kate over a steaming bowl of delicious beef stew served with a generous slice of buttered homemade bread. It was a wonderful meal, and John's guitar playing seemed soothing to him. Being out of the storm and in the presence of a beautiful, charming lady was a real stroke of luck.

After the empty bowl had been taken away by an efficient and taciturn Almira it was replaced by a huge piece of apple pie. With his coffee cup refilled, Quince began to relax all the more. He was in no hurry to go back into the rain. Kate Bender seemed genuinely interested in him, where he lived, and where he was headed. A very caring young lady, for sure.

From the back room, he heard the old man tell the younger one to play "Jeannie with the Light Brown Hair" on his guitar. This was a tranquil song that caused him to think even more on the beautiful, auburn-haired girl sitting across the table from him.

Quince was from Tulsa, in the Indian Territory, he told the lovely girl while eating what he thought was the best apple pie he had ever tasted. His aunt in Kansas City had passed away unexpectedly. He was sent by his family to settle her estate.

Cautiously and with a caring demeanor, Kate told him of Choctaw Charlie's capture in Parsons. She was very careful not to say the word "killed." They couldn't be expected to know of that so soon. Should this young man not be carrying a sum of money, they didn't want any suspicions aroused.

Young Quince Stallings showed obvious relief at Kate's statement. He patted his vest pocket and told her that he *had* been worried about being robbed, and this outlaw was notorious. Then he mentioned that he had successfully sold his aunt's estate for nearly three thousand dollars. Quince was obviously proud of that fact. It was more money than any of his family had expected him to return with.

Kate Bender watched as her father moved stealthfully to position himself behind the wagon canvas. She could see his outline through the flimsy covering. Keeping an alluring smile pasted on her visage, she waited for the outline of a blacksmith hammer to appear. Kate knew her Pa could see the back of the man's head as easily as she could observe his movements.

A few more moments. A sprinkling of pouty smiles and batting green eyes from Kate. Finally Quince Stallings leaned back against the canvas, laughing at one of his own jokes.

There was a dull, slapping sound, and the traveler recoiled from the cloth with an expression of disbelief painted on his wide-eyed face. He fell heavily onto the table, his head coming to rest in the half-eaten piece of apple pie.

Kate, her smile gone now, grabbed the man by his hair and raised his head from the plate, which she extracted with obvious concern. When she looked the dish over and found it wasn't broken, her smile returned. China serving plates cost money. Mama would have been displeased if it was cracked.

John placed his guitar carefully on the bed. As he came through the doorway, he extracted his razor-sharp Bowie knife from its hidden sheath.

Within a few minutes the traveler's throat was cut, and his body dumped into the gullet of the old well under the table along with the rain slicker and hat.

John led the man's horse into the distant hills. Returning soaked, he stripped off his wet clothes and hung them by the stove to dry. Soon, he was playing a tune on the guitar again — the same one he was playing before being interrupted.

Almira took the two apple pies from the oven, after looking them over to make certain they were perfectly done. She placed them on a shelf to cool. Then she checked the fire, adding a few pieces of wet oak. That would not be a problem, she knew. Soaked wood, when added to an established fire, soon dried out and burned well. It did however, cause the temperature to drop until the fire returned. Making a mental note to allow more baking time, she slid the two uncooked pies into the oven, closed the door and sat down for a short rest.

Kate sat back at the front dining-room

table, across from the canvas, no longer tired. She was anxious for nightfall, when they would strip the body in the hole beneath her and add up their take. San Francisco was growing closer. Choctaw Charlie wouldn't bother her anymore, and her breasts could heal now, without his biting on them. Neely Wells, the sheriff, wouldn't be like that, she thought. He might even be gentle with her. In some of the books she had read, men treated their women with kindness, even love. That would be a new experience for her. She would never find out about Neely if her Mama didn't tell her to do it with him, though. Kate was a perfect child. She never did it with any man unless her Mama told her to.

Almira told John to play "Amazing Grace." When he did, Kate began singing. She loved that song.

William Bender went back to tool sharpening. It was still raining out. They probably wouldn't have any more customers today. That was just as well, he thought as he took time to slice a piece of plug tobacco off with his pocketknife and plop it into his mouth.

Tomorrow would be a busy day. They had to plant another apple tree in a nice deep hole. At least the rain would soften the earth.

The Lord always provides.

FIFTEEN

Neely felt just as if a knife had been driven in his heart, then twisted. Kate all but ignored him on her way into church that morning. He sat dejectedly alongside John Bender in the wooden church pew, wondering what dark deed he could have done to incur her wrath.

When Neely turned to look at Kate, who was stowed away and nearly hidden between the bulk of Almira and William, John would roll his empty face around to gawk blankly at him. After a couple of John's baleful stares, Neely decided it was more pleasant to watch the preacher drone through his sermon.

A steady patter of rain on the church roof made Pike Rogers's invocation seem even more boring and long-winded than usual. Even Eppie, the preacher's wife, finally nodded her head and dozed off. She started snoring loudly from her seat in the front pew. After several loud snorts Mrs. Saunders, who was seated behind her, reached forward and tapped her rather firmly on the shoulder. Eppie threw a Goosey Hooper fit, accompanied by a yell that would have done justice to a coyote.

An obviously vexed Reverend Rogers hastily drew the service to a close. This was a relief to everyone except his wife. The entire congregation knew she was in for her very own special sermon once the preacher got her home.

When Kate Bender was leaving the church, walking close between her folks, Neely came up from behind and placed his hand on her right shoulder. It took all her strength not to cry out or show any discomfort. In spite of everything, she still made a slight gasp. "Is something wrong?" Neely asked in a concerned voice.

"Oh Neely, I'm sorry," Kate replied, unsmiling and hard-eyed, glad his hand was gone from her bruised shoulder. "I'm not feeling very well today."

"I'm sorry," Neely said. "Is there anything you need? Can I get you something from the store?"

Kate's attitude changed like a black cloud fleeing the sun. "You're *so* sweet to me, Neely. Why, I think you're the nicest man," she said, beaming at him and batting her green eyes. "But I'll be all right in a few days. It's nothing a little rest won't cure." Kate planted a quick kiss full on his lips in front of what must have been half the town of Parsons. Neely felt as if he'd turned the color of a beet.

Still smiling that cute, pouty, sexy smile of hers, Kate quickly wheeled around to walk alongside her mother to go climb into that decrepit-looking wagon of theirs.

Neely stood dumbstruck in front of the church in the gentle rain and watched as the two Bender men took time to cut huge chunks of black tobacco from a twist, using a one-blade pocketknife. After stuffing them in their mouths they drove away, leaving twin ruts in the muddy street. His beloved Kate, sitting beside her somber mother, looked straight ahead, never turning her head or waving him farewell.

He took the western scout hat he had been holding respectfully against his chest and placed it on his already wet scalp. After shaking his head in a questioning manner, he turned and walked the muddy path that led from the church to The Grand Hotel.

Pausing in front of the door for a moment to scrape mud from his boots and shake water from his coat like a wet dog, Neely nearly collided with Ben Chatterhorn when he turned to head for the dining room.

"Your friend, Lute Thompson, is inside drinking coffee," Ben said in an unusually pleasant tone. "He came by the bank yesterday and signed the reward papers. Then, of all things, he opened an account and left the money there. *All* of it."

Neely was glad the banker was in a good mood. After that comment he'd made earlier, he hadn't been really anxious to see him again anytime soon. "I don't think Lute's going to drink like he used to," Neely replied.

"Of course he will," Chatterhorn replied with an air of authority. "Once a drunk, always a drunk. He insisted on being paid for burying those two outlaws, so I went ahead and gave him the money. I expect he'll be soused by tonight, for sure."

"Let's not underestimate him, Ben. Those outlaws made the same mistake."

"Oh, he'll get falling down drunk, just like I said," Ben retorted, looking down his nose with a cocky, self-assured sneer.

It was a relief, seeing that uncharacteristic niceness leave the banker. Neely watched as Chatterhorn spun and walked off down the boardwalk without even a hint of stiffness. *Nothing like a big deposit to cause a money-*

226

lender to forget about being shot in the ass, he thought with a grin.

After a few steps Ben Chatterhorn stopped, turned around with an almost puzzled look and said flatly to Neely, "By the way, that was a good job you did taking care of those outlaws."

It was a morning of surprises for Neely Wells. First, Kate made him feel unwanted, and now Ben Chatterhorn actually paid him a compliment. In all of his memory, he couldn't remember that pinched-faced old banker ever saying a good word about anybody.

His head was spinning with questions when he walked into the hotel dining room and took a seat across the table from Lute Thompson. Over a lot of small talk, mostly about the much-needed rain, he devoured a huge plate of fried chicken, mashed potatoes and gravy, hot biscuits, and string beans.

After the table had been cleared, Neely scooted his chair back, bit the end off a long nine cigar, and began filling the room with smoke. With a voice full of concern, he told Lute about Kate Bender's strange behavior.

"In my long and varied experience with women," Lute said with a twinkle in his eye, "I've found that about every twenty-eight days or so they *all* go nuttier than a shit-house rat."

Neely shook his head seriously and said, "No, it's not *that* simple Lute, I'm sure of it. She treated me like I was a stranger. Do you think what happened with the shooting and all had anythin' to do with it?"

"One thing's for certain — you'll never figure out what goes on in a female mind. They're a lot like horses. You think you have them all figured out, so you get relaxed. Then one day you let your guard down, just a little. The next thing you know, they've thrown you and you're sittin' on the ground wonderin' how you got there."

"What should I do, Lute — to get her back?" Neely questioned.

"You ain't lost her. The next time you see her, things will probably be back to normal. I've been tryin' to tell you — women just like to twirl your rope once in a while. It keeps you thinkin' about them."

Neely chuckled. "I see your point. Works, too, that's for sure." Then a serious look crossed his face and he said, "I've not heard a thing on the wire about Greasy Haynes. Do you reckon he's dead?"

"Probably not. I think he takes more killin' than what we gave him. That bullet in his belly will keep him low for a while. You may have put another hole in him, too. But my gut feelin' tells me he'll be back in action one day."

This was not what Neely wanted to hear. Kate was out there on the prairie, nearly alone. He didn't think the Bender men, especially John, would be a lot of protection from an outlaw like Greasy Haynes. There was no doubt about it — he would have to keep a watch over Kate himself.

To add to an already bewildering day, Lute Thompson paid for Neely's dinner at the hotel. Then, just to keep him even more off balance, he paid the rent for his undertaking parlor up through the end of the month. This was the first time since Lute had taken over the business that the rent payments had ever been paid ahead of time.

The befuddled shopkeeper walked slowly back to his store in a drizzling rain. His head had begun to hurt from thinking about all that had gone on in the past few days. For so long, things had been simple, without changes. Now nothing looked the same to him. *Maybe Lute's right,* Neely thought through the red fog that now filled his head. *Perhaps it's normal to feel like this when smitten by a woman.*

The Benders were holding one of their family conferences. All four of them were sitting at the front dining-room table. Kate and Almira took the side next to the canvas, the one with the backrest. Kate was careful not to place her hair against any of the dark brown spots on the covering; they might still be somewhat sticky. Almira, on the other hand, leaned back heavily against the stained wagon canvas.

The body of Quince Stallings still lay crumpled in the old dry well under their table. After some discussion it had been decided that since it was Sunday and raining they would put off planting him in Ma's orchard for a spell. No one planted trees in a rainstorm. That might attract attention.

When they had gotten home from church, John descended the rickety ladder into the well while William and Kate kept a sharp watch out for visitors or more customers. It took him just a moment to retrieve the dead man's wallet and personal possessions from his pockets.

Another quick moment and the trapdoor was closed, the rug laid smoothly out again. All was in readiness for new business.

Meticulously, Almira counted out the money from Quince's wallet onto the table. Two thousand, eight hundred and fifty-seven dollars. The figure brought smiles to all their faces. John grinned so widely that a river of tobacco juice squirted from his mouth and ran down the front of his already stained shirt, to come to rest on his pants.

Ma Bender noticed this and looked at her son with a narrow-eyed gaze Kate and William had learned to recognize with trepidation. It was the same look she gave their customers, just before hammer time.

John, noticing none of this, kept his empty-headed expression and said, "That's a lot of money. Do we got enough for San Francisco now?"

"No, son, we don't yet," Almira said in a too sweet voice. "We had forty-one thousand when we got here. The two thousand from the man by the river we used to set up our business with. The bounty hunter Kate killed only had a hundred dollars on him. We got five hundred off that fat cattle buyer, and now we've got this." Almira beamed. "We'll put three thousand in our travelin' money. The rest will go for business expenses. That means we need another six thousand dollars. Then we're out of this place forever. We'll have a wonderful life once we get to California and San Francisco."

"Mama, tell us about it. What it will be like when we get there," Kate pleaded.

A smile crossed Almira's face. She enjoyed

this. There would be no new customers today, most likely, with the rain and all.

With Kate and William listening intently while John drooled tobacco juice, Almira Bender once again painted a beautiful picture in their minds.

As always, Ma ended her family talks with a quote from the Bible. Almira never was one for a lot of accuracy in her excerpts. It was the thought that counted as the preacher always said, anyway. This afternoon her quote was a familiar one from the book of Psalms: "Follow the teachings of the Good Book and you shall receive the desires of your heart."

Even John, with a faraway look in his eye, his mind still in that willow-the-wisp place called San Francisco, joined in with the others and said, "Amen."

It felt good to be together, a family with a goal. And their desires were becoming closer every day. All it would take would be a few more of the right customers. Then they could leave this barren prairie forever.

No longer poor innkeepers on a grassy Kansas plain, they would be wealthy socialites, living in a new town full of trusting rich people, *very* rich people.

The Lord always provides.

■ ■ ■ ■

PART 2
ALMIRA'S ORCHARD

■ ■ ■ ■

Hell is truth seen too late

H.G. Adams

"It sure is hard to look at a pretty girl and tell if she's a goddess or a bitch."

Lute Thompson

Sixteen

"Shit," Neely mumbled as he tossed a piece of wadded up paper toward his round wastebasket. It rolled around the edge for a few seconds, then fell from the rim to land on the floor and join another dozen or so like it.

Lute Thompson watched the ball of paper fall from the basket with a wry grin. He was sitting in his usual chair at the south end of Neely's rolltop desk. As had become his habit, he leaned the chair back against the wall at a precarious angle.

In the past few months Lute had taken up Neely's habit of smoking those strong, black, long nine cigars of his. He bummed them from him as often as he could. They seemed to smoke better when he didn't have to pay for them. This morning, however, Neely was in another one of his increasingly bad moods, so Lute had plunked down a half dime on the counter, helped himself to a pack, bitten the end off one, spit it in the general direction of a brass spittoon, and taken his usual seat. "If they ever made a game out of gettin' a round ball into a basket, you would be the world's worst," Lute cracked.

"What the hell is goin' *on* around here?" Neely said with anger and desperation in his voice. "This mornin', I got my eighth telegram about someone comin' up missin' around these parts. I've been plottin' them out, and every damned one of them has decided to drop out of sight somewhere between Independence and Fort Scott. This puts Parsons and my district smack dab in the middle of trouble. Every mother's son of them expects me to find what happened to them, and stop the problem sometime last month."

"It's a thankless job, being a lawman. When you do your job, like when you handled Choctaw Charlie and Vance Tobe, you're a genius. When you simply don't know what's goin' on, you're a fool. It comes with the office, and there's not a thing you can do about it, Neely."

"*You're* the one who took care of those robbers, Lute. We all know that."

"Yeah, but I'm not the sheriff. That task, thank goodness, is all yours. I've done my share of being a lawman. Now I'm real happy just to plant 'em after someone else plugs 'em."

"Lute," Neely asked seriously, "do you think Greasy Haynes is the one knockin' these people off?"

"That's a possibility, but I doubt it. Three months ago, he got the shit shot out of him. It took at least a month or more for him to heal up good enough to get back to the job of outlawin'. Four travelers disappeared without a trace durin' that time."

"I know — all of them in my district."

"My guess is Choctaw Charlie's gang weren't the only ones out there a killin' and robbin' people. I found out durin' my Ranger days that there's some really bad ones around. A lot of times you just don't have a clue who they are until they've been in business for a while. Sometimes it's the ones you least expect.

"I remember one time down in Rio Grande Country, cattle were being rustled and moved across the river into Mexico. Those outlaws weren't any too kindly to those they rustled from, either. That bunch simply killed them all so there wouldn't be any witnesses.

"This went on for nearly six months. A lot of good people died, and we still didn't have one clue as to who was behind it.

"Skinny Skinner and Josh McCabe were finally sent from Austin by Captain Bernard to help me out. I'd been in that God-forsaken, barren country for over five months, following one wild-goose after another. Those cowboys and ranchers kept right on gettin' killed, and I still didn't have a single clue except that there was four of them. You could tell that by their tracks.

"Let me tell you, Neely, that is dry, rough country down there. Even the lizards have to carry canteens or they'll die of thirst. Once those outlaws got into the rocks — and there was no shortage of those — I'd lost their trail. By the time I found it again, they were already across the river and into Mexico.

"It sure was good to see Skinny and Josh show up. I was about ready to bite the bullet and hand in my badge. Then I expect I'd have taken up another trade that didn't require a lot of thinkin', like being a storekeeper or somethin' like that."

Lute's smile grew as he watched his friend grimace. Then he continued, "Well, as luck would have it, the second night out we made a cold camp on a greasewood-covered knoll, overlooking a couple of *vaqueros* who were watching over a couple dozen of the rankestlooking Texas longhorns you ever laid eyes on. Those cow's hides draped over their bones like a wet sheet on a skinny whore. You wouldn't have thought a self-respectin' rustler would've had anythin' to do with stealin' them.

"Then, around midnight, we heard the gunfire. The moon was full bright, and you could make out four riders plain as could be. They just rode right into that Mexican cow camp and killed those two *vaqueros* while they were sleepin'.

"Now, old Skinny is more than a tolerable good rifle shot. He blasted two of them out of their saddles while Josh and I mounted up — we'd kept our horses saddled, just in case — and we had those other two lookin' down our gun barrels in short order.

"Well sir, we had the town preacher and the bank president caught red-handed. The two Skinny had shot turned out to be the owners of the biggest hotel and restaurant in Del Rio.

"One of the hotel owners — Biggs was his name — took another bullet to convince him he was dead.

"It was over sixty miles of rough trail back to the jail at Del Rio. We was pretty sore at the two that were left, the way they killed those cowboys, and all. Also, it was a long trip to undertake with a pair that was likely to try to escape. We decided it would be a lot easier to bring them back if they was already hung. They were as guilty as John Wilkes Booth, anyway.

"The hardest thing in the world to find in that God-forsaken country is a tall tree when you need one. Finally, we spotted this finger of rock sticking out over the trail from the top of a little mesa. It was perfect. Just high enough for a good hangin'."

Lute's grin fled from his face. He reached over to Neely's desk, picked up his coffee cup, and took a long sip. Holding the cup close to his chest with both hands, like a priest clutching a chalice, Lute Thompson continued his tale in a quiet, somber tone. "Killin' a man is never easy. At least I pray to every god there is that it never gets easy for *me.* That's when you've lost your soul.

"Anyway, Josh made up a noose — that Josh is a right handy fellow with a rope — and we got the rope wrapped around that overhanging rock all proper like. Why, that hangin' knot he made would have done anyone proud. Then this preacher starts a bawlin' like a baby, quoting scriptures between sobs just like he was standin' behind a pulpit. His favorite verse seemed to be the one from the Old Testament and the Ten Commandments — Thou shalt not kill. Of course he was referring to *us* a hangin' *him,* not about him just a killin' those two *vaqueros* in cold blood, not to mention all those other innocent ranchers and cowboys this bunch had murdered, either. I kind of lost a lot of respect for sanctimonious parsons on account of that man.

"We hung him first, mainly just to cut down on his cater-waulin'. The banker was being rather decent about the whole thing. I guess he looked at it like a business deal that went bad."

Lute set the coffee cup down, and a sparkle returned to his eyes along with his usual grin as he said, "Well sir, Josh's rope knottin' worked just perfect. I said he was a good hand with a rope. When we took those four outlaws' bodies into Del Rio, you never saw such an uproar. But you know, to this day a cow grazin' down there in that country is as safe as a baby in its mother's arms."

"So you're saying we ought to hang Chatterhorn and the preacher?" Neely quipped with a wry smile.

"Couldn't do a lot of harm, especially that hawk-nosed, old moneylender with a scar on his ass. I reckon we should cut the Bible-thumper some slack, though, with him being a new daddy and all." Lute was beaming now. He had won a five-dollar bet from Roland Langtry, a quarter from Goosey Hooper, and a steak dinner at The Grand Hotel from Neely, all when Eppie Rogers's blessed event finally occurred.

Most everyone in the town of Parsons was wondering whether or not the reverend and his wife would name their new son James or possibly some version of Acts, which would be the next Book of the New Testament. The possibility of Eppie's baby being a girl wasn't even considered.

The general consensus was that an Acton Rogers would join his brothers Matthew, Mark, Luke, and John in their father's progression through the New Testament.

When Lute Thompson started telling folks it would be a girl, he was asked to put his money where his mouth was — and did. Lute's intuition had been correct, and the preacher's rotund wife had given birth to not one but *two* redheaded, bouncing baby girls, named Ruth and Esther — from the Good Book, of course.

Lute had been enjoying the steak he won from Neely at a packed Grand Hotel dining room when Roland came to his table and plunked down a five-dollar gold piece.

242

"How did you guess?" the saloonkeeper asked.

"Why, it was a simple matter," Lute replied loudly enough for all to hear. "Our preacher man isn't hampered by any picayune plans, like I'd first thought. He's a plannin' to screw his way through the whole Bible, not just the new part."

A red-faced Roland Langtry wheeled hurriedly and left the dining room. The hushed conversations and wide-eyed stares Lute received from some of the other patrons didn't bother him in the least. He looked at it like a politician who had just delivered a controversial speech. It would give this little town something to talk about for quite a spell that wasn't a matter of life or death, or of any real consequence at all.

Lute's attitude was that any hard frontier town needed to focus once in a while on things other than work or dying. The fact that he had done his part so well made Neely's huge steak dinner taste even better. He felt *very* civic-minded that evening.

Fresh cups of coffee were poured by Neely from his well-used pot, which by now looked like a lump of coal with a handle attached.

"I ain't seen the Benders in town for a

while. How's things with you and Kate these days?" Lute asked. Neely frowned. They had skirted this issue for some time, now. He knew how much his friend was enamored of Kate and had avoided the issue — until now.

"They're a going to church over in Cherryvale these days. I reckon that inn of theirs is keepin' them mighty busy. I rode out a few times, and Kate was so busy helpin' her Ma we didn't have a lot of time to visit. Lots of people are stoppin' by there. The food's mighty good, and Almira's apple pies are the talk of the whole county. That apple orchard of theirs is a lookin' mighty good, also. They must spend a lot of time choppin' the weeds out of it, by the looks of things."

"You want to talk about it?" Lute asked softly, a caring look in his brown eyes.

"About what?"

"Neely, old friend, it's written all over your face like a bad story, and has been for weeks."

"It's that obvious?"

"Yeah, it sure is."

"It's Kate Bender."

"Hells bells, Neely, tell me somethin' that all of Labette County doesn't already know."

"Look at this," Neely said as he reached

in a precariously stacked pile of papers on his desk. He extracted a copy of the Cherryvale newspaper and handed it to Lute. It was obviously well-handled, and folded open to show a large box ad that had been circled in black ink.

Lute read the advertisement over for a long, wide-eyed moment, then exclaimed, *"Hell's fire and tarnation!* Neely, I think Kate's been around her Ma too long."

Neely glared at the paper with a frown when Lute tossed it back onto his cluttered, rolltop desk. He had read that ad a hundred times. It was in large black print, and proclaimed:

"PROF. MISS KATIE BENDER
Can heal all sorts of Diseases; can cure Blindness, Fits, Deafness and all such diseases, also Deaf and Dumbness.
 Residence, 14 miles East of Independence, on the road from Independence to Osage Mission one and a half miles South East of Norahead Station,
Katie Bender.

This was one of the few times Lute Thompson had ever felt at a loss for words. He sipped indifferently at his cup of coffee with a far-off look on his face. Lost in thought for a long moment, he shook his head and said, "I've always kind of fancied myself as being a knowledgeable man at most things, including the fairer sex, there's no question about it. But this one sure caught me on my dumbshit side. What the hell is she up to, Neely, trying to become a gypsy?"

"Maybe it's her Ma's idea — to drum up more business for their inn."

"Could be. It sounds like somethin' Almira would come up with, for sure. I think we can rule out William or John. Those two couldn't stumble on an idea between the both of 'em."

"I tried to talk to her, ask her about what she was doin', but she just kept scurryin' around the place and paid me no mind."

"Women in general like to spin your spurs once in a while, but this is more serious than that. If I were you, I'd start countin' my blessings that you didn't get all tangled up more so with her than you did. Like I was tellin' you, when you marry a girl her whole family comes along as part of the package."

"You're probably right, Lute," Neely said with a sigh. "But I think I'd better ride out there in a day or two and see them. This time I'm going to make it official. I've got to ask them about all these missin' travelers. They may have seen one or two of them, or know somethin'. That cattle buyer, Cal Olson, was in their inn gettin' drunk just before he dropped out of sight. I know that, for sure. Maybe someone else got a little too much whiskey under their belt out at the Bender's and said somethin' I can use."

"When you go, let me know. I'll rent a horse from Goosey and come along with you."

"I'd appreciate that. Only I'm going to deputize you, and we'll let the Labette County Trustee pay for the horse rental and your salary for the day."

"I like that even better. Makin' ole Ben Chatterhorn come up with money pisses him off more than hangin' him ever would."

"One thing that I wonder on most of all is why hasn't anybody found some bodies. The only person we know for sure that got themselves killed in these parts was that man the freighters found by the Verdigris River."

"Can't answer that, Neely. In my experience, most outlaws are generally a lazy bunch and just leave their victims layin' out for the buzzards. Take that darling of humanity you tried to shoot full of holes — Greasy Haynes. Now, can you imagine him lyin' patiently in wait for just the ones coming through this country packin' money, killin' them real neat like, then buryin' them where no one would find them? Of course, there's also the matter of a horse to be dealt with. No, whoever is robbin' these travelers is clever and most of all, organized."

"That's another thing that puzzles me, Lute," Neely continued in a worried tone. "It seems most everyone that's turned up missin' was on business and carryin' a sum of money with them. How in the hell could a bunch of robbers know if someone was carryin' money or not?"

"They wouldn't. Most generally, killers like Choctaw Charlie's bunch just does them *all* in that goes by, and sorts it out later."

"Yeah, that's what bothers me most. It has to be like you say, someone organized, informed, and coldblooded as a rattle-snake."

Lute stood up slowly, cracked his knuckles, arched his back, and said with a broad smile as he placed his coffee cup back in its usual place on the shelf, "We could just go ahead and hang the preacher and ole Chatterhorn to see if it would do any good."

"I reckon we ought to wait for a tad more evidence first, just to be on the safe side," Neely replied, a tight smile forming underneath his handlebar mustache as he watched his friend leave the store.

It felt good to the shopkeeper-turned-sheriff to have a smile on his face again. Kate Bender had built his hopes high only to bring them crashing down, like a Kansas twister hitting a barn.

In the past few months, Neely had fallen into, and now possibly out of, love. He had been involved in shootings, killings, and an attempted bank robbery. It seemed to him that now nearly every sheriff's office west of the Mississippi was looking to him to find eight missing people. All for the grand sum of twenty-five dollars a month.

The summer had shaped up to be a dry one, again. In spite of the early rains, the rolling grasslands had turned a sickly shade of brown. Neely knew all too well that this year's wheat crop was already stunted from drought and heat. Even if Pike Rogers's fervent prayer meetings were successful in persuading God to send some rain to La-bette County, it would still be a miserly harvest.

Neely had been so preoccupied with what had started out as his part-time lawman's job that he had sorely neglected his general store. Several times — far too many, his books showed — he had simply flipped the sign in the window to read CLOSED and gone about the business of being the sheriff.

Sometimes he had left Maude Saunders in charge. She was a middle-aged widow lady who lived in a falling down shack stuck in the middle of a few acres of brush-covered land on the edge of town. Maude's husband, Claud, who was never thought of as being any too smart, proved this fact two years ago when he attempted to repair the pump head on his windmill during an electrical storm.

After Lute had laid the crispy farmer to rest in the local cemetery, the town of Parsons banded together to help Maude raise her brood of three sons and four daughters. Nearly every business went out of their way to hire her to do tasks that needed to be done.

It was soon discovered that Maude Saunders and her not-so-bright husband had been a good match. Once the owners of the Grand Hotel hired her as a cook. The first day she made a dozen pans of cornbread that defied any efforts to slice them, even using a bucksaw. They were ultimately tossed out back into a wash, where they lay intact for weeks, resisting the efforts of every stray dog or wild bird in town to make even a small dent in one of them. Eventually a cloudburst washed the lot of them into the creek and out of the town of Parsons. No one hired Maude Saunders as a cook after that.

When Neely finally took the time to go over his ledger books, he quickly figured out he shouldn't have hired her as a store-keeper, either. Inventory had been sold on credit and not entered into the record, or the wrong person's name shown as the buyer.

Maude wasn't a thief, just not any too smart. Nothing was missing that couldn't be accounted for — eventually. Neely was certain everyone who bought things on credit would own up to the bill, even if they never paid him. Farmers were for the most part, extremely honest people. It annoyed him that he now had to question every one of his regular customers who came into the store to find out what, if anything, they had bought on credit. Then he had to straighten out the ledger entries — something else to do when he was already behind in nearly everything.

Inventory needed to be done. This fact hit him like the lightning bolt that had fried Claud Saunders when he realized he was nearly out of long nine cigars. He hadn't taken Lute Thompson's starting to smoke

251

them into account.

Two solitary packs sat in a lonely corner of what used to be a fully stocked, glass cigar case. Neely loved his cigars. He always kept a pan full of water with a sponge floating in it inside the display to keep the cigars from drying out. In the dry heat of a blistering Kansas summer, the pan needed filling every day. The waterless pan and petrified sponge that looked back at him through the glass told Neely that Maude certainly wasn't going to keep his shop anymore. She had been told repeatedly to keep it filled. He would still hire her to sweep and mop. She was good at simple things like that. Maude had even done a good job of cleaning Choctaw Charlie off the jail wall. She came up with the idea of whitewashing the whole inside of the cell, which worked well. When she finished, there wasn't a spot of blood remaining to upset future residents.

Neely slid the door of his cigar case open and filled the metal pan with water. He frowned when he felt a pack of the cigars. They were as dry and crisp as the surrounding prairie.

He shook his head sadly and closed the door, hoping to moisten his meager supply. Taking a notebook and pencil, he began making a tally of items to order. Normally, he would post the list to a supply house in Kansas City. Being dangerously close to running out of cigars, however, constituted an emergency worthy of a telegram.

Carefully, Neely composed his order. It cost but little more to add a few items to the wire. He was lost in thought when he heard the door slam unusually hard and the sound of heavy boots stomping on the wood floor.

He looked up into the white-bearded, stern face of a stocky man wearing a ten-gallon felt hat. The stranger was wearing a large revolver underneath a Confederate officer's jacket. The question of why anyone in his right mind would be wearing a long coat in the heat of a Kansas summer crossed Neely's mind. Then the man said sharply, "I'm Jefferson Davis Cowell, *Colonel* Jefferson Davis Cowell." The man let his proclamation hang, as if he were announcing the arrival of President Grant himself.

Neely looked the man over with a blank expression. There *was* something vaguely familiar about him. Looking past the stranger through his lone, street-side window, Neely saw three mounted men, one holding the reins of a saddled horse that he felt belonged to the colonel.

All three of the men were wearing guns,

and there were rifles in scabbards attached to their saddles. Like the man facing him, they looked angry and unforgiving, carrying the same narrow-eyed expression Lute Thompson had worn when he went up against Choctaw Charlie's gang.

It felt to Neely as if the temperature had dropped thirty degrees inside his store. Through pinched lips, he asked, "What can I do for you, Mister Cowell?"

"That's *Colonel* Cowell, sir."

"Well then, what can I do for you *Mister* Colonel Cowell?"

The dried up cigars and overloaded ledger books had taken their toll on Neely Wells's sense of humor. Also, he was finding out that diplomacy was not always the best approach to use when dealing with people.

The bearded man's eyes flared, and for a brief moment Neely thought he was going to pull his gun. Then the stranger's eyes softened slightly and he said, somewhat apologetically, "I'm sorry if I offended you, but my men and I are bone tired. We have been riding for days. We've taken up rooms in the hotel, The Grand, I believe it's called. You *are* the sheriff, are you not?" The man's English was too correct, his words measured.

"Yes, I am."

"Then, once we have bathed and rested, I shall be back to talk with you. I need some information."

"What about?" Neely's success at acting tough was working so well that he wasn't about to quit now.

Once again, the man's eyes narrowed and he said gruffly, "My brother was through this lovely hellhole of yours a while back in pursuit of some outlaws. He hasn't been heard from since. Sheriff, we *are* going to find him — with or without your help, no matter how long it takes — and then take care of whatever other business we find needs done."

"You are going to abide by the law while in my district?" Neely felt his statement came out in the form of a question, much to his chagrin.

"Of *course* we will, sheriff. We are law-abiding people. It's just that sometimes the law needs a little help, is all."

The bounty hunter. That's who this reminds me of, Neely thought. Then he said abruptly, "Wade Cowell, the bounty hunter who was after Choctaw Charlie's gang, he is your brother?"

Jefferson Davis Cowell's expression never changed as he hissed, "Yes sir, he is, and we are here to find him. That outlaw was not a match for my brother. He brought in many a man smarter and meaner than this Choctaw Charlie. I assure you, sir, we *will* find out what happened to him. I shall return later in the day."

Neely watched as the bearded man in the Confederate coat spun smartly with military precision and went through the door to join his armed companions. As soon as the door closed, he rolled his eyes with a look of quiet resignation and said, "Ah, shit!"

SEVENTEEN

Almira Bender was very pleased with her apple orchard. All the saplings had rooted well and were growing at a prodigious rate. Nearly every morning, while a coolness still hung in the air, the entire family turned out to water the trees.

The well that John and Seth had dug produced an abundant supply of clear, good water, with only a hint of the harsh alkaline taste that was so common in the limestone hills of southeast Kansas.

John turned the crank on the windlass. Each trip with the leaky, wooden bucket brought up about eight gallons of cool water. Six or so finally made it into smaller buckets. Then William carried the water and dumped it into circular ditches or water rings dug around the bases of the sapling trees.

The Benders knew a windmill would be a lot easier and more efficient. The blades spinning in the nearly always present Kansas breeze would turn a gear box that would raise and lower a clanking sucker rod. Each stroke would bring up a gallon or two of water. All that would be needed was a tank to store it in. Then hoses could be run and ditches dug.

With none of the backbreaking cranking of loaded buckets from the depth of the well, there would be a continuous supply of water for the orchard and vegetable garden. By installing a little piping, they would also have water running inside their inn and to the barn for the horses and cows.

Windmills cost money, and John Bender's labor on the crank was free, or at least nearly so — he did eat enough to founder a draft horse, and chew copious amounts of tobacco. His redeeming qualities were his immense strength and his willingness to do whatever Ma or Pa told him to do. Also, building a windmill took time. They wouldn't be here long enough to get any real benefit from it, anyway. That was a certainty.

Under eight of the trees, John and William had dug holes of nearly five feet in depth and three feet around. Into each of these, a body of one of their "customers" had been forced. By placing them into the holes with their legs against their chests, John only had to jump up and down on them a few times to leave plenty of room for sufficient dirt to replant the apple trees.

While John was cranking water from the depths of the well and William carried buckets to dump in the tree rings, Almira and Kate carefully hoed and raked around the base of each sapling. They took extra care to make certain all of the twenty-four trees looked identical, without a single weed growing inside the water rings. Ma Bender's fledgling apple orchard gave the look of being simply well-cultivated. It was the mark of good, caring farmers, who planned to be around when their trees finally bore fruit.

Once the watering of the orchard, livestock, and small garden were all completed, the Bender family retired to their inn. The stifling heat of the day had yet to come.

Not that it wasn't hot inside their living quarters. The large, cast-iron cookstove required a fire be kept in it all day, regardless of the temperature outside. Bread had to be baked, stews simmered, coffee boiled. When one ran a restaurant such as theirs, they had to be prepared. Someone might order bacon and eggs, or even a steak with fried potatoes. All had to be in readiness.

With the windows and doors open, the perpetual breeze kept it bearable. The only problem with that was the flies. They came in droves, lured by the smell of food. It was a mystery to the Benders as to how the flies could find their hidden trapdoor under the rug. But they did, flocking to it, outlining the opening.

Ma's theory was that dried blood gave off a scent only flies could follow. A sack of quicklime was dumped into the open trapdoor during the dark of night. It had little success. The pesky black insects still congregated to outline the old well.

Flyswatters wielded by John and William kept them fairly well at bay. John enjoyed swatting flies. Getting more than one with a single swat became a game with him. He would have liked to be able to count up his day's kill, but he always gave up when he got to twenty, which came early in the day.

The fact that they were so near their goal of fifty thousand dollars brought smiles and excitement to all but Ma Bender. She seldom smiled, anyway, but lately had been in a worse mood than usual.

William guessed it was possibly the heat, or maybe one of those female problems he had seen cures advertised for. If he really believed a bottle of it would keep Almira from complaining, he would buy a case. But since he'd never in his entire life run across a female that didn't have *something* to bitch about, he felt it was just a hornswoggle to separate an honest man from his money.

Kate Bender, on the other hand, knew the cause of Mama's irritability. The idea of her becoming a healer and spiritualist was Almira's. At the time, it had seemed like a good one. Kate could ask intimate questions, find out about finances and places where money was hidden.

The ad placed in the Cherryvale paper had brought only poverty-stricken farmers' wives looking for some miracle to cure themselves or one of their children.

Kate played along, reading tea leaves or, if there were no tea, coffee grounds. Sometimes she would look into a large quartz crystal that she had brought with her from Missouri, mumbling some mysterious sounding words she thought up at the time. Kate would always promise a cure, saying it would take a while, maybe a long while, before the cure would work.

The Benders were very careful to charge little or nothing for Kate's "services." They didn't want much attention directed their way. The spiritualism plan had brought them a lot more attention than they wanted.

Twice, there had been potential customers seated alongside Kate, leaning heavily back into the stained canvas. The auburn-haired, beautiful girl had them to the point of talking — or bragging — about how much money they had, John waiting with his well-used hammer. Then some farm family had barged in, hoping for an impossible cure for some little kid or some such, ruining the Bender's entire day.

San Francisco loomed closer than ever. Nearly forty-nine thousand dollars had their hidden lard can bulging. Those two customers who barely escaped might have made the difference, if it hadn't been for that damn ad.

Almira was wanting to leave in the worst way. They had planted eight customers in her orchard. One of them had been the bounty hunter, and he didn't really count as a paying customer — Kate had simply meant to protect Choctaw Charlie. That plan hadn't worked out, either. It would have been good if it had. Having a well-known outlaw stalking about sure would have taken some pressure off them. Now there were people just disappearing for no good reason. Soon the law would be investigating more than would be comfortable. That was a certainty.

The incident in Missouri had taught them that they might have to leave quickly, only this time they had a plan. They were prepared for what they would do.

Every day, while waiting for that final customer or two to come into their inn, they would go over their escape plan. John was the reason for the repetition. It was a plan. He couldn't kill it, he couldn't eat it. Therefore, he couldn't understand it. They needed him to do what he had to do if they were going to make San Francisco, and constant practice was the only way he would get it right.

It was understood by everyone but John that *he* might not make it to California, but that would be no great loss. Especially in Kate's view, it wouldn't.

Midday had come, bringing with it a hotter breeze and more flies. John's flyswatter was caked with parts of the dead insects. He had just squashed five with one swat, or at least thought he had. He was cutting a large chunk of tobacco off a twist with his hidden Bowie knife as a reward for being such a good flykiller when a horse nickered in front of the open door.

Quickly he slipped the knife back into its sheath. When John turned to check on their visitor, he could see why the rest of his family looked happy.

A slender young man swung from the saddle of his well-groomed palomino with the grace of a dancer, his silver spurs glinting in the bright Kansas sun.

The horse's saddle was obviously handmade, Mexican style. Bright conchos and shimmering ivory and metal inlays were set into well-oiled leather. It was a *very* expensive saddle.

Once the palomino had been tied to the hitching post, the stranger turned to swagger toward the door. A smile remained on the Benders's faces. This young man was dressed like an Eastern dandy. Polished brown leather boots set off his store-bought clothes. He sported a goatee beard and muttonchop sideburns that were as jet black as his obviously long hair, which was nattily covered by a white, bowler style straw hat with a red ribbon band.

He walked with an air of authority. The Benders had learned early on that arrogance is generally born of wealth. When the man's piercing blue eyes fixed on Kate, a look came to his face that had California written all over it.

The man smiled at Kate like a cat looking at a canary in a cage. Hungrily. With a toss of her long, auburn hair and practiced batting of her green eyes, she returned the stranger's smile.

Kate always enjoyed these times, when she was the center of a man's attentions. At least, she did if Mama didn't make her go too far with a man, like she'd had to with Choctaw Charlie. The whiskey Kate could now freely drink was the best part. It seldom was a problem getting a customer to buy her whiskey. Her sweet smile alone could often accomplish this.

Then, when the man left — out the door if he was broke or someone who happened to live nearby, or dropped through the trapdoor under the table with his head caved in if he was neither — there was usually some whiskey left in the bottle. That made it all worthwhile. Kate Bender loved whiskey more all the time. It made her feel warm, comfortable. And it helped her forget about David. Beautiful, perfect David. The wonderful son that she dreamed about often. David, who her half-wit brother had so surely killed.

"Boone, Tip Boone, is the name, miss. And yours?" the stranger asked politely, drawing Kate from her reverie.

"How nice of you to drop by, Mister Boone. My name is Katie Bender. My mother, Almira, and my father, William, and my brother, John," she answered sweetly, while pointing out each family member in turn. "Please come and sit by me," she purred to the obviously awestruck young man.

Tip Boone hung his straw hat on a nail by the door and slid onto the seat Kate offered him, the one with the comfortable backrest. She slid in closely alongside him.

To the young man's relief, John and William left after making some statement about having to go work on the barn. Almira retired to the kitchen area, busily banging around pots and pans.

"You look like a man who could use a drink of good whiskey to get that awful trail dust out of your throat. Am I right?" Kate questioned with a voice of honey.

A wide-eyed Tip Boone reached into his pocket and tossed a five-dollar gold piece onto the table. "Only if you join me."

"Mama, please bring us a bottle of whiskey. The *good* kind," Katie said, turning to look through the open doorway.

Almira Bender brought in a bottle along with two glasses and set them on the table, wearing the closest thing to a smile she was ever able to muster. On her way back into the kitchen she reached quietly under Kate's pillow and brought out her small hammer, leaning it handily against the wall, just in case. She had a feeling about this customer, and as the Good Book admonished: "Set thine house in order."

John's heavy blacksmith hammer was certainly more effective than Kate's dainty one. However, this customer's eyes were constantly moving, searching, making Ma worry that the young man might be as skittish as a colt. The presence of one of the men could cause problems. Ma Bender didn't like problems. She and Kate could handle this just fine without them. This man simply reeked of money.

"Darlin'," Almira said loudly from the kitchen, "I'm goin' down to the barn for a spell and help out the menfolk."

As soon as Kate heard the door close, she poured the glasses full of good Kentucky bourbon. Tip Boone's eyes widened as the beautiful girl with auburn hair chugged a half glass without wincing. His afternoon of surprises was just beginning. Kate unbuttoned her blouse, nice and slow, while batting her green eyes at the young man.

Tip Boone helped himself to a shot of whiskey. He needed it. Never before had such a beautiful girl been so forward or available to him in his life. Abandoning himself to the moment, he kissed Kate, sliding his sweaty hand inside her blouse. She just giggled and pulled him closer. He couldn't believe his good fortune.

"You seem like such a nice man," Kate purred in his ear.

"Little darlin', whatever you want is yours," Tip replied while massaging her breasts.

"I want to leave this place, go somewhere nice, but that takes money," Kate replied. "My family is *so* poor."

"That's no problem, none at all. My folks are worth a fortune. . . ."

Kate's hands were under the table now, doing what she had to do. "You have enough money with you, to take me away from here?" Kate asked in a loud voice.

Tip thought his loving had caused Kate's lusty question. He took his hand from inside her blouse and placed a finger across his lips in a silencing sign. "We can leave here right now and go any place your heart desires," Tip Boone whispered, but he didn't need to bother to be quiet. The canvas curtain did little to keep out sound.

Almira Bender was silently standing behind the curtain, holding Kate's hammer. It always worked, just slamming the door and then walking back in. People were so trusting.

Swinging the hammer with both hands, Ma hit the back of the man's head square on. Tip flew from the wagon canvas to sprawl across the table. Kate barely managed to keep him from spilling the bottle of whiskey. She frowned when his head struck the glass, spilling its contents. *Such a waste.*

Tip Boone was still shivering when John and William got there after being called up from the barn. They were both surprised how fast it had gone. Usually this took longer.

John reached out, grabbed the man by his long hair, pulled him from the table, and threw him to the floor in one quick, practiced motion. Then he saw Kate standing, holding the whiskey bottle, her breasts nearly falling from the open blouse. John gave Kate a long stare that caused Ma to give him a full-handed slap to the back of his head.

"Keep your mind on business, boy. That's your sister. Show her some respect!" Almira screeched.

"Yes, Ma," John mumbled as he obediently opened the trapdoor and scooted the customer's still quivering body to where his head hung over the open hole. Then using his razor-sharp knife, he cut the man's throat.

"Kate," Almira commanded, "you and Pa keep a lookout. We're going to pick this one clean right now. If he's got enough on him, we can leave right away."

William immediately went to the front door. Kate followed, buttoning her blouse. Pa Bender especially liked this plan. Digging holes was a lot of work. Just leaving the body in the old well held a lot of appeal.

Nothing moved in the hot Kansas afternoon. A couple of circling buzzards were the only living things William and Kate saw from the front of their lonely little inn.

"Why that lyin' son of a bitch." The voice was Almira's. When father and daughter looked through the door, they could see John and Ma had undressed the man and both were standing back looking at the body with angry eyes. "Thirty-six dollars," Almira lamented. "William, go look in his saddlebags."

When Pa did so and found nothing but a rain slicker and a change of clothes, Ma Bender became more angry than they had ever seen her, and she had some *very* bad days.

"John, hand me your knife!" she said,

270

bending over the naked body.

"What are you gonna do, Ma?" William asked carefully from the doorway.

Almira gave him a look that he hoped he would never see on his wife's face again. She took the knife and said loudly, "When the Lord gives you lemons, you make lemonade." Then she started cutting.

William and Kate went to take the palomino into the barn, glad to leave. Only John stood silently smiling and drooling tobacco juice, as he watched his Mama at work.

EIGHTEEN

"So, our lost bounty hunter had himself a brother who was a colonel in the Confederate Army?" Lute asked Neely over steaming bowls of beef stew during dinner at The Grand Hotel.

Lute had been paying for their meals ever since coming into that reward money. His undertaking business had been doing well, also. He seldom talked to Neely about burying people unless he felt the law should be involved. Ever since the bank robbery attempt, all of Lute's clients had died of agreeably natural causes. There had surely been enough of those, an even half-dozen in the past month, bringing his supply of coffins to the lowest level since he started in the business.

The undertaker's biggest concern lately had been that some tragedy might strike, like a wagon overturning. That would clean out not only his last two coffins but his bed, as well. He had been sleeping on those two caskets for so long they felt just right. Breaking in fresh sleeping coffins would be as painful as buying a new pair of boots. To be prepared for any new disaster, he had toiled all morning in the hot sun, busily sawing and hammering. The product of his efforts was a half-finished coffin. As he was fond of saying, "I can cut a board twice, and it's still too short." Carpentry wasn't to be counted among Lute's talents.

When Neely told him about Jefferson Davis Cowell and the three men he'd brought along with him, Lute made a decision. After dinner, he'd hire Goosey Hooper and the barber's son, Albin, to help him build up his coffin inventory. He figured he would need them for sure, now. This Cowell fellow didn't sound like a reasonable man, and unreasonable people with guns generally meant trouble. Bad trouble.

Neely looked tired, drawn, and plainly worried when he said, "After this colonel got himself and his men checked into the hotel, they've been askin' questions all over town. When I came to join you, they were headin' into Chatterhorn's bank."

Lute felt it was time for lighter conversation, after all this was dinner. Anybody knew a person shouldn't wake snakes over a good meal. "I imagine he'll make a big deposit in ole Scarbutt's bank. Then they'll hang *you* for dereliction of duty. And here I am, down to my last two buryin' boxes. Do you have any idea the hardship that'll cause me?"

A spark returned to Neely's eyes. He crumbled a chunk of cornbread in his stew and said, "Hell, I ain't worried. I owe Chatterhorn a passel of money."

Lute studied on that for a moment and said, "I reckon you're right about bein' safe. Scarbutt likes his interest better than a whore likes to see a cattle drive hit town."

After dessert, a generous slice of apple pie not nearly as good as Almira Bender's, it was time for serious talk. When Lute took a long nine cigar from his pocket, Neely noticed only two remained. He reminded himself to send that telegram to Kansas City on his way back to the store, or a real disaster would strike, for sure.

Once the table was enveloped in a cloud of smoke, Lute said earnestly, "I suppose we ought to heel ourselves and go visit this Colonel and his group personally. You *are* the sheriff, and you have the right to see what they're up to."

Automatically, Neely felt for the gun that wasn't there. Lately he had quit wearing it. He knew Lute was right, that he should always go armed, but that revolver seemed to always get in the way. It caught on items in his store. Womenfolk always looked at him a little scared like when he waited on them while wearing it. The thing was a nuisance for a storekeeper. "I suppose you're right," Neely answered. "Let's go by the store and then we'll go visitin'."

Lute waited patiently outside the telegraph office while Neely sent off what appeared to be an urgent message. The duo nearly collided with Ben Chatterhorn as they left the hotel.

"Neely, Mister Thompson, I was hoping to run into you," Chatterhorn said.

It was a mystery to Lute why having money in the bank gained him the title of *"Mister."* He'd always been happy just being called "Lute." He guessed it was one of those things you had to put up with if you were a wealthy man. For him, it was a healthy incentive to spend it fast.

The banker continued, "Colonel Cowell and his men paid me a visit. They are very concerned, as I am, about his brother's disappearance and the vanishing of those *other* folks, also."

And it's bad for banking business. They were all carrying money, Neely thought when he replied, "We're looking into that. I was planning on deputizing Mr. —" he caught himself just in time — "Lute, and we're going to spend a day out that way asking questions."

"Yes, that's a good plan but what I want you and Mister Thompson to do is this. You are to visit everyone who lives along the Osage Mission road — every one of them — and tell them we're calling a township meeting in two days. We're holding it at the schoolhouse, six o'clock in the evening. I want all of them to come."

"So, you want Lute to help?" Neely asked Chatterhorn. It would be a lot easier to bring up paying Lute for his services and renting a horse from the livery if it seemed like his idea.

"Certainly. We're going to need Lute's services until this terrible matter is resolved." Lute relaxed a little. That "mister" thing was beginning to irritate him. The banker continued, directing his gaze at the undertaker, "Come by the bank later today. The township will pay you twenty-five dollars for a month's work — same as Neely."

A dollar a day for a month didn't quite equal twenty-five dollars to Lute's way of figuring, but he decided to keep quiet about it. He might be unlucky and have a dry spell. Sometimes he could go a month with nobody dying.

Neely was feeling better. He wanted Lute's help. Hell, he *needed* it. A month was more than he could have hoped for. "I'll make arrangements with Goosey for a horse and saddle and tell him to send you the bill," he said, causing a pinch to come to the banker's face.

"Uh, uh, OK," Chatterhorn sputtered. "Now, about Colonel Cowell and his men. The colonel is a respected man who is running for congress. All of them have offered to act as unpaid deputies. I've already sworn them in and issued badges. They understand they are to act only under your orders." He spoke to Neely, but his eyes were on Lute. "I want to stop this scourge to our fair land, and we *are* going to accept their help."

Shit, Lute thought, *leave it to politicians to royally foul things up.* He knew from experience that Chatterhorn was forming a lynch mob. "Folks around here know us and we know the country," Lute replied. "I think it would be best if the colonel and his bunch stayed in town, at least until after the meetin' and we have need of them."

Ben Chatterhorn thought on that a moment, adding up in his head how much money four men would spend over two days, and said, "Yes, that's a good idea. We don't want to unnecessarily alarm our citizens."

"We'll leave tomorrow at first light," Neely announced with an authority he didn't feel.

As Lute and Neely walked away down the creaking boardwalk, Chatterhorn called after them, "And wear your *guns,* for pete's sake!"

Colonel Cowell and his men were in The Rose Saloon when Neely and Lute caught up with them. Both *were* wearing guns and badges now, only Lute's was a Texas Ranger star. He hadn't worn it for years, but since he'd never officially quit he felt it was appropriate. Also, it might make a good impression on the colonel. Lute knew full well that keeping this bunch under control would take a *lot* of doing.

Jefferson Davis Cowell spun around to meet them with military precision, his narrow gray eyes fixed on Lute's Ranger badge like a hawk spying a field mouse. "And who might I be addressing, sir?" he asked sharply, looking at Lute. He already knew who Neely was from their earlier meeting, and felt he would be no problem to handle. He assumed this thin man with the hard, brown eyes, wearing a Texas Ranger badge on his shirt, was Lute Thompson. He wasn't so sure about being able to handle him.

"I'm the *regular* deputy around here — Lute Thompson."

"Glad to meet you. These are my two cousins, Edward and John Stern, and my nephew, Carlton Cowell," the colonel said, sweeping his arm toward three men bellied up to the bar.

Lute sized them up. The two cousins looked trail-tried, with sunbaked wrinkles etched into their brows, cold-looking eyes, and faces that would crack if they ever smiled. Carlton was the exception. He was young, maybe not yet even eighteen. His nervous, flighty manner said that he had rather be anywhere but there.

The shiny badges they all wore plainly pinned on their shirts for all to see caused both Lute and Neely to grimace. The fact they were also heavily armed caused Lute's frown to run deep. "You expectin' to find some one in *here* that needs shootin'?" Lute asked the colonel blandly, glaring at the guns. "Those whores upstairs are a rather gentle lot, I've found."

"We're here as deputies, duly authorized by your township," Jefferson Davis Cowell retorted angrily.

"That may be, but you're under *our* orders. And your orders are to leave those guns in your room. Right now, we have no idea what happened to your brother, or anyone else for that matter. I'd take it right personal if someone got hurt that didn't have it comin'," Lute said firmly.

Ed Stern spun around toward Lute with a snarl, his fist clenched, drawn back to strike. He never got the punch off. Lute pulled a gun quicker than anyone could see and struck the Arkansan alongside his head with the barrel. The man fell heavily to the barroom floor in a heap. "Like I said, we don't want anyone gettin' hurt around here," Lute declared in a mild manner without changing his expression or taking his eyes from the colonel.

"I'll explain it to him as soon as he finishes his nap," Cowell replied.

The colonel had heard many stories about Lute Thompson from the locals. He had heavily discounted most of them. That was a mistake he wouldn't make in the future. There was not a lot of doubt in Cowell's mind that his brother was probably dead. The only reason he was there was to find out who was responsible, kill them, and go back to Arkansas with his brother's body and give him a proper burial. Perhaps this Texas Ranger could be a real help.

Jefferson Davis Cowell had no wish to

remain in Kansas any longer than absolutely necessary. He had been struck by a heartfelt desire to run for Congress. When the urge hit him three years ago, his first action on the matter had been to change his middle name from the ignominious one his mother had given him at birth to one much more desirable to the voters in a state full of Southern sympathizers. A man with the middle name of Ulysses wouldn't garner a lot of votes in Arkansas.

Putting on his best "Trust me" smile, Colonel Cowell said, looking at Lute and Neely at the same time — a skill he thought necessary for a politician — "Please excuse my cousin's rash actions, sir. I assure you we only wish to help. We will act only under your directions in the future. Our firearms will not be worn in town."

Lute looked down at the unmoving form of Edward Stern for a moment, flashed his eyes at the colonel, and said, "I never had doubt one about your seein' things our way."

Jefferson Davis Cowell let the perceived insult slide. A few years earlier he would have seen just how tough this Ranger was. A man who is practicing up for a political career, however, must control his temper.

"We're ridin' at first light," Lute said with

a wicked smile — he was thoroughly enjoying this. "While you folks rest yourselves, we'll make sure the township meetin' is well attended."

"I think, sir, I would like to accompany you — to get to know this lovely country of yours better," Cowell said.

"You've changed your mind about Labette County for the better, I see," Neely said.

"I was distraught earlier, sir, this is a place to be proud of."

"We'll do just fine by ourselves. We don't want to upset people by havin' a bunch of strangers come ridin' in on them," Lute said firmly.

"I must insist that one of us accompany you, someone who knows my brother," Colonel Cowell said.

Lute looked at Neely and said, "The man does have a point. We'll take the young'un — Carlton — with us. He shouldn't spook anyone."

Colonel Jefferson Davis Cowell's neck couldn't have gotten redder if his throat was cut, but he forced a thin-lipped smile and said, "That will be acceptable, gentlemen, thank you."

"Meet us in front of the general store at daybreak," Neely said loudly to the wide-eyed Carlton Cowell.

When he left the saloon, Lute watched out the corner of his eye as a cold beer was dashed into the face of the man on the floor in a vain attempt to awaken him. When they came to the boardwalk and turned to head toward Neely's store, Lute said, "That colonel is going to be trouble. Not only is he as full of shit as the bottom of a year-old bird's nest, he's a politician, to boot."

"I always thought the two went together, like a hand and a glove," Neely joked.

"You know, you're right," Lute grinned. "Only problem is, when politicians get things stirred up, it's left to people like us to straighten out their messes."

Neely, no longer smiling, said, "Lute, I think we have our work cut out for us."

"I *know* we do," Lute replied seriously.

NINETEEN

The sun was a red blaze on the eastern horizon when a nervous Carlton Cowell met Lute and Neely at the appointed place, shaking Neely from his reverie. He had been looking at the fiery sunrise thinking of the old adage, "Red skies in the morning. Sailor take warning." Neely hoped that saying applied to bone-dry Kansas grasslands as well as the ocean. He felt the ocean already had plenty of water. This was not the case here. A rainstorm would be a welcome thing, indeed, even if Pike Rogers took credit for it, which he knew he would.

The preacher couldn't lose, to Neely's way of thinking. If the drought continued, it was God's will, not *his* fault. Should a good frog strangler come, it was due to his diligence in calling all those prayer meetings.

Neely remembered Lute Thompson saying that when it rained one time for forty days and forty nights, giving Noah and his animals a well-known boat ride, Southeast Kansas had received less than an inch.

"When I told your uncle no gun wearin' in town, I really didn't expect you to show up unarmed," Lute said to Carlton when he rode close enough to see he had no weapon.

"M— m— my uncle told us to do what you said, and you said no guns," Carlton stammered, obviously intimidated by the Texas Ranger.

"Well, that's all right, son," Lute said soothingly. "We'll take care of any outlaws that happen to be about. You'd most likely shoot yourself or one of us instead of the bad guys, anyway."

Carlton Cowell kept his red face toward the ground while he waited for the sheriff and the famous Texas Ranger Lute Thompson to mount up for the day's task. He didn't think this was going to be a good day. It had already started out bad, and he felt it was just going to go downhill from there.

"How's Ed Stern this morning?" Neely asked the young man in a cheery voice, hoping to build his spirits some. The boy just didn't know how to take Lute yet. Before the day was out, he would either be giving birth to a sense of humor or bawling like a baby. That much was a given. "His left eye's all swole shut. He can't see out of it, and his head hurts him powerful bad," Carlton answered in an obviously scared voice.

"I wouldn't concern myself none about his head," Lute boomed. "He's probably never had a lot of use to put it to, anyway. Otherwise, he'd have figured out not to pick a fight with a peacelovin' man like me."

Neely saw tears beginning to swell in the boy's eyes. In his distress, he looked more like ten years old than seventeen. *You're going to do a lot of growing up today,* Neely thought.

"Well, let's get to ridin'. We've got a lot of country to cover and folks to visit," Lute said, wheeling his horse around.

Neely rode alongside Lute. The wet- and wide-eyed Carlton followed at a respectful distance behind. They turned left when they came to the road to Independence. Heading west, away from the red sun, Neely couldn't find a speck of cloud in the sky. "You know, Lute," Neely said loudly, scanning the sky with his eyes, "sailors don't know gunpowder from mouse turds when it comes to predictin' the weather."

Carlton Cowell, from Arkansas, was certain now — he *was* going to have a bad day.

The sun was its usual blazing yellow color and hanging overhead in a dry and hot blue sky when Neely, Lute, and Carlton hitched their horses to the rail in front of The Bender Inn.

A lumbering freight wagon pulled by a team of draft horses and loaded to the breaking point with saw logs was in the distance, heading toward Coffeyville. White clouds of limestone dust rolled in its wake, obscuring the men on the wagon.

Lute noticed fresh ruts in the dirt under their feet. The freighters had just left The Bender Inn. He thought for a moment he should ride ahead, stop them, and visit. They might have some ideas as to where all these people dropping off the face of the earth were. That would be a welcome change. Every farmer from the town of Parsons to where they stood hadn't a clue as what was going on. Everyone was, however, glad something was being done about it. All said they would attend the township meeting. At first, it was a mystery how every single person they talked to knew all about the disappearances. Then Neely remembered Joe Peeples, the telegraph operator. He was a well-known gossip. Once a few beers passed his lips, Joe would tell everything he knew and then give his opinion on things he didn't know, whether people were interested or not. And Joe Peeples *liked* his beer.

A grumble shook Lute Thompson's flat belly. He decided to let the freighters go their way. He was hungry. The thought of Ma Bender's delicious apple pie caused a second rumble to hit his gut and made him forget all about the freighters. His only hope now was that he wouldn't have to look at Almira or John when he ate it. To contemplate either one for even a short while would put man or animal off his feed. Now, Kate was another matter. She might be batty as a cage full of loons, but that was Neely's problem — he was the one that had been lovestruck. Kate Bender's looks were something to behold. She was a beauty, a rare and beautiful flower. How she kept her attractiveness living out here as she did was only part of the mystery to him.

There was something about Kate Bender that bothered Lute. It was nothing he could put his finger on. Perhaps it was the fact she was just *too* pretty and sickly sweet. His personal tastes in women ran more to earthy ladies like Annie Mitchell. At least with Annie, he always knew where he stood, good or bad. With Kate, he felt it would be hard to even guess.

Lute loved to read. He read everything he

could get his hands on. Dime novels were his favorites. The plots were so ridiculous that he really enjoyed them. Once he had read about a lizard called a chameleon. These creatures supposedly changed colors to match whatever background they were placed against, a female tactic if ever there was one. Maybe Kate was better at it than most.

Carlton Cowell followed the sheriff and ranger into The Bender Inn. He was careful to keep some distance between them. He was beginning to feel a little better about the day. The two lawmen seemed to make fun of most everything. This was totally strange to him. His father and all four of his uncles, including the missing bounty hunter, Wade, never joked about anything. Around them, everything was always serious, a matter of concern.

Carlton had been raised to believe people who made fun of others were weak-minded. Now his uncle, the famous Civil War colonel and soon to be congressman, actually seemed to be in awe of the Texas Ranger, who seemed to do nothing *but* poke fun. He wasn't sure now just what to think.

Then he saw Kate Bender. The stunning girl with long hair that shone like copper in the sunlight ran to give the sheriff a hug and kiss. Carlton's heart fell to somewhere near his kneecaps. He had been right all along. This *was* going to be a bad day.

Lute and Neely slid onto the bench with a comfortable-looking backrest, leaving Carlton to sit on the plain, plank bench across from them. Not that he noticed. The boy's mind and eyes were only on Kate. He had reached the age when girls caused an urge to strike him that he didn't quite understand but certainly did enjoy.

"The freighters that just left finished off the last of Ma's special liver and onions," Kate purred with a mischievous look in her eyes and a hint of sorrow in her voice. "But we can fix up most anything else."

After the three finished their dinner of Ma Bender's fried chicken and were chasing the last crumbs of apple pie with cups of black coffee, Neely told them about the meeting and why it was being called.

"So, the bounty hunter's brother is a congressman?" William asked, standing behind the grocery counter.

"Just wants to be at this stage, but he's so full of sh— nonsense, he might just make it," Lute said with a hint of redness on his cheeks. He'd forgotten about Kate being in hearing distance. A man never cursed in front of a woman. With Ma Bender, now, he might make an exception, but the boy sitting across the table needed to see how a gentleman behaved in the company of a lady.

Almira's pan banging in the kitchen grew louder. The Benders all agreed the meeting was a good idea and said they would attend.

Neely noticed that Carlton left Kate's presence with the slowness of molasses running in January. After some not-so-gentle urging from Lute the boy was mounted on his horse, and they all headed off west along the dusty Osage Trail road. There were a lot more folks to see, and they needed to get moving if they hoped to get back to town before dark.

The dust from the departing horses' hooves had barely settled before Ma Bender took John's fly swatter from his hand and began beating Kate across her shoulders with it.

Tears streaming down her cheeks, Kate Bender stood stone still while her mother flailed away with a rage. She deserved it. She shouldn't have killed that bounty hunter. A perfect girl doesn't cause problems like she had. Her mother would tire of it soon, and Mama was always sweet to her afterwards. *Spare the rod and spoil the child.*

Once Ma's rheumatism started paining

her shoulder, she handed the flyswatter back to John. He frowned when he noticed that the handle was badly bent and a piece of the end was missing, also. That would cut down on his fly killing considerably.

William had watched with his usual complacency, waiting for Almira to settle down so they could have a talk. Judging a family conference was in order, he went to the kitchen and cut one of his wife's apple pies, giving an extra large slice to Kate.

After the pie had been eaten, coffee cups filled, and Kate had finally quit sobbing, William decided it was time for business. "We've got until after that damn meetin', I'd guess," he said.

"Don't you swear in front of the children," Almira admonished. Then directing her look at her daughter, she said, "Katie, dear, don't you see what you caused? Here we are, on the brink of our goal, and now we may have to leave before we're ready. I was thinkin' of *you.* We need that money so you can be happy once we get to California."

"Yes, Mama," Kate said meekly.

"I'd guess they're goin' to form some mob and go search the country," William said. "They'll go through this place like a doctor lookin' over a sick baby. We need to be gone by then."

"That meetin's not until tomorrow night. There's still a chance. Katie darlin', you unbutton that blouse of yours some," Almira said hopefully.

Kate did as she was told, causing a lecherous gawk to come to John's face. She said nothing. Without a doubt, she had caused her Mama problems.

"I reckon we might still get lucky, at that," William said.

"The Lord always provides," Almira declared.

The hot sun hit Kate's raw shoulders like a whip when she went to stand outside the open front door of The Bender Inn. Never mind. The problem the family had was her fault. Carefully, she folded her blouse open and leaned back seductively against the searing rough wood. *Bait for the trap.*

When the three tired horsemen rode into Parsons, it was late evening. The sun had dropped below the horizon, bringing an agreeable coolness to the air. Carlton Cowell was feeling better about the day. The two lawmen were certainly different from anyone he had ever spent time with.

During the trip back he rode alongside them. He had even summoned enough courage to laugh at some of their jokes. A few of the tales the Texas Ranger told caused him to wonder as to their truthfulness, but after what happened to his Cousin Ed he felt it prudent not to say anything. Lute actually seemed to have developed some respect for his Uncle Jefferson. Twice he had referred to him as an excellent grafter. Carlton didn't know what that was, exactly, but it sounded important. His uncle loved compliments. He made a note to call him that at the first appropriate moment.

And there was that beautiful lady at the inn, Kate Bender. In his short lifetime, Carlton had never laid eyes on a more desirable girl. Too bad that old man Neely Wells had her attentions. He knew he would dream of her for the rest of his life.

"Well, we've done all we can do today," Lute said as Neely and he dismounted to lead their horses into the livery stable. "I enjoyed your company, son. I'm truly sorry we didn't find out a thing about your uncle."

The young man said his good-byes and rode to the hotel to see his family. He hadn't thought much about his Uncle Wade all afternoon. Carlton Cowell had been thinking about Kate Bender.

TWENTY

It had been a night of fitful sleep for Kate Bender. Her back and shoulders burned as if they were afire, keeping her awake. On occasions, when she was able to doze off, the dream visited her again, hurting her worse than her mother ever could with a whip.

David, her perfect son, died anew. Mama holding his struggling little body so tightly. His head submerged in a tub of dirty wash water.

Stifling a cry, she shifted her body to another position, rekindling the pain. Now they were forced to run again. Mama promised once they were in California she would be happy. The Lord knew how hard she tried to be a perfect child. Kate Bender had faith. The Good Book said it plain, and even the Reverend Rogers intoned it from the pulpit — "The desires of the righteous shall be granted." It was just so difficult to *be* righteous and honor your mother and father. Especially in her mother's eyes, it was.

She vowed to be a better daughter. The deep pain across her shoulders *was* a needed lesson. Kate would have to be perfect to go to San Francisco and inherit the promised dreams. Soon, very soon, they would leave this windblown prairie and go live in a castle on a hill.

There was nothing to slow their departure this time. No little David to worry about. John had seen to that.

Kate lay on her side. Her back was far too raw and painful for her to sleep on it. Drawing a feather pillow into a ball, she hugged it close and loving. Her half-wit brother's broken snorting blared from the bed above. With each of his snorts, her hatred for him festered like her welted skin.

As she hugged the pillow and remembered David.

Placing Kate outside the front door of their inn with her blouse nearly open attracted only a pair of out of work cowboys. They were so broke they even tried to talk Ma down on the price of whiskey.

Much to Kate's relief, her father threw them out. At first, they didn't want to leave.

Both were acting like dogs in heat. Pa grabbed one, wrapping the cowboy's arm around so hard that when it broke it sounded like a snapping tree branch. The Benders were glad to see them go. They needed paying customers.

The morning was shaping up as a monotonous repeat of yesterday and the day before. The freighters made their usual stop. Mostly, they dropped by to stare at Kate Bender. If they ate in the inn, they could look longer. The old woman cooked up a good meal, to boot.

This morning, Kate moved stiffly when she waited on them, using none of her pouty smiles to cause them to tarry. Freighters weren't wanted or needed around The Bender Inn, not now. Time was running out.

Almira Bender worked in a black cloud of anger as she fixed breakfast for her clan after the freighters left. Even John sensed her rage and quietly nursed his coffee, keeping his eyes on his cup.

"Are we a gonna go to that meetin' tonight, Ma?" William asked carefully, making sure she was far enough away at the time so he could duck anything thrown his way.

"We've got to, you fool," she growled from the kitchen, "even if we get a passel of payin' customers today. It'll take those fools a while to get this far, pokin' their noses around. If we leave *now,* they'll know it was us all along."

"You're right, Ma," William answered. "We'll all go and make like we're as concerned as all get out."

"Time, that's what we need most of all. After a couple of days even an Indian won't be able to track us," Almira said, coming to the table, her cold eyes fixed on John. He kept his gaze fixed on his coffee cup. "Where's your dictionary?" Ma asked him in a voice that sounded cold and unforgiving, like a rattlesnake's buzz.

John winced without looking at her and mumbled, "I think it's on the shelf by my bed."

"You think! — you *think!*" Almira was screaming now. "You have to know. The whole family's countin' on you, and you just *think* you know?" Ma grabbed up the flyswatter from the table and started to hit him. She thought better of it, and laid it down, unused.

Ma Bender had learned it was best not to hurt John by beating him like she did Kate. Once, in a red rage, she'd grabbed a stove poker and hit him across his shoulders. Holding the badly bent poker, she'd seen a look in John's unblinking eyes that told her

298

another tactic was in order. "No supper and no apple pie for you today," Ma said, no longer screaming. Her voice went to sickly sweet. "John — son — the family's a countin' on you. If we're goin' to San Francisco, you have to be ready."

"Yes, Ma," John replied sheepishly. "I'm powerful sorry, I'll keep it in my pocket, for sure."

"That's my good boy," Almira replied.

John slid from his seat. Keeping his head bowed, he picked the small dictionary from his crate shelf, thrust it into his shirt pocket, and headed out the back door. Not bothering with his knife, he bit a huge chunk of tobacco off a black twist.

As soon as John was safely out of hearing, William asked, "Do you think he can manage what we're askin' of him?"

"He only has to be a little smart for a day or two," Ma said, "just to give us a chance."

"I'd hate to lose that boy. He's a lot of help some days," William replied.

"We got our plan. If John does what a good son is supposed to do, the Lord will look after him," Almira said.

"I've heard it said that God looks after fools and drunks, so I reckon he's got half a chance — he don't drink much," William said hopefully.

■ ■ ■ ■

It was early afternoon. A lack of paying customers kept Almira in a foul mood. William had joined his son to sit in the shade of their barn and chew tobacco. The doe-eyed, Jersey cow and her rapidly growing calf were more agreeable to be around than Ma when she was having a bad day, or a good one, for that matter.

They were attempting to wean the calf. It was penned alongside its mother, and made desperate attempts to reach her through the log fence. Finally it gave up and began bawling. John seemed to enjoy this. Since his Ma had berated him, nothing had brought out his usual mindless grin until the calf began its pitiful bellowing.

William noticed a dust cloud growing in the distance. As it grew closer he could make out a spring buggy with a surrey top pulled by a single horse. The rig was driven by a lone man dressed in what appeared to be a suit — strange dress, for travelers generally resorted to more utilitarian clothing. Closer scrutiny showed a slight figure wearing a sunbonnet by his side. When the buggy pulled to a stop in front of their inn, William stood up, spat out his chew, and said, "Come along, son, we may have us a job to do."

When William and John made their way through the back door, they noticed with delight that both travelers were already seated with their backs against the canvas. Kate was happily chatting with them. Almira had sliced two generous pieces of apple pie and was placing them on plates.

John had a puzzled look on his face; he was trying hard to remember where he left his hammer. William left his son's side and strode through the entranceway with a smile to make his greetings. His impression from the barn had been correct. The man was impeccably dressed, wearing an expensive business suit and a satin black cravat. Close-cropped hair and a neatly trimmed mustache spoke of learning. William knew money and education did not necessarily go together. "I'm William Bender. Welcome to our inn," he said, extending his hand.

"Doctor James Lewis, sir. We've heard you folks make the best apple pie in the county. Sarah, here, and I are looking forward to a slice," the doctor said with a benevolent glance at the shy, slight, blond-haired girl by his side.

"Sarah is going all the way to Kansas City," Kate said happily.

William looked closely at the little girl. She was perhaps six years old, skinny, gaunt, and drawn. She had the pasty complexion of someone who never went outdoors. "She sick?" he asked the doctor.

"She's going to be fine. There's a hospital in Kansas City where Sarah can be operated on. I don't have the facilities in Cherryvale to carry it out there," Doctor Lewis replied.

Ma Bender came to the table and set a piece of pie in front of each. The sickly girl only looked at hers, while the doctor dug right in. It was obvious whose idea it was to stop for pie. "Operations like that must cost a lot of money," Almira said with a sad look on her face.

"Yes, you are correct there," Dr. Lewis answered, "but we live in the wonderful town of Cherryvale. The citizens there have worked hard and raised funds to pay for Sarah's operation."

"Praise the Lord," Ma Bender intoned. "Just how much money did they raise? Do you have enough?"

"My, how good of you to inquire," Dr. Lewis replied between mouthfuls of apple pie. "You never know how much these things will cost. I have over five hundred dollars that was raised. Should you like to make a contribution, it would be graciously accepted."

"We'll do our part to help end Sarah's suffering," Almira said sweetly. She patted the little girl's head lightly and went to the kitchen.

Kate was standing by the open front door, keeping watch. She really hoped these travelers wouldn't be paying customers, but now there was no question. John could be seen standing behind the canvas holding his hammer.

The little girl with the cornsilk hair, picking at a piece of Mama's pie, reminded Kate of David. Her son had to die so they could flee. Now this child must do the same. It wouldn't be easy. John's hammer would most likely be able to hit the doctor. Then Mama would make her take care of the screaming girl. This would take all of her resolve, but she could do it. She *had* to, if she were to be a perfect child and go to San Francisco.

When Kate saw her brother draw the hammer back, she closed her eyes against tears and repeated:

"Honor thy mother and thy father."

TWENTY-ONE

"If bunkum could be set to music, he'd be an entire brass band," Lute whispered to Neely, causing a needed smile to cross his face.

Ben Chatterhorn was prancing around in front of the crowd like a revival preacher. Behind him, on a shiny blackboard, nine names were written in large, white letters. The ninth one had come in on the wire only a couple of hours ago — a young man by the name of Tip Boone, last seen in Independence.

The banker was plainly enjoying being the center of attention. The little, red frame schoolhouse was packed to overflowing. Opening the front doors had made standing room only for those in the street in front of the school.

The Benders had come early enough to get a bench. Kate returned Neely's smiles, batting her green eyes and tossing her long auburn hair. This caused the sheriff to sincerely hope this would all blow over soon so that he would have the time to run his store and court Kate in the manner she deserved. Neely felt if he could get Kate away from that strange mother of hers things would be different, the spiritualism thing forgotten.

Lute Thompson kept glancing at the crowd with a worried look. He had seen lynch mobs form before. It was a contagious disease that spread like a prairie fire over dry grass, each person urging the other on, inciting them to do things they would never normally do. Probably not a man here tonight would ever kill, on his own. Ben Chatterhorn was working the crowd into a fever pitch of anger and fear. They didn't know who they were angry at, or afraid of. This made the killing mentality ever easier. It was a different matter when names and faces could be put to it. But this crowd was getting so infected that Lute knew it wouldn't matter now who got lynched. They wanted to hang someone just so they could settle down again, the killing urge sated.

"And so it is decided, my fellow citizens," Ben Chatterhorn boomed, looking at the assembled crowd with fiery eyes, "to rid the county of Labette — our *homes*, ladies and gentlemen — from this scourge of lawlessness, we shall search every square foot of our fair land. No stone will be left unturned, and no canyon or stream will escape our quest."

Ben took time for a drink of water. He didn't really want one, but thought the pause would help hold his audience's attention. Strutting to the blackboard, he swept his bony arm at the list of names and continued, "Those names belong to fellow human beings. Their very names cry out for justice. Are we to turn a deaf ear to their cries? Not here, not in Labette County, Kansas, we will not."

The roar and applause from the crowd was deafening inside the little building. Ben Chatterhorn, who was clearly having the time of his life, noticed that only Neely Wells, Lute Thompson, and the Benders were not applauding his speech.

Holding up his hands for silence, the banker continued. "We will move in two groups. One headed by our sheriff, Neely Wells, and the *famous* Texas Ranger, Mister Lute Thompson."

If Lute had had a long nine cigar in his mouth, he would've bitten it in two. Being called both famous *and* mister in front of a crowd was too much. Lute had joked once about hanging Chatterhorn and the preacher to see if it would do any good. Right now he would have been real happy to whip the horse from under ole Scarbutt. No joking about it.

Ben Chatterhorn shouted, "The other group will be led by our esteemed guest and future congressman from Arkansas, Colonel Jefferson Davis Cowell — a man whose own brother's name is written on this board!"

Neely noticed that Lute's eyes had become cold, dark slits. The only other time he had seen this was during the bank robbery. He felt it would be a good plan just to be quiet and listen as the banker continued. "We will begin our search at eight o'clock in the morning. Before we leave here tonight, make arrangements with your chosen leader. The search teams will work west from our fair town of Parsons and not stop until we reach the Verdigris River. This will take time, ladies and gentlemen. I feel bad asking you to leave your farms and families, for what we are doing will take three days or more to accomplish. But I assure you, the homes you return to will be safe havens, peaceful isles in a sea of lawlessness. This scourge will be el—"

A shot roared through the packed room. Women put their hands over their ears while the men looked wildly about to find out who was shooting, and at what. They didn't have long to wait.

Lute Thompson was standing alongside Ben Chatterhorn in scant seconds, a smoking revolver in his hand pointing skyward. Some noticed the small round hole in the ceiling above where the Ranger had been sitting, especially Perry Thomas, the custodian. He knew he had a roof patching job to do now. There was no real hurry. The next rain might not come for weeks.

For one of the few times in his life, Ben Chatterhorn was both speechless and afraid. He wanted to upbraid Lute for his rash behavior, but then he looked into the Ranger's eyes. The only other time he'd seen eyes like that was on a diamondback rattlesnake. The banker decided to graciously give Lute Thompson the stage.

"All right, folks," Lute said in a loud but calm voice. His gun was holstered and he held both hands out, palms down. "Now, just relax everyone. No one has been shot, and I'd like to keep it that a way. I just want to add a couple of things to what our *esteemed* civic leader *Mister* Ben Chatterhorn, has been sayin', and I want your full attention while I'm sayin' it."

The banker put on his practiced poker

face and stood close to Lute. He thought it best if he acted as if this had been his idea all along. "What I want to say is," Lute continued, "we don't know *what* happened to any of these people. And if they met with foul play, we don't have one clue to *who* did what. Mister Chatterhorn says this is a law-abiding county, and I know for a fact it is. What we will do is search and see if we can find out *what* happened to these people. Then the *law* will take care of *who.* A mob lynching someone is not the law. It's murder, and will be dealt with accordingly."

"Lute Thompson is right, ladies and gentlemen," Chatterhorn intervened, somewhat less enthusiastic than he had been. "I asked him to tell everyone we're just forming a search party. Once we figure out what's going on, our fine sheriff and deputy will take care of the problem. I don't want anyone taking the law into their own hands in Labette County."

A grumble ran through the crowd. Lute and Neely both noticed it started where the four unsmiling Arkansans were gathered. It stopped as quickly as it began, and silence filled the room when Kate Bender came forward to position herself between Lute and Ben Chatterhorn. There was a short stool the teacher used to stand on when she needed to make a point. Kate kicked it forward and hopped up on it. "This is a time to band together," Kate said in a surprisingly strong voice. "We have a duly elected sheriff, Neely Wells. I, for one, give him my support." She surveyed the silent crowd for a long moment, as she had seen Pike Rogers do, then added, "Everyone here tonight who is for law and order in Labette County and agrees to uphold the direction of our government, please — let's show them our support."

Holding her hands out, Kate began loudly clapping them. Ben Chatterhorn quickly began following suit. Soon the entire room was shaking with applause. Even Colonel Cowell, with a stern look on his face, began clapping.

After the meeting adjourned, Neely found Kate in the milling crowd and went to her and said, "Thank you for what you did tonight. I really appreciate it."

Kate found his hand and squeezed it gently. "It's something I had to do," she purred. "Folks need to know who's in charge."

"I'll not forget this, Kate," Neely said to her.

Kate rolled her green eyes at him and said, "Neely, darling, it was the least I could do.

Mama wanted you to know the Bender family is always ready to help out the law." She squeezed his hand tightly. Then, with a swirl of auburn hair, she left to join her departing clan.

Darling. She actually called me darling, was all Neely could hold in his mind until Lute placed a hand on his shoulder, bringing him back to the problems at hand. "Well, I think that went well," Lute quipped.

"I don't think Chatterhorn thought so."

"Ole Scarbutt needed some settlin' down, is all."

"He *was* gettin' a mite carried away with himself."

"Yeah, and takin' half of the folks here with him. At least now maybe we won't have a mob we can't keep under control."

"Kate really helped us with her talk."

"That surprised me, Neely. I think she really does care."

"Once this matter is over, I'm goin' to court her proper."

"Problem is, it's only startin'. We have a passel of people showin' up tomorrow mornin'. We'd better get prepared. I don't know what this bunch will dig up, but we've got to keep an eye on that Cowell outfit, for sure."

With Kate Bender pushed momentarily

from his mind, Neely could see concern in his friend's face. He wished fervently that someone else, anyone else, was wearing the badge that felt so heavy pinned to his shirt. He felt like a man who was in water over his head and didn't know how to swim. If it hadn't been for Lute and Kate —. "Let's go talk it over. I have got a pot of coffee on," Neely said.

"I reckon a cup of your coffin varnish won't do no harm," Lute replied.

As the two men walked together in gathering darkness, a grin crossed Lute's face. It was one of those wicked ones he got on occasion.

"Well, what's so blamed funny?" Neely asked.

"It just crossed my mind. I'll give you ten to one ole Scarbutt never calls me *mister* again."

Late that night, while most folks in Labette County were lost in their dreams, a decrepit old wagon plodded slowly northward along the Osage Mission Trail. The yellow light of a waning moon swimming in a sea of blackness shone slightly over the four figures seated on it. A stiff wind blowing from the east filled the twin tracks the wagon left on

the road with a powder-white dust, conceal-
ing any evidence of its passing.

TWENTY-TWO

"I'm getting too old for this," Lute grumbled as he slid his lanky frame into a chair across the table from Neely at The Grand Hotel.

It was nearly dark outside, and both men were bone-tired from the first day of a fruitless search. The only high point of the day had come when Lute decided to look inside a spring house in back of the Reverend Pike Rogers's parsonage.

Behind a gunnysack, in a hidden compartment, he found six bottles of whiskey. Grabbing up a couple, Lute made certain enough members of the search party saw them to create a good rumor.

A red-faced and chagrined preacher denied any knowledge of their existence, saying the last minister, a heathen Methodist, must have left them. When Neely gently reminded him of the fact that the spring house wasn't even built then, the thoroughly distraught preacher felt it was a good time to go work on next Sunday's sermon.

The colonel's search party didn't report uncovering even a stash of whiskey. They had taken the northern half of the county, Lute and Neely's group the southern. What they were looking for even the searchers weren't certain. Bodies left lying in the open or buried in shallow graves were most likely. Some of the more imaginative lookers, using iron rods, probed the soft mud around creeks and even the holes beneath outhouses.

Only the first two miles west of town had been combed during the first day. Neely realized that at this pace it would take several more days of looking to move the search out of his district. He was very anxious to get this over with. The colonel's crowd was making him nervous. And there was Kate.

Colonel Jefferson Davis Cowell and his group selected a table as far away from Lute and Neely as they could get. Ed Stern kept shooting cold glances at them, using the one eye he could see out of. His other eye was still hidden inside a purple mass of swollen flesh. Ben Chatterhorn had taken a chair next to the colonel and was talking up a storm.

"It's sure hard to figger what makes politicians tick," Lute said quietly, smiling at Chatterhorn.

"Ain't that the truth," Neely replied. "I'll be real relieved when Cowell goes back to Arkansas."

"We all will. Only thing is, he's not going to leave until he finds out what happened to his brother. I can't say that I can fault him none there."

"I reckon not," Neely said with a sigh as he started carving on a steak while keeping a nervous eye on Ed Stern, "It'll just be a relief to get this thing over with." Then he added dryly, "Well, tomorrow's another day."

"That, my friend, is the only thing we know for sure," Lute stated as he spread a heavy layer of ketchup over his well-done steak.

Seth O'Malley had gone a long time without seeing Kate Bender. His father had kept the lovestruck youth tied to chores for most of the summer. In spite of the drought their farm had produced a fair crop of stunted corn. Over supper last night his dad had said it would be a neighborly gesture if they stopped by the Bender's tomorrow on their way to town and asked them if they would like to buy a few wagonloads of the corn for animal feed.

While a coolness still hung in the morning air, Seth hitched up the buckboard with zeal. His father watched in amazement as to just how fast his son could move when the spirit called him. He wasn't sure if the hope of seeing that pretty Bender girl or the fact they were going on to Cherryvale for supplies was the moving force. It had been weeks since the boy had been off the farm.

When they hopped on the wagon to leave, he noticed that Seth was wearing a fresh boiled shirt. When he caught a heavy whiff of shaving cologne, there was no question left in his mind; his son was growing up all too quickly. Brock O'Malley clucked his tongue, popped the reins, and headed the wagon toward the Bender's with his aromatic son by his side.

Both noticed the circling of large, black birds against a blue sky long before they reached the inn. At first they thought, or hoped, that an animal had died and the Benders had dragged it some distance away so it could be devoured by buzzards. As they got closer, they could plainly see this was not the case. The vultures were circling directly over the Bender's barn and corral. With growing concern, Brock flicked the reins and put his team of horses into a faster gait.

When they pulled their wagon to a stop in front of the inn, the plaintive bawling of a calf could be heard from the barn. A wide-eyed and obviously worried Seth jumped from the seat and headed for the sound, causing a cloud of buzzards to take flight. By the time Brock got the brake set on the wagon and joined his son, the boy was standing open-mouthed, a look of disbelief on his face, staring into the pen.

The Jersey milk cow lay stiff and dead, partially eaten by birds. Her udder had burst from lack of milking. Penned next to her, but far enough away to prevent its nursing, was the bawling calf. Brock opened the corral gate to allow the suffering animal to drink water from the trough it could see but not reach.

While the calf drank greedily, a stunned Brock and Seth stood together in shocked silence. Nothing moved in the still morning air. The Bender Inn, only a couple of hundred feet away, was ominously quiet. Both knew there could be no one inside, not with the calf's loud bellowing.

The flock of vultures that had taken flight from their meal of the dead Jersey cow flew lazily over the pens. A few wheeled in the clear sky, to glide silently and land behind the barn. Without a word, the concerned father and son ran to see what was in back of the building that attracted the birds.

Seth let out a shocked cry when he saw the dead horse. It was still hitched to a buggy with a fringed surrey top. Even after the damage the vultures had done to the dead animal, Brock could see where a close-range shotgun blast had torn into its chest.

Running wildly now, father and son headed for The Bender Inn, afraid of what they might find. The back door was locked, barred from inside. Quickly making their way to the front, they saw the door was padlocked from the outside. With mounting dread the O'Malleys pressed their faces to a window pane. To their relief, everything inside looked to be in order. At least, it was as well kept as they had ever seen it. There were no bodies lying about. "It looks like they just up and left, son," Brock said somberly. "Their wagon and team's gone."

"Dad, no one would leave a little calf like that and that horse hooked to a buggy —" Seth sobbed the words, tears streaming down his cheeks to drop onto his boiled shirt, no longer looking like a young man. His face was that of a scared boy.

Brock hadn't told his son about the shotgun blast to the horse. The sight of the dead animals alone were enough for the youth to bear. He knew that something terrible and violent had happened at this place. Also, he felt that whatever the incident was the immediate danger had passed. From the evidence the buzzards left, the cow and horse had most likely been dead since yesterday.

Placing a firm hand on his son's shoulder, Brock guided him back to their wagon. Reaching under the plank seat of the buckboard, he took out a battered, single-shot twelve-gauge. He flicked open the breech of the gun to assure himself it was loaded. Cradling the shotgun in the crook of his arm, he turned to his thoroughly unnerved son and said, "Seth, you take the wagon and go to Parsons and fetch the law."

"Dad, I — I don't want to leave you here," the lad sobbed.

"You do as I told you, son," Brock said firmly, acting braver than he felt. "I'll be all right. There's nobody about, and I have a gun should trouble come. Now you git, and do as I say. We need the law here, and time's a wastin'."

Seth O'Malley puckered his face into a frown to keep from crying outright. He couldn't be seen like that. He'd already done enough tearing. It was just that calf and its mother. If they had only been penned together, or left to run —. He didn't believe it was possible anyone could be so cruel to an animal. Trying hard to keep his mind on what his father had told him, Seth climbed onto the seat and goaded the horses into a trot.

Brock watched as the buckboard became a dust cloud on the road to Parsons. He hoped the boy wouldn't wind the horses too much. Carrying his old shotgun, he walked back to the barn. He chased a pair of determined vultures from the dead horse's body. There was no question in his mind that the sheriff would want to see where the close-range shotgun blast killed this hapless animal. He would have to keep the birds away until the law got there.

"Someone's sure in a hurry with that buckboard," Lute said as Neely and his group rode along the main road, heading for the Miller farm.

Neely looked into the distance. It always amazed him how Lute could see something long before anyone else. A faint, billowing cloud of white dust was coming their way, for sure. It was still maybe a mile away, but there was no question about it, whoever was driving that wagon was in a big hurry. No one ever pushed horses that hard without a good reason.

Both sheriff and deputy looked back at the ragtag band of volunteers following them. Goosey Hooper and, strangely enough, Carlton Cowell, were among them. The rest, eight in number, were farmers, and all looked the part, haphazardly armed with whatever ancient gun they owned that might actually shoot. Lute sincerely wished in vain that Neely and he were alone. A person driving horses wildly down a road always meant trouble. And it only took a single bullet from a gun, ancient or not, to make worse trouble. "Let's go see who's in such a dadblamed hurry," Lute said loudly to the group as he spurred his grey to meet the oncoming wagon.

Once the wagon stopped it took a moment for the dust to settle enough to make out who was driving the buckboard. It was just a kid. Chalk-dry, white dirt had covered him from head to foot. The only places on him that weren't dirty were wet lines on his cheeks. The boy had been crying. Neely thought he recognized the pasty driver. "Seth — Seth O'Malley? That you, son?" he questioned gently.

"Mister Wells, Sheriff, you got to come

quick. It's awful. My dad's there." The boy sobbed loudly, his voice breaking.

"Where, son? Tell me where, and settle down," Neely said.

"The Bender's place. You've got to get out there!" Seth squawked.

Neely's face became as white as the O'Malley boy's. *Kate* was the only thing on his mind now. Everyone in the party heard what the kid had said, and no one asked any questions as they all spurred their horses to head for The Bender Inn, leaving a sobbing, dust-covered boy sitting on a buckboard in their wake.

Brock O'Malley walked calmly from the back of the barn to meet the group as they rode hastily to The Bender Inn and dismounted. When he saw a large party of strange men with the sheriff, he leaned his old shotgun against the barn before going to see them. He had lived long enough to know that some folks were just plain trigger happy when they got worked up. Few would shoot an unarmed man, however.

As Brock grew closer, he could see his guess was right. At least three rifles were pointed at him.

"Put those guns away, you blasted idiots," Lute yelled when he saw what was going on, "That's the boy's father!"

Somewhat sheepishly, three farmers pointed their squirrel guns to the ground. Loudly enough for all to hear, Brock told what he and his son had found. Neely was obviously relieved to find out there were no bodies, just dead animals.

Looking at the dead horse still hitched to a buggy, they could see plainly where a shotgun blast had ripped into it. Goosey looked it over closely, dancing around the animal as if the ground were on fire. "I know this horse!" Goosey exclaimed excitedly. "I sold it to a Doctor Lewis from Cherryvale last year. She was a good horse, too. There was no cause to shoot her."

Lute looked the milling crowd over carefully. With not a lot of surprise, he noted that Carlton Cowell was no longer among them. Four men were sent to explore the area, from the barn to the rounded hills. Lute was careful to make sure the three men who pointed guns at Brock were among them. He didn't think there were any innocent folks in that direction they could shoot.

The Bender Inn and home was locked up tight, just as Brock had said it was. The fact that their old wagon and team of horses were missing gave hope the Benders were just on a short trip. But that calf penned away from its mother made no sense.

Faces pressed against the window panes showed nothing out of the ordinary. Neely was plainly puzzled. He hated to break into their home. As far as he could tell, though, there was no reason to. Whatever happened there must have transpired near the barn. But that horse — and what happened to the person driving the buggy? Questions grew like the grumblings of the men standing around the locked building.

"I reckon we ought to go inside," Lute said to Neely.

"What that would do to help I don't know, but we've got to find out what happened to that buggy driver and the Benders. Maybe they left a note or something," Neely answered hopefully.

Motioning people out of the way, Lute drew his forty-four, took aim at the brass padlock on the front door, and fired. The lock exploded into pieces. Placing the gun back in its holster, Lute opened the door wide. A cloud of black house flies hit him, along with a revolting stench.

Lute had been a Ranger and an undertaker long enough to recognize the smell for what it was. Decaying flesh had an odor like nothing else. Instinctively, he started breathing through his mouth.

A couple of farmers pushed their way past the Ranger, only to spin around with a gasp to leave the inn, holding their hands over their mouths.

"Lute, what is it?" a thoroughly shaken Neely asked.

"There's something dead in there, for sure. The smell would gag a maggot," Lute answered, still standing in the doorway. No one, it seemed, wanted to join him. The two farmers who tried to push past him were now alongside the house, puking up their breakfasts.

Lute's brown eyes scanned the shelves back of the Bender's grocery counter. When he saw what he was looking for, he took a deep breath and plunged through the swarm of flies, quickly grabbing up a green bottle. He ran to the clean air and inhaled deeply. "This is camphor oil," Lute said to answer the unasked question as to what the bottle contained. "Wipe some on your upper lip and it'll kill the smell a bunch. It's an old undertaker's trick."

The green bottle was passed around. All did as Lute instructed except the two sick farmers, who made it plain they weren't going back inside, no matter what.

Swatting at the hordes of flies, Lute,

Neely, Goosey Hooper, and a few ashen-faced farmers plunged into the open door of The Bender Inn.

A hurried search showed no source of the stench. Then Neely saw a circular outline of black flies under the table and pointed it out.

"That's the old dry well, the one the Andersons started. William Bender said it was to be a fruit cellar," Brock O'Malley shouted at them through the open door.

Lute pushed past Neely, went to his knees, and pulled the rug from under the table, causing a fresh mass of flies to swarm. A hinged, half-circle wooden door with a leather lifting ring met their gaze. There was no mistaking the dried bloodstains around the closed door. "Shit," Lute exclaimed.

"Oh my God." Neely choked.

"Well, we might as well open it," Lute said grimly as he grabbed the leather ring and threw the trapdoor open with a loud thud.

The stench that bellowed from the Stygian blackness of the old well was more than any human being could take. Holding their breath, everyone ran for the outside and fresh air.

Of the men that were inside, only Lute was somehow able to push down the gagging urge to vomit. Even he was having a tough time accepting what was probably in the depths of the old well.

After Neely composed himself he asked Lute, "Do you think it's the Bender family down there?"

"God only knows, but whatever's down there is —" Lute looked into Neely's eyes — "something I'll take care of."

The thunder of approaching horses caught everyone's attention. What looked to be maybe a hundred mounted men were riding hard toward The Bender Inn. Colonel Jefferson Davis Cowell and his nephew were in the lead.

Thank you very much, Carlton, Lute thought when he saw the not-unexpected group approach. He suspected all along the young man had joined with their group just to keep his uncle informed as to what they were doing.

Colonel Cowell leaped from his horse, tossing the reins to his nephew. With a worried expression, he strode to where Lute and Neely were standing in front of the inn. It only took them a moment to fill Cowell in on what they knew. With a look of determination, the colonel walked into the Bender's, only to return gagging. "My God, what an awful smell!" he exclaimed.

"We'll have to air it out before anyone can

see what's down there," Lute said. "No one can take that stench."

Neely, who had been looking the inn over with determination, said, "You men ever move a building? We'll need some poles from the corral. We can pry the place up and use those poles as rollers, then we'll move the building from the old well. That'll air it out."

The colonel barked orders to his men to follow Neely's directions. In a few minutes, the flimsy inn had been levered onto rollers and slid to one side, exposing the old well and open trapdoor to the bright Kansas sun.

None of the mass gathered around seemed anxious to peer into the maw beneath the door. With a grim look, Lute smeared a fresh helping of camphor under his nose. He then took a mirror from The Bender Inn and walked to the old well with it. Reflecting light from the sun with the mirror, he was able to light up the dark hole. The bloody and bloated bodies of a man and a little girl lying on their backs stared sightlessly from the depths. "My God! There's a girl and a man down there!" he exclaimed.

A murmur ran through the crowd. Colonel Cowell used some of the camphor as he had seen others do, and joined Lute. When the reflected light passed over the face of the dead man in the well, Cowell said with relief, "That's not my brother."

No one could make out what the Texas Ranger said to the colonel. Lute grabbed the Arkansan by his shirt and angrily drew him face-to-face. Whatever words were passed, Colonel Cowell seemed to agree with Lute Thompson's version. Wearing a rather subdued look, the future congressman climbed onto the ladder they found leaning against the well opening and descended into its depths.

Using the block and tackle that was left hanging so conveniently to the crossbeam, the man's body was hoisted from the depths. Colonel Cowell carried the slight body of a little girl up the ladder under his arm like a rag doll. When the mass of men assembled around the old well and saw the dead girl, curses, murmurs, and sobs racked the crowd.

Death was not an uncommon thing for these men to deal with, but murder, especially the murder of a little girl, was more than most of them could comprehend. Cries from the ones who looked at the bodies were, "Boys they've had their throats cut, and the man's got the back of his head caved in!" They were working themselves into a fever pitch.

At Lute's urging, Neely fired his pistol into the air, quieting the crowd. Standing on a chair he had taken from the inn, the sheriff looked to the horizon and noticed with a sinking feeling that horses and wagons of all descriptions descending on them. *Bad news travels fast.* "OK, boys, now calm down," Neely barked. "The first thing we need to know is who these people are. Now let's have some order, and let folks take a look at the bodies."

Without argument, most moved away from the bloated corpses, allowing others to look at them. All shook their heads sadly and left. Then Doc Clemmons walked up and scrutinized the bodies sternly. "That's Doctor Lewis from Cherryvale, and the girl is Sarah Claremore. He was taking her to Kansas City for an operation," he proclaimed loudly in one of the longest specches he'd ever given.

A loud murmur racked the crowd. First a little girl, and now a doctor. What could be worse?

Neely felt he was losing control. There were now well over two hundred people milling about. The fact that Kate and the Benders weren't in the well gave him a little relief. But now he had two murders to solve, and he *was* the sheriff.

Goosey Hooper was happy to be on the outside of the crowd. He hated looking at dead bodies. They unnerved him. Backing up a little to let the growing crowd have more room, Goosey stepped into the soft, fresh earth under one of Almira Bender's apple trees and sank up to his ankle. His gasp of surprise caught the attention of a couple of farmers, who yelled out, "Boys, we've found a grave!"

Pushing Goosey aside, a horde of men approached, carrying shovels. They didn't have to dig deep to find what they feared. In short order, the naked and mutilated body of a man lay beside a mound of earth.

Lute, Neely, and Doc Clemmons pushed their way to the scene. "That man fits the description of Tip Boone," Lute said after looking over the remains.

Doc made a hasty examination. "His head's caved in like the other man's, and his liver's missing," he said loudly.

"My God," Neely said before he was dashed aside by more men with shovels who started digging underneath an adjoining tree.

Lute and Neely stood together in the distance as body after body was unearthed from beneath the apple trees in Almira Bender's orchard. Some of the corpses were badly decomposed, obviously having been buried for some time. All had the backs of their heads caved in and their throats cut.

Neely felt ill, shaky. Lute put an assuring hand on his shoulder and said, "Neely, I'm sorry. Now we know why the Benders aren't around — they're the ones that done the killing."

"Not *Kate,* for God's sake. She couldn't have known."

"She *had* to know. That canvas behind their table, the stained one — they hit them in the head with a hammer. There's no other explanation, and from the looks of those bodies they've been doin' it for some time."

With feet of lead, Neely Wells followed Lute into The Bender Inn. Shakily, the sheriff examined the canvas and looked at the bloodstains under the table that had been covered by a rug. Then Lute held up a hammer he saw lying on the floor in the living area behind the stained wagon covering.

When Neely saw the blacksmith hammer, he looked it over closely and said numbly, "That's the hammer I sold them the first day they came into my store. John wanted it."

Under a pillow on a lower bunk bed, Kate's bed, Neely found a smaller hammer, the kind a shoemaker might use. He felt as if he had found another body, only this was Kate Bender's. Lute was right. He knew that now. The canvas, the hammers, the old well with a trapdoor under the table; the evidence was simply *there*. He could no longer ignore it, or hope. With a growing lump in his throat, Neely gently laid the hammer on Kate's pillow and said, "They played me like a fool, Lute. This place was *built* for killing. My God, how could I have been so stupid?"

"No one could have known. That's what they depended on. Who would ever expect an entire *family* to be killers, for pete's sake? All the time I spent Rangerin', I never even heard of anythin' like this," Lute said gently.

"Let's get out of here," Neely said, his voice showing anger. That made Lute feel better. He knew if his friend didn't get mad he'd break down.

When the pair left the inn Ben Chatterhorn, who had just come on the scene, called to them, "They've found the colonel's brother."

"Oh, shit," Lute mumbled as Neely and he made their way through the growing crowd.

Colonel Cowell was kneeling by a badly decomposed body when they got to him. He was obviously taking it hard, his upper lip quivering. Lute wondered how he could identify the body. There was not a lot left to tell who it was. Then the colonel pulled a small, silver ring from a bony hand. "I gave him this years ago," he said brokenly, handing the ring to Lute. "His initials are engraved inside," the colonel said without looking at it.

Lute rolled the ring so that the sunlight hit inside the band. The initials W.C. were etched there, as the Arkansan had said they would be. Looking the colonel in the face, he returned the ring and said sincerely, "I'm sorry."

"How many bodies do we have out here, for God's sake?" Ben Chatterhorn demanded loudly.

Neely sighed. "We've got — let's see — eight, and there's still a lot of trees left in the Bender's orchard."

"The Benders," Chatterhorn screamed, "where *are* they?"

"That's a mighty good question," Lute answered. "When we *do* find them, we'll have the folks that did these killin's."

An incredulous look crossed Chatterhorn's face. "What do you mean?" he yelled.

Neely came forward and told what they had found. The stained wagon canvas, the hammers, everything. When he was finished,

Chatterhorn looked pasty sick, and for once had nothing to say. Colonel Cowell quietly listened to the sheriff's theory. No one noticed as he left to join his cousins.

"We've found another one!" some stranger yelled, throwing dirt from a shallow hole with a shovel.

Neely didn't look to the site of the digging. His eyes were focused on the rapidly swelling crowd. He guessed there were well over three hundred people here now, the numbers increasing steadily. Some of the men had begun taking things from the inn, souvenirs from those some were already calling, "The Bloody Benders."

"When is it going to end?" Neely asked no one in particular.

"It's just beginning," Lute answered somberly.

"Over here!" someone yelled brusquely. It was Doc Clemmons, who was kneeling by the remains of Wade Cowell. Neely, Lute, and Ben Chatterhorn pushed their way through the milling crowd to reach the doctor. He was holding the small hammer, the one Neely had found under Kate's pillow. He had rolled the broken skull over, and with a flourish showed how the small hammer fit into every hole that had been hammered into Wade Cowell's head. "This is the weapon," Doc proclaimed.

With steely eyes, the sheriff of Parsons, Kansas, looked to the horizon — as if he could see the Benders sitting on that old wagon of theirs heading off — and he said loudly for everyone to hear, "I'll get those sons o' bitches."

■ ■ ■ ■

PART 3
THE LORD GIVETH,
THE LORD TAKETH

■ ■ ■ ■

What matter if I stand alone?
I wait with Joy the coming years;
My heart shall reap where it has sown,
And garner up its fruit of tears.

John Burroughs

TWENTY-THREE

The Benders loved traveling by train, especially John. He sat quietly looking out the window, empty-eyed, his open mouth drooling brown tobacco juice as the miles clacked away. Almira liked the service. A fawning black man with silver hair catered to her every whim. It felt so good to her, being waited on by someone else for a change, that she actually tipped him a silver dollar for bringing her a glass of sherry.

Kate was giddy with happiness, looking forward to the promised land called San Francisco. William, on the other hand, was quiet, morose, lost in thought. He knew they still had a long way to go, and telegraph wires traveled faster than any train or stagecoach.

The Benders never went back to their inn after the town meeting in Parsons. Once they came to the Osage Mission Road, William had turned north. When they reached the outskirts of the railroad town of Thayer, the decrepit wagon was abandoned, left with the hapless horses still hitched to it.

Each carrying a suitcase containing everything they felt necessary for their journey, the Benders walked the final half mile to the train station. A black leather purse slung over Almira's shoulder held what they needed most, cash money. Their entire fortune of nearly fifty thousand dollars was in that pouch Ma Bender cradled so lovingly next to her body, all of it in easily carried paper money.

With the morning sun, the Benders boarded a northbound Leavenworth, Lawrence, and Galveston Railroad train, using tickets purchased under the name of Gebardt. Once reaching the town of Humbolt, the family changed trains. This time they bought tickets on the express to the Indian Territory town of Vinita, under the name of Flickinger.

It was dusk when the train grunted into the station in Vinita. The tired clan rented two rooms in a first-class hotel within walking distance. Kate and Almira thoroughly enjoyed having a room to themselves. For the first time, Kate was able to stretch out in a tub of hot water without having to worry about John.

The family met in the dining room for a festive dinner. Bottles of chilled wine were savored with a meal of quail and pheasant for the women. John and William each devoured a huge cut of blood-rare porterhouse steak smothered in mounds of onions. The Flickinger family believed in traveling first class.

Later that night, while Kate and Almira were stretched out on the unaccustomed luxury of feather beds, William and John walked to the other side of the railroad tracks to a dimly lit, smoky, and noisy saloon. It didn't take a long time for them to find what they were looking for and make arrangements.

Ernst Sykes, a rotund man of nervous disposition who would never look anyone in the eye, met the two Flickinger men for breakfast, as agreed. He had made a career out of running houses of pleasure, and was always on the lookout for new opportunities — especially if someone else's money was available.

Two hard-looking prostitutes accompanied Sykes. The women gave their names as Mary White and Susan Buckman. The young man, John Flickinger, stared at them with an open mouth so long that his breakfast was cold when he finally devoured it in a few huge mouthfuls.

This was nothing new to the women. They were used to being looked at, with or without their clothes on, as long as the man or men paid them for the privilege, of course.

It was a mystery to Sykes as to why these two men wanted to finance opening a whorehouse in the West Texas town of Santa Angela. The older man, who did most of the talking, said they had information that a military fort was to expand and they wanted to take advantage of the situation. What puzzled him even more was why only these two ladies were to go with them on this trip. To his way of thinking, the more girls working, the more money earned.

Sykes decided not to ask a lot of questions of these men. After all, they were financing the venture. He had learned early in the game that prying into another's business could be downright hazardous to your health. The last owner of his present stable of whores hadn't been so prudent. He made the mistake of inquiring about where a customer came by all those gold coins he was spending so freely. The stranger's answer was to shoot the nosy pimp through his large middle. This had pleased Ernst Sykes a great deal. It had left a vacancy for him to easily fill, and spared him the task, and saved the cost of a bullet to boot.

The few questions Sykes had were answered when the older man started counting out hundred-dollar bills to young John. Cash talked in a way that solved all problems. Ernst didn't particularly like the idea of this John Flickinger accompanying them on the trip. He didn't give the impression of being any too smart, however, and he thought he could handle him with words. If that didn't work — well, it was a long trip, and accidents could happen.

When the eight o'clock express train puffed away from the Vinita depot, two men and two women were on board as first-class passengers carrying tickets to Denison, Texas. They were well on their way when the conductor made his rounds. Ernst Sykes noticed all four tickets were under the name of Flickinger. No matter. They were on their way, money in hand.

After the train had rattled out of sight leaving behind a cloud of smoke hanging in the still morning air, William sighed, clucked his tongue, and walked to the hotel with a heavy heart.

Kate and Almira were packed and ready to board the stage. Both women looked refreshed and happy, eager to be on their way. Ma carefully went over the money in the privacy of their room. William took five hundred dollars, folded it, and stuffed it into a hidden pocket in his belt. Once again they rehearsed their travel plans.

The two women were to journey together. William was to go another route. They felt certain any lawmen on their trail would follow the four people on the train. After all, they reasoned, the Benders had left on a train. It was reasonable to think they would continue doing so. Two men and two women traveling together under the name of Flickinger almost guaranteed any lawmen would pursue that lead.

Kate and Almira, now known as Kathy and Alma Griffith, were to make their trip by stagecoach to Salt Lake City, Utah Territory. William, now calling himself William Goode, was to travel alone, along lesser routes through Dodge City and Cheyenne, eventually meeting Kathy and Alma in Salt Lake City.

Once they were reunited, their plan was to stay in the Mormon city for some time, maybe as long as several months. It would be a simple matter to pass themselves off as recent converts to the Church of Latter Day Saints. No one would ever suspect a family of pious Utah farmers of being the Benders from Kansas.

Should John survive his journey of deception, he was to send a telegram to Salt Lake City. There was little doubt in Almira's mind that the message would never come. At least she hoped it wouldn't. From here on, John could be a problem, and she hated problems.

William didn't go to see his wife and daughter off on the stage. It wasn't wise that they should be seen together. After the women left he stayed in his room to await the afternoon stage that would take him back to Kansas. When he ran his hand over his face, the newly emerging beard felt rough and satisfying. *I hope the boy remembers not to shave,* he thought. A lump formed in his throat when he thought of John. It was a strange feeling for him to experience, worrying over someone, but the boy was his son. And here his wife was, nearly certainly sending him off to get himself killed.

Ma and the preacher both always said the Lord looked after his own. William comforted himself a little with this thought. After all, John always did what he was told. He was a child who always honored his father and mother. Surely the Lord would forgive him his shortcomings and see him safely to Salt Lake City.

When the afternoon stagecoach pulled out of Vinita, William Goode was on board, still thinking of his son, John.

TWENTY-FOUR

Neely and Lute rode back to Parsons under a black sea of winking stars. Both were still too stunned over the events of the day to be tired. This was the first time in Neely's memory that Lute Thompson had been at a loss for words. The grim-faced Texas Ranger kept his pinched eyes focused on the now well-worn, dusty road.

Before darkness brought a halt to the excavations at The Bender Inn, eleven bodies had been laid side-by-side in a gruesome display. Neely guessed that as many as four hundred people had appeared on the scene.

Ma Bender's fledgling apple orchard resembled a battlefield. Holes riddled the field like shell craters. The only bodies found outside of those in the old well, however, were in a line under a single row of trees, leading to the hope that possibly no more corpses remained to be exhumed.

349

Dispatches had been sent to Parsons, Cherryvale, and Independence for enough coffins to hold the victims. With wagons carrying the caskets had come more flocks of people, all of them armed and incited to the point of rage. Rumors and accusations flew rampant. Anyone who lived in the area, especially those close to The Bender Inn, was suspect as being involved with these terrible crimes.

Early in the afternoon, Lute had told the O'Malleys to leave. Seth placed a halter on the Jersey calf and tied it behind their wagon, forcing the struggling animal to leave its dead mother. The Ranger had seen mob violence before, and knew the insanity seemingly normal people could work themselves into. Even Lute Thompson, however, had never seen a crowd in such a fever as this one. He felt the O'Malleys would be safer at home. To make sure, he sent two armed men he felt he could trust along to watch over them.

There was no controlling the souvenir hunters. Already, pieces of the inn itself were being stripped and carried away. At Lute's urging, Neely had taken the hammers for evidence. Aside from the two they found in the inn, another was taken from the barn. All three were rattling in Neely's saddlebags as the distraught sheriff rode into Parsons.

The town was simply alive with people. Yellow lantern light flickered from most windows. Saddled horses were tied to every hitch rail along the main street. Lute and Neely both grimaced when they saw the milling crowds of grumbling armed men outside The Rose Saloon and The Kansas Schooner. They knew whiskey and blind anger was a bad mix.

"Well, old friend, it's been a bad day, for sure," Lute finally said with a slight twinkle returning to his eyes. "You lost your girl, and I've lost my bed. Been sleepin' on those coffins for years."

Neely tried to force a smile, but it wouldn't come. "I'm afraid we've got more trouble," he said grimly, eyeing the gathering in front of The Rose.

"We'll have to have a little talk with them," Lute said, reining his horse into Goosey Hooper's livery.

After the spastic stablehand unsaddled their horses, the duo walked the short distance to the general store, Neely carrying the leather saddlebags containing the Bender's hammers. Even by the waning moonlight, the men could see stacked coffins spilling out from under the lean-to alongside

351

Lute's undertaking parlor like cordwood.

Lute was even more upset when he found the sacks of quick lime unused and lids nailed tight to the caskets. He knew if he didn't open each coffin and give the decaying inhabitants a good dusting, he would catch billy hell from everyone for a mile downwind. That would have to wait, though. If something weren't done to calm down the mob, there would be more bodies added to the collection, and probably none of them would have had any more to do with the Benders than Moses. Also, he was fresh out of coffins. "You got a couple of scatterguns?" Lute asked.

"I've got two ten-gauge double barrels in the store, both new."

"With any luck we can put them back in the same condition."

"Lute, there's a whole mob in The Rose — we can't shoot them all," Neely said as they walked into his store.

"You don't have to rein in but one or two. There's always a passel of followers behind a couple of big-mouthed leaders. I've a good feeling the one with the biggest mouth will be our would-be congressman."

Neely grabbed two shotguns from a rack and laid them on the counter. Taking out a box of double-O buckshot shells, he broke one gun open and thrust a pair of the red and brass cartridges into the breech and slammed it shut. Tossing the loaded ten-gauge to Lute, the sheriff then loaded the other. Each stuck a handful of cartridges in their pockets and walked from Neely's store into the dusty, dark main street of Parsons.

Standing silently side-by-side in the middle of the road, Neely noticed that Lute had cradled the shotgun in the crook of his arm and cocked both hammers. He did the same. With the big gun lying heavily in his grasp, Neely Wells headed for The Rose Saloon with a growing feeling of anger. In the pale light Lute noticed that his friend's eyes were narrowed to coal-black, emotion-less slits.

Neely jabbed his way through the milling crowd into the saloon. A couple of farmers were soon holding their sides in pain where the sheriff had used the shotgun barrel to convince them to move. Roland Langtry was standing on a whiskey barrel at one end of the saloon, ranting like a stump preacher. When he saw the two lawmen he grew silent, a smirk on his face. Neely noticed no one was behind the whiskey barrel. He swung the big shotgun around and fired, sending the oak keg flying into splinters and Roland sprawling onto the barroom floor.

The swiftness of Neely's action, along with the explosion of the shotgun in the packed room, got everyone's attention, surprising even Lute.

Roland Langtry jumped to his feet. A shocked, white expression replaced his smirk as he felt himself all over to make sure he wasn't shot. After the saloonkeeper decided he didn't have any holes in him, he turned to Neely and started to say something. A quick glance at the black opening of the ten-gauge that was pointed at him gave Roland cause to think this wasn't a good time to argue with the sheriff. Meekly he shifted his gaze to the plank floor and dropped his arms listlessly.

Neely slapped a fresh shell in the shotgun and, walking behind the counter, hopped up on a chair. From there he jumped up on Roland's polished walnut bar and began pacing up and down it, sweeping the big gun at the murmuring crowd. "Who the hell is the law around here?" he yelled at no one in particular. "I asked, who the hell is the sheriff around here?" This time Neely held the cocked shotgun with a steady hand and pointed it at Roland Langtry.

"You are," the now meek saloon owner answered softly.

"I can't hear you!" Neely boomed, keeping the gun steady.

"*You* are, dammit," Roland squawked, his voice nearly breaking.

"Well, I'm glad we've got that settled," Neely replied in a loud voice, swinging the shotgun back to the crowd. "Now, does anyone here have another opinion worth getting their ass shot over?" he boomed.

A nervous twitter ran through the group, but not a person, it seemed, had anything to say to Sheriff Neely Wells.

"Boys," Neely continued, "anyone here who takes the law into his own hands, I'll personally hang — or shoot — whatever it takes. Now think about it. Your wives and family need you at home, not hanging from a rope because you acted like a blamed idiot. Go home to them and let us do our job — and I mean *now,* Goddammit!"

Lute Thompson was wearing a satisfied grin as he watched the murmuring crowd rapidly disperse into the darkness. Through the open batwing doors of the saloon he could see word had also hit across the street, as The Kansas Schooner bunch starting thinning out. One of the comments Lute overheard was that the sheriff had gone nuttier than a peach orchard boar and was out to kill anyone who disagreed with him.

After the saloon had emptied, Neely kept

pacing up and down the bar, nervously swinging the double-barrelled ten-gauge. Roland scowled every time the sheriff turned, thinking of all the scratches Neely's hobnail boots were making in his shiny bar. There was no way he was going to say anything about it. He could get the scratches sanded out; being shot by a crazy person was permanent.

Lute carefully lowered the hammers of his shotgun against the firing pins. Using the droning tone of a cowboy trying to calm a spooked horse, he looked up at Neely and said, "I don't think anyone's gonna give you cause to shoot them tonight. Let's go back to your store and boil up a pot of coffee."

Making one last scan of The Rose Saloon, Neely had to concur with his friend's assessment. Aside from Lute, only a shaken and subdued Roland Langtry remained in the room. Uncocking the shotgun, Neely hopped gracefully from the bar. He spun to give the saloon owner one final scowl. Then Lute placed a hand on his shoulder and said happily, "Well, I think that went well."

As Lute and Neely walked back to the general store, they noticed most of the lanterns that had been flickering yellow light through closed windows were now out, and the saddled horses were gone.

Lute was feeling immensely proud of Neely. He had recovered from the shock of the day in the only manner he could. The Ranger had noticed that some people let catastrophes stay inside them, where they start eating away like a cancer. At least his friend had gotten a little heartbreak out of his system tonight, and nothing but a whiskey barrel got hurt. Neely had been so worked up by the time they got to The Rose he hadn't paid any attention to what Roland was saying from his temporary perch on top of the empty keg. The saloonkeeper had been telling everyone to settle down and behave themselves or he was going to close the bar. There was no doubt in Lute's mind that someone would mention this little detail to Neely; he sure didn't plan to.

One major point of worry still bothered him. It was Colonel Cowell's bunch. He would have bet his refurbished hearse that Jefferson Davis Cowell was the one trying to work the crowd into a frenzy, and it turned out he wasn't even in town. The last time Lute remembered seeing him was at The Bender Inn, when his brother's body was being placed in a coffin. Maybe he was in Cherryvale or some other town, causing problems. At least he wasn't in Parsons. As Lute followed Neely into his store, weariness crashed over him like an ocean wave hitting shore. He was glad this day was finally over and Colonel Jefferson Davis Cowell was among the missing.

Under a dark covering of towering elm trees alongside the slow running waters of the Verdigris River, the man who dreamed of being a congressman from Arkansas sat slumped in the saddle of his horse.

With a feeling of detached numbness, the Civil War hero Colonel Jefferson Davis Cowell watched in waning moonlight as John and Edward Stern tamped newly turned earth firm with the backs of their shovels. Carlton came from the darkness downriver, dragging a few pieces of freshly cut, green brush. The Stern brothers walked to the edge of the river, drew back, and threw their shovels into the black water. The two men then went to help young Carlton use the brush to rub out all evidence of their digging. Once the dank earth had been scoured, the pieces of scrub were also tossed into the Verdigris to slowly drift away.

The three then directed their efforts to a pair of dead horses that were lying in shallow water, still wearing harness and traces. John Stern took a gleaming Bowie knife and slit the animals' bellies open. Carlton and

Ed began stuffing river rocks into the body cavities of the horses. Once they were certain the dead animals would stay submerged until the crawdads and catfish had done their work, Ed stood up and gave a low, muted whistle to Whitey Whitmore and Ralph Benson, who were on the other side of the river standing alongside their saddled horses. In answer to the sign, the men picked up ropes and tied them securely to their saddle horns and urged the horses away.

Colonel Cowell watched in stony silence as the two animals slid beneath the swirling, murky water. Once the dead horses had been dragged to the center of the river, Benson and Whitmore stopped their mounts, untied the ropes, coiled them tightly, and threw them into the waters with a heavy toss.

With a cold, detached look, the colonel surveyed the scene. He had done all he could. They had been lucky to have the time to cover their mistake. A couple of travelers would have been no problem. They could have joined the Sullivan family in the now obscured hole. If an armed party had shown up, however, Cowell knew he would have been hung along with his relatives and the two farmers from Parsons — probably from the same elm tree where they had hung the wrong people.

Looking at the shadowy forms of Whitmore and Benson across the river from him, Cowell shouted, "You boys go on home now. Just remember, you were as much a part of this as anyone else. It was a mistake, plain and simple."

The two men slouched down in their saddles and rode off into the night. It *had* been a mistake, Colonel Jefferson Davis Cowell reflected grimly. He had been in too big a hurry to extract his revenge and get back to Arkansas and his campaign.

After the decomposed body of his brother had been nailed into a coffin and sent off to Parsons in a rattling wagon, he had called his group to one side of the crowd. Whitmore and Benson joined them. The two farmers had been with them since their arrival. They liked the way the Arkansans paid for whiskey and talked tough.

"Men," he said, "that sheriff and burned-out old Ranger couldn't pour piss out of a boot. Those damn Benders killed a lot of people other than my brother, and I, for one, am not going to let them just ride off. They left on a wagon and there were four of them, so they're traveling slow. I'm betting they went for cover, and the river would be the best place to hide. Let's split into two groups and find those bastards — and when we do, we'll show 'em as much mercy as they showed those poor souls they massacred."

Fired into a red rage, the colonel, Benson, and John Stern headed upriver and the others downstream, with a plan to meet where they'd parted at full dark.

Carlton's group found nothing. When they arrived at where they were to meet up with the colonel, an excited Ralph Benson was there. "We've found them," he exclaimed, "and we've already got them hung!"

Riding fast in the fading light, they soon came to the bend in the river. Under huge green trees stood a lone wagon. Four figures dangled lifelessly from a high limb. It was obvious they had been stood in the wagon, ropes placed around their necks, and had it driven from under them. Carlton rode close to the still bodies and looked wide-eyed at the young, blonde girl dangling in the moonlight, her black tongue protruding through swollen lips. "Uncle, who *are* these people?" Carlton screamed.

"They're those Goddamn murdering Benders!" the colonel replied loudly with just a hint of trepidation in his voice, when he remembered that his nephew was the only one in the group who had actually seen the Benders.

Carlton was in too much shock to do more than mumble, "It's not them." Then he said, louder, "I ate dinner at the Bender's. Uncle, it ain't them you've hung."

"Oh, my God," was all Colonel Jefferson Davis Cowell could muster.

When you make a mistake, bury it, was the colonel's answer. There was no alternative, actually, outside of being hung themselves. With a numbness brought on by their deeds, the group had broken up the wagon and buried it and the dead family in a deep hole dug with shovels they had found in the wagon.

By candlelight, Cowell thumbed through the contents of a chest they found under the wagon seat. Sullivan was the family's name, after all, just as they had said. They were Baptist missionaries going to start a new church in Nebraska. No one had expected them to answer to the name of Bender. There were four people traveling together, two men and two women, heading away by an old wagon.

Along with the personal items found in the box, Colonel Cowell discovered nearly four hundred dollars in an envelope. No one wanted to touch the money. When Carlton mentioned they would be no different than the Benders if they took it, his words hit like a knife.

They would like to have burned the wagon and the money, but a fire might have drawn attention, so everything was thrown into the hole and covered over. All evidence of a family named Sullivan was concealed.

Wordlessly, the group rode off slowly into the darkness.

Lute and Neely had both slept poorly. When the first light of day shone through the lace curtains of the windows in front of his store, Neely went and ripped them off and used them to start a fire in the stove. As soon as he had a pot of coffee boiling, Lute came in.

The Ranger was dressed and wearing his guns. Dark circles around his eyes made Neely wonder if Lute had even slept at all. He realized he probably looked just as tired or even more so.

Over cups of steaming coffee both made small talk, neither of them anxious to speak of the Benders. They knew that subject would be around for a long while.

A light knock on the door caused Neely to go open it. A red-eyed and somber Jefferson Davis Cowell met his glance. The man was so tired he was shaking. "I'd like to take my brother's body now. We're going home," Cowell said softly.

"He's out back — in the lean-to," Lute said, coming to the open door.

A hitched wagon was parked on the street. Ed Stern was in the driver's seat. He kept his one good eye looking straight ahead, avoiding Lute's gaze. Carlton and John were both mounted on horses and leading the colonel's roan. None of them seemed to have anything to say.

Wade Cowell's wooden coffin was carried up and slid into the freight wagon. "I bought the wagon and team from Mister Hooper," the colonel said to stave off any questions.

Lute hadn't gotten any quicklime into the coffins yet. He had planned to do it that morning. He thought about saying something, but the colonel would figure the problem out soon enough on his own, and Lute didn't much like the man, anyway.

"How much?" Cowell questioned blandly to Lute.

"Huh?"

"For the coffin, how much do I owe you?"

"Oh, fifteen dollars."

Colonel Jefferson Davis Cowell handed the money to Lute, walked stiffly over to his horse, and climbed on. Then Ed Stern flicked the reins and the wagon headed off. None of the Arkansans looked back as they headed down Main Street, away from Parsons.

"I wonder what got their goats?" Lute asked. "They were sure full of piss and vinegar for a while. Now somethin' up and happened to their vinegar."

"Well, I expect we ought to count it as a favor. Probably the fact he's found his brother is the problem."

"Don't seem like his style, but I reckon you're right. With that bunch out of the way, it's just one less thing to worry on."

When they got back to their coffee both cups had cooled a little, allowing them to drink it without sipping. Neely swigged a much-needed mouthful, leaned back in his oak swivel chair, looked at Lute, and asked, "Well, what do we do now?"

"Nothing we can do until we figure out where the Benders have gone to. I expect they're long gone, possibly leavin' right after the town meeting that night. They had plans, for sure."

Neely winced as he remembered how Kate had come to his defense. All that time she was playing him like a fiddle. "Reckon we ought to go out there to the orchard and see if they found any more bodies?"

"Won't do no good that I can see. We can't do anything for the dead except find those that caused them to be that way."

"Every lawman in these parts probably knows about what happened by now, Lute. Do we just wait?"

"No one can travel without leavin' a trail. We can't just go off without some idea where they went. A telegraph wire can travel faster than a wagon or a train. I'm goin' to dust down the coffins after breakfast and pack a travel kit. You best get some clothes packed yourself, and see old Scarbutt for a passel of money. When we get word of where they're a headin' we could be gone for a while."

"You think they took the train?"

"Wouldn't you want to get away as quick as you could if you'd killed twelve people?"

"Eleven, Lute, there was just eleven yesterday."

"Nope. Remember back to about the time the Benders showed up, and those freighters found that man by the river with the back of his head knocked in? I'm a bettin' that if we dug him up, one of those hammers you have in the drawer over there would just fit in that hole in the back of his skull."

"Oh, my God."

"I don't reckon God had much to do with it," Lute replied. "Those Benders come from a hotter climate. They're regular Hell Benders."

Chatterhorn had given Neely three hundred dollars with a surprisingly small amount of argument. The banker was already catching his share of fallout. When Neely was there, one family had come in and closed out their account, saying they were moving away.

That a bunch of murders were bad for business was a certainty he couldn't deny. The sooner the Benders were caught and brought to justice, the sooner things would return to a profitable norm for the banking business.

It was mid-morning before Joe Peeples flew into Neely's store with a telegram. Nothing could have been more welcome. It seemed a hundred people had come by wanting to know what the sheriff was doing just sitting around on his butt.

Lute had seen Peeples enter the store, and followed behind him in a near run to read the telegram with Neely. It was from the City Marshall of Thayer, Kansas, and said that four people meeting the Benders' descriptions had boarded a train there two days ago. The name they used was Gebardt. Yesterday, a wagon was found still hitched just outside of town. The wagon had two front wheels narrower than the rear.

"It sure as hell took them long enough to get the word out," Neely spat.

"Never mind," Lute said. "Now we know how they left, and we've got us a trail. Joe, tell Goosey to saddle our horses and make arrangements to get them back from Thayer once we get there. The sheriff and me are goin' to be gone for a while." Shifting his gaze to Neely he said, "Let's get rounded up. We've got ourselves a manhunt."

TWENTY-FIVE

To Almira's way of thinking, stagecoach travel was a lot rougher method of traveling around the country than rich folks should have to endure. Train travel was downright luxurious compared to the swaying, dusty, and slow-moving coach Kate and she left Vinita, on.

The way the stage wallowed back and forth in a slow, even motion caused her to think of a boat on the ocean. She had heard that wealthy people, like them, could book passage to Europe on a sailing ship and have a private cabin all to themselves and be waited on hand and foot for the entire voyage. No one deserved such luxury more than Almira. She had worked so hard the past few years to make their dreams come true.

Once they were in San Francisco living in luxury on Nob Hill, it wouldn't be long before Kate would attract a wealthy beau, a man of affluence. Then she would look into a nice cruise. Paris in the springtime was said to be most beautiful. No one had a right to spend the rest of her life steeped in luxury more than she. Living by the Good Book had its rewards, for sure.

Seated across the coach from Almira, Kate noticed an amiable look on her mother's face and smiled happily at her through the billowing dust. Kate's beauty was a pleasure to her Ma. It was a deep, natural attractiveness she had never been blessed with. And it was so usable in this world of men. There was no doubt at all in Almira's mind that her daughter would have a rich husband in short order, a man who would take good care of his wife's parents. If not, she certainly knew how to handle disrespectful men who didn't follow the teachings of the Good Book and honor their mother and father. A good inheritance would be nice, too. Kate was young. Her beauty would last for years.

Almira's reverie didn't last long. Only an hour out of Vinita on the dusty road to Tulsa, a rifle shot split the still air. Quickly she shuffled the black leather purse containing their future under her left arm. There was cursing, then a confused jumble of voices from outside the stagecoach as it jerked to a stop. Another rifle cracked, followed by the loud boom of a shotgun. There was a sound, as if someone had dropped a sack of potatoes to the ground from the driver's seat; after that, silence.

A burly, unkempt man smelling of stale whiskey was sitting alongside Kate — much closer than was necessary, to her way of thinking. He pulled a small revolver from his tattered coat and shouted, "We're being robbed!"

Color fled Almira's face like a white cloud crossing the sun. She was ashen and shaking when the door next to her flew open and the twin black barrels of a shotgun protruded into the stagecoach. The pistol the man next to Kate had pulled made a dull thud as it hit the wooden floor. He was holding both hands palm open.

"Right smart of you," the man holding the shotgun said matter-of-factly. "We ain't going to hurt no one if you'll see things our way."

Kate smiled her best winning smile at the young man holding the shotgun. She noticed his red beard was neatly trimmed, and he had the most beautiful, twinkling, blue eyes she had ever seen. The robber returned her smile and said politely, "If you folks will be kind enough to get out for a spell, you

371

can continue your journey right soon."

"You thieving son of a bitch! I'm not leaving this stage!" Ma screeched.

The shotgun swung to point at Almira's ample middle. No longer was the young man smiling when he said, "Lady, my name is Jesse James, and it's a matter of pride that I've never shot a woman before, but in your case I might make an exception."

"Let's do as the man says, Ma," Kate said sweetly.

Almira scowled deeply but said nothing as she swung her bulk from the thinly padded seat and jumped to the ground with a grunt. Jesse's gun followed her every movement.

"Please, sir," Kate pleaded, beginning to cry, "we're on our way to take care of my father. He's bad hurt and needs our help."

"Then you're carrying some money, that's good," Jesse said happily.

Almira shot Kate a scowl that would kill a thistle patch, then glared at the robber and said, "God's commandment is, 'Thou shalt not steal.' Don't you have any respect for the Good Book?"

" 'It is more blessed to give than receive' — Book of Acts, Chapter twenty, verse thirty-five, lady," Jesse quoted with a twinkle in his eye. Then he shouted over his shoulder, "Cole, bring a sack for these folks to fill."

Kate looked through misty tears to the man Jesse had yelled at. He was young, also, about her age. The man called Cole casually flipped his pistol back into its holster and walked toward them with a sickly grin. Another man mounted on a horse kept a rifle pointed at the driver of the coach, who kept his hands held high. A man Kate remembered as being the guard was sitting on the ground leaning against a wheel, keeping his hand pressed to a bloody shoulder. He seemed more angry than hurt.

Cole walked up to Kate. While he looked her over with a yellow-toothed, hungry sneer, he pulled a canvas sack from his belt and opened it. Jesse James stepped alongside the man holding the bag and said to the three passengers, "Hand it over, and please be quick about it," all the time keeping the shotgun pointed at Almira.

The large man who had been sitting by Kate slowly took a leather billfold from his jacket and dropped it into the sack.

"Come *on,* sir," Jesse urged.

With a deeply furrowed frown, the man tossed a gold pocket watch and a handful of gold coins after the wallet.

Then Jesse's twinkling blue eyes focused

on the black purse Almira was clutching tightly. "Give it up, lady," he demanded.

"Oh my poor husband — we need this for doctors," Ma sobbed.

"Blazes, you're wearin' thin," Jesse grumbled as he took his free hand and grabbed the purse away, breaking the strap as he did so. All that time he kept the double-barrelled shotgun pressed into Almira's belly.

Jesse backed off a few steps and cradled the gun in the crook of his arm while he unsnapped the purse and he examined the contents. His eyes widened. When he looked at Almira and Kate, he was beaming. "Your old man must be powerful sick," Jesse said as he reached in and took out a few bills and handed them to Kate before he tossed the purse into Cole's money sack. "Don't let it be said that Jesse James and Cole Younger ain't charitable," Jesse said graciously to Almira. Then he looked Kate over closely and shifted his gaze back to Almira. "Mother and daughter, huh? Who would ever o' thought it?" Then Jesse placed a pair of fingers to his lips and let out a shrill whistle. Two mounted men led a pair of saddled horses from a dense grove of trees.

Jesse James and Cole Younger went to the horses and jumped easily into the empty saddles. Before turning to ride off, Jesse took one final look at Almira, clucked his tongue, shook his head questioningly and said, "Who'd o' thought it."

Almira and Kate stood side-by-side and watched with teary eyes as California rode away, tucked in a canvas sack carried by the outlaw Cole Younger. All their hard work and planning gone in less than three minutes. "It ain't fair," Ma sobbed, "it just ain't fair. We worked so hard for what we got."

The man who was riding alongside Kate produced a silver flask from his pocket, took a drink, then offered it to Almira saying, "There's a passel of dishonest people in this world who have no respect for law and order."

"Ain't it the truth," Ma answered, taking a large drink of the whiskey.

Kate counted the money Jesse had handed her — two hundred dollars. That gave them five hundred — she had three hundred stuck in her blouse. If the robbers had suspected money being there, they would have searched her, for sure. Cole Younger would have been bad. He had the same cold look as Choctaw Charlie. Now Jesse, on the other hand — being searched by him wouldn't have been so bad, not bad at all.

William didn't mind traveling by stage-coach. He didn't have to hitch or unhitch horses, and there was always a decent meal at the way stations. It was nice being a man of means. Most nights there was a fluffy, soft, feather bed to sleep in. He was pleasantly surprised to find it wasn't necessary to sleep alone, either. After all the years of waking up to the sternness of Almira, it was a pleasant experience to have a pretty face next to him in bed.

William didn't want to do this every night, though. Ladies were only willing if he paid them. He wanted to save his money for Dodge City. That was where the real fun lay. Faro was his game, and no place held higher stakes for a man who really knew how to play than Dodge City. And William was the best at cheating there was. He was just itching to buck the tiger once he got to where the stakes were high enough to make things interesting. *Hell,* he thought, *I might turn my five hundred into more money than Ma's carryin'.*

He smiled at the thought, then slapped the naked bottom of the fat Indian girl who was lying alongside him, snoring. She rolled over and gave him a snaggle-toothed grin. The girl was possibly fifteen years old, but her hard face spoke of years of men. No matter. William had paid her for the whole night. He didn't like hired help sleeping on the job.

Denison, Texas, was as far as John, Ernst, and the two whores could travel by train. The rest of the journey to Santa Angela and Fort Concho would be by wagon. John was unable to understand why the train couldn't go all the way. To his way of thinking, those tracks they ran on could be thrown down ahead of the train easy enough. And he really liked train travel. John was so angry about losing the train that he bit off a huge chunk of tobacco with a snarl.

After getting rooms in the local hotel and the whores taken care of, Ernst and John went wagon shopping. At Ernst's urging, John bought a spring surrey. It was a new type of conveyance to John, who was only used to a freight wagon, and a decrepit one, at that. This wagon was shiny black, with a gray fringed top to keep the sun away.

Two spry horses were hitched to his new wagon and John sped around what there was of Denison, Texas, driving wildly and squirting tobacco juice from the corner of his mouth at every turn. This was a lot of fun for John, who had never dreamed a wagon could move so fast. It cost a lot of money, but Ma had said once they got to California money wouldn't be a problem. For all he knew his Ma and Pa were already there.

Returning to the livery stable with a grin, John Bender paid the asking price for the surrey and horses — a wealthy man never haggled over the price of something. This wagon was nearly as much fun as riding the train. Paying the liveryman extra to unhitch the team and board the horses until morning, John took an extra bite of tobacco and walked back to the hotel with his good friend, Ernst Sykes.

After dinner and drinks — lots of drinks, all paid for by John — the young man retired to his hotel room. He got undressed and lay back on the bed. Earlier he had thought of trying out one of those bathtub contraptions, but he'd had a bath the night before they'd left the inn, so he couldn't see any urgency in the matter.

John had just fired up a cigar — a real good one, the man at the bar had told him. It cost a whole dollar. Suddenly there was a knock at the door. Cracking it slightly, he saw the two smiling whores, Mary and

Susan, standing there wearing flimsy nightgowns. The one he thought was Susan — John had a hard time remembering names — held a full bottle of whiskey.

"Can we come in, big boy?" the blonde purred.

John's mouth fell open, and the cigar hit the floor as he let them in and they stripped their nightgowns off. In all his adult years he had desired women, for some reason he didn't completely understand.

He used to go into the trees and pleasure himself with his hand on occasion. His Ma had warned him that if he did this, he would go blind. That was a crock. He could see as good as ever. Women might be better, but the only one he'd ever had a decent chance at was Kate, and she'd made it plain if he ever did it to her even once he wouldn't have the equipment left to do it again.

Now there were two willing girls. John grabbed up his cigar, placed his arms around the whores with a grin, and led them to his bed.

The next morning, John had to admit women were better than the palm of his hand, a lot better. The whiskey didn't hurt any, either, and the best part of it was they'd only asked him for twenty dollars for all their hard work.

Twenty-Six

"So far, this is as easy as followin' a telegraph line," Lute quipped to Neely as the train puffed and groaned its way into Denison, Texas.

"It hasn't been a brain strainer, that's for sure. They didn't even change their first names. They just went from callin' themselves Gebardt to Flickinger," Neely answered.

"I'd of reckoned them to have more sense, partner. When things get too easy you'd better worry."

"Just changin' their last names and travelin' together sure isn't what I'd expect."

"That bothers me a lot. It's as if they want us to find them," Lute said. "I'd expect them to scatter like a covey of quail and meet up somewhere after a spell. Now we're probably just a day or so behind them, and this here is the end of the track. Unless they doubled back on us, from here on out we travel on horseback and we can make up that day easy. I never met a woman who didn't lollygag around a bunch, and they got two of 'em to contend with."

"They'll hang Kate, won't they, Lute?" Neely said. It sounded more like a statement than a question.

Lute looked at Neely uncomprehendingly and blurted, "Hell's bells, they knocked the brains out of half the people in Kansas, not that the people were usin' them at the time. Of course she'll hang, right alongside that apple pie–bakin' Ma of hers."

"I know," Neely answered softly. "It's just that I'll have to do it."

"Well," Lute said, "we've got to catch them before we can string them up." Then the Ranger's face brightened. "This here's tough country. They just might get themselves killed before we get a chance at them."

Neely sighed as the train jerked to a stop at the Denison station. He grabbed his hat from the vacant seat beside him, pressed it on his head, and said, "Well, whatever, let's get those sons of bitches."

A dirty frame building on the bad side of town, the depot looked like all the others they had stopped at. A quick inquiry to the ticket agent answered their questions. He remembered two men traveling with women getting off the train yesterday. One of the men was drooling tobacco juice. They had gone to the hotel, and no, he hadn't sold them tickets leaving town.

Lute and Neely went to the baggage car and claimed their saddles and packs. Tossing them on their shoulders, the pair walked toward town. A heavy mass of brown clouds had settled in, and the temperature dropped steadily. "Just what we need now, a blue norther," Lute grumbled.

"What's a blue norther?" Neely questioned.

"In Texas, it's a storm that comes out of the north. The wind blows like hell, and it gets so danged cold your nuts turn blue."

"Oh, I see," Neely said, trying to button the collar of his shirt while balancing his saddle.

The first thing they had to do was the same thing the Benders would have had to do, buy horses. Denison had two livery stables, one at each end of town — "So they can get you coming or going," Lute had remarked. The first one they came to was the Acme Livery. The man who ran it was surly about Lute's questions. Neely talked Lute out of discussing the man's sour attitude with his fists, and the pair walked the dusty and cold length of what passed for the main street to the First Class Livery Stable.

Jeb Tatum was the proprietor, and in contrast to the other liveryman he was friendly and over-talkative. He was all excited about the early norther hitting, and how long and hot the summer had been, going into intricate detail as to how many lizards had died of sunstroke, and the creeks going dry.

Neely looked the country over and decided the only time any creek around there held water was when a cow took a piss in it. He was anxious to get the job done and go back to Parsons.

Lute seemed put out when Neely stopped the liveryman's storytelling to ask about any strangers that might have hit town in the last couple of days. The Ranger was a good liar in his own right, but he was in the presence of genius, and Jeb Tatum was going at it at a pace that would keep them there all evening.

The liveryman didn't seem to mind the change of topic. He just liked to talk. "Why, yeah, I sold some folks a real nice buggy yesterday. It was a spring one, it was. Had a genuine split leather top cut in a fringe around it, and all new harnesses. And the horses — let me tell you, they were a pair, spirited as a saloonkeeper come cattle drive time."

"Tell us about the folks who bought it. What did they look like?" Neely interrupted.

"The guy with the money that bought the rig, well, he was a young'un, he was. Didn't seem any too smart. Then agin, being smart ain't no guarantee of makin' money, is it?" The liveryman cackled at his humor for a moment, and continued. "He liked his tabbacky, drooled it all over the place. He paid my askin' price for the rig, to boot. Hell's fire, everyone likes to haggle, but not him — just whipped out the cash, paid me, and left — him and another man."

Lute and Neely smiled at each other, *John Bender.*

"They had a real spree in the hotel last night. I reckon they must have bought drinks for everyone a dozen times. My head sure was a poppin' this mornin' when they left. That young'un had this blonde wrapped all over him when they pulled out."

"Blonde!" Lute and Neely both exclaimed.

"Yeah, a blonde whore. The other gal was a whore, too. Two things I know for sure is horseflesh and whore flesh. Them gals were whores as sure as a Baptist stump preacher's God happy. Yup, yup."

"Tell us all about them," Lute said, showing his Texas Ranger badge.

The liveryman's smile fled, "What did they do, kill someone?"

"A lot of someones," Lute replied. "The guy squirtin' tobacco juice all over the countryside is John Bender, from Kansas."

"Oh shit. You mean the Bloody Benders, like in the paper?"

"One 'n the same."

"Oh shit, *oh* shit!" Jeb Tatum exclaimed. "No wonder the short hairs on the back of my neck stood up and I got a headache when they came in."

It took the liveryman a while to explain what the Bender bunch looked like. This was the most exciting thing that had happened to him in years. He wasn't going to waste a moment of it.

Lute and Neely bought a pair of horses before leaving the livery stable. As anxious as Jeb Tatum seemed to be to help them catch the Bloody Benders, his attitude didn't seem to extend to not making a profit. He'd charged the lawmen top dollar for two horses, then asked them to pay the night's keep for them. It was of no real consequence, and by the time they had checked into the hotel and gotten their first cup of coffee in the dining room, the liveryman's excursion into their pockets was forgotten. After all, it was Chatterhorn's money.

"We've been hornswaggled, Neely," Lute said as he lit up a long nine cigar. They had run out of smokes on the train from Thayer. It had been a rough trip until they got to Vinita and found a supply of long nines. The store had charged twice what Neely did for them, ten cents for nine cigars, but it was either pay the price or start chewing tobacco. When they thought of John Bender, they decided to buy the cigars, no matter what they cost.

"From what we know now, it's just John we're a chasin'," Neely said.

"The question is, for how long have they been split up? Jesus, I knew this was too easy. Should have known better."

"The Benders are devious, but maybe they ain't that smart. It's pretty certain John's not much smarter than a day-old mule. My guess is they'll join back up when they think things have quieted down."

Lute took a long puff on his cigar. "This guy they call Sykes and the two whores, I'm willin' to wager they've been hornswoggled, too. They're headin' off together for some reason of their own. Ma Bender had this all planned out. We get John, and they get away."

"Why, they wouldn't sacrifice one of their family just to buy some time, would they?" Neely leaned back in his chair for a moment, a faraway look in his eyes, then answered his own question. "Of course they would. That family is capable of anything."

Lute smiled and said, "See, I told you — to catch outlaws you have to think like 'em. It ain't easy, them being crazy and all, but you're gettin' the hang of it."

Neely smirked at Lute through a cloud of smoke and said, "We should catch up with them tomorrow."

"Yep, if those plug horses we paid two prices for don't go tits up on us, we should be lookin' at John Bender's lovely face before the day's out. A wagon doesn't travel real fast. Add a couple of females to it, and it's goin' even slower."

"Do you think John will tell us where his folks are?"

"He might take a passel of convincin', but few people are willin' to hang by themselves. We'll find out rather soon," Lute said as he put out his cigar and started covering his blackened steak with ketchup.

The blue norther never came. The clouds

made a swing to the east after peppering the town with hail. Jeb Tatum seemed only slightly upset that the weather cleared up. The Benders were a bigger story than a storm. The lawmen had eaten breakfast before sunrise. The liveryman had their horses saddled as he'd promised.

Under a breaking, blue Texas sky Lute and Neely headed southwest on the road to Fort Worth, their breaths steaming white in the chill morning air.

By midday the weather had turned downright hot. Their coats had been stowed in their packs, and shirtsleeves rolled up. "Weather seems to change a lot faster in Texas," Neely commented.

"Oh, down here you get all four seasons, generally all four of 'em every day."

"I see your point," Neely said, then asked, "How do we know they haven't turned off on one of these crossroads? There's wagon tracks everywhere."

"We *don't* know, but it's a sure bet they've got a destination in mind. These other roads mostly just lead off to ranches. When you track someone you got to remember they've got a place in mind. Most of the time they head straight for it."

"What about the other times?"

"That's when you come home skunked,"

Lute said simply.

Lute saw the wagon long before Neely did. The Ranger drew up his hand to signal they were stopping, then pointed out a speck on the mesquite-dotted plain. Once Neely's eyes focused, he could make out the gray fringed top on the buggy. "They're stopped, and there's only one horse hitched. Somethin's wrong," Lute said. Neely took his word for it. He had a hard enough time just making out the surrey. "This could be a trap. I'll ride off to the right and circle in. You head off to the left, and come in on the other side of the wagon."

"What if they start shootin'?" Neely asked.

"Well, shoot back," Lute said, pulling one of his pistols and spurring his horse.

To Neely's surprise, no one did shoot at him. When they cautiously approached, he saw Lute ride up and jump off his horse. He rode in with his gun held ready and quickly searched the site for John Bender. He wasn't there. Lute was standing by the buggy. A blonde girl sat leaning against a wheel; a darker haired girl was bent over the blonde, her hands pressed to her face. Then he saw the body.

Neely slipped his revolver back into its holster, rode up to Lute, and dismounted.

He tied his plug horse to the wagon to keep it from heading back to Denison and went to join Lute.

"Ole John's had a busy day," Lute said, not taking his eyes from the blonde. The girl had wide, pain-glazed eyes. Crimson red blood seeped through bandages on her left arm and side.

"He just went crazy," the brunette sobbed. She appeared unharmed and nearly hysterical.

Neely walked a few feet to where Ernst Sykes lay, staring at the blue sky through sightless eyes. His throat had been cut and his belly slit open, his guts spilling out as if from a butchered hog.

"What's your name?" Lute asked the brunette gently, taking hold of her hand. "We're the law. No one's goin' to hurt you now."

The girl wrapped herself around the Ranger and cried, "Mary, my name's Mary. Susan — how's Susan? He cut her bad."

"Let's take a look," Lute said softly, passing the girl called Mary to Neely. He bent down and pulled the bandages back. He kept a blank look on his face for the girl's benefit as he looked at the deep cuts. A stab wound went completely through her left arm just above the wrist. More serious than that was a deep gash that ran from her breast to her neck. White bone showed through the cut in several places. "You'll be all right, honey," Lute cooed. Then he said loudly, "We need some whiskey and a sewing kit."

Mary looked at him numbly and stammered, "Sykes — he always carried a flask."

Neely went to the dead man, bent over him for a moment, and returned carrying a bloody silver decanter. Lute took the whiskey and said once more to the stunned girl, "We're goin' to need a needle and thread. I've got some stitchin' to do."

Mary fumbled through the wagon for a while, coming out with a small wooden box. She was shaking so hard she nearly dropped it. Lute poured the whiskey into the blonde's cuts. The pain caused a brief scream. Then, mercifully, she passed out. While Lute stitched damaged flesh back together, Mary told what had happened.

It seemed the blonde girl had been sitting alongside the man she knew as John Flickinger. As a tease, Mary said, the girl had picked John's pocket, and he caught her in the act. He snarled, came up with a knife they didn't know he had, and started cutting. Ernst Sykes was riding behind them and tried to stop him. John had thrown the man from the wagon and gutted him in an instant.

After killing Sykes, he started smiling again. He took his wallet back, bit off a mouthful of tobacco, cut one of the horses loose, and rode off bareback toward Fort Worth. Mary couldn't understand why he hadn't killed her.

Lute stitched the ugly wound closed as well as he could. Using some clothes the girls had in the wagon, he put thick bandages tightly around the blonde, then lifted her unconscious form and laid her gently in the back of the buggy.

It took some time to repair the cut harness and arrange things so the one remaining horse could pull the wagon. Mary told them the horse John had rode off on was a piebald — black and white spotted with a white face and black tail, uncommon markings. That would make John fairly easy to follow, once they got back to trailing him. Right now they had to get the girl called Susan to Fort Worth, and a doctor.

Lute was surprised the blonde hadn't bled to death before they got there. As vicious as the cut across her side was, the stab through her wrist had cost the most blood. The girl was white as a bedsheet, and her breathing was coming in shallow gasps. If she made it to a doctor she might live. Lute had seen people who were cut up worse survive. At least the bleeding had mostly stopped now.

Sykes's body was tossed into the wagon. Neely rode behind, leading Lute's horse, and Mary sat in back, cradling Susan as best she could, crying all the while. Lute drove the wagon slowly, taking care not to hit any hard bumps that might tear loose some of his stitching efforts.

It was pitch dark when they reached Fort Worth. Lute had lived there before, so he knew where the hospital was and headed straight for it.

The doctor on duty was so drunk that Lute and Neely carried the girl in themselves. The doctor might have dropped her. Once they had Susan in a bed, the sodden sawbones cut the bandages and examined her. She had been unconscious ever since Lute had poured whiskey in her cuts. "If she don't get a blood poison, she'll live," the doctor said, looking at them with blood-shot eyes. "Have to take off her arm, though. The bandage cut off the circulation, and the flesh died. Gangrene will set in before morning if I don't cut it off."

Lute looked devastated. "I didn't mean to do nothin' but stop the bleedin'."

The doctor staggered and looked at Lute.

Noticing his badge, he said, "Ranger, if you hadn't dressed her like you did she'd be dead. It was a lucky thing for her you showed up. That was a tolerable job of stitching, too. Now you get out of here and get some rest. I'm going to trade her arm for her life, and I don't need you here looking over my shoulder while I'm doing it."

Leaving the hospital, they went to the wagon containing Skyes's body. After tying the horses behind it, they wearily climbed aboard. Lute sat on the backseat with Mary, who was sobbing softly. He put his arm around her protectively and said, "Go ahead and have a good cry. That's all we can do for her tonight."

Mary White did just that. By the time the buggy creaked to a stop in front of the marshall's office the front of Lute's boiled shirt was wet, and stained by running makeup. He didn't seem to mind as he nearly carried her in to see the local lawman.

Ben Murphy was on duty by himself. He remembered Lute from when he used to live there and Rangered under Captain Zackary Bernard. After exchanging pleasantries, Lute and Neely explained why they were there. Ben was taken aback to find one of the Benders was about. The story of the

"Bloody Benders" was becoming well-known. Even *Harper's Weekly* magazine had sent a reporter and sketch artist to the slaughter house. All across America, people had the opportunity to see renderings of the grave digging and the Bender's humble inn where the grisly murders of unsuspecting travelers had occurred.

The fact that an entire family could be in on such a horrible plan fascinated the Texas marshal. He could have talked and asked questions for hours, but when Lute mentioned how tired they were, Ben Murphy apologized and said he would take care of Sykes and their horses. He then accompanied them to a nearby hotel. Mary was done with her crying. Now she wore a blank, emotionless expression as they walked through the still night.

An angry hotel proprietor threw open the door, upset about being awakened so late. Neely was surprised to find it was after midnight. When the innkeeper saw the badges and was told the story by Marshal Murphy, he became overly friendly. Mary was seen to her room and the hotel owner — his name was Russell — brought them cold roast beef sandwiches from the kitchen. Neither Lute nor Neely realized they were hungry until they took a bite. After the sandwiches were devoured Neely pulled off his boots and stretched out on one of the two iron-frame, single beds.

Lute fired up a long nine, slouched into a chair by the window, and stared out into the darkness. After a short while he said, "You know, Neely, a woman has a rough row to hoe in this life. They need a man to help them out, but all too often they get kicked around." He took a long drag on his cigar, sighed, and continued. "That blonde reminded me of Annie. Something like that could happen to her."

Neely's snoring told Lute he was talking to himself. He crushed out his cigar, pulled his boots off, and went to sleep in his chair, staring out the window at the twinkling stars and thinking of Annie Mitchell.

Over breakfast the next morning Lute and Neely turned down Ben's offer to send a posse along with them after John Bender. They could travel faster by themselves. The marshal had done a lot of early morning detective work, however. Late yesterday, a man riding a piebald horse had bought a saddle from the Ace Livery Stable. A clerk at the general store had sold a big man who drooled tobacco juice a Colt pistol, a Sharps buffalo gun with a scabbard, a hundred rounds of ammunition for each gun, four twists of cheap tobacco, a bedroll and travel pack, and, of all things, a small brass telescope.

"That's our darlin'," Lute said.

"Did the clerk see which way he went?" Neely asked.

"Even better than that. He asked the closest route to Titusville," Ben replied.

"Oh *shit!*" Lute exclaimed.

"What's Titusville?" Neely asked, suddenly concerned.

"If the devil owned Titusville, he'd rent the place out and live in hell, where he'd have a better class of people to contend with," Lute quipped. Then, looking at the marshal, he asked, "I thought the Rangers would have cleaned that nest of vipers out by now — what happened?"

Ben took a long sip of coffee, pinched his lips, and said, "It's a matter of jurisdiction. It seems Texas claims Titusville is in New Mexico, and not our affair. New Mexico says it's in Texas, and they refuse to do anything about it. So it just keeps going."

"Like a boil on a baby's ass," Lute sputtered. Turning to Neely he said, "It's an outlaw colony. Anyone with a price on his head can go there and not have to worry about the law. Ole John will fit right in. Hell, he might be made mayor."

"You'd best hope you catch him before he gets that far," Ben Murphy said.

"I think John may be a little smarter than we were givin' him credit for," Lute said. "He's bought a buffalo gun and a telescope. You can blow a man out of the saddle from a quarter mile away with a Sharps, and with that telescope he can spot us comin' a lot farther away than that, so he can have plenty of time to get all prepared for an ambush."

"He doesn't know we're after him," Neely said hopefully.

"Maybe not us in particular. But you can bet your last cigar he's expectin' someone to be after him," Lute said, "or he wouldn't have bought that telescope."

After picking up their horses Lute and Neely stopped by a store and bought some supplies, including a Sharps rifle. Long nines were a nickel a pack, so they stocked up on that, along with coffee and what few staples they could carry. They were going to travel fast. Lute said there were a lot of rabbits and deer in West Texas, so they also bought a light tin frying pan, some lard, and salt.

As they rode together from Fort Worth to take the westerly trail toward Titusville, Neely noticed a huge home on a knoll overlooking the town. It was a sprawling, colonial-style mansion with white pillars in front. "Quite a home," he mentioned casually.

"That's my ole daddy-in-law's place," Lute said, to Neely's surprise. Lute had never told him he had been married. "He owns the newspaper and half a dozen businesses in town," Lute said. Then a smile crossed his face, "He said he hit town with nothin' but two dollars and a hard-on. I reckon he's still got the two dollars."

John Bender was tired. He had ridden all night and was still angry about the whore picking his pocket. His Pa and Ma had warned him that not all people lived by the Good Book, that some folks were dishonest and would try to take advantage of him. He had showed them he wasn't stupid. *An eye for an eye.*

At least Ernst Sykes had told him about Titusville. To his way of thinking, it would be a good place to lose anyone on his trail. His daddy had told him some bad people might come after him to take his money. Sometimes they wore badges to get you to trust them.

Fort Concho was just another town. Titusville, he was told by Sykes, was a place where you wouldn't have to worry about folks carrying badges. If someone tried to get his money before he got there, he was ready for them. He reined his horse to a stop atop a low hill. Taking the telescope from his saddlebag, he clicked it slowly into focus. Looking carefully down the road he had just traveled, he grinned when he saw nothing. After folding the telescope, he stuck it back into its place. Taking his Bowie knife from its hidden sheath, John sliced off a huge chunk of tobacco and plopped it into his mouth.

Bloodstains, he noticed unhappily, were still on his blade. When he made camp tonight he'd try to remember to clean it. Once his knife was sheathed, he spurred the piebald horse on, riding west under a blue Texas sky.

TWENTY-SEVEN

The past several days of stagecoach travel had taken its toll on Almira and Kate, and dark circles underlined their eyes. They had scrimped on lodging and meals to save money. In spite of their economy, the cost of getting to Salt Lake City had reduced their money supply to nearly two hundred dollars.

Ma had been in an even blacker mood than usual after Jesse James and Cole Younger took their fortune. The first night after the robbery, Kate had expected her Mama to beat her for her indiscretions. Instead, Almira had curled up on the bed in a tight ball and sobbed for hours, finally dropping into a fitful sleep still wearing her traveling clothes.

Kate felt sorry for her mother, and spent the rest of the trip trying to put up an optimistic front, saying as cheerfully as she could that it wouldn't be hard to recoup their lost wealth once the family was re-united. They could simply go back into business. This time, they would pick a location where they'd attract a better class of clients. When Kate reminded her Ma of the single customer in Missouri that donated over ten thousand dollars, she seemed to perk up. After Kate said the word "Missouri" she cringed, waiting for a hard slap from her Mama, or worse. It never came. Almira seemed to actually enjoy talking about all the money they had made. Also, Ma was sweeter to Kate than she had ever been. Kate viewed her Mama's niceness with trepidation — she knew that when she finally received her well-deserved whipping it would be a bad one.

The driver of the stage came to help Almira disembark when they arrived in Salt Lake. It was a lot chillier there than it was in Kansas, and her rheumatism was acting up. Kate picked up the two bulky suitcases containing their belongings and started walking toward a hotel they could see in a distance. A sandy-haired young man named Tate immediately politely offered to carry their bags. He identified himself as a Mormon who was leaving on the next stage for his mission. Tate smiled broadly when Kate said they were recent converts to the faith.

He nearly tripped and dropped the suitcases before they had gone far. Kate's blouse was partially unbuttoned, showing more cleavage than the awestruck Mormon had ever seen.

The Hotel St. Cloud, it turned out, was owned by Tate's parents Ira and Sarah Newman. It was a three-story, wood frame building containing fifty rooms. On the lower floor was the largest dining room Kate or Almira had ever seen. Rows and rows of linen-covered tables stretched the entire distance of the building. Even though it was the middle of the afternoon, nearly half of the tables were filled with people eating.

Almira Griffith explained pitifully to the Newmans how they had been robbed by bandits of all their money while crossing Wyoming on their way to live near the Temple. Her husband and son had stayed in Ohio to sell a little parcel of land they owned, and would be joining them shortly. The entire Griffith family had seen the light and converted to Mormonism, due to the efforts of a dedicated missionary like their son Tate was going to be. Almira gave the young man a close hug. She was standing by Kate, and this afforded him one last, hungry look at her firm cleavage before he had to hurry to catch the stage.

What the Benders had heard about Mormons was true — they took care of their own. The concerned Newman family immediately offered the women jobs in the hotel and gave them each a shiny new Book of Mormon, theirs unfortunately having been lost when they were robbed by those terrible outlaws. A stern-faced Ira Newman showed them to their room. Unlike his son, he had no problem letting Kate carry the heavy bags.

The quarters allotted to Kate and Almira was a dark and windowless little room in the basement containing a pair of iron-frame beds with wooden slats instead of springs. Two small kerosene lamps were set on the only other piece of furniture, a plain wooden table with a tree limb wired to a broken leg to keep it from collapsing.

"The salary is a dollar a day," Ira said firmly. "Almira, you can do the cooking, and Kate, you can wait tables in the dining room. We start work at four in the morning. That means you'll get off at four in the afternoon. You eat your meals in the kitchen. The washroom is upstairs. Wash your clothes in the sink.

"Sunday is a day of rest," Ira continued. "We — and you folks — will go to Temple at ten o'clock. Oh, and please don't burn your lamps unless you are studying the Bible. Coal oil costs money. Well, you get yourselves organized, and we'll see you in the kitchen tomorrow morning bright and early."

"Mister Newman," Kate asked respectfully, "the dollar a day, is that for each of us?"

Ira looked aghast and replied sternly, "Money is the root of all evil. Of course the dollar a day is for *both* of your services. Good day."

After the hotel owner left by the narrow, creaking stairs, Kate and Almira set their bags on the hard beds and began unpacking, fixing their clothes on nails driven into the dingy walls. After hanging up a couple of her black dresses, Ma flung herself onto the bed and began sobbing pitifully.

"Mama, it'll be all right," Kate implored. "Pa will be here soon. He'll have some money with him, and we'll leave this place and be in business before we know it."

Almira sat up, dabbed at her eyes with a handkerchief, and said, "You're right, child, we'll be out of here in a short time. As *our* Good Book says, 'The righteous shall inherit the earth.' If I only had my hammer, the nice little one that don't pain my arm when I swing it, I'd do a little inheritin' from *that*

405

son of a bitch right shortly."

"Patience, Mama. Pa will be along with some money before you know it, and we do have over two hundred dollars they don't know about."

"And keep it that way," Almira mumbled. "Otherwise they'll expect twenty of it for that damn Temple of theirs."

"Yes, Mama. Now let's unpack our clothes and get some rest. Tomorrow is going to be a long day."

"They're all goin' to be long ones until we get to California."

"I know, Mama, but it's just for a little while," Kate cooed.

"Yeah, we'll be back in business right shortly," Almira said as she swung herself from the bed with a grunt and started hanging up more clothes with a sickly grin on her face. Kate noticed her Ma's expression and started looking around the room for a stick or something that her Ma could use to beat her with. Luckily, there was nothing.

Her rheumatism is paining her, Kate thought. Otherwise she would have gotten her deserved whipping. She hadn't been a perfect child, and a bad daughter deserved her beatings. Kate shrugged her shoulders and unpacked the rest of her belongings. She would feel a lot better once her Mama had whipped her and gotten it out of her system. A lot better.

William headed out of Dodge City as fast as he could on the stolen mule. He would rather have taken off on a horse, but the mule was saddled and the farmer who owned it was roaring drunk. William didn't think the man would be sober enough to miss the mule until he was long gone.

Things had not gone as he had hoped. The faro dealer at the Long Branch was a card cheat, that was for sure. It was just that William couldn't understand *how* he'd cheated him. At first he had won. At one time he was ahead by nearly a thousand dollars. Then he started betting heavy — fifty dollars a hand. A man couldn't get rich if he didn't play for high stakes. That was his view.

Once William started playing for big money, the dealer never lost. The young man with a pockmarked, sickly face had dealt the cards with a loving ease.

William watched the cards with an eagle eye, but could never see anything underhanded going on. And he *had* won at first, with just a small amount of cheating on his part. Hand after hand, his stacks of gold coins had grown smaller, along with his temper. Every attempt he made at stacking the deck failed, for some reason he couldn't understand.

It was nearly midnight when the unsmiling dealer scooped up the last of William's hard-earned money. He had jumped back from the table and reached for the pistol stuck under his belt. The young man with the wan complexion had a gun pointed at his middle before he ever got a grip on it.

The dealer slid a twenty-dollar gold piece across the table to him with his free hand and advised him to leave town for his health. William took his hand from the pistol and picked up the coin with a snarl. He wanted to kill the cocky, cheating dealer, but there was something about him that told William that would take a lot of doing. He stuck the single coin in his pocket, turned, and trudged from the saloon to the sound of laughter.

He stole the mule and rode hard toward Salt Lake City. He knew a mule couldn't make fifty miles a day. A horse would have been better. They weren't as smart as mules, and he could have ridden it nearly to death and then stolen another. He sure couldn't buy one, not with only twenty dollars to his name. When he got to Salt Lake and Almira, there would be no problem with money. It would just take him a little longer than he planned to get there, was all.

Briefly he thought of son John and hoped he was still alive. Perhaps, he thought as he rode the plodding mule under a sea of stars, one day John and he would go back to Dodge. There was a dealer there who needed killing real bad. He would never forget the card cheat's name; it was John Wesley Hardin. If it took years, he would shoot him. No question about that.

John Bender was beating a direct path to Titusville. He was pushing the piebald hard, much harder than he should, he knew. His Pa had told him, however, that most likely some bad men would be after him. Also, he was just plain homesick for his folks.

He stopped briefly at way stations to grain and water his horse while he ate steak dinners. None of them had any whores, to his disappointment. If they had, he would have stayed long enough to enjoy one. He really liked whores. The only thing was, he'd have to watch his money around them from now on.

After he left Titusville he could slow up a little. If what Sykes had told him was the truth, there would be no one after him once he got there. He had a plan, and the money to carry it out. With those after him dead, he'd have plenty of time to stop at all the whorehouses he wanted.

Several times he had stopped on high ground and scanned his back trail, using the telescope. Twice he had seen a distant dust cloud on the road. *It could have been a dust devil,* he told himself, *or a wagon.* When he thought on his Pa's warning, however, he knew he was being chased. No one kicked up a dust cloud unless they were in a big hurry. Dust devils didn't follow a road, either.

Both times he'd seen the dust cloud, he had spurred his horse hard enough to draw blood, and pushed on. Sykes had said it was a seven-day ride to Titusville. If he made it in five, that would be just right.

"He's a gonna kill that horse if he don't slow down," Neely spat out through the dust that caked his face.

"Wouldn't that just be too bad? I wouldn't mind runnin' our little darling all the way back to Parsons tied behind a horse, now that you mention it," Lute said.

"I'm not so sure these high-priced plugs we're a ridin' won't croak before John's does. Neither one of 'em would make decent buzzard bait."

"You need a more positive attitude, Neely. We know where he's a headin'. Hell, he's left a track like a train. We could almost follow him by the tobacco juice alone."

Lute and Neely had been trailing John Bender for six hard days. After leaving Fort Worth they had traversed some of the hardest, most barren country Neely had ever seen. He thought Kansas was dry when it didn't rain for a while. This country was so dry and barren it looked to him as if even God had given up on it.

The only time they took to rest was in the cowtown of Amarillo. They checked into a hotel, soaked the dust from their bodies, and ate a decent meal. After stocking up on a few supplies and long nine cigars, they had ridden north at daybreak.

Neely said that anyone could have followed John Bender's trail, even Al Jennings, the shoemaker back in Parsons, and he was blind in one eye and couldn't see good out of the other. John stopped often to eat. He liked his steaks. The piebald horse and his tobacco drooling weren't easily forgotten by the stationmasters.

From Amarillo, they rode until they came to the Canadian River. Turning west, they took a little-traveled trail along the south bank. Lute stopped, got off his horse, and examined some fresh tracks. "From the looks of things, our boy is just ahead of us and pushin' as hard as ever," he said.

After Lute had remounted, he turned seriously to Neely and unpinned his Ranger badge. "We're getting a mite close to Titusville, Neely. You best do the same," Lute said, putting his star into his saddlebag.

Neely looked at his badge, frowned and asked, "What do you mean?"

"Oh, Sam Titus — the lovely who runs the town — and some of his cohorts don't like lawmen. They sometimes shoot just when they see a badge. Matter of fact, ole Sam generally kills anyone he don't take a shine to."

Neely buried his badge in the bottom of his bag, turned to Lute, and said through pinched lips, "*Now* you tell me!"

"Why, Neely," Lute said with a feigned look of surprise, "you never asked."

Lute headed off on the trail alongside the muddy river. Neely shook his head, sighed, and hurried to catch up.

The lawmen made camp underneath a clump of willow trees in a bend of the river that night, stopping when a blazing red, Texas sunset painted the western sky. While they watered their horses Lute took a piece of cloth and strained some of the roily water into their black coffeepot. After examining what was left in the cloth, Lute turned up one side of his mouth and said, "We could just boil this without the coffee and have soup." He dumped out a couple of tadpoles, a water spider, and a few unrecognizable wiggling objects.

"I'd rather have coffee, I think," Neely said as he watched a tadpole flip its way into the river and swim away. "If you'll build a fire I'll go shoot us a rabbit."

"Sounds better than river soup, for sure," Lute said, as he made a pass in the river with the coffeepot.

Neely hadn't gone a hundred feet before the biggest rattlesnake he'd ever seen hissed a warning at him and coiled to strike. He jumped back, from reflex. Neely didn't have any special fear of snakes. He just didn't like it when they startled him. He'd seen a dead tree branch by the river — one of the few pieces of natural wood in West Texas, he guessed. Retrieving it, he went back to the buzzing snake and teased it with the stick until the rattler raised its head high to strike. Instantly, Neely drew the branch back and swung hard, nearly taking the snake's head off. He took his pocketknife, finished the job, then skinned the still wiggling rattler. It was the biggest one he had ever seen, maybe six feet long and as big around as his arm.

Lute had a fledgling fire started when Neely came in with the skinned and still writhing snake. "Desert delight, and more meat than two rabbits," Neely exclaimed proudly.

"Kinda puny for a Texas rattler," Lute quipped, eyeing the snake. "Must have been a sick one, or at least the runt of the litter. Should have gone with the soup."

Neely grinned, tossed the rattlesnake onto a patch of grass, then went to the riverbank to cut some green willow sticks to roast it on.

After the snake had been cooked and eaten, without further comment from Lute, they sat in gathering darkness around the fire, sipping on strange-tasting black coffee.

"We're about twenty miles from Titusville," Lute said seriously. "John will be there before us now, no doubt about it."

"What do we do about it?"

"Sam operates on the capital system. How much money do we have left?"

Neely brought his billfold out of a saddlebag and counted the money slowly by firelight. "Hundred and fifty-five dollars," he said.

Lute frowned, "If John's got a hundred and sixty, our goose is as cooked as that snake."

"We can't give up now," Neely pleaded.

"Ain't a plannin' on it. I haven't seen ole Titus for a spell. He might have mellowed out some."

"You *know* him!" Neely exclaimed.

"Oh yeah, I didn't tell you, did I? Sam Titus was a Fort Worth marshal before he went crazy."

"Oh, shit!"

"I'd save that comment until tomorrow," Lute said, tossing out the last of the rancid coffee. "Let's get a good night's sleep."

"*That's* Titusville?" Neely asked loudly. They were on a low, grassy knoll above the Canadian River. About a quarter of a mile away, perched precariously on a red sandstone cliff above the slow-moving, murky water, was a string of ramshackle, wooden buildings, maybe twenty in number. A pole corral held possibly thirty horses. Numerous goats and chickens and a few pigs could be seen wandering around the shabby structures looking for food. A profusion of empty cans and bottles was strewn down the cliff behind the shacks, spilling into the river. Aside from whispers of smoke from chimneys, no sign of life was apparent.

Neely felt the cold grip of his Colt with trepidation. He was scared and tired, having slept but little last night. Desperately he had hoped they would catch John before he got to this outlaw settlement. That was not to be. He didn't need Lute's eagle eyes to spot the piebald horse that was saddled and tied to a hitch rail in front of the largest building on the row.

"I wouldn't go pullin' that gun if I was you," Lute said. "There's probably a few buffalo rifles a pointin' at your middle right now. Let's ride in and see if ole Titus has some coffee brewed."

Neely shot a glance at the desolate country around him — thinking it was a pathetic sight as the last thing he might ever see in this world — and followed Lute into Titusville.

As they rode slowly down the dusty street, keeping both hands on their reins, Neely could hear the metallic click of guns being cocked from inside the shacks. Aside from the plodding of their horses, it was the only sound in the still Texas air. Looking over his shoulder, Neely saw maybe a dozen men walk into the street behind them, all carrying rifles that they kept pointed at them.

When they came to where John's horse

was tied, Lute stopped and waited. Neely rode alongside him and did the same. From the open door of the single large building a fat man with flaming red hair and a scraggly beard walked up to them. A pair of pistols rode low below his ample middle. To Neely's surprise he kept them holstered. A half-full whiskey bottle was in one hand, the other was wrapped around an obviously scared, wide-eyed Mexican girl who looked to be no older than fourteen.

The man squinted into the sunlight for a moment and said in a gravelly voice, "Well if it ain't Lute Thompson, and as cocky as ever. You've come a long way to die."

Lute smiled at him, "Good to see you too, Sam, and for your information I'm feelin' right fine." His smile faded when John Bender came from the dark building wearing his mindless grin and drooling tobacco juice.

"Howdy, Sheriffs," John said happily. A fat Mexican girl wearing nothing but a blanket wrapped around her came smiling to his side and hugged him. John gave her a big kiss, leaving a smear of black juice on her dusky skin.

"You git on your way now, boy," Sam Titus said coldly to John.

With a look of regret John gave the girl

one last hug, walked to his horse and climbed on. Turning to the lawmen, he was smiling broadly as he said, "Won't be seein' you agin." He spat a load of tobacco juice at Lute, wheeled his horse, and rode slowly away, heading west.

"Why don't you two get down and stay a spell?" Sam said in a more pleasant tone. "My boys will take those guns. This here's a law-abidin' town. Don't want no one gettin' hurt."

When Lute and Neely dismounted, a Mexican with a sickly, yellow, snarling face took their guns and stuck them in his belt. "We keel 'em now, boss?" he asked.

"If you want to kill somethin', go kill one of those stinkin' goats, and make it a good one this time. The last one you shot was so damn stringy a dog couldn't even eat it," Sam growled.

The Mexican glowered, but turned and walked away. "Come on inside. We've got some talkin' to do," Sam said roughly, grabbing the girl by his side and heading inside the dark saloon.

Lute and Neely followed. The place smelled of stale whiskey and rotten meat. Flies buzzed around the only window in the place that opened onto the river. Sam chugged down the last of the whiskey from his bottle and tossed the empty through the window to crash onto the littered riverbank. "Sit down," he demanded, nodding at one of the two plank tables.

Lute swatted a mangy cat out of a chair, scooted up to the table, and sat down. Neely joined him. Sam plopped into a chair across the table from them with a grunt. "Maria, get some more whiskey and three glasses," he yelled at the young girl, who ran off quickly to do as she was told.

"That man who just left — do you know who he was?" Lute asked.

"Of course I do," Sam answered. "It was my Cousin Early, from Abilene."

"He was John Bender from Kansas, and he's killed a lot of innocent folks," Lute replied.

"Too bad it warn't him. This bein' a law-abidin' town, I'd o' turned him over to you," Sam said.

"How much?" Lute asked.

"Your distrust pains me, old friend," Sam said as a shot rang in the distance. "Hope you like roast goat — that's what we're eatin' for supper — but to answer your question, I reckon my memory might improve for, say, five hundred dollars."

Lute frowned and said, "That man's a criminal, and we mean to take him back."

419

"Well, sir," Sam said, as Maria set the glasses out and filled them with whiskey, "talkin' about the law, we have a law here about carryin' a gun. Seems the fine's a week in jail. Now since I'm the judge, you're guilty. Drink up and count yourself lucky it ain't a hangin' offense."

That evening the bolt on the windowless, stifling shack that passed for a jail slid open. The yellow-faced Mexican came in with a plate of evil-smelling goat meat and a jug of cloudy water. Two other men carrying shotguns stood outside the open door.

The Mexican sneered at them, slammed the door when he left, and locked it.

"Why didn't he kill us?" Neely asked. "I know John paid him to do it."

"He wouldn't kill a Ranger. That's the last thing he'd do. I knew that all along. He knows for sure twenty more would come hang him and burn this place down."

"After a week we'll never pick up John's trail."

"Titus knows that. It'll keep his reputation, and the Rangers will ignore him — for a while, anyway."

"What do we do about the Benders?"

"You remember earlier on this trip I said sometimes you come home skunked? Well,

420

we're lookin' the striped kitty right in his ass. Hope you like goat meat. I think we're gonna have so much of it we'll be buttin' our heads on things before the week's out."

Twenty-Eight

John Bender rode easier now that he knew no one was chasing him. He couldn't understand why Neely Wells and Lute Thompson would come all that way just to steal what money he was carrying. He tried hard to think of another reason why the law would be after him, and came up blank. All he did was try to live by the Good Book and do what his Ma and Pa told him to.

The knowledge that his pursuers were dead was a comfort to him. It had been expensive — that fat crook charged him three hundred dollars — but he had to admit Ernst Sykes had been right. In Titusville you could buy anything.

Christina, the Mexican whore he'd quickly bedded there, only charged him a quarter for her favors. John thought heavily on this and finally realized he'd been cheated before by the two whores from Vinita. They had charged him twenty dollars for one night.

Of course there were two of them, and it was his first time. He tried to add up how many quarters were in twenty dollars. After a while he gave up on the matter. He still had money. In the future he'd be more careful not to be taken advantage of because of his trusting nature.

The Mexican whore had begged John to take her with him when he left Titusville. She told him that he could have her any time and any way he wanted. It would be nice, not having to pay for it. *Maybe that's why men get married,* he thought, *to save money.* Then he remembered how his Ma yelled at Pa, and how unhappy he seemed at times. Finally John decided that as long as he had money he wouldn't get married.

Following the twisting and turning Canadian River, it took John five days to reach the New Mexico Territory settlement of Raton. Behind the town were the biggest hills he'd ever imagined. It was late summer, and he was surprised to see some of the more distant ones had snow on them. John didn't like snow. It was cold, wet, and miserable stuff to put up with.

The first thing he did when he hit town was sell the piebald horse and saddle. When the liveryman offered him another ten dollars for his rifle he decided to sell it, too.

The thing was a bother to carry on the train. The telescope was another matter. He loved it. The way it brought faraway things close was a fascination.

John was furious to find there was no train he could ride to Salt Lake City where his folks were. He settled down some when the agent told him he could take a stagecoach to Cheyenne and he could ride the train to his destination from there. He was mystified to find that the place called Salt Lake wasn't in California, as he'd thought, but in Utah. John couldn't understand where Utah was, even when the frustrated station agent showed him on a map. It looked close to California, anyway, so he grudgingly bought a ticket to Cheyenne. At least he wouldn't have to put up with snow on a stagecoach.

He had been so concerned with getting on another train he nearly forgot to do what his Ma had told him. When he saw the telegraph office, he remembered. Taking the small dictionary from his pocket, he sauntered into the small building. The agent watched with a perplexed expression as John took a lead pencil and his dictionary and spent a long while at the counter composing his message.

He nearly made the telegram out to Almira Bender. Then he saw a note in the dictionary where his Ma had written for him to send it to Almira Griffith. Then he remembered that for some reason he'd forgotten, *his* name wasn't Bender anymore, either. That was too bad, Griffith was harder to spell. But he knew he had to do what his Ma said.

Carefully and slowly, using the dictionary, he composed his message to Almira Griffith, Salt Lake City. It read: MADAM. GNU. OMNIPOTENT. MUTUALLY. WAX-BILL. JOHN.

The telegraph operator shook his head when he read it. He studied John's expression, and decided it wouldn't be wise to ask him any questions, so he sent the message as written. When he paid the agent, John received two quarters as part of his change. He asked the operator bluntly where the whorehouse was, causing the operator to raise an eyebrow and give him a wry smile.

Leaving the office, happy with himself that he'd done well and remembered what he was to do, John felt in his pocket and came up with another quarter. He had two hours before his stage left, and three quarters. Biting off a big chew of Brown Mule tobacco, he grinned as he held the quarters in a sweaty hand and walked to the distant white house with the red lantern hanging on the porch, swaying in the wind.

Almira had never really expected John to send the telegram she held in her hands. It was good that he had, now that they were broke. John was a usable commodity. Strong as an ox and nearly as stupid, he would do anything she told him.

The fact that he had survived, leading the law into Texas and throwing them off their trail, wasn't a complete surprise. Almira had read every paper she found left in the dining room. At first she saw many accounts of the "Bloody Benders," as they were now called. She always expected to read, but never did, that John had been caught or killed — hopefully killed. He knew where they were, at least what city they were in. If John had been captured, Kate and she would have had to run. Where to run to was the question they had asked themselves several times. William hadn't shown up, and they were getting concerned. Pa was needed to help them get into business again.

When Almira got back to their dreary little room in the basement of the hotel, she lit a kerosene lamp for light. She opened the Book of Mormon and laid it on the table in case she received a visit from the owner. He was a slave driver of the first order. During

426

a twelve-hour shift, hired help was only allowed to sit down for fifteen minutes to eat a meal. The rest of the time, the wooden straight-back chairs in the kitchen hung on the wall. "Idle hands are the devil's playground," Ira loved to say.

Sitting down on her hard bed with a grunt, Almira grabbed her dictionary from the table, moved it close to the light, and began reading. She knew pretty much what it would say, anyway. All she had to do was find each word John had written, read down five words, and use it. A simple code, one John could understand. Quickly it translated to MADE GOAL ON MY WAY. JOHN. Kate would like to know this, but it would be a while. She was working late another night. For the last three days Kate had put in sixteen hours straight — all for the same salary. John was coming. She knew that now. If William would just show up, they could get back into business. Almira was so tired of working such long hours, and to add to her woes her rheumatism was acting up. William *would* come. She grabbed her Bible and started reading it closely. *The Lord always provides.*

"Mule, if you weren't a mite faster than me a hoofin' it all the way to Salt Lake by shank's mare, I'd shoot ya and make me a supply of jerky out o' your worthless carcass."

William Bender was sitting under the only shade tree on a trackless prairie, talking to his hobbled, stolen mule. He had his pistol out and pointed at the animal, who was grazing nonchalantly away at a patch of half-dead grass by a muddy creek. He cocked the gun and aimed behind the mule's ear. "Once we get to Salt Lake, you blamed nuisance, I'm a gonna pull this trigger," he growled as he lowered the hammer with his thumb and stuck the Colt back into his belt. The mule kept grazing, ignoring him completely.

"Should o' stole a horse. The only good thing is, I expect your owner is damn glad to see you gone." He was talking to himself. The mule didn't seem to pay him any mind, taking all the fun out of his complaining. "No one would make a big fuss over stealing a worthless mule."

It was a good thing no one did come after him, he reflected. This mule — he called him "Shitty Red" because he had a red cast and stopped dead still in the road every few miles to take a shit — wouldn't cover more than twenty miles a day. Once Shitty Red had covered what he felt was the required distance, he'd just stop for the day. Short of someone building a fire under him, the mule refused to budge another inch. William had considered a fire, but the grass was so dry he felt he'd burn Western Kansas and himself up along with Shitty Red, so he kept plodding along west at his twenty miles a day.

A prairie dog popped out of his hole a few feet away and let out a shrill whistle, drawing William's attention. Slowly he pulled the gun from his belt and took aim. When he shot the prairie dog, the mule didn't even flinch or miss a bite of grass. "You could've at least *thought* you was shot, you son of a bitch," he growled as he got up to clean his still quivering supper. It was the middle of the afternoon, but he knew he wasn't going any farther today.

As he skinned and gutted the prairie dog he added up how far he'd come in the past nine days and wondered if he was in Colorado yet. He doubted it. At the rate he was moving, it would take another ten days just to reach Cheyenne. He hoped fervently he would encounter a lone traveler with a decent horse, maybe even one carrying money. So far, all he had seen was a couple of wagon trains and a lot of grassland. The only good side of Shitty Red was he always seemed to stop for the day by water. The mule at least had a little sense. William meant to shoot him, anyway, the first chance he had, as soon as he acquired less stubborn transportation.

After leaving the little town of Raton, it had taken the swaying stagecoach only four days of traveling twenty-four hours a day to get John to Cheyenne. He was taken aback to find the snow stayed on the high hills to the west. It was a little chilly at night, but to his amazement they didn't have to plow through any of that cold snow.

In Cheyenne, he found that a first-class sleeping car only cost twenty-five dollars more than a regular ticket. He had the money, so he paid for the finest accommodations. John had been looking forward to riding a train again. The fact that he had little money left after buying the ticket didn't bother him. Ma had lots of money. She was in Salt Lake. And he held a ticket to go there. A first-class one, at that.

Two days on the puffing and hissing train passed far too quickly, to John's way of thinking. He sat by a window for most of the trip, chewing on Brown Mule and watching the countryside roll by. He liked how fast trains went. Someone said they ran as fast as thirty miles in one hour.

Meals cost what seemed like a lot of money. During a stop in Salt Wells, John paid a dollar and a quarter for a piece of dry ham and a plate full of burnt potatoes. He felt he'd been cheated, but there were some folks about wearing badges so he grudgingly paid the bill and left quietly.

He'd remembered not to shave. When he looked in a mirror he realized his Pa was right. He did look better with the black scraggly beard — John Griffith cut a handsome figure.

When he stepped down from the train in Salt Lake City, he didn't know where to look for his Ma and Pa. This town was a lot bigger than he was used to. He figured there must be literally hundreds of people living here.

When he counted up the last of his money, it totaled nearly ten dollars, so he decided to have a steak dinner. Someone on the train had said you could get a really good one at the Hotel St. Cloud. He told himself there was plenty of time to find his Pa after he ate. Grabbing up his pack, he walked off looking for the hotel with the strange name.

"Ole Chatterhorn was as mad as a peeled rattler," Neely remarked as Lute and he left

431

the bank to take the familiar boardwalk to his general store. Goosey had received their earlier telegram and met them at the Thayer Depot with a pair of horses when they arrived on the morning train. During the ride back to Parsons, Goosey filled them in on all the bad publicity the Benders had caused in Labette County, and told them that Chatterhorn, being the banker and the county trustee, was catching billy hell from newspapers and everyone else for his inability to apprehend an entire family of murderers.

"Don't take it personal that he fired you," Lute said. "Scarbutt's a politician. The first thing any decent stuffed shirt, windblowing, piss-proud son of a bitch like him does when things go a little wrong is fire everyone. Nothing is ever *their* fault. He probably thought he'd make governor some day. Now he'll be lucky to get elected to sweep the courthouse."

"Well, I'll have more time to spend runnin' my store."

"He did give us our month's pay. That's a minor miracle," Lute said.

"It was a surprise when Sam Titus let us go with our money and guns. Hell, I thought we were dead for sure."

"Oh Neely, like I told you, Sam wasn't

going to start shootin' Rangers."

"You ain't a Ranger anymore, Lute. All you've got is the badge."

"Glad you didn't inform ole Titus of that detail. It does feel good to be home, don't it, though?"

"It'll be a lot nicer when the Benders are caught. That's all folks are goin' to talk about — how we let 'em get away, and all."

"Hell's bells, we chased those Hell Benders dang near a thousand miles from here. That ought to count for something. Look at the bright side — now you don't have to worry about hangin' anyone, just sellin' the rope," Lute said smiling. A serious expression crossed his face and he stopped walking, sniffing the air.

"What's wrong, Lute?" Neely asked.

"Oh nothin' really. I just realized if there was a customer at my place that needs attention we'd have known it by now, the way the wind's blowin' and all. I think I'll go see if Langtry can cash this voucher of Chatterhorn's. There's someone I want to see."

"Give my regards to Annie," Neely said cheerfully as he watched Lute turn and walk away toward The Rose Saloon, whistling.

Kate didn't recognize John when she saw him in the dining room devouring a porterhouse steak. It wasn't just the beard and the fact that he was dressed rough and dirty like most of the Mormon farmers who ate there. John was sitting in Sarah's section. She was simply too busy to pay any attention to what went on out of her area.

Ira Newman ran the dining room of his Hotel St. Cloud like a prison guard, to Kate's way of thinking. There was room for sixty people to eat, thirty in each section. Two waitresses and a cook was all the help the owner would hire. When things got a little slow, everyone pitched in to wash dishes — everyone except Ira, that is. He continually strutted around the place with his hands folded behind his back, cheerfully visiting with people, always asking if they needed anything.

Most of all, Kate needed a new pair of shoes. The old ones she wore rubbed blisters on her feet. Lately, they had begun to bleed, and Ira refused to let her have the time off to shop for new ones.

When John saw Kate waiting tables, he couldn't understand why she was doing that. Rich folks got waited on in restaurants. They didn't do the waiting. After he finished his huge steak, he wiped the grease from his hairy face with his shirtsleeve and went to talk with her.

"John!" Kate was so shocked she nearly dumped a bowl of chicken and dumplings. There was a lot to explain, and Kate knew it couldn't be done here. Also, there was no telling what John would blurt out. She delivered the meal, then ran to him and threw her arms around him, hugging him tight. John was so surprised he was speechless, just as she hoped. "Don't say anything," she whispered in his ear. "We've got trouble. Remember, we're Mormons and your name is Griffith — from Ohio."

"Who's this?" Ira demanded. He was standing behind them. It seemed that any time Kate slowed down just a little, there he was.

"He's my brother, John," Kate said. "My Pa's been delayed, so he sent him on to be with us."

"This is no place for pleasantries. There's work to be done. I can let him have a room tonight for a dollar. You can visit after you finish your day. Come along with me, young man," Ira said firmly, leading a stunned John to the lobby.

After he paid for his steak and room, John pulled out a twist of tobacco and started to slice off a chew with a pocketknife. He'd been told to never take the Bowie knife out in public. It might start folks to talking.

"Young man, you are not to use that vile tobacco in *this* hotel. It's against our teachings. You must know that!" Ira shouted.

John gave him a look that caused a ripple of fear to run through the hotel owner like a cold chill. "Of course you're new to our faith, and old habits are hard to break," Ira added apologetically. There was something about Kate's brother that told him not to yell at him again. Ever.

It was late evening and the sun was setting before Kate and Almira came to John's room. He had passed the afternoon sitting by the open window watching people on the street, chewing tobacco and spitting the juice into a flower pot.

Tearfully, his Ma told him how they were robbed of all their hard-earned money by those terrible outlaws, Jesse James and Cole Younger. Then Ma asked him how much money he'd come with.

John thought hard for a moment and said, "I had ten dollars, then paid a dollar for my steak and another for the room, so I got seven left," smiling proudly.

"You had a thousand dollars when we split up," Almira hissed.

"But *you* had all the rest," John said simply.

Kate noticed Ma looking around the room for something to hit John with. To distract her she said, "We ain't heard a thing from Pa, and we're gettin' mighty worried."

Almira couldn't find anything that wasn't breakable to pound on John with — something they wouldn't have to pay for — so she calmed down a little and said, "We'll lay low here for a while. We're gonna go back into business, son, with or without your Pa, but we'll wait a spell longer. Kate and me, we have jobs here. I asked Ira real sweet like and he said you could keep the fires goin' and sweep the place out for your room and board. You do as you're told and don't talk none or sass back, and no chewin' that damn tobacco in front of anyone. These Mormons just ain't normal folks, son, but we won't have to put up with 'em much longer. We'll make California yet."

John thought back on the map he'd seen on the wall in Raton, and he knew his Ma was right. They were a lot closer to their goal of California. "OK, Ma, I'll do what you tell me. I'm powerful fond of my chewin', but I'll remember," he said.

"Your name is Griffith — don't forget that, John," his ma said firmly. "Don't talk if you aren't asked nothin'. We're from Ohio, too. You keep your mouth shut and we'll be in California soon."

"OK, Ma," John answered, squirting tobacco juice into a begonia. "I only wish Pa'd show up."

"He will. Just have faith. Like the Good Book says, 'Good things come to he who waits'," Almira said.

"Yeah, Ma. I'll do what I'm tole and wait for Pa."

"That's a good boy. We've got to get some rest now. Katie dear, let's go to our room."

John observed that his sister looked at him coldly and never said much, and after she'd been so sweet in the dining room. Women were a mystery to him, how they acted so strange at times. He sure liked them, though, a whole lot better than before. They said their good-byes and left his room. Kate was limping, he noticed, and wondered why.

He cut a huge chunk of Brown Mule and sat down by the window again, only now he wasn't just watching people — he was hoping to spot his Pa so they could go to California.

Shitty Red had finally gotten William to the Oregon Trail, at least the part of it that dipped down along the South Platte River in Northeast Colorado. At twenty miles a day he was growing tired of looking at grassland. The only good part was that lately there had been a lot of buffalo. He'd gotten close enough to a herd to use his pistol and killed a calf. The liver roasted on a stick over a small fire had been delicious, much better than prairie dog.

Twice he had seen parties of Indians, but to his surprise they had ignored him. Finally he realized the Indians probably didn't want the mule he was riding any more than he did. "Well, Shitty, at least your worthless hide's good for something," he told the mule that afternoon after they had stopped for the day.

Now that he was on a main trail it didn't take him long to meet up with some fellow travelers. The lone wagon he met was just what he'd been hoping for — a single family heading west all by themselves.

Orman Redd and his wife, Martha, along with their three young girls, were heading for Salt Lake, too. They were happy to have a convert to Mormonism riding along with them. With all the murderous redskins about they felt safer now.

William tied his mule behind their wagon when he quit for the day, giving the animal no choice but to continue traveling. He barely caught himself before he called the mule "Shitty Red." No Mormon would use such language. William rode on their extra saddle horse, a high-spirited gelding. It literally danced along the road. It was nice having decent transportation again.

Mrs. Redd cooked up a delicious buffalo stew for supper. It was the first decent meal he'd had for a while. William felt a pang of regret when he cut her throat late that night. He took care to slice their bodies up more than was needed; he wanted the Indians to be blamed.

William was pleased to find a change of clothes that fit him; he'd thought Orman was about his size. By yellow moonlight, he washed himself and buried his bloodstained clothes some distance away so they wouldn't be found.

Rummaging through their trunks by the flickering light of a coal oil lamp, he found just over three hundred dollars. He had hoped for more, but that was enough for a first-class train ticket to Salt Lake. The feisty gelding would have him in Cheyenne soon.

He shot the two draft horses that had pulled the wagon, just like he'd heard that Indians did. Then he walked over to Shitty Red who, true to form, had his head down, eating grass, ignoring him completely. William looked the mule over for a moment. Then he removed the hobbles and halter, freeing the animal.

When William rode away under a star-studded sky, the only thing left alive at the campsite alongside the Oregon Trail was a red mule, casually grazing on stunted grass.

Twenty-Nine

"All of it! Ya fool woman, you lost *all of it*!" Almira cringed and started crying. Kate and John had never seen their Pa so red-faced angry, or Ma fall to pieces like this.

William had been in Salt Lake City two days before he found his family. "Now I know why the bank ain't heard of you like they was supposed to. That's how we was to find each other, through the bank. You couldn't put any money in the damn bank because you lost it all, ya idiot!" William shouted, livid.

"Pa, they shot the guard. It was Jesse James and Cole Younger. There was twenty men ridin' with them, and we didn't have a chance," Kate said.

Almira was lying facedown on her hard bed now, blubbering loudly. John had a wide grin on his face. He was enjoying this immensely.

William seemed to calm down when Kate

talked to him in her soft voice. She had always been able to quiet him when he got riled. "You just can't trust nobody no more," William mumbled. "I don't know what this world's comin' to."

"We can start over, Papa," Kate said optimistically. "There's piles of money comin' out of the gold camps up north. A miner came through a couple of days ago with a fortune on him. He tried to get me to leave with him. He said they were minin' a hundred thousand dollars a week in a place called Idaho City."

William's face brightened, and Ma sat up and started daubing at her eyes with a red handkerchief. "That much in a week — just think of it," Pa said dreamily.

"We've saved over two hundred dollars," Almira sobbed meekly.

"I've got a hundred," William said firmly. "Give me your money — you ain't done a good job of hangin' on to it — I'll buy us a wagon in the mornin' and we'll head out to this Idaho City. We can't stay around here. There's too many people and too much law."

Kate reached inside her blouse and took out a wad of bills and handed them to her Pa. John kept his eyes on the source of the money with a wide-eyed grin, hoping there

443

were whores in the place called Idaho City.

"Hon," Ma said softly, "the man that runs this place has lots of money, an' he's been awful mean to us. He won't even let John chew his tobacco. Maybe we could kill him before we leave and take his money."

"You get dumber every day, woman," William growled. "We ain't wanted for nothin' hereabouts. We wait until we get to where the gold is and it counts for somethin' when we do away with a body. Bump off a Mormon here in Utah, and we'll have a hundred of 'em chasin' us. I swear, Ma, you'd get us hung if it wasn't for me."

"Sure Pa, you're right. It's just that he's been so mean," Almira said pleasantly.

A dumbstruck look crossed William's face; he wasn't used to Ma being so agreeable. "You'll get over it. Now get some sleep. We'll leave as soon as I buy us a wagon and team in the mornin'," William said. Then he added, "And we ain't gettin' no shittin' mules to pull it with, either."

Pa stormed out, slamming the door, leaving his family wondering why he'd started hating mules.

It took the Bender family nearly a month to traverse the more than three hundred rugged miles to Boise, Idaho Territory. The wagon William had bought was nearly as decrepit and worn as the one they had abandoned in Kansas, but at least the wheels lined up. Ever so slowly, the days creaked by as the two old horses struggled to pull the heavy dray wagon along the rutted roads.

The weather began to turn cold, threatening an early winter. The family had stopped in Brigham City and bought heavy coats, thick blankets, a large canvas to fashion a makeshift tent — they had other uses for the canvas later on, it was a business expense — and a rifle to shoot game with. Even with their scrimping, the Bender's money supply was running out. They realized that when they got to Idaho City there wouldn't be enough left to buy a building and start an inn as they hoped to do.

They were forced to stop early every day. The twenty miles a day William had covered riding Shitty Red now seemed like a long distance to him. A quantity of firewood had to be chopped and gathered to cook food and keep out the night cold; game had to be hunted down, killed, and cleaned; the horses had to be unhitched and hobbled so they could graze. Then, their shelter for the night had to be arranged. The canvas was fastened to one side of the wagon and stretched out to poles driven into the ground to make an open-sided tent. It wasn't much for warmth, but it kept rain off.

When they were in Brigham City, Almira had wanted to put wooden stays over the wagon bed to cover it like other folks did; also, she wanted a small stove to cook on. Pa had told her she'd have to make do, they just didn't have enough money. There were other things they needed more — a gun and ammunition to hunt with, for one thing, and a couple of good blacksmith hammers for another. Ma didn't grumble, to everyone's surprise. She didn't have the same spunk she had before Jesse James and Cole Younger robbed their stage. Most of the time Almira just sat quietly, staring at the distant mountains, a faraway look in her eyes. Kate was afraid she was sick. William was just glad to have her quiet for a change.

The only time Ma really said much anymore was during their nightly prayer meetings. This was something Ma had started insisting on. Ever since they'd left Salt Lake City she'd had a Bible squeezed tightly in her hand. John didn't mind the after-supper prayers too much. They weren't nearly as bad as what the Mormons did — sitting around with their hands folded listening to some long-winded preacher ranting away while the food got cold.

After the supper dishes had been washed up and what food supplies they had stowed back in the wagon so some varmint couldn't get at them, Kate would put on a pot of sage tea. They didn't buy coffee when they stopped. It cost money. There was lots of sagebrush free for the gathering, however. A few handfuls of leaves added to water and boiled for a while made a drinkable brew, especially if they sprinkled a little sugar in with it.

Over cups of steaming sage tea, the Benders would sit under the canvas, huddled around a crackling fire. The nights were growing increasingly colder, and Ma wore a black shawl over her shoulders when she opened the Bible. She read inspirational passages over and over again, droning on into the night. John wondered why she never told them about California anymore. He never asked her, though. He just chewed his tobacco and listened respectfully, like his Pa.

Almira closed her Bible sessions with a long prayer, asking God for an outflowing of profit from their business ventures. Every night she ended the meetings by saying, "And the Lord always provides." Then, with the last of the sage tea drunk and the prayer meeting over, the fire was built up for the cold night. The family wrapped up in thick blankets and slept the sleep of the weary to the music of distant coyotes.

The Benders made a temporary camp on the outskirts of the budding town of Boise. Poles were cut from trees and the canvas was draped over them and the wagon to keep out the wind. Now they could sleep in the back of the wagon, off the cold ground.

Idaho City, where the gold was, lay a day's ride to the north. William had insisted the family stop here, away from their goal for a while, so they could check things out. Ma and Kate could find work in town to build up their money, while John and he took the horses and went to Idaho City, looked things over, and planned their future business.

Ma found a job right away, cooking in the Fairmont Hotel. The only work Kate could find that paid the kind of money they needed was working upstairs in the Snake River Saloon. It meant putting up with a succession of dirty miners and cowboys, but the money was good. The proprietor said a pretty young thing like her could make ten or twenty dollars a day. Then he offered to pay her a dollar to try out the "merchandise," as he called it. Kate didn't like doing that, but she'd done worse to help her Ma — a lot worse. Kate felt nothing while the saloon owner grunted away on top of her; she kept her gaze on the ceiling and thought about California. After a few minutes, she had a silver dollar and a job that paid better than waiting tables, and was a lot easier.

William didn't much like Kate's line of work, but since it paid so well he kept his thoughts to himself. John was simply flabbergasted at the price of whores in Idaho. He was glad when his Pa told him they were leaving for Idaho City tomorrow. That was where the money was. Soon he would have lots of dollars to spend.

The Bender men saddled their horses and left as soon as there was enough light to travel by. Yesterday they'd paid twenty dollars for the two saddles — every dollar Kate had made the day before.

Their horse's hooves crunched in the heavy frost as they rode north. Once the sun rose the weather turned warmer and more agreeable, as did William's nature, especially after they stopped to chat with some folks fixing a broken wagon wheel. John and he pitched in to help them. After the wheel had been repaired, the grateful men nonchalantly told them they were bringing in over twenty-five thousand dollars' worth of gold. Then they opened an iron-bound wooden chest and showed them the nuggets, pounds of yellow, glistening metal. A fortune.

There were three of them, all armed with pistols, and a shotgun lay against the seat of the buckboard. There was nothing William and John could do but exchange pleasantries and continue on. Kate had certainly been right about the gold. All they had to do was a little planning, and they might be richer than before. The miners they met had been so trusting. William liked that quality in people. It made his work easier.

Idaho City was a larger and more bustling town than William had thought it would be. He realized now he should have brought his family here. This town bristled with a lot more money and activity than Boise did. No matter. John and he could get a really good stake here all by themselves. He felt it in his bones.

It was getting late so they rented a cramped room in a log frame two-story hotel. The clerk charged two dollars for the use of two bunk beds along a plank wall.

This was a high price for such accommodations, but William paid the bill with a smile. He knew folks couldn't afford to live there if there weren't a lot of money about.

After a few drinks in The Elkhorn Saloon that night, William was ecstatic. Even if you took all the wild stories and cut them in half, or even believed a tenth of them, there were fortunes being dug from the creeks around there on a regular basis.

Some of the miners paid for their drinks with gold dust. Two shots of rotgut whiskey allowed the barkeep to a three-fingered pinch from a leather pouch. William thought the pudgy bartender was hired because he had fat hands. It certainly wasn't for his personality. When a patron ran short of money or gold, the barkeep nodded to a pair of scruffy bouncers who threw him out the front door, none too gently. Only paying customers were welcome in The Elkhorn.

William kept his attentions on one miner who had an exceptionally heavy poke and was getting exceedingly drunk. Late that night, when the miner staggered from the bar, he and John paid for another quick drink and left, turning down the dark dirt street in the direction the drunken miner had taken.

One quick swing from the hammer hidden in William's belt under his felt coat, and they had a sackful of gold. After dragging the man between a couple of buildings, John and he went to their small hotel room. By flickering candlelight, they quietly added up their take. There were nearly five pounds of nuggets, probably nearly a thousand dollars; with gold, it was hard to tell. When they'd cashed in the gold the man they killed in Kansas had on him, they'd learned that natural gold wasn't pure. Pure or not, they had gold, and there was plenty more available. The Benders were beginning to recoup their lost fortune.

When a happy William and John went for breakfast the next morning, it came as a pleasant surprise to hear that the miner they'd robbed hadn't died. He was at the doctor's with a cracked skull but was expected to recover. Robbery wasn't too uncommon, nothing to get folks all worked up over. Besides, there was a lot more gold where that came from.

Most of the big nuggets were coming from a place called Moore Creek, they'd been told. Saddling up, they headed for the source of Idaho City's wealth. By midday, they had looked most of the mining operations over from a discreet distance, finally finding what they were looking for. Using John's telescope, they carefully watched a lone man shoveling gravel through a long wooden box. On occasion, he stopped and grabbed a yellow nugget from the sluice and dropped it into a leather bag.

Carefully, William and John scoured the area, making sure the man was alone. After a while, they made their move. "You stay here, John," William said, taking off his gun and handing it to his son. "We don't want to spook him none."

William stuck the blacksmith hammer under the back of his belt and covered it with his long coat. When he dismounted his horse, the heavy sack of gold in his pocket felt as if it might slow him down, so he handed it to John. "Keep an eye out with that telescope in case anybody comes around. Once I bust his head, come on in," he said.

"Sure, Pa," John answered while biting off a chew of tobacco.

The miner saw William walking from the timber toward him and stopped shoveling. When he saw that the bearded man was unarmed and smiling, he relaxed and leaned his shovel against the sluice box, extending his hand. "I was a hopin' someone might drop by. It gives me a good excuse for a breather," the miner said happily.

William grasped the work-calloused hand and said, "I'm glad I could help. Malloy's the name, Frank Malloy. My brother Sam's supposed to have a claim hereabouts. Have you made his acquaintance?"

"Nope, can't say I have, but there's a new bunch upstream," he said, turning away to point. "Now he jus' might —"

William's hammer struck as quick as a rattlesnake before the miner finished talking. The back of his head exploded with a crimson spray. *This man wasn't as lucky as the one last night,* he thought.

William picked up the heavy bag containing the nuggets and looked to see if John was coming. He was so busy wondering where his son was that he didn't see the two men come out of the trees behind him, carrying a deer slung under a pole. When the men got close enough to see their partner draped over the sluice box, they dropped the deer and cocked their rifles. William spun at the sound, but it was too late; they had him in their sights from fifty feet away. With a sigh, he threw up his hands and waited for his son to rescue him.

Porcupines were something John had never seen. They were strange, laughable-looking animals all covered with stickers, and the one he was teasing with a stick was causing him a lot of fun. When the porky got angry from being poked, it danced around, then swung its tail with startling speed and swatted the stick. Again and again, John made the tortured animal slap his stick heavily. Finally he got too close, and caught some quills in his leg. To John's surprise and pain, the stickers wouldn't pull out without a lot of effort. He gritted his teeth and slowly worked them out with his Bowie knife. John made a mental note to never play with one of *those* critters again.

The harried animal had climbed a pine tree, and was huddled near its crest. John thought about shooting it, then remembered he was supposed to do something. He rubbed his leg, then took the telescope from his saddlebag. When the glass clicked into focus, he got a worse shock than when the porky slapped quills into his leg.

His Pa was wrapped in heavy ropes, and two men carrying rifles were marching him away at gunpoint, heading upstream. There was another mine working just out of sight around the bend. He didn't have much time. Quickly folding the telescope closed, John looked for his rifle. Finally he remembered he had sold it somewhere. *Shit,* all he had was his Pa's pistol. Staying in the cover of the heavy larch growing alongside the creek, he ran to get ahead of the men leading his Pa away.

Before John got to where he could head them off, he heard loud shouting and cursing. Sneaking to where he could see what was going on without exposing himself through the thick growth, he saw that a half-dozen miners had joined the men who had his Pa. He cast a pained glance at the pistol he held in his hand. There were more men now than he had bullets for. John felt a rising panic. He was so confused he was shaking. Nothing like this had ever happened to him. His Ma or Pa had always been there to tell him what to do. He finally decided he'd best go ask his Ma. She would be angry with him, for sure. Even more than his Ma's scoldings, he dreaded the fact that when she was mad at him he had to do without supper, and he was already hungry. The breakfast they had this morning was a skimpy one.

As he rode back to Boise leading his Pa's horse, a thought occurred to him. He was surprised at himself for not thinking of it before. He didn't have to tell about playing with that stickery animal. It would be a simple matter to make up a story about a bunch of bad men with guns catching his Pa. There wasn't anything he could do about it. There were so many of them. It wasn't his fault. Ma had told the same story when she lost all their money. It worked for her. Smiling at how smart he'd gotten, John took a big bite out of his plug of Brown Mule and spurred his horse into a faster gait.

Sheriff Wolfgang "Wolf" Noonan and his deputy, Ray Scarbrough, listened with stern expressions while the miners told them what had happened. The burly prisoner with a gray-streaked, black beard and long greasy hair refused to say a word, snarling with an upturned lip when questioned.

From the evidence and what the miners had told him, the man was as guilty as sin. Then Wolf remembered the miner who was knocked out and robbed last night. The prisoner had used a hammer to kill Lane Cooper a little while ago. The man who was robbed could have been hit by a hammer, too.

Wolf remembered there was something in a Wanted poster about people getting killed with hammers. He went to his desk, opened a drawer, and leafed through some papers for a moment. Finally, taking out a Wanted flier, he studied it and the taciturn prisoner closely. "Ray, go get ole Pete, the barber. He's probably sober enough to shave a man, since it ain't dinnertime yet. Tell him to bring his razor and hot water. We're gonna see what our hammer swinger looks like without his whiskers," Wolf said loudly enough for everyone in his office to hear.

William's eyes narrowed, and his face hardened at the sheriff's words, but there was nothing he could do now. *When I get out of here, that John's one dead son of a bitch,* he thought. Looking the situation over, he realized getting out of here might be a tall order. The windowless jail cells he saw down a dark corridor were new — heavy steel bars set in massive quarried stone. To make matters worse, that damn deputy had slapped leg irons on him. Now they were going to shave him. If they made a connection with Kansas — *surely not,* it was impossible. This sheriff wasn't *that* smart. Even if they didn't figure out who he was, William knew he was in deep trouble. The rugged, angry miners who filled the room were ready to lynch him. If they didn't, maybe Ma and Kate would break him out. Then he'd kill John.

Pete, the barber, wasn't sober. Scraping the man's wiry beard off with a mostly dull straight razor, he made a number of small, bloody cuts in the prisoner's face. To everyone's surprise the huge man never even flinched. Finally he wiped the now clean-shaven man's bloodied face with a hot towel and stepped back so the sheriff could take a close look.

Wolf had the Wanted poster he'd taken from the desk in his hands. Carefully he looked the prisoner over, then the poster, slowly and deliberately doing it again. A broad smile crossed Wolf Noonan's face. "Welcome to Idaho City, William Bender. Shame we can't hang you today, but there's some folks in Parsons, Kansas, that would like to see you again."

THIRTY

Joe Peeples was so excited when he raced into Neely's store that he collided with a pickle barrel and nearly fell. He spun around, feeling in his pockets with both hands. Lute and Neely were both in the store sipping cups of coffee. It had been raining slowly all day, and few people had ventured into the store. No one had died for a spell, and Lute's coffin supply was built up, so they had been enjoying the quiet day.

"You been takin' some of Goosey's nerve medicine again?" Lute asked flatly.

"They got him! It just came in on the wire!" Joe said excitedly.

"Why, that's good news," Lute drawled, "or it might be, if we knew who the hell you was talkin' about."

"Bender," Joe spurted out, finally finding the telegram. "Old Man Bender — they've got him in jail in Idaho. They want someone to come and identify him."

"Jeez, Neely, we did better than we figured, scarin' those folks all the way to Idaho. I thought running them a thousand miles away counted for somethin'. Now we find out they kept right on skitterin'," Lute said, grinning.

Neely didn't join Lute in his humor. "Anyone else caught, or just William?" he asked seriously.

"All the telegram said was William Bender," Joe answered.

"You can bet your last dollar John and the rest of them aren't too far away," Neely said. Then he added, "But I'm not the sheriff anymore. Scar— Chatterhorn's the man you need to talk to."

"Yeah, we don't have any law now," Joe lamented.

Lute and Neely knew what he was referring to. After firing Neely, Ben Chatterhorn hired a tough-acting, big-talking man from Missouri to fill the job — at a hundred dollars a month no less.

Marsh McFadden was the new lawman's name. He'd spent most of his time hanging around The Kansas Schooner drinking beer and threatening to close Roland Langtry's saloon. This new sheriff had tried to get Roland to give him free drinks and whores and

461

had gotten thrown out for his efforts. Langtry was so angry that he'd spent a pile of money sending telegrams around trying to find out a little about McFadden. It turned out that before leaving Missouri, Chatterhorn's new sheriff had relieved a couple of banks of their money at gunpoint. A pair of marshals had taken him away in handcuffs last week, leaving the banker with a really red face and Parsons without a lawman.

"Grab yourself a cup of coffee, Joe. It'll settle your nerves," Lute said. "I'll go down to the bank and fetch ole Scarbutt. Tryin' to get him to act smart is like tryin' to train a turkey, but he is the county trustee."

Chatterhorn stomped into the store with a frown, grabbed up the telegram, and read it carefully. "They're not even certain it's him," he said haughtily. "They want me to go to the expense of sending someone that far? Why, the cost would be terrible."

"They need somebody who's actually seen the Benders," Lute said simply. "The rest of the family's probably in the area, too."

"I — the township has already spent a lot of money and received nothing in return," Chatterhorn said sharply, causing Lute's neck to show red.

"Ben, if the Benders are brought to justice folks will think a lot better of things," Neely said.

"That's true. However, the township has no funds left. The governors posted a reward of five hundred dollars for each of the Benders. If you're so certain it's him, Mister Thompson, why don't you go collect it?" Ben asked.

Lute's eyes narrowed. Neely noticed Lute didn't have a gun handy, so he relaxed a little. "OK, by God, I'll just do that!" Lute boomed. "Go down to that cracker box you call a bank and draw me out five hundred dollars of that reward money I got settin' in there. I'll leave this afternoon."

Chatterhorn started to say something, thought better of it, wheeled, and left the store.

"You don't have to do this," Neely said.

"Oh, I've got a passel of money, an' I never seen Idaho. Supposed to be pretty country. Everyone around here's healthy as a damn horse. They'll last 'til I get back. Besides, that John shouldn't have spit tobacco juice on me in Texas. I'm still tolerable pissed at him over that," Lute said, his humor back.

"How long you expect to be gone?" Neely asked.

"I'll take the train when I can. Who knows, maybe three weeks. I'll send you a telegram when I've got somethin' to say," Lute said as he left to pack for the trip.

When they were alone, Joe said, "I thought Chatterhorn was gonna get himself shot again, for sure."

"If Lute ever does shoot him, you can bet it won't be his ass that's bleedin'," Neely said seriously.

John was taken aback by his mother's reaction to the news that Pa was caught. He had expected her to at least yell at him. Instead, she threw herself on a blanket in back of the wagon and started wailing. Ma's sobbing hurt him worse than a cussing out. Kate was working; when she found out what happened to Pa, she would yell at him, for sure.

After a long while Ma finished her bawling, sat on the back of the wagon, and wiped tears from her eyes with a dirty dishcloth. John thought of something that might perk her up. He took the bag of gold from his coat pocket and handed it to his Ma. "Pa got this for us last night," he said proudly.

Almira *did* brighten. "How much is here, do you think?"

"Pa said maybe a thousand dollars."

"The Lord does provide, don't He?" She thought for a minute, then said, "John, you hitch up the wagon and I'll walk to town and get Kate. You be ready to leave when we get back."

He quickly sprang to the task as his Ma wrapped herself up in a black felt coat and started walking to Boise. If he hurried and worked hard, maybe they could have his Pa back real soon. John missed his Pa, and felt real bad about what happened. As he worked, the pain from the porcupine quills stuck in his leg reminded him of his wrongdoing.

Wolf Noonan received a telegram from Parsons saying a man by the name of Lute Thompson, who knew the Benders, was on his way. This strengthened his resolve to keep his prisoner alive. He had been a lawman in gold camps for years, starting in Virginia City. He knew full well miners got themselves worked up into a lynch mob really easy. He'd made up his mind they weren't going to string up this prisoner. He hired a half dozen deputies that he could call on if problems arose.

Old Man Bender — if that was actually who he had in his jail — was shackled to the cell with a leg iron. Catching a famous killer like one of the Benders would be good for his reputation, and might mean a raise in pay. No mob would get this man if he had anything to say about it.

The man locked in the cell had yet to say a single word. He'd kicked at the deputy when he tried to hook the leg iron to the cell, and it had taken five men to finally wrestle the man into submission. Not only was he as strong as an ox, he was a killer. Whether or not his name was William Bender, he'd killed a man with the hammer they'd found in his belt. Regardless of who he was, Wolf knew he'd hang. He just hoped it *was* Old Man Bender; he needed a raise in pay.

William sat morosely in his cell, weighing his options. This damn lawman just had to figure out who he was. That was a real pisser. Now he'd heard someone say Lute Thompson was on his way, adding to his woes. The more he thought about his situation, the more desperate it looked. The leg iron hooked to his right leg and an iron bar was the worst. He had a pocketknife hidden in his boot, under a leather flap he'd had Ma sew in for just that purpose.

It wasn't a large knife or a particularly good one, having only one blade. He remembered it already had one blade broken off when they took it from the man they'd killed alongside the river when they first came to Kansas. If he could just get it pressed against a deputy's throat, it was a passport out of there. *But that damn leg iron.* The sheriff was the only one with a key to it. If he didn't get free from it first, killing a deputy wouldn't do him any good, and would likely just cause him more trouble. Come night he would have to do something. He couldn't wait. Cursing John under his breath, William Bender planned and hoped.

"We just can't go off and leave him, Ma," John pleaded.

"Yer Pa's a smart man. He'll be all right. But we can't stay here. If they figure out who he is, the law'll know to look for the rest of us — you want to hang, boy?" Almira said.

John felt a strange lump in his throat. His Pa was in Idaho City in bad trouble, and now his Ma was making him leave. It was all his fault, too. He would be in deep trouble when his Pa told about what he had done. Then he thought for a moment; if his Pa *didn't* get out, no one would know of his shortcomings, and he wouldn't get whipped. Feeling better now, John climbed on the wagon seat and flicked the reins. They would be a little ways from Boise before it got too dark to travel. Ma said they were going to another gold camp, a place called Sumpter in Oregon. John hoped it was closer to California. He needed money. The price of whores up where it was cold was outlandish. And Ma always said when they got to California money wouldn't be a problem. Before they had gone two miles, John had forgotten all about his pa, and was thinking of whores and wondering if his ma would fix supper for him. He was awful hungry. He didn't notice Kate sitting behind him staring at him with dark, cold eyes.

William knew it was a desperate act, but he was in a desperate situation. There was no way John or anyone else was going to bust him out. *Hell, John probably couldn't find Idaho City again.* The ticking clock on the wall above the loudly snoring deputy showed it to be two A.M. He had to do it now. It would be better to have a foot missing than be hung in front of a jeering crowd. He slid his belt from the pants loops and tied it as tight as he could around his leg above the shackle.

He looked the knife over and shook his head. *I need a bigger knife,* he thought. *Cutting the bone with this piece of shit is damn near impossible.* Then he decided to cut through at the ankle joint, below the shackle. There was just gristle holding his foot on. He'd butchered pigs before, slicing off their feet for pickling. His foot wasn't any different. Carefully, he felt below the two knots of his ankle.

With a grim smile, William realized he wouldn't have to saw through bone to remove his foot. *Once I cut it off and I'm free of the leg iron, I'll scream for the guard. He'll think I can't reach him, but I will. With my knife to his throat, he'll help me. I'll take guns and a horse. After I cut the bastard's throat I'll ride north, hide in the wilderness until my stump heals up. I'll be free.*

William cut an end from his leather belt, folded it, folded it again, placed it in his mouth and bit down hard. *I can do this. I have to do this, and then I'm going to kill John.* Anger welled in him like bile as he took the one-bladed knife and did what he had to do.

Damn, Ray Scarbrough thought when he woke up with a start and noticed what time it was. He hadn't planned to doze off. His wife was right — once he got to sleep, even thunder couldn't wake him. It was after seven. The sheriff would be here soon, and want his morning coffee. Wolf had warned him about sleeping on guard duty. He hurried outside, scooped up an armload of firewood, and had a roaring fire in the potbellied stove and a pot of coffee boiling by the time Wolf came in.

"How's our prisoner this mornin'?" the sheriff asked, motioning with his head to the dark corridor of cells.

"Never heard a peep out of him all night," Ray answered truthfully. "I'll go see if he wants a cup."

Taking a kerosene lamp from the desk, Deputy Scarbrough went to the back of the jail and looked in the only occupied cell, the one holding the man they thought was William Bender. "Oh my God!" he yelled when yellow light flashed through the cell bars. "Wolf, get in here!"

Grabbing a pistol, the sheriff ran to see what the trouble was. The deputy was ashen-faced, and shaking so hard the lantern light flicked eerie shadows through the bars over the bloody form that lay unmoving on the cold floor. "Get the key!" Wolf shouted. "I'll keep him covered. He might be playin' possum."

"I don't think so," Ray said somberly, moving the light to show he was standing in a pool of thick, red blood.

"Jesus," Wolf said, grabbing the lamp and looking into the cell. "He's cut off his goddamn foot and bled to death. *Shit!*"

"Just like an animal."

"What?" Wolf asked.

"An animal caught in a trap will chew its leg off to get away," Ray said, going to get the key to open the door. "Who'd a thought a man could do that to himself?"

"This was William Bender, not some wild animal," Wolf said firmly.

Returning, the deputy opened the cell door, looked down at the still, gray figure with a snarl frozen on his face, and asked, "Are you sure?"

"Professor" Layton Kane was Idaho City's only undertaker. Supposedly he had been a scientist of some repute in Europe. Rumor was, he'd gotten into bad legal problems there and hurriedly emigrated to the United States. One thing was certain — he loved using big words and drinking good whiskey.

Looking over the body through gold-rimmed glasses that rode on the end of his nose, the professor clucked his tongue and said, "This man is dead of exsanguination."

"Huh?" Deputy Scarbrough questioned.

"Means he bled to death," Wolf answered with irritation in his voice. Placing a hand on the undertaker's shoulder he asked, "Can we keep him some way, so the man comin' from Kansas can at least identify him?"

"Oh, the weather is much too warm during the day. I'm afraid we're experiencing what you call an Indian summer. Keeping him from deteriorating will be difficult, very difficult."

Wolf Noonan knew what the word "difficult" meant. "How much will it cost?" he asked.

"Oh my, I'm not even certain it can be done. My studies show the Egyptians were capable of preservation by using a calcifying pool," the professor said.

"Never heard of any Indians called E-gipshuns before," Ray said.

Wolf and the undertaker ignored the deputy, and the professor continued, "I have the necessary chemicals, and for a fee of, say fifty dollars, we may be able to keep Mister Bender around for centuries."

"Fifty dollars!" Wolf sputtered, trying to add his hoped-for raise up in his head.

"Well, let's say thirty," the undertaker added quickly. "I've never done this before. It will take a lot of research and work. The first thing I have to do is remove the deceased's viscera."

"Take out his what?" the deputy asked.

"He's got to gut him," Wolf answered curtly.

"Oh," Ray said, wishing he'd never asked.

"Well, let's get him over to your place and try to pickle him for a while," Wolf said, grabbing up the one foot still attached to the stiff body.

THIRTY-ONE

Lute Thompson traveled for nearly eight days to get to Idaho City and William Bender. He had been able to take the rattling train from Thayer all the way to a place called Corrine, in Utah. From there, he had to travel by stagecoach.

He had gotten a good chuckle out of a travel brochure describing the town of Corrine as "the Chicago of the Rockies." Apparently some railroad magnate had named the place after his daughter. Lute decided if Corrine herself was as ugly and badly built as the town, she was definitely an old maid.

Even though the Transcontinental Railroad had been running through there for well over three years, the town was a collection of unpainted, clapboard buildings and tents. To Lute's way of thinking, Corrine made Titusville look prosperous. Even the hotel and the restaurant where he tried in vain to eat an antelope steak were crude huts made by stretching canvas tightly over peeled logs. This dining room was no different than most he had encountered on his trip. The time allotted for stopovers was short, and customers were required to pay for food in advance. Nearly always, Lute's dinners were set down in front of him just when the "all aboard" sounded.

When the time came to leave in the stage for Boise, he hadn't been able to slice a single bite from his steak. He choked down the potatoes and carried the steak with him when he left, to keep them from serving it to some other fool. Lute guessed the same leathery piece of meat had been sold several times before. His knife only added to the scratch marks already on it.

Lute tossed the steak to a starving mongrel before climbing on the stage. Through the departure dust he grinned when he saw the restaurant owner chasing the dog down the street hoping to retrieve his livelihood.

The swaying stagecoach traveled twenty-four hours a day, stopping only briefly at way stations to change horses and allow the grimy passengers time for a hurried meal and a visit to the outhouse.

Lute was red-eyed and thoroughly exhausted when he finally arrived in Boise. It was late afternoon, and the next stage to

Idaho City didn't leave until eight the next morning. Grateful for the chance to sleep on something that wasn't moving around all the time, he checked into the Fairmont Hotel.

After soaking layers of trail dust from his body in a tubful of steaming hot water, he went to a barber shop. Once the stubble of beard was shaved away and his hair trimmed, he started feeling better. When he devoured the first really good meal he'd had lately — a well-done beefsteak covered with mounds of ketchup — he went back to his room and slept like a log for twelve straight hours.

Refreshed after his long rest, Lute ate another steak for breakfast. He then strapped his revolvers on, stuck a handful of long nine cigars in the pocket of his newly laundered boiled shirt and happily went to catch the Idaho City stage. He was getting anxious to see William Bender again.

The ticket agent ruined his day when he told Lute the man they thought was William Bender was dead. There wasn't time to ask any details. The stage was leaving.

Lute had been disappointed with the scenery around Boise. He thought Idaho was supposed to be completely covered with trees. Mostly he had seen sagebrush-covered

hills. Now that the stagecoach was travers-
ing some really beautiful country, his mind
was elsewhere. None of the other passengers
traveling on the stage with him knew any
more about the Benders than what the station agent had told him.

It took nearly eight hours to reach Idaho
City. The time seemed to crawl by at a
snail's pace. In the worse way Lute wanted
to bring the Benders — at least one of them
— back to Parsons. They had made fools of
him and his friend, Neely Wells. He believed
the twelve people they had murdered in
Kansas were just a small part of the total
number this family had actually killed. He
felt if it were possible to catch just one of
them alive, and they were lucky enough to
get them to talk, the cases on a large number
of unsolved murders or disappearances
might be closed. If this man was indeed William Bender, then Kate, Almira, and John
would surely have known of his death long
before. They could be anywhere by now,
almost certainly still plying their deadly
trade.

When the stage groaned to a stop in Idaho
City, Lute consoled himself with the
thought that the Wanted poster didn't say a
thing about the Benders having to be alive.
All he had to do was identify the body to be

in for a share of the reward money. Then, at least the trip wouldn't cost him too much.

The weather was surprisingly warm for that time of year. Lute had gained a lot of experience with dead bodies these last few years, and as he walked to the sheriff's office he was hoping they had an ice-house. That was the only sure way to keep corpses looking like their true selves for a while.

"I'm Lute Thompson, from Parsons, Kansas," he said to the big man with the chiseled features sitting behind the desk, whittling away on a stick. The large pile of shavings by his side showed he'd been at the task a while.

The sheriff looked up, unsmiling, and kept whittling. "Sorry you made the trip, Mister Thompson. I sent a wire when the prisoner kicked the bucket, but you'd already left."

"You had him in jail. What the hell happened to him — he get himself lynched, or did you feed him an antelope steak?" Lute said curtly.

Wolf quit whittling and laid the stick on his desk. He looked Lute over closely, wondering what he meant about the antelope steak. Scooting the chair back from his desk, he folded the blade on his pocketknife, stuck it in his pants pocket, walked around the desk, and offered his hand to Lute.

"Wolfgang Noonan is my name. Most folks call me Wolf. You'll have to forgive me. I'm still a little upset over the matter, myself. Coffee?" he asked, nodding to a pot sitting on a black, potbellied stove.

"Yeah, that'd be nice."

The pot was drained and another boiling when Wolf finished telling about how the prisoner had been apprehended. Then he went into great detail as to how the man had used a knife concealed in his boot to cut his foot off, just to get out of a leg iron and attempt an escape.

"He must have underestimated the pain and passed out, then bled to death," Wolf said somberly.

"Your deputy that was watchin' over him didn't hear anything, like a lot of yellin' and hollerin'?" Lute questioned unbelievingly.

"Said he never heard a sound. When Ray goes to sleep you could shoot him dead and he wouldn't know it until he woke up the next morning. He told me he was awake all night, but I doubt that. He's a good deputy, though, and who would've thought a man would cut his own foot off?"

"There's a lot about the Benders that's hard to believe," Lute said. Then he asked, "Where's the body? I hope you've got him packed in ice. If the man's William Bender, he'll be mighty easy to recognize, even if he is a little peaked."

The sheriff looked down at the floor, kicked some of the wood shavings from his whittling around for a moment. Then he mumbled, "I'm afraid we've got a little problem."

Lute's eyes widened. "Just how *little* of a problem are we talkin' about?"

"Well, our undertaker, Professor Layton Kane, took the body to his place and tried to use a calcifyin' pool to preserve him, like the Egyptians did," Wolf said.

"Tried *what*?" Lute blurted. "Didn't he just pack him in ice?"

"All the ice that comes to town is used in the saloons to keep the beer cold," Wolf said. "If the weather hadn't got so blamed warm, we could've spared a little, but the professor said he thought it was possible to embalm him and keep him around for years without him spoilin' none."

"What I don't like is the 'thought' part and the 'tried' part," Lute snipped. "Can we go to this professor and see for ourselves?"

"That would probably be the easiest way." Wolf sighed, leading Lute out the door.

Professor Kane's undertaking parlor was a long, low building constructed of peeled logs. It sat on the lower part of the main street in what a preacher would consider the area of town that needed the most work. Kane's parlor was the only business on the block that wasn't a saloon, gambling hall, or house with a red lantern hanging on the porch.

"Nice location," Lute said agreeably as the sheriff steered him toward the front door.

Wolf smiled, "Ain't a far piece to carry 'em, that's for sure, and the professor don't have a long walk to come home at night."

Sounds like my old days, Lute thought. He hadn't been on a drunk since the trouble started with Choctaw Charlie, and that had been months ago. It seemed as if the longer he went without drinking, the less he desired it. Annie never complained when he was drinking, but she'd told him lately that she fancied him better when he was sober. He liked it when Annie gave him a compliment. Also, it was nice waking up in the morning without his head hurting.

The professor was sitting slumped at a wooden table staring at a glassful of whiskey with bloodshot eyes when Lute and Wolf came into the parlor. Stacks of crude plank coffins of various sizes lay stacked along the log walls like firewood.

"This here's Deputy Lute Thompson from Parsons, Kansas," Wolf said. "He's come to see Old Man Bender."

Lute wasn't an official deputy, but he knew he'd get a lot more cooperation if they thought he was, so he'd pinned his badge on before getting off the stage.

"Welcome to Idaho City, sir," the professor said in precise, measured words. "Just give me a moment to compose myself, and I will accommodate your wishes."

When Kane reached with his right hand to pick up a towel from the seat of an empty chair, Lute noticed he was shaking so much he could hardly grasp it. The undertaker tossed the towel around the back of his neck and grabbed the other end and the glass of whiskey with his left hand.

Using the towel, he slowly pulled his hand containing the whiskey to his mouth. Lute realized he had such bad shakes that this was the only way he could get the liquor to his mouth without spilling it.

The professor chugged the large glassful of bourbon without blinking. With a satisfied sigh, he set the empty glass on the table, tossed the towel after it, turned to Lute, and said, "Nectar of the gods, gentlemen. Through the ages, all great men have enjoyed its redeeming qualities. Take Napoleon, for example —"

"Could you just show him Bender," Wolf interrupted.

"Ah yes, Mister Bender. How unfortunate. If you would accompany me to the rear of the building," the undertaker said, staggering making an attempt to stand. After a moment the sheriff helped him up.

Lute followed the pair with a growing feeling of dread and concern that he'd made a wasted and expensive trip to Idaho.

The professor and Wolf stopped at a claw-foot bathtub along the back wall under a window. Both looked into it and shook their heads sadly. When Lute came alongside, all he saw was a milky looking, gelatinous mass which filled the tub. "Well, what's this stuff?" Lute asked curtly.

"I'm afraid it's all that remains of Mister Bender," the professor said sadly. "There was a small difficulty in translating what chemicals were needed from the ancient texts."

"He botched it," Wolf said flatly.

"I can see that," Lute said.

"When I saw my efforts at preserving the subject for your scrutinage were going awry, I made a valiant attempt to save the head," the professor said. As he leaned on the sheriff for support, he reached into a wooden crate and brought out a gleaming white skull and handed it shakily to Lute.

"It wasn't a thirty-dollar effort," Wolf said with a frown.

"He's lost a little weight since I last saw him, but it's Bender for sure," Lute said, beginning to laugh. At first he'd felt like shooting the undertaker. Then when he saw the irony of the situation, he couldn't help but laugh out loud. "Those damned Benders are a pain in the ass even after they're dead."

Wolf Noonan couldn't see anything funny in the situation. He was out thirty dollars, and a raise in pay. "You could have just packed the head in ice. The Elkhorn could've spared that much," he growled at the professor.

"Gentlemen, if you'll excuse me, I think I'll be on my way." Lute chuckled, turning to leave, still holding the skull.

"Sir, that skull belongs to me," the undertaker said firmly.

Lute flicked out a pistol with his free hand and stuck it under the professor's nose so quickly that even Wolf couldn't follow his draw. "This is evidence, and I'm taking it with me, *sir,*" Lute growled.

"You're welcome to it if you want it," Wolf said. He'd never seen anyone draw as quickly as Lute. He decided the man from Kansas could have anything he wanted without any argument over it. "Here, take a gunny sack to carry it in. We don't want to upset any of the locals," he said, handing Lute a bag.

"Obliged to you," Lute said jovially, holstering his gun and sacking the gleaming white skull. "Gentlemen, I wish I could say it's been a pleasure."

"I am sorry," Wolf said sincerely. "We did try, you know."

"That's all a steer can do," Lute said over his shoulder as he left carrying the sack, leaving the professor and Wolf arguing over the thirty dollars.

Lute stopped by the telegraph office before taking a room in the hotel and sent a message to Neely Wells. It read: SAW TUBFUL OF BENDER. SKUNKED AGAIN. HOME SOON. LUTE. The operator couldn't understand what there was in the telegram to make a man laugh so.

Late that night while Lute was sleeping peacefully in the hotel, Wolf and the professor were in the cemetery digging up a grave by moonlight. The undertaker had eventually told the sheriff why he was so reluctant

485

to give up Bender's skull.

Zack Reeves, the owner of The Elkhorn Saloon, had offered him fifty dollars for it. He felt that the skull of William Bender displayed prominently behind his bar would be a wonderful conversation piece and would draw tourists who wanted to see the skull of one of the most famous killers in history.

After giving the matter some thought they decided it was pretty hard to tell one skull from another. Zack would pay fifty dollars for whatever skull the professor brought him.

Another foot or so of digging and the saloon owner would have his conversation piece, Wolf would get his thirty dollars back, and the professor, twenty dollars to buy whiskey with.

Best of all, they avoided a fight with the man from Kansas. Both men were immensely happy with themselves as they threw dirt from an open grave under a towering pine tree in the dark of night.

THIRTY-TWO

After leaving their camp near Boise the remaining Benders made only a few miles that first day before darkness called a halt to their flight. Almira sat slumped over in the wagon bed, wordlessly cradling the leather sack of gold in one hand and her Bible in the other, like a caring mother holding her children.

John shot a couple of jackrabbits while there was still enough light to draw a bead. He skinned and gutted them while Kate gathered wood and started a fire. Ma just sat humped up like a sick bird, doing nothing toward fixing John's supper, to his disappointment. It had been a long, hard day for him, too.

Kate didn't yell at John, to his great surprise. She even fried the rabbits up for him and made a dutch oven full of hot biscuits. Ma refused to eat anything, climbing into the back of the wagon again and rolling up in a blanket. Kate seemed more concerned over her mother than what had happened to Pa, much to John's relief.

Once he had drenched the last biscuit in molasses and devoured it, John tossed some more wood on the fire. Cutting a large chew from a plug of Brown Mule with his Bowie knife, he wrapped a felt blanket over his shoulders and leaned against the wagon wheel.

Ma and Kate stayed in the back of the wagon, talking in whispers so quiet John couldn't hear them. He felt bad about what had happened, and worried some of it might have been his fault. What he wanted most now was for his Ma to sit by the fire and tell of California. He always liked to hear what their life would be like there. It cheered him up. But his Ma didn't come to talk to him. He spat a load of tobacco juice into the fire. The resulting hiss was louder than the hushed tones coming from the wagon behind him. John wondered what they could be talking about.

Tomorrow would be a better day, he told himself. His ma said Pa was smart and could take care of himself. Maybe his pa would catch up to them soon. He knew he'd get a whipping when he did, but it would be worth it to have someone to talk to.

Finally, exhaustion overtook him, and he drifted off to sleep and dreamed of California.

The next morning Almira seemed more like her old self. After a short walk into the sagebrush-covered countryside, she came back to the wagon, fried up salt pork, and made another batch of biscuits. John felt better when Ma called him dumb for leaving his Pa to the law yesterday. Also, the coffee brightened his day. Kate had brought a sack of it with her from Boise. John really liked his coffee — boiled-up sagebrush wasn't nearly as good.

Before John hitched the horses to the wagon for the day's journey Ma called a family meeting around the campfire. "If the law figures out who Pa is, we might be in trouble," Ma said. "They'll be a lookin' for two women and a man travelin' together, so here's what we're gonna do. I'll ride in back, and if we meet anyone I'll roll myself up in that canvas so's they can't see me. John, you and Kate are man and wife, travelin' by yourselves."

John was giving Ma his full attention now. Being married gave a man privileges that didn't cost a dollar.

"We can't take a chance usin' our first

489

names, either, at least not for a while. John, now pay attention. If anybody at all asks your name, it's *Jason* Griffith. That's not a whole bunch different. Now tell me your name," Ma commanded looking John in the eye.

"Jo— Jason. My name's Jason, Ma," John said meekly. He was getting confused. "Jason Griffith."

"That's a good boy," Ma said soothingly. "Now don't you ever say the name 'John' again until I tell you it's OK. Katie dear, you'll use the name Susan."

"Yes, Mama," Kate replied.

Vaguely, John remembered something about a girl named Susan, but no matter how hard he thought on it he couldn't recall who she was. He decided to keep his mind on his new name. Ma would be real angry with him if he forgot that.

The day creaked by slowly as John urged the pair of old horses west. He chewed his tobacco, and Kate sat by his side. It was a good feeling having her sit close to him like she was. Always before, his sister had sat as far away from him as she could get.

When they met anyone on the road, Kate would snuggle even closer, so close John could smell her heady, sweet perfume. Then she'd whisper in his ear that his name was Jason, while Ma rolled under the big canvas in the bed of the wagon. He felt good about being married, and wondered how long it would be before he could get what a husband wants. Kate told him it was just a "pretend" marriage. He didn't understand that part. To John, married was married. He should get something for his efforts, and not have to pay for it.

John was thinking so hard about his state of matrimony that he didn't notice the posse of armed men until his sister scooted closer to him and said loudly, "Jason, dear, let's stop and see what these men want."

With a start, John reined the slow-moving wagon to a halt. Two stern-faced men wearing badges and carrying rifles rode up to talk. Four more armed men kept their distance.

"Howdy ma'am, sir," a big man with a long, black beard said, tipping his slouch hat while peering into the wagon. "Where you folks headin' to?"

"My husband, Jason, and I are going to Oregon," Kate said, "is there trouble about, sir?"

"We're lookin' for a couple of women — one of 'em is old and as mean and ugly as a she bear — and a clean-shaved man by the name of Bender. They're murderers from Kansas. The old man was caught in Idaho City yesterday. Came over the wire this mornin' he's dead. Sheriff up there thinks his family might be around. You seen anyone suspicious?"

Kate squeezed John's hand so tightly her nails dug into his flesh. "No sir," Kate said, shaking her head. "My husband and I are Mormon missionaries from Salt Lake City. We're trying to make Oregon before the snows hit."

"Well, you folks keep a watch out. I don't reckon they're about, but if they are they won't hesitate to kill you," the lawman said.

"Thank you, sir," Kate said sweetly, "but we're doin' the Lord's work. He'll look out for us."

"If you run across the Benders, you'll need the Lord *and* a gun, from what I know about them," the lawman said gruffly. Then he turned to the other men, waved his arm, and shouted, "Well, let's get to goin'."

As the posse rode away, kicking up a cloud of dust, Kate's hand began shaking. John flicked the reins, starting the wagon moving forward. Almira's low sobbing could be heard from inside the rolled up canvas, over the groaning and creaking of the wheels.

■ ■ ■ ■

Ma stayed wrapped up in the back of the wagon until they made camp for the night. Kate spotted a secluded site in a grove of trees near the Boise River, some distance from the main trail. With any luck they would be left alone for the night.

While John unhitched the horses Kate helped Ma unroll herself from the canvas. When he came back carrying an armload of firewood he was shocked by his ma's appearance. Strands of black hair were pasted to her face with dry tears and her eyes were red as beets from crying.

Almira sat down with a loud grunt and leaned back against a wheel of the wagon. "The Lord's supposed to look after those who live by the Good Book," she lamented in a hoarse voice while staring blankly past her children at the clear, roaring river. "Now Pa's gone, and the damn law's lookin' for us."

"I'm sorry, Ma," John said sincerely. He didn't like seeing his ma like this.

"I just don't know what Pa must have told them," Almira wailed, ignoring John. "He must have told them who he was, *the bastard!*"

John's mouth flew open. He'd never heard her talk like this about his pa.

"It'll be all right, Ma," Kate said sweetly. "Remember, the Lord always provides."

"The bastard told them who he was," Almira said, still staring at the river. "Now they know we're here. It's just a matter of time until we all hang. The Lord has given us up." She had the Bible clutched in her hands, holding it to her chest so tightly her knuckles showed white. "Oh Lord, look after thy servants in their hour of need."

"Go see if you can shoot a deer, or some rabbits for supper," Kate said quickly to John. "I'll look after Ma."

Grabbing up the rifle, he couldn't get away fast enough. Women's crying made him nervous. As he worked his way silently along the river, John tried to understand what was happening. His pa was dead. He knew that now. It couldn't have been his fault; no one had gotten mad at him over what happened in Idaho City.

Ma was in a bad way. She acted really sick, too. Maybe she would get better and tell about California again. He hoped so. This talk about being hung disturbed him. All he'd ever done was live by the Good Book and honor his father and mother. Surely that wasn't anything to be hung over. If the law caught him, he'd tell them he'd just done what his Ma and Pa told him to do, and they'd let him go, for sure.

A deer so young it still had a few white spots on its tan coat was drinking from the river when John came from the trees. The fawn looked up with big, innocent eyes, trying to decide if this strange creature was dangerous and it should run. John dropped it with a head shot before the deer made up its mind. He gutted the animal, skinned the carcass, then washed it clean in the clear cold water. Draping the little deer across his shoulders, John headed back to camp. Hunting always made him feel better when something was worrying him. This time was no exception. His ma would get over being sick. They were close to California now; he just knew it couldn't be much farther. It wasn't his fault at all about what happened to Pa. John had a smile back on his face and a spring to his step. Then the sound of a gunshot split the still air.

Quickly, John tossed the deer onto a sagebrush. With a shaky hand, he reloaded the rifle, upset with himself for not doing so after shooting the deer. His pa always told him, "An unloaded gun won't do you any good when you need it."

His first instinct was to run straight into

their camp and see what was the matter. He was certain that was where the shot had come from. Then he thought of all the armed men he'd seen earlier, and decided to circle around and come in from another way.

As carefully as he could, John kept to heavy cover, moving to where he could see the wagon without being seen himself. He looked for saddled horses, men with guns, anything out of the ordinary, and saw nothing.

Kate stood alone alongside the wagon looking down at something. Cautiously, John crept from his cover and walked into camp, keeping the rifle ready. When he saw his ma still leaning against the wagon wheel sleeping and Kate holding his pa's pistol, he relaxed. Probably just a rattlesnake. Nothing to worry about.

"I shot us a deer," John said coming around the wagon. "What'd you shoot? I was afraid there was trouble. . . ." Then he saw a small black hole in his Ma's forehead, between her eyes; a stream of syrupy blood dripped slowly from the wagon wheel she lay slumped against.

"She killed herself, John. She said she couldn't go on without Pa," Kate said quickly and soothingly.

John dropped his rifle onto the ground, ran to his ma and knelt down. "Oh Ma," he sobbed, "we was near to California."

Kate put a soft hand on her brother's shoulder. "Our Ma was sick, John. She had a cancer. The doctor in Salt Lake City told us she didn't have long to live."

"We don't have a Ma or a Pa now," he wailed between wracking sobs.

"Ma said to tell you to be strong. I'll help you now. There's just the two of us. We have each other."

Kate watched as John rolled himself into a ball on his dead mother's lap and began crying loudly. A look of hardness washed the mask of grief from her face as she went and picked up the rifle John had dropped. She placed the pistol and rifle in the back of the wagon alongside the pouch of gold she'd pried from Almira's dead fingers before John got there.

She decided to let him cry it out. Briefly, the thought crossed her mind this would be a good time to get rid of her brother, too. A rifle bullet in the back of his head while he was drawn up in a ball would remove a problem from her life. Kate had use for her brother, however — at least for a while. She couldn't kill him now. John's help might be necessary for her to reach her goal. She needed a considerable amount of money before going to San Francisco. She needed to meet the right people, young men with lots of money, more money than she could dream of, and occasionally Kate had some very good dreams. Consoling herself with the design of killing John later, she started gathering firewood for the nightly fire.

Ma had increasingly become a problem. Ever since they were robbed of their money, she'd been having strange ideas, like the Lord had abandoned them and the law was going to hang her. When they were working at the hotel in Salt Lake City Ma started waking up at night sobbing that spirits had come to her in dreams. She claimed she saw the faces of their "customers" telling her if she gave herself up to the law she wouldn't hang.

After a while, Almira became afraid to go to sleep. She didn't like for the spirits to come. She said her only hopes from hanging were in the Lord's mercy and that leather-covered Bible she squeezed so hard at night her fingernails bled.

Today, when Ma heard the lawman say Pa was dead, it seemed to push her too far. Ma declared they were to give themselves up. The spirits had told her she wouldn't hang. She was to tell the law it was William's idea, that she just went along to keep him from killing her. Kate knew better. She also knew the law was looking for *two* women and a man. A problem. Kate sent John out to shoot something for supper so she could be alone with Almira. Before Ma lost her mind, she had taught her how to handle problems. Kate had learned well. *Like mother, like daughter.*

John would believe anything she told him — Ma's suicide, the cancer story. He was like a well-trained animal. He didn't understand about them pretending to be married, but she could control him, at least for a while. Eventually, he would become a major problem, but Kate knew how to handle problems.

THIRTY-THREE

The cashier at the Virtue Bank in Baker City, Oregon, didn't bat an eye or ask a question when John laid the heavy sack of gold on the counter. It was a common occurrence in that part of the country. The bearded, tobacco-drooling miner was no different from hundreds of others who walked through the doors in hobnail boots, except for the pretty, auburn-haired girl clutching his arm.

The banker was so taken aback by seeing such a beautiful woman that he had difficulty concentrating on weighing the gold. After a short time, the purity of the precious metal was determined. "This wasn't mined around here, was it?" the cashier questioned idly, causing John to jump and squirt a stream of tobacco juice onto the polished wood counter.

"No sir," Kate answered quickly. "We had a claim in Colorado Territory, but it ran out on us. We brought all we mined with us to start over in this beautiful country."

"Good choice," the banker said happily, looking at Kate. "There's more gold around here than Colorado will ever have. Auburn and Sumpter in particular are doing exceptionally well."

"I've been minin'," John said simply, causing the cashier to look at him strangely.

"My husband and I are goin' to run an inn. We're not really too good at minin'," Kate interjected.

The cashier wondered briefly just what this beautiful girl's husband *was* good at as he wiped tobacco juice from his counter with a white cloth. "Seventy-three ounces at six hundred fifty fine. Let's see, that's just over nine hundred dollars. Would you like that in bills, or perhaps to open an account?" he asked hopefully.

"We'll need the cash to buy a business. The town of Sumpter sounds nice. My husband, Jason, and I will ride out there this afternoon," Kate said.

The banker smiled as he started counting out stacks of bills. "A man by the name of Seldon McEwen has a place for sale on the main road. It's a few miles out of Sumpter, but you may want to stop and see him. He's got a powerful urge to go to California, and

501

will sell cheap."

"Why thank you Mister — ?" Kate asked.

"Jennings O'Brian, ma'am," the banker said, looking into her batting green eyes. "Tell Seldon I sent you. And you folks are?"

"Susan and Jason Griffith. If everyone's as nice as you, I'm sure we'll just love it here," Kate purred.

The cashier watched dreamily as the beautiful girl led her tobacco-chewing husband out of the bank. *There goes one nice lady,* he thought.

The banker was right. Seldon McEwen was very anxious to sell. The rotund, cigar-chewing man had a wild look in his eyes when he told Kate and John of a big gold strike he'd heard about in California. He wanted to go there so much that he would take two hundred dollars for his property right now, throw what he felt he could carry in his buggy, and leave the rest. Kate counted out the money, and McEwen gave them a bill of sale and a deed that he'd had notarized in advance, hoping for such an opportunity.

While Seldon McEwen hastily went about his business of preparing to pull up stakes, Kate and John looked over their purchase. The place fit their needs perfectly. It sat a discreet distance from the main road to Sumpter and Baker City — where the gold shipments were moved — in a thick, sheltering grove of huge pine and tamarack trees.

John was especially pleased to have a cookstove again. Seldon had also left an elk hanging in the woodshed. This was great news. *If only Ma would cook it for me,* he thought. Then he remembered she wasn't with them anymore.

Kate and he had buried her along the brushy banks of the Boise River. She had shot herself because she was sick and missed Pa. John wondered why his sister had insisted he dig such a shallow grave and made him carry all those round rocks and cover Ma's grave with them. When he'd finished no one could tell anyone was buried there, he noticed. Most folks put up a wooden sign telling who was laid to rest. Kate wouldn't let him even put a stick in the ground.

Before they left the next morning, he told Kate he needed to go to the bushes for a few minutes. While John was gone, he gathered up a sparse handful of dying summer flowers and left them under a rock over his ma's grave. Kate never knew. He missed his ma a lot; also, his sister couldn't cook as good as his ma, either.

Later that day, Kate made him turn the wagon around, back toward Boise. Then they drove a long distance cross country, unhitched it, and saddled their horses. "We have to travel fast," his sister had said. "We're going to make a lot of money, then we'll go to California, like Ma and Pa wanted us to. I'll take care of you, John. Just let me handle things. We'll get there, trust me."

All his life, John had been told what to do. Obediently, he followed Kate's instructions. Ma had said Kate and he were married now. He remembered his pa had always done what his ma had told him to do. Now that Kate was his wife, he guessed he had to do the same. The only problem with that was Kate said their's was a pretend marriage, and in no uncertain terms told him she'd cut his goodie off if he tried anything with her. It confused him, why she talked to him like that, but he had no doubt his sister meant what she said, none whatsoever. He liked his goodie, so he decided to leave her alone until they got to California. Then he'd have money for whores. They never told him he couldn't do it, or threatened his goodie.

Two weeks after John had nailed a crude sign to a post by the main road that read

504

GRIFFITH INN-MEALS AND DRINKS, it had become the most popular stop on the road to Sumpter.

Kate was the draw. Her efforts at cooking weren't nearly as good as her mother's, much to John's displeasure. None of the miners or freighters that stopped by the inn ever complained though. A woman of any kind was a rarity in this remote area. A beautiful woman, even if she was married to a hulking, taciturn man, was a jewel to be admired.

The bubbly lady known as Susan Griffith was always so sweet to them. She showed great concern and interest in what they were doing. Also, she showed more cleavage than most of the men had ever seen. When she bent over to serve food or refill coffee cups, the miners were awestruck.

Eventually, only three men were allowed lingering glances at Kate's charms — Enos Kent, John Penny, and Robert Vose. The trio had been bragging to Kate for some time about the richness of their mine. Enos, especially, was smitten by the lovely lady, telling her that tomorrow they were bringing out the largest shipment of gold to ever come from Sumpter.

When the miners left to return to their mine, Kate walked to the door with them.

Taking Enos aside, she placed a soft hand on his shoulder and whispered something in his ear. No one else could hear what she said. The red cast that flowed onto the young man's face spoke volumes to his partners. With a spring to his step, Enos literally bounded from the inn to their wagon, leaving under a cloudy sky.

John watched morosely from an uncut pile of logs as the miners departed. That was all his sister had him doing of late; cutting firewood. She said it was going to be a long, cold winter and they needed a large supply. Already, he had five cords neatly stacked behind the inn. He felt that was plenty. It seemed to him she wanted him out of the way for some reason. With a fresh fever of anger, John attacked a log with his axe, sending woodchips flying in the cold, still air. If he wanted supper, he knew, he had to do what he was told.

Darkness came early to the Oregon mountains in wintertime. The crackling fire Kate had roaring in the cast-iron cookstove gave a welcome feeling of warmth inside the little inn. A fresh pot of coffee was boiling and the smell of baking apple pies added to the serenity. A wagon freighting supplies into the gold camp was stopped outside. Two freighters were enjoying steaming bowls of elk stew and biscuits, while John sat alone in the corner quietly honing an edge on a meat cleaver as Kate had instructed him to do.

Across the Powder River on the flank of a tree-covered mountain, a large man sat under a covering of tamarack that still retained their needles. Hunkered under a heavy buffalo hide with a brass telescope, he carefully studied the inn across the canyon from him. The light was failing, but the man had patience. He had watched mountain lions stalk their prey. They would single out a solitary deer from the herd and concentrate solely on the hapless animal. Sometimes it took them a long while, but they always caught it.

The man clicked the telescope into better focus, trying to make out the movements inside the cabin, where yellow lantern lights were flickering through foggy windows. It was too dark. Tomorrow was another day. He had patience. Just like a lion, he had been stalking his prey a long while. He carefully folded the spyglass closed, slid it back into its leather case, and started rubbing bear grease into his long, stringy red hair.

THIRTY-FOUR

Day brought a thick gathering of gray snow clouds to the Elkhorn Mountains. Except for areas of shadow where rays of sun never gave their warmth, all of the earlier snows had melted. This storm gave promise of the first true snow of winter, one that would still crown the rugged mountain peaks behind the Griffith Inn when the summer solstice came.

John had spent the entire day in the still cold, cutting more firewood as Kate had ordered him to do. The sound of his axe striking the wood echoed eerily in the unmoving air. It amazed him how any noise he made was exaggerated by the cold. This was the first thing that had entertained him since coming to this place. Kate told him to stay out of the inn because he scared the customers. He was also beginning to wonder just what his sister was doing to get them to California.

The weather was supposed to be a lot warmer there, at least that was what his ma used to tell him when they had their family gatherings. John missed those meetings. He missed many things that he'd once taken for granted, his ma's cooking most of all. And he missed having his pa to talk to. Up here in this cold place, there was no one Kate would let him visit with.

Four well-dressed men in a surrey had just left the inn. John watched as they headed toward Baker City. A few fluffy, white snowflakes as big as chicken feathers were beginning to float to earth from an iron-gray sky. He placed his calloused, blue hands to his mouth and tried to warm them with his steamy breath. The thought struck him now that there were no customers. He could go inside. Besides that, it was getting dark and he was hungry, so hungry even some of Kate's cooking would taste good. Also, he determined it was time for his sister to tell him when they were going to California. He was getting awfully tired of cutting firewood. There were a lot of trees in Oregon; at the rate Kate was going, he'd have them all cut and stacked in racks before they left for California.

John came in the back door, closing it quickly before Kate could begin yelling at him about letting all of the heat out. He held his hands over the stove for a while, savoring the warmth, trying to get up enough nerve to ask his sister some questions about what she was doing toward getting him to California. When the feeling finally returned to his numb hands, he poured a boiling cup of coffee and blew on it. Looking at Kate through the steam, he finally got up enough nerve. "Kate, when are we gonna go to California, like Ma said we could? It's awful cold here, and I'm tired of cuttin' wood."

"Don't *ever* call me Kate, you dummy," she scolded. "If I wasn't around telling you what to do, you'd already be hung." Then her voice mellowed. John could be unpredictable when riled. Like Ma used to say before she lost her mind — *You can catch more flies with honey than vinegar.* "Jason," Kate purred, "you know we have new names now, better names for our own good. I know you have a hard time rememberin', but this is something you can't forget."

"I'm sorry," John said, looking at the floor and shuffling his feet.

"Of course you are. This time it's all right — no one was here — but if you forget when we have a roomful of customers, we'll both be in a lot of trouble."

"I won't make no more mistakes, I promise. But I'm sure tired of cuttin' wood in the cold. An' I wanna go to California like we always were gonna," John pleaded.

"You're right, Jason, we need to leave here. We can't do like we used to. A hammer would point right to us. What we have to do is make one big pile of money off one customer."

"OK, K— Susan," John stammered.

"That's good, real good. Now listen to me. We may make our haul tonight. Remember those three miners that drive the big wagon with four horses?"

"Uh huh," John nodded agreeably, even though he didn't remember. He'd been cutting firewood.

"Well, they've been braggin' about bringin' out a big gold shipment. The way I understand it, they can't mine any more until spring, when the river thaws out. This is all the gold they mined this summer." Kate brightened and squealed, "Jason, they're supposed to be here any time! If they show up, we kill them. And then we'll take their gold and go to California."

This was the first good news John had heard in a long time. He grinned and took a big drink of coffee. It was so hot it burned his mouth, and he spat the scorching liquid

511

onto the floor and Kate's dress. He was agreeably surprised when she didn't scold him.

"You get Pa's pistol and make sure it's loaded," Kate said, trying to hide her displeasure. A double-barrelled twelve-gauge shotgun loaded with buckshot leaned against the wall, hidden behind her coat. She had bought it from Seldon McEwen for ten dollars. Kate knew she could most likely only shoot two of the miners with it. John's help might be needed. Then, with the customers dead, she could do what she had to do to make it look like a robbery. Two more shells for the shotgun were in her apron pocket. It might take both of them to bring John down. He was tough, that was for certain.

John, happy now that he was finally going to California, sat his coffee on the stove and took a huge bite of Brown Mule. Chewing tobacco was better than coffee, and didn't offer so many surprises. He took his pa's pistol from a shelf and spun the cylinder to check if it was loaded. Satisfied, he snapped the loading gate closed and stuck the pistol under his belt.

Kate went back to cooking. John scooted a straight-back chair next to the stove, leaning it against the back wall. He slouched into it, soaking up the wonderful warmth. John hated cold weather. Impatiently, he chewed his tobacco and waited for their ticket to California, where it was never cold, to come in the front door.

When the back door to the inn flew open with a crash, John was so startled that he tried to spring from his precarious seat on the leaning chair, getting his legs in a tangle. He fell to the floor with a thud, sending his pistol skidding across the plank floor, coming to a stop underneath the cookstove. Kate screamed loudly, upsetting him even more. John had never heard his sister scream before. He tried to reach the pistol, but only succeeded in burning his arm; the gun remained out of his reach. Pulling his razor-sharp Bowie knife from the hidden sheath inside his pants, John jumped to his feet with a snarl, only to look Greasy Haynes in his bloated face.

I know this man, John thought, confused as to why someone he knew would kick the door in. The big man with long, stringy, red hair had a pistol pointed at him for some reason he couldn't fathom. Kate, ashen-faced and shaking, was backed close to the cookstove, by the intruder.

Greasy Haynes would like to have told them how glad he was to see them again.

Since he had no tongue, all he could do was make a low growling sound like a dog. He had come a long way for this. Ever since he first laid eyes on the beautiful Kate, he had wanted to cut on her in the worst way.

When Jesse James had taken him into his gang, his belly was still leaking a vile smelling fluid from where he'd been shot robbing the bank in Kansas. Since he hadn't healed properly, Jesse made him hold their horses when they robbed a stagecoach just out of Vinita. That was when he saw Kate again.

He had patiently followed her ever since; waiting, watching, planning. Of all the women he'd cut, Kate would be the prettiest. She was undoubtedly the toughest. With any luck, she would last for days. His wide grin showed yellow teeth as he fired the pistol into John Bender.

The force of the bullet drove John back against the wall, wide-eyed. He didn't understand what had happened to him. Something felt wrong in his groin; when he put his hand there it came back wet with blood. *I've been shot,* he thought, *why doesn't it hurt?* Then he got angry. He felt for the knife in his hand. It wasn't there. Through wide, shocked eyes, John saw the Bowie knife lying on the floor, where he had dropped it when the man — he couldn't remember his name — shot him.

John started for his knife. He staggered and nearly fell. His legs wouldn't do what he asked of them. The red-haired man cocked his pistol to fire again, making a loud click that echoed in the silence. Kate noticed that Greasy Haynes's cold eyes were fixed on her brother. Using his brief inattention, she quickly grabbed the boiling hot enamel coffeepot from the stove and dashed its contents into the glowering man's face.

The shock of the boiling coffee hitting him caused the fat man to pull the trigger of his pistol. When the unaimed bullet shattered his hip John reeled and fell to the wood floor.

Now, believing John was no longer a threat, Greasy Haynes turned his attentions to Kate Bender. The hot coffee hurt — half of his bearded face and one eye had already begun to turn beet red — yet he grinned at Kate with a sickly, cold grin. For the first time in her life she felt real fear.

John curled into a tight ball on the floor and began crying, just like he had done when his ma died. He had never really been hurt before, not so much anyway. The racking pain that now struck him like a red-hot iron was scaring him. He didn't know what to do. A long, guttural sob escaping his lips, accompanied by a stream of tobacco juice, drew Greasy Haynes's attention.

Kate wheeled desperately, but to no avail. The big man caught her arm in a vise-like grasp. Dragging her with him, Greasy began kicking the groaning, prostrate form of John viciously with his hobnail boots. Kate screamed loudly for him to stop, that she'd do anything he asked of her. Greasy Haynes didn't stop kicking John. Instead, he drew Kate's arm up along her back, nearly lifting her from the floor. All Kate could do now was scream, loud and long.

Nothing she could have done would have brought more pleasure to Greasy. He loved hearing women scream. It was the only real pleasure left to him. The soft thudding of his heavy boots striking the crying man on the floor only heightened his arousal. He loved it. *This could go on for hours.*

"What the hell is that?" John Penny exclaimed when he reined the wagon to a stop in front of the Griffith Inn.

The three men grew as silent as the cold mountain evening and listened carefully while flakes of snow drifted lazily to earth.

A desperate, pained scream crackled through the still air from inside the cabin. "It's Susan," Enos blurted, "someone's hurting her."

The miners hadn't really been expecting trouble, but it was better to travel prepared. There was a lot of gold in the strongbox under the seat of their wagon. All three had loaded pistols stuck under their belts, and a Sharps rifle was leaning against the seat. John Penny grabbed the rifle and ran to the door of the inn, cocking the hammer as he threw the door open.

Greasy Haynes tossed Kate onto the bloody form of her brother as if she were a rag doll, then turned with a cocked pistol and an animal-like growl to face the intruder who had the gall to take him away from his pleasures.

The shocked miner threw the Sharps to his shoulder and aimed at the brutish man with long, greasy red hair. John Penny was so shaken by the viciousness of the scene that greeted him that he didn't aim well. When the Sharps boomed inside the inn, a chunk of the big man's upper arm exploded. Unfortunately for the hapless miner, it wasn't the arm that held the pistol. Greasy Haynes fired a return shot, hitting the man full in his chest, knocking him through the open door. He made a soft thud when he hit the ground at his stunned partner's feet.

Robert Vose bent low and ran into the inn,

firing as fast as he could at the hulking figure holding a pistol.

Greasy Haynes felt the bullets strike him like stings from an angry hornet. He'd been shot before. It just took a while to heal up. He tried to shoot back at the man, but he couldn't cock the hammer. For some reason his right arm refused to do his bidding, hanging listlessly along his side. Dropping his useless pistol, Greasy pulled one of the knives he carried. With a loud growl, he ran the short distance to the miner who now held an empty gun. With one vicious stroke, he slit his belly open to his chest, lifting him from the floor. With eyes showing disbelief, Robert Vose slowly fell into a pool of his own blood, dead before he hit the floor.

After witnessing the quick demise of his two partners, Enos kept a respectful distance from the red-haired giant who seemed to soak up bullets with impunity.

From outside the inn, Enos cocked his forty-four caliber pistol. Holding it with both hands, he took careful aim at the red-haired man's heart and fired. He saw a black hole appear exactly where he had aimed. Greasy Haynes gave him a yellow-toothed snarl and drew back the knife to throw it at Enos.

Quickly, the miner cocked the hammer

again. As he looked down the barrel of his pistol he saw the silvery gleam of the Bowie knife over the brute's head. He fired. The sound was deafening, louder than before. He waited for the knife to rip into his body. Instead, the man with the knife collapsed heavily onto the wood floor of the inn and lay unmoving. Behind him, framed in yellow lantern light, Susan Griffith stood holding a smoking shotgun in her hands. "Oh thank God," she said shakily, "he was going to kill us!"

Enos walked warily to the body of Greasy Haynes from fear more than anything, he placed his cocked pistol to the big man's ear and fired. The red-haired giant never moved. Satisfied the danger had past, the miner stuck his pistol back in his belt with an unsteady hand and surveyed the carnage. His two partners were dead, but at least the beautiful woman seemed unhurt. "You OK, ma'am?" he questioned uncertainly.

"Thanks to you," she answered, "but my bro— husband is bad hurt."

Enos didn't catch what the girl said and he walked over to the whimpering, bloody man he knew as Jason, dragged him to the wall, and propped him up. After a quick look Enos said, "He's bad shot, ma'am. We ought to get him on the wagon and to the

519

doc in Baker City once we patch him up some."

"Yes, of course. I'll get somethin' for bandages. I think the big man was here to rob all of you. Did you bring the gold, like you said?"

Enos pressed a folded handkerchief where a stream of blood was pumping from John's groin, causing the wounded man to gasp. "There's a fortune in that wagon," he said idly, keeping his attentions on John's wounds. "I guess it won't do my partners any good, now. I wonder how that man knew we was carryin' gold."

The steel barrels of Kate's shotgun pressing against the side of his neck were the last things Enos Kent would ever wonder about.

Then, except for her wounded, mewing brother, Kate Bender was the only one left alive inside the bloody cabin.

"John, can you hear me?" she asked loudly, "It's Kate." She slapped his pale face.

John Bender rolled his eyes at her. "I'm hurt. Can we go to California now? I'll get better," he mumbled.

"Remember Missouri, John?" she asked.

His head slumped to his chest. Kate slapped him harder this time.

"What'd you hurt me for? I'm already bad hurt. I want to sleep," John answered with a raspy voice.

"Remember Missouri?" she repeated.

"Uh huh."

"Do you remember David?"

"Uh huh."

"When we had to run, and he was too little to travel, what did we have to do, John?"

"Don't know."

"Oh, but you *do,* Brother. And it was your fault. *Remember?*"

"Uh — uh."

"You played with a snake, and made us have to run. Little David, *my* David, couldn't travel fast. Now *you* can't travel, John. What *should* I do?"

"Don' know —"

"Well, *I* do, brother," Kate Bender said firmly.

Through pain-glazed eyes, John watched Kate unfold his Pa's straight razor, the one with the ivory handle he loved so much. He tried to bring his arms up to defend himself, but simply couldn't make them move. *"Kate, don't!"*

"Remember David," she said happily as she drew the sharp blade across her brother's neck. Then it was done.

Kate dragged the body of the slain miner into the inn, then closed and bolted the door. Calmly now, looking herself over, Kate saw she was covered with blood. She filled a tin dishpan with water and placed it on the stove to heat.

After her bath she felt better, more relaxed. This was one of the few times lately she'd been able to take her clothes off and bathe without having to worry about John. *That's one problem I don't have anymore,* she thought as she slipped into clean clothes. Taking care to dress warmly against the cold, Kate slid her already packed suitcase from under her bed. Almost as an afterthought, she piled her bloody clothes in a heap in the front of the inn next to Greasy Haynes's body.

A spattering of blood was on her fingers from handling the stained clothes. She carefully washed them clean in the dishpan and dried her hands. She pinned up her long, auburn hair and pushed a slouch hat one of the miners had worn over it. From a little distance, no one could tell her from a man.

Kate Bender put on her heavy coat, happy no blood could be found on it. Picking up her suitcase, she left the inn by the back door so she wouldn't get any blood on her clean boots.

It was nearing full dark now as she tossed her bag into the bed of the miners' wagon.

She brushed snow from the seat and climbed aboard. The last thing she did before leaving was open the lid on the heavy box under the seat of the wagon and run her fingers through the mass of gold it contained.

Slowly, the creaking wagon faded from the inn. Snow was coming down now at an increasingly heavy rate, filling the tracks made by the departing wagon, obscuring any evidence of its passing.

Epilogue

I

The first thing Lute Thompson did when he got back to Parsons was build a glass-sided display case for the skull he had carried back with him from Idaho City.

It cost him a smashed finger and several panes of broken glass to complete, but he felt it was a worthwhile effort. The grinning skull had cost him dearly. While there was little doubt in his mind that the skull was William Bender's, there was no way to prove it, which meant no reward. At least now he had something to show for his money.

The second thing Lute did was ask Annie Mitchell to marry him. She had never expected any man to ever want her again, at least for no longer than one night. The overwhelmed, teary-eyed blonde had choked out a "yes" to Lute's question.

Lute helped her pack what few belongings she had, then moved her into the hotel until the wedding. Roland Langtry was upset at losing one of his best moneymakers, but had the common sense to force a smile and wish them well. Whores were easier to come by than a new set of teeth.

After Lute had gotten her settled and left for the night, Annie took a long, hot bath. She slid between the clean, white sheets in a bed she would share with no one. As she lay there in silence a lump formed in her throat, a burning lump that brought tears to her eyes. When she woke the next morning her pillow was still moist with happy tears.

II

From the Baker City *Bedrock Democrat,* November 18, 1872.

SLAUGHTER NEAR SUMPTER

A ghastly sight greeted two freighters when they stopped at the Griffith Inn at McEwen for a meal yesterday. The foully murdered remains of four local men and one outlaw were found strewn about the little cabin. Robbery was the apparent motive and the scene gave evidence of a violent struggle.

Three of the murdered men were known to be carrying a quantity of gold they had mined near Sumpter: Robert Vose, Enos Kent, and John Penny. These three honest, hardworking miners were bringing the fruits of their summer's labor, believed to be over seventy thousand dollars, to Baker City.

It was thought they stopped by The

Griffith Inn, well-known in the area for delightful accommodations, for refreshments when they were besieged by outlaws. Jason Griffith, husband of Susan Griffith, proprietor of the inn, apparently made a valiant effort to help the miners in their fight against the robbers and was killed and mutilated for his efforts.

One of the outlaws also paid the supreme price for his sordid deeds. The body of a man wanted in the Indian Territory by the name of "Greasy Haynes" was found riddled with bullets, giving evidence that the brave men fought their attackers with vigor.

Sadly, the lovely wife of the dead innkeeper, Susan Griffith, is missing and believed abducted by the vile robbers. That some of her bloody clothing was found at the scene of the slaughter gives great fear for her safety.

Sheriff Greenwald has raised a large posse of men. Unfortunately the heavy snowstorm which continues unabated has delayed their departure. The sheriff promises as soon as the weather allows he will have a force of nearly a hundred men looking for the outlaws.

The Reverend Samuel Peters has called a special prayer meeting to ask the Almighty for the safety of Susan Griffith and to help in the capture of the unknown band of robbers who have invaded our sanctity.

Services will be held at the United Methodist Church at seven P.M. We urge all concerned citizens to attend.

III

Colonel Jefferson Davis Cowell lost heavily in his bid to become a congressman. His friends and supporters felt he hadn't campaigned nearly as hard upon his return as he should have, blaming his melancholy on his brother's death.

After the colonel returned from Kansas and buried his brother's remains in the family plot, he seemed to lose interest in the election. His wife wondered why he refused to touch her anymore. When she asked him what the problem was he didn't answer her, and took to sleeping by himself in the spare bedroom. Late at night she could hear him sobbing through the thin wall.

A week after his defeat in the election, a hired hand found him hanging in the hayloft. Only two of his cousins and his nephew, Carlton, showed no surprise that the Colonel hung himself over just losing an election.

IV

Lute and Annie were married in the church on a cold, clear day in late November. Why Pike Rogers agreed to perform the ceremony at all, let alone in his church was a matter of much discussion. Soiled doves such as Annie Mitchell were simply never to mingle with the decent people of Parsons.

The preacher performed a brief ceremony, slurring his words through a swollen lip and squinting at the Bible with a black eye. He told folks who asked that he had run into a door in the dark. When they saw Lute Thompson's skinned knuckles, they decided Lute must have been holding the door when the preacher ran into it.

The couple moved into a large, frame house on the outskirts of town. It was on a few acres of land, backed up against a tree-lined stream. Neely was concerned that Lute might move his undertaking parlor to his home, but he didn't. Every day but

Sunday he kept his usual schedule at his business, and drank coffee in Neely's store.

On Sunday mornings Lute and Annie would walk arm in arm to the church and listen to the Reverend Rogers's sermons. After a few weeks of dropping money in the collection plate all was forgiven, and in order. Annie began to be invited to church socials and, much to Lute's delight, her past was forgotten.

V

On a cold, blustery day in March, Roland Langtry was filling the coal oil lamps that were on a wagon wheel hanging over his bar. It was dark from the storm, and as far as anyone could guess at least one of the lamps must have been burning when the ladder broke, or he fell. The resulting fire not only incinerated the luckless saloon-keeper and The Rose Saloon, but an entire block of Parsons, Kansas, as well.

Ben Chatterhorn's bank was one of the buildings in the path of the fire. His wild yelling and attempts to form a bucket brigade to fight the conflagration were to no avail. The wind drove the flames with such speed that by the time the firefighters were organized all they could do was douse water on buildings in the next block and let the fire burn itself out.

Once the embers had cooled some, Ben Chatterhorn poked and scraped numbly through the smoldering remains of his bank. The fireproof safe he had bought at a bargain price turned out to not be fireproof, at all. Its doors had sprung open from the heat, leaving only a few handfuls of half-melted gold and silver coins.

Aside from the bank, Chatterhorn had owned the entire block, including a large note on The Rose Saloon. He also owed a mortgage to the Bank of Independence, covering the business block and his home, as well.

Ben Chatterhorn had never been inside The Kansas Schooner before, since it was competition for what used to be The Rose Saloon, his property. That evening, the stone-faced banker went there and exchanged some fire-blackened coins for a bottle of whiskey. Then he took a table in the back where he could be alone and slowly began to work his way to the bottom of the bottle.

VI

"You know I've been thinking the town could use another saloon," Neely said to Lute a few days after the fire. "The store business isn't real good. Mostly I sell on credit and I never get paid."

It came as a pleasant surprise when Lute answered, "Before ole Roland decided to burn down half the town, I took my money out of ole Scarbutt's bank. Annie and I've been thinkin' on what to do with it. Why don't we go partners? I've always wondered what a bar looks like from the other side."

The general store was gutted to accommodate a massive cherrywood bar that filled the entire north wall of The Prairie Clipper Saloon. Lute had ordered it custom-made in Kansas City. A special shelf was built in the center to display the grinning skull of William Bender. Neely took the three hammers he had taken from The Bender Inn and mounted them on a polished walnut board. He hung the hammers next to the skull. Then Lute and he backed off to check their handiwork.

"He was near to bein' your daddy-in-law," Lute remarked, looking at the skull.

"I like him better this way," Neely said, "he's a lot less trouble."

"Yeah, I reckon," Lute said. Then a smirk crossed his face. "You'll have to admit that daughter of his was a real knockout."

VII

From the society page of the San Francisco *Chronicle,* June 20th, 1873

In what promises to be the social event of the year, this Saturday, Mr. Orland K. English will take Miss Kate Griffin as his wife in an extravagant ceremony to be held in the Episcopal Church.

Mister English is a well-known financier and real estate magnate who made his fortune in the Comstock Mines some years ago. Aside from his vast real estate holdings, Mister English is a director of the First National Bank and quite active in the Republican Party. It is widely believed he will run for the office of senator when that post comes up for election.

Miss Griffin came to San Francisco last December from England, where she had been studying singing with a Professor Shoen for the past year. Sadly, Miss Griffin is an orphan, her parents having died from pneumonia while engaged in gold-mining operations in Colorado.

The wedding ceremony will be attended by many dignitaries including the mayor and our governor. After an ocean cruise to visit the south of France, the couple will be at home in Mr. English's stately mansion "Bel Aire" situated on Nob Hill.

VIII

Ben Chatterhorn received the same treatment from the Bank of Independence that he had dealt others over the years: they foreclosed on him. Never one to believe in paying good money for fire insurance, he was now a broke and beaten man who turned more and more to whiskey.

One day while he was in town drinking up what little money he had left, his wife packed the few of their possessions she could carry, including a handful of coins Chatterhorn had gleaned from the ashes of his bank, and left Parsons on the afternoon stage, never to return. Chatterhorn stayed so drunk it was two days before he realized she was gone.

After a while, Lute and Neely began feeling sorry for the homeless man, who had begun sleeping behind buildings at night. Lute said he was afraid Ben might build a fire to warm himself up and burn the rest of the town down.

Ben Chatterhorn was given Lute's old bed on a pair of coffins in his undertaking parlor and an occasional plate of beans, in exchange for swamping out their saloon.

When a fresh face appeared in The Prairie Clipper, Chatterhorn would immediately latch onto them and point out the grinning white skull of William Bender and the three hammers mounted behind the bar. As long as the strangers bought him drinks, he told exciting stories of Choctaw Charlie and the family of killers known as "The Bloody Benders."

AFTERWORD

The case of the Bender family remains unsolved to this day. Much of the written information available is contradictory in nature, and fogged by the passage of time. For the purposes of this fictional account I have adapted my own time frame as well as many of the more popular stories of the Bender family and the aftermath of their killings.

Perhaps the best ending for the Bender family is inscribed on a Kansas State historical marker alongside Highway 160 west of Parsons, a mile from the actual site of The Bender Inn. It reads, in closing, ". . . The earth seemed to swallow them, as it had their victims."

Ken Hodgson
Mertzon, Texas

CPSIA information can be obtained
at www.ICGtesting.com
Printed in the USA
FFOW04n0042020514
5213FF